S0-AVP-852

GOLEM
IN
THE GEARS

GOLEM
IN
THE GEARS

Piers Anthony

A Del Rey Book

BALLANTINE BOOKS • NEW YORK

A Del Rey Book
Published by Ballantine Books
Copyright © 1986 by Piers Anthony Jacob

All rights reserved under International and Pan-American Copyright
Conventions. Published in the United States of America by Ballantine
Books, a division of Random House, Inc., New York, and simultaneously
in Canada by Random House of Canada Limited, Toronto.

Manufactured in the United States of America

Table of Contents

XANTH

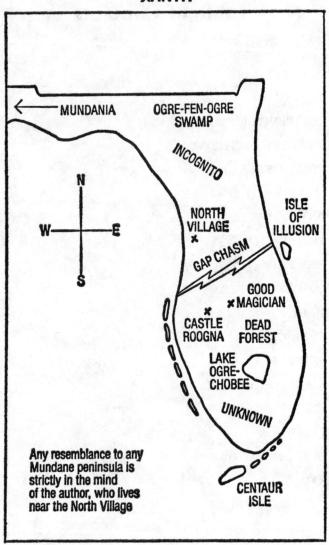

MUNDANIA

OGRE-FEN-OGRE SWAMP

INCOGNITO

N
W — E
S

NORTH VILLAGE
x

ISLE OF ILLUSION

GAP CHASM

GOOD x MAGICIAN

CASTLE ROOGNA x

DEAD FOREST

LAKE OGRE-CHOBEE

UNKNOWN

CENTAUR ISLE

Any resemblance to any Mundane peninsula is strictly in the mind of the author, who lives near the North Village

GOLEM
IN
THE GEARS

1

Quest

Grundy Golem stretched and bounced off his cushion. He looked at himself in the mirror, not totally pleased. He stood the height of a normal man's spread-fingered hand, and that was fine for sleeping on a cushion but not all that great when it came to making an impression on the Land of Xanth.

It was a nice new day. Almost, he was able to forget that he was the least significant of living creatures. When he had been a true golem fashioned of wood and rag he had longed to be a real living thing, supposing that he would be satisfied if only he could become flesh. At last he had won that goal and for a time he had believed that he was happy. But slowly the truth had sunk in: he was still only a handsbreadth greater than nothing.

No one took him seriously. They thought he had a smart mouth because he liked insulting people; actually it was because he was trying desperately to cover over his deepening awareness of his own inadequacy. When he used his talent of language to make some other person or creature feel low, he felt a little higher himself—for a moment. But now he knew that this was a false device, and that his mouth had mainly brought him the contempt of others. He wished he could undo that damage and make of himself a genuinely worthwhile and respected person—but he didn't know how.

Meanwhile, he was hungry. That was a consequence of being real: he had to eat. It hadn't been that way when he had been a true golem. Then he had suffered no hunger, pain, or calls of nature. But he liked it better this way, he decided, because he also felt living pleasures.

And living miseries. . . .

He slid down the banister and scrambled out the window that was normally left open for him. He landed in a clump of toadstools that had sprung up overnight, knocking several over. Unfortunately, a small toad had been sitting on one.

"Clumsy oaf!" the toad croaked, righting himself. "Watch where you're going!"

"Listen, frogface," Grundy retorted. "This is *my* path! You have no business here."

"I was on a toadstool, as I have a perfect right to be," the toad protested. "You just came barging through!"

The creature had a case, but Grundy didn't care. His irritation with the situation—and with all of Xanth—caused him to react in the familiar way that he wished he didn't. "Know what I think of that? I'll bash all these stinky things to smithereens!" And he grabbed up a stick and laid about him, knocking over toadstools right and left. Grundy was no giant, but they stood only about knee-high to him, and were easy to dispatch.

"Help!" the toad croaked. "Berserker on the loose!"

Suddenly there was a stirring throughout the weedy region beside the castle wall. Toads appeared, hopping in toward the summons—small ones at first, then larger ones, and finally one huge one.

Grundy realized he was in trouble. He tried to scramble up to the window, but the monster toad oped his ponderous maw and speared the golem with his tongue. The tongue was sticky; Grundy could not get free. The toad retracted it and hauled Grundy in.

"Eat him! Eat him!" the massed toads cried. "Teach him to leave toadstools alone!"

Grundy clutched at a half-buried rock, managing to halt his progress toward the maw. But now the little toads hopped on him, pounding him with their feet, and one of them wet on him.

Disgusted as well as frightened, he grabbed that toad and heaved it into the maw of the giant toad. The maw closed. The tongue released Grundy and snapped back home. Evidently the giant toad didn't mind what he ate.

But the little toads minded. "Get that monster!" they croaked, and snapped at him with their tongues. They couldn't do him much damage singly, but as a group they might. He tried to dodge the snapping tongues, but there were too many.

In addition, the giant toad was catching on that it hadn't eaten the whole thing. It reoriented on him.

Then Grundy spied a hypnogourd. That might help! He ran to it and dived behind it, so that its peephole was facing away from him and toward the toads. As the giant toad opened its maw and lined up its terrible tongue, Grundy shoved the gourd around so that the peephole bore directly on it.

The big toad looked—and froze. Its gaze had been trapped by the gourd.

"So there, filth-tongue!" he cried. "Now you're stuck!"

But the little toads weren't stuck. They averted their gazes and came leaping at him. One landed on his head, bearing it down. Grundy shook the creature off, but in the process caught a glimpse of the peephole himself.

Suddenly he found himself inside the gourd. He was standing amidst giant wooden gears. The huge toad was there too, and had a leg caught between two of them. The gears were drawing it slowly but inevitably between them, crushing it.

"Halp!" it cried. "I'm gonna croak!"

"Well, you were gonna eat me!" Grundy retorted. But he didn't like this; it was too ugly a demise.

He tried to pry the toad out, but the gears were too strong. Then he saw a small, loose gear. He picked it up and jammed it next to the toad's leg. As the two turning gears ground together, the loose one was crunched. In a moment the moving ones shuddered to a stop.

Now a huge stallion appeared, virtually snorting fire. His hide was midnight black, and his eyes glinted blacker. "I should have known!" the Night Stallion snorted. "A golem in the gears!" There was a subtle flicker.

Then Grundy and the giant toad were back in the real world, out of the gourd. Grundy realized that they had been ejected. The big toad's leg was whole, but it seemed to have lost its appetite.

Grundy realized that he had suffered the ultimate indignity: he had been rejected by the hypnogourd! *No* one had any use for him!

He scrambled again for the window, and this time made it. Fouled with the sticky spittle of the giant and the wetting of the midget, he fell inside. What a mess!

But worse than the ignominy of his present condition was his realization that he was of so little account that even a toad could humiliate him. It wasn't just a matter of size; it was an almost total lack of respect. He was a nobody, socially as well as physically.

What use was it to be a living creature, if he was of absolutely no consequence?

He found a bucket of wash water left over from yesterday's scrubbing

of a floor, and labored to get himself clean. While he worked, he came
to a conclusion, an answer to his question.

It was *no* use to live without respect. But what could he do about it?
He was what he was, an insignificant creature.

As he ran across the room, he heard stifled sobbing. He paused, for
now he also cared about others. He was seldom able to show it in ways
they appreciated, but he did care. He looked about and discovered that
it was a plant—a small green stem that looked rather wilted. Grundy's
magic talent was the ability to converse with other living things, so he
talked to the plant.

"What's the matter with you, greenface?"

"I'm w-wilting!" the plant responded.

"I can see that, potroot. Why?"

"Because Ivy forgot to w-water me," the plant blubbered. "She's so
wrapped up with her mischief that—" It tried to squeeze out another
tear, but could not; it had no water left.

Grundy went to the bathroom, climbed up on the sink, and grabbed
the damp sponge there. He hauled this down, dragged it across the
floor, and to the plant. Then he hefted it up and squeezed it in a bear
hug, so that water dribbled into the pot.

"Oh, thank you!" the plant exclaimed as it drank in the moisture.
"How can I ever repay you?"

Grundy was as selfish as the next creature, but he didn't see any way
the plant could do anything for him, so he elected to be generous.
"Always glad to help a fellow creature," he said. "I'll tell Ivy to give
you a good watering. What's she doing that's so distracting?"

"I'm not supposed to tell . . ." the plant demurred.

Now Grundy saw what the plant could do for him. "Didn't I just do
you a favor, wiltleaf?"

The plant sighed. "Don't tell I told. Ivy's a terror when she gets
mad."

Grundy well knew that! Ivy was eight years old and a full Sorceress;
no one crossed her without regretting it. "I won't tell."

"She's teaching Dolph to be a bird, so he can fly out and look for
Stanley."

Grundy pursed his tiny lips. That was mischief indeed! Dolph was
her little brother, three years old and a Magician who could change to
any living form instantly. Certainly he could become a bird and fly
away—but just as certainly that would be disaster, because, if he didn't
promptly get lost, he would get eaten by some airborne predator. This
had to be stopped!

But Grundy had promised not to tell. He had broken promises before, but he was trying to steer a straighter course. Also, if he told on Ivy, he would be in immediate and serious trouble. He had to find some private way to stop this.

He went through the motions of breakfast, but found no answer to his problem. He saw Ivy going to Dolph's room and knew he had to act —without admitting what he knew. So he pretended to encounter her accidentally, intercepting her in the hall. "Whatcha up to, kid?"

"Go away, you little snoop," she said amiably.

"All right—I'll play with Dolph instead."

"Don't you dare!" she said with moderate fury. *"I'm* playing with him."

"We can both play with him," Grundy suggested. To that she was unable to demur, because she didn't want to give away her secret by being too insistent.

Dolph was up and dressed and ready to play. He was a handsome little boy with curly brown hair and a big smile. "See—I'm a bird!" he exclaimed, and suddenly he *was* a bird, a pretty red and green one.

"Ixnay," Ivy whispered, but Dolph was already changing back, pleased with his accomplishment.

"Can I go out and fly now?" he asked.

"Why would you want to fly?" Grundy inquired as if innocently.

"He doesn't," Ivy said quickly.

But Dolph was already answering. "I'm going to catch a dragon!" he said proudly.

"No, he isn't!" Ivy cried.

"That's very good, Dolph," Grundy said. "What dragon will you catch?"

"No dragon!" Ivy cried.

"Stanley Steamer," Dolph said. "He's lost."

Grundy turned to Ivy as if surprised. "What's he talking about? You know he's not allowed to go out alone."

"I told you not to snoop!" Ivy said furiously. "It's none of your business!"

"But you can't send Dolph out! If anything happened to him, your father would ask the walls of Castle Roogna who put him up to it, and then your mother would—"

Ivy put both hands protectively against her backside, knowing where her mother's wrath would strike. "But I've got to rescue Stanley!" she wailed. "He's my pet dragon!"

"But nobody even knows where he is," Grundy pointed out. "Or even whether he's—" He had to break off, because it would not be smart to utter the dread conjecture in Ivy's presence. Stanley had disappeared when a monster-banish spell had accidentally caught him. Of course he wasn't a monster; he was a pet, but the spell had not distinguished one type of dragon from another. Naturally Ivy had pestered Good Magician Humfrey about Stanley's whereabouts, but there were so many dragons in Xanth that Humfrey's spells had not been able to isolate Stanley. Or so Humfrey claimed. Humfrey was younger than he once had been, and probably his magic wasn't up to snuff, but he wouldn't admit that.

"Somehow I'll find him," Ivy said resolutely. "He's my dragon."

There was some justice in that claim. Nobody could hold a dragon unless that dragon wanted to be held, and it had been friendship that held Stanley. Ivy had perceived him as her friend and her pet, and her enormous and subtle magic had made him so. Grundy was sure Stanley would have returned to her, had he been able. The fact that he had not returned strongly suggested that he was dead.

And Ivy would not give up the search. Grundy knew her well enough to accept that. Yet if she were not dissuaded, both she and her family might in the end suffer much greater distress than the loss of one little dragon—such as the loss of a little brother. Ivy was a Sorceress, but she was also a child; she lacked adult judgment.

Grundy could neither tell on her nor allow her to proceed with this foolish project. What was he to do?

It occurred to him that there was a noble way out of this dilemma—a way that just might bring him some of the esteem he craved. "I'll find him for you," he said.

Ivy clapped her hands in the way that little girls had. "You will? Oh, thank you, Grundy! I take back half the mean things I've said about you!"

Half? Well, half a loaf was evidently all he rated. "But while I'm doing it, you mustn't do anything yourself," he cautioned. "That could mess it up."

"Oh, I won't, I won't!" she agreed. "Not until you bring him back."

In this manner Grundy found himself committed to a Quest he strongly suspected was futile. But what else could he have done? Ivy needed her dragon back, and he needed to be a hero.

Grundy had no idea how to proceed, so he did what anyone in that situation would do: he went to ask the Good Magician. He caught a ride with a passing thesaurus who was going that way. The thesaurus was a very ancient breed of reptile who had picked up an enormous vocabulary during its centuries of life; it made for an interesting dialogue while they traveled. However, it had the annoying habit of never using a single term where several similar ones could be squeezed in. For example, when Grundy inquired where it was going, it swished its heavy tail and replied: "I am departing, leaving, removing, embarking, going, traveling for distant, remote, faraway, separated regions, zones, areas, territories, districts." By the time they reached the Good Magician's castle, Grundy was glad to bid it farewell, adieu, good-bye, and good riddance.

Now Grundy stood before the Good Magician's castle. Each time he had approached it over the years, it had looked different from the outside, but very little changed inside. This time it was suspiciously ordinary: a circular moat, gray stone walls, scattered motley turrets, and a general air of indifference to external things. Grundy knew this was illusory; Humfrey was the Magician of information, and though he was young now, he generally did know what was going on. He didn't like to be bothered about inconsequentials, so he established barriers to intrusions, on the theory that only folk with sufficiently important concerns would navigate them.

Well, Grundy had a concern and he knew he had to get past three obstacles to win entry. What he didn't know was what they were or how to nullify them. He would simply have to move ahead and do what he had to.

He stepped up to the edge of the moat. The water lay there, rippling at him. Naturally there was no way for him to cross; the drawbridge was up. Well, he would simply have to swim.

Swim? First he had better check out the moat monsters!

"Hey, snootface!" he called. Moat monsters were always varieties of water serpents and vain about their appearance.

There was no response. Well, he could handle that. "Say, grass," he said to the verdant bank. "Where's the monster?"

"On vacation, ragbrain," the grass replied.

Grundy was surprised. "No moat monster on duty? You mean I can safely swim across?"

"Fat chance, stringfellow," the grass replied. "You'd get eaten up before you got five strokes."

"But if there's no monster—"

The grass rustled in the breeze. "Suit yourself, woodnose."

Grundy didn't trust this. "How can I get eaten, if there's no monster?"

But the grass had been ruffled. "Find out for yourself, clayface." Obviously it had some notion of his origin, though he was no longer composed of string, rag, wood or clay. He didn't really appreciate its attitude, perhaps because it was so like his own.

Something was definitely amiss. He bent to poke a finger in the water, but an anticipatory rustle across the lawn alerted him. So he plucked a blade of grass, evoking a strenuous protest from the bank, and poked it in the water.

In a moment it dissolved into sludge. This mote was filled with acid! Some obstacle! If he had tried to swim in that . . . !

He scrounged for a small stick, and poked that in the moat. It dissolved more slowly, being dead and more solid. He located a pebble and tried that, and it didn't dissolve at all.

Now he knew that the acid only affected animate material. Unfortunately, *he* was animate. He would have to use some sort of boat to cross, to keep his flesh clear of the liquid.

He searched the premises, looking for a boat. Naturally there was none. He heard a popping noise and discovered a popcorn plant, but that didn't help. He took a kernel of the corn on general principles, however; one never could tell when something might be useful in some obscure way.

Then he found a giant snail shell. The snail had long since passed away, but its hollow shell was beautiful, gleaming iridescently. But what use was an empty snail shell?

Suddenly he had a notion. He took hold of the shell and dragged it toward the moat. This was a job, as it weighed more than he did; he could have crawled inside the thing! But that just might be what he needed.

He shoved it to the moat and nudged it in. It floated with the hollow aperture up, and it did not dissolve. He pressed down on it, but it contained a lot more volume of air than he could displace; he could not push it below the surface of the liquid. Good enough again!

Grundy hauled the shell back on shore, then made another tour, locating several long twigs of wood. He brought them back, set them inside the shell, and launched it again. Then he climbed in himself, carefully. It supported his weight. Now he was floating!

He took a twig and used it to pole off from the bank. He settled himself as comfortably as he could inside the shell and used a flattened twig to paddle the craft. He had a snailboat!

Before long, his wooden paddle dissolved, and he had to use another. He had to paddle carefully, so as not to splash any of the acid on himself. Progress was slow, but the moat was not broad; he judged he would make it safely across if he didn't panic. Just as long as no monster appeared at this stage!

No monster appeared. Monsters didn't like acid any better than living golems did. An armored serpent might withstand the corrosion, but how would it protect its eyes and mouth?

In due course he nudged his way to a landing inside the moat, and stepped carefully to shore. One hurdle down.

He stood and looked about. He was on a fairly narrow beach between the moat and the wall. The beach curved around the island that was the castle. The wall was vertical and fashioned of flat, polished stone; he could see his reflection in it, but he couldn't catch so much as a fingerhold for climbing. He would have to walk around until he came to a suitable entrance.

He walked—and soon encountered a large animal. It was a unicorn! There were very few of them in Xanth; they seemed to prefer to range in other pastures. This one was a fairly disreputable-looking creature with a burr-tangled mane and a gnarled horn. It snorted as it spied him and pawed at the sand with a forehoof.

"Hi there, warp-horn," Grundy said in equine language with his usual politeness. "Why don't you clean up that stinking coat?"

"I'll clean up the sand with *you,* you midget blot," the unicorn replied with unprovoked bad humor.

Oops—this was evidently another obstacle. "I don't suppose you'd care to let me pass, so I can go on into the castle," Grundy said.

"I don't suppose you'd care to take a bath in the moat," the unicorn replied in the same tone.

Grundy made as if to scoot under the creature, for there was no room to pass on the side. The unicorn made as if to spear anything that tried that route. It was obvious that he could not get by; the animal was set to prevent it.

The golem stood back and considered. How could he pass a creature who was determined to prevent it and had the ability to enforce the restriction? There had to be a way.

He had a notion. He turned and walked away. He could circle the castle in either direction, and reach the entrance either way. The unicorn did not pursue him, perhaps too stupid to realize what he was doing.

Grundy walked three-quarters of the way around the castle—and stopped. There was the unicorn, facing the other way, horn lowered warningly. Obviously it had backed up to the entrance place, used that wider region to turn, and had come to block this route too. It wasn't stupid after all; it had known that it couldn't protect the entrance by chasing the golem around the castle.

Well, maybe he could trick it into letting down its guard. Or make it so mad it miscalculated. Grundy had a rare touch with insults, when he put his beady little mind to it. "Say, founderfoot, did they put you out here so you won't stink up the inside of the castle?"

"No, they put me out here so *you* wouldn't stink it up," the unicorn replied.

Hm. This might be more of a challenge than he had thought. But Grundy tried again. "Did you get that horn caught in a hole in the ground? No self-respecting creature would carry a broken spear like that!"

"Did you get that body caught in a shrinking violet?" the unicorn responded. "No self-respecting midget would use it."

"Listen, knot-mane, I'm a *golem!*" Grundy exclaimed. "I'm *supposed* to be this size."

"I doubt it. That body is way too small for that mouth."

Grundy swelled up to his full diminutive height, ready to spew forth a devastating torrent of abuse—and realized that the unicorn was winning the contest. *It* was the one that was supposed to be getting mad!

He would have to try some other tack. Well, if he couldn't beat it, maybe he could join it. "What do you want most in all Xanth?" he inquired.

"To get rid of pesky golems so I can resume my snooze."

"Apart from that," Grundy said unevenly.

The unicorn considered. "Well, I do get hungry, and meals are far apart. I'd sure like a nice snack of something good."

That was more promising. But Grundy wasn't sure how he could provide such a snack. "If you let me into the castle, maybe I could get you some nice hay or something," he suggested.

"If I let you into the castle, maybe I'll get my hide tanned before I'm ready to leave it," the unicorn said.

"Maybe I could get you a snack without going in," Grundy said.

"I'd be glad to have a snack without you going in," the creature agreed.

Somehow that didn't sound promising. Grundy stared across the moat, where the grass was green and the brush was leafy. Surely there was plenty there to distract the unicorn—but the unicorn couldn't cross to it, and Grundy himself would not be able to carry enough across in the snailboat to last for more than one mouthful at a time.

He spied a tall green plant that sported several tassles. That jogged his memory. Maybe there was a way!

"What kind of a plant are you?" he called in plant language. The unicorn couldn't understand that, of course, so it didn't know what he was doing.

"I am a popcorn plant," the plant replied proudly. "I have the best popcorn on the bank!"

Grundy turned to the unicorn. "Unicorns don't like popcorn, do they?"

"Of course they don't," the creature agreed, its mouth watering.

Aha! He remembered correctly. Unicorns liked all kinds of corns, because they were magically related.

He returned his attention to the popcorn. "You don't look like much to me," he sneered in plant language.

The plant huffed up and turned color. "I'm the top pop!" it proclaimed. "My kernels pop harder than anyone's!"

"They do not!" Grundy retorted. "I bet they fizzle!"

"Fizzle!" the plant snapped, outraged. Its ears turned an angry red. "I'll pop off so hard you'll think it's an explosion!"

"I think it's a fake!" Grundy said.

The plant's corns became so hot that the tassles browned and shriveled, and the leaves around its ears split apart. The kernels popped with the heat, first a few, then many, until it did indeed resemble an explosion. Popcorn puffs flew out in every direction, a number of them arcing over the moat and peppering the castle wall.

"Popcorn!" the unicorn exclaimed, eagerly snatching up the fallen pieces.

"But unicorns don't like popcorn," Grundy reminded it.

"Get out of here, golem!" the creature cried angrily.

"As you wish." Grundy retreated to the unicorn's rear, toward the gate, and the creature was so distracted by the delicious popcorn puffs that it didn't notice. Grundy moved on up to the gate and through it without further opposition. He was inside the castle!

"Very clever, you little morsel," a voice growled.

Grundy looked, startled. He was in a moderately sized court with a dirt floor, and before him stood an ant lion. The monster could snap him up in a moment, if it wanted to.

"I'm just trying to get in to see the Good Magician on important business," the golem said nervously.

"Indeed." The ant lion yawned, showing its enormous feline teeth. It was playing cat-and-mouse with him, knowing that its six insect legs could overtake him anytime. "I doubt you are smart enough to rate any of his time."

"Sure I am!" Grundy retorted hotly. "I'm just not big enough to get by all you monsters."

"I will make you a deal," the ant lion said, stretching languorously. "Prove you are smart, and I will let you pass."

It was up to something. But Grundy realized he had nothing to lose; he was already in its power. "How do I do that?"

"You play me three games of lines and boxes," the ant lion said. "If you can defeat me, I'll let you enter. If you lose, I'll consume you. That's very fair, isn't it?"

Grundy swallowed. He was not entirely pleased with the terms. "Suppose we tie?"

"Then I will let you enter anyway. I can be magnanimous to an intellectual equal. To make it even easier for you, I will even grant you the first move each time."

Grundy still didn't like this. But he was aware of two things: first, he really had no choice, as he could not otherwise get in to see the Good Magician, and second, he was a pretty good player of lines and boxes. He could probably win. "I agree," he said.

"Excellent!" the ant lion said heartily. It leaped suddenly into the air and came down with its six legs straight. It was a fairly massive creature, so each leg sank into the dirt as it landed. It stepped out of its tracks, and six neat depressions remained. Then it jumped again, this time landing a little to the side. The three right legs landed in the dents left by the three left legs before, and the three left legs made three new dents.

The monster stepped carefully back. There before it was a neat pattern of nine dents, forming a large square with one dent in the center. "There is the board," it announced.

"That's only enough for four boxes!" Grundy protested.

The ant lion extended a claw and contemplated it. "So?"

Grundy decided not to protest further. A small game was the same as a big one in principle, after all, and he did have the first move. He stepped up and scratched a line with his foot between a corner dent and the center dent on his side.

The ant lion reached across and scraped another line, from Grundy's center dot to the other corner dot. One side of the figure was complete.

Grundy drew a line from a near corner up to connect to the middle dot on that side. The ant lion made another, completing that side. Grundy drew one along the side closest to the ant, and the ant completed this one also. Then they each put a line in the fourth side. Now the figure was a large box—and Grundy realized he was in trouble.

He had no choice now but to draw a line from the center dot to one of the sides. That would set things up for his opponent to complete a box with his line, and then use his extra turn to complete another box, and so on through the figure, winning. He had been trapped into a game he couldn't win.

"Move—or forfeit," the ant lion said with satisfaction.

Grundy sighed and moved. Whereupon the ant lion did exactly as expected, filling in all four boxes and marking his neat letter A's in each. Grundy had lost badly.

"I think I'll give you the first move for the next game," Grundy said.

"By no means," the ant lion said firmly. "I promised you the advantage of the first move every time, and I am a creature of my word."

"But—"

The monster extended another claw and studied it significantly. Grundy realized that he had to accept this generosity.

What was he to do? The advantage clearly lay with the second player —and that advantage was going to get him consumed by the monster!

Then Grundy remembered something. There just might be a way! He had not played such small games before, but the principle should hold. The key was in the fact that a player did not *have* to complete a box if he did not want to, provided he was able to make some other move instead. That seemed like a losing strategy, so it was seldom employed, but it had its points. He would use it here.

They started the second game of their appointed three. Grundy started exactly as he had before, and the ant lion continued as before. They completed two sides of the outer square. Then Grundy made his surprise move: he drew a line to the center.

The ant lion stared. "But you're giving away a box before you have to!" it protested.

"Nothing in the rules against that, is there?"

The ant lion shrugged with all three sets of shoulders. "Nothing in the rules against foolish moves," it agreed, and completed the box, marking its A in it. Then it put its bonus line in the opposite side, to avoid giving Grundy a similar gift. Grundy filled in the last free spot. Now the diagram looked like this:

The ant lion got ready to draw his line—and paused. There was nowhere he could move, without setting Grundy up for three boxes and victory. "I'll be cursed!" it exclaimed. "You set me up!"

"Merely playing the game to win," Grundy replied modestly.

With imperfect grace, the ant lion drew a line at the edge, and Grundy filled in the rest, marking G's in three boxes.

The score stood at one victory each. The ant lion was very thoughtful as they commenced the deciding game. This one started as the others had, but when Grundy offered the sacrifice box, the other declined it, choosing instead to continue around the rim. Now Grundy was nervous; could this force the win back to the lion?

Then Grundy saw the other side of the key. He moved in and took the first box himself, and used his bonus line to fill in the last available free space. It didn't matter which player took the box and the bonus line; that extra line shifted the advantage to the first player. The configuration now was this:

The ant lion stared at it for a long time. Finally it shrugged, and filled in a line. Grundy filled in the remaining three boxes.

"I learned something today," the ant lion said philosophically. "The ploy of the proffered box, which is disaster whether accepted or declined. I congratulate you, Golem; you have proved yourself to be smart enough to pass." And the monster stood aside and allowed Grundy to enter the castle.

Grundy's little knees were weak. In retrospect he realized that the Good Magician had surely known about the way to reverse the game, so that it represented a fair test of ingenuity. But how close he had come to failing that test!

Now he walked through another gate, and there was the veiled Gorgon. "What kept you, Grundy?" she inquired solicitously.

Grundy didn't have it in him to make a smart reply. "I just want to see the Magician."

"By all means. But be careful; he's grumpy today."

She ushered him into the Good Magician's office. Humfrey was perched on his high stool, poring over a monstrous tome. That was par for the course. He was now about twelve years old, physically, having recovered that far from the overdose of Youth Elixir he had suffered five years before.

"Magician, I need advice on—" Grundy began.

"Go away," Humfrey grumped.

"I just want to—"

"One year's service—in advance."

This was of course standard procedure for the Good Magician. But Grundy had been shaken by the experience with the ant lion, and his natural manner of expressing himself surged to the fore. "Listen, you rejuvenated freak! You're such an idiot you've missed the obvious for five years! You can be any age you want to, anytime. I can give you back a century of your life, with one sentence. Then you'll owe me a hundred Answers!"

This got the Good Magician's full attention. "Prove it."

"All you have to do is dunk a stick of reverse-wood in a cup of Youth Elixir. Then it will—"

"Become Age Elixir!" Humfrey finished, amazed. "Now why didn't *I* think of that?"

"Because you're an—"

"I heard. Very well, Golem—you've earned your Answer. Ask your Question."

"I've earned all the Answers I want!" Grundy exclaimed.

"No. You have done me one service that I may exploit to my satisfaction. How many years I use it for does not relate; it is *your* year that counts. Ask."

Grundy realized that the Good Magician, like the ant lion, was a creature of no compromise. At least he had what he wanted.

"How can I find and rescue Stanley Steamer?"

"Oho! You're doing something about that!" Humfrey glanced at his open book. "It says you must ride the Monster Under the Bed to the Ivory Tower."

"You mean you had it open to the place all the time?" Grundy demanded indignantly.

"Is that another Question?"

Grundy ground his teeth. The Good Magician didn't give *anything* away for nothing, unless the visitor was a Magician. "At least tell me where the Ivory Tower is!"

"Do you want to pay your year's service before or after I give you that Answer?"

"You gnomish cheapskate!" Grundy raged. "I just gave you back your age, hardly a minute ago!"

Humfrey's lips quirked. "And what have you done for me lately, Golem?"

Grundy stormed out of the room. The Good Magician hardly noticed; he was back poring over his tome.

2

Snortimer

Back at Castle Roogna, Grundy remained disgruntled. He had belatedly realized that the Good Magician hadn't even told him that Stanley Steamer was at the Ivory Tower; he had just said to ride the monster there. Who could guess what complications would manifest at that point? On the other hand, Humfrey also hadn't said that the quest was useless. He might not know for sure whether Stanley was alive, but at least he had enabled Grundy to find out.

First he had to explain things to Ivy. He suspected that would not be easy—and he was correct.

"You want to take Snortimer?!" she demanded indignantly. "He's *my* monster!"

"But all you do is ignore him or tease him," Grundy pointed out.

"That's beside the point," she said, assuming her Little Lady manner. "He belongs under my bed, nowhere else."

"But the Good Magician says I have to ride the Monster Under the Bed to the Ivory Tower, and he's the only Monster Under the Bed I know well enough to ask."

"The Ivory Tower?" she asked with a mercurial shift of mood. "That's where Rapunzel lives!"

Grundy hadn't thought of that. Rapunzel was Ivy's pun-pal, who sent her periodic boxes of puns in exchange for the mundane scraps Ivy sent. It had always seemed to Grundy that Ivy had much the best of the bargain, and he wondered why Rapunzel continued with the arrangement. But what could Rapunzel have to do with the missing dragon? Surely she would have notified Ivy if Stanley had turned up there!

But he decided it was better not to raise such issues with Ivy; no good could come of it. "Do you want Stanley back or don't you?" Grundy demanded gruffly.

"Oh, pooh!" she said. "Go do it, then. But if anything happens to Snortimer, I'll never forgive you!"

So Grundy went to talk to Snortimer, the Monster Under Ivy's Bed. Such monsters were an interesting species, because only children and credulous folk could see them at all; normal adults didn't even believe in them. Since Grundy was small, he had no trouble perceiving the monster—and because he was small, he had always stayed well out of reach. Now, with some trepidation, he approached Snortimer's lair.

"Snortimer," he called from a safe distance.

Something twitched in the dusky recesses beneath the bunk.

"Snortimer, I know you understand me," Grundy called. "I'm speaking your language. Come out from under there; I need your help."

A big, hairy hand poked out from the deep shadow, as if questing for something to grab. That was of course the speciality of the species: grabbing children's ankles. Some mean children would dangle their feet down and snatch them away just before getting grabbed, but most children were properly terrified.

"Listen, Snortimer, I have a Quest. I need your help."

At last the monster spoke. "Why should I help you?"

" 'Cause the Good Magician says I have to ride you to the Ivory Tower to rescue Stanley."

Snortimer considered. "It'll cost you, golem."

Grundy sighed. He should have known that nothing about this Quest would be easy. "What will it cost?"

"I want romance."

"What?"

"I've been eight years under this bed, grabbing at Ivy's ankles and hiding from her mother. The same old grind, day after day. There must be more to life than this!"

"But that's what Monsters Under the Bed do!" Grundy protested. "They have no other purpose than to grab at children's ankles and hide from parents."

"Then why am I supposed to help you?"

Snortimer had a point. Obviously there was more to such a monster's life than ankles. "Um, just what do you mean by romance?"

"I don't know. But I'll know it when I find it."

"Why don't you just crawl off to another bed and find a, uh, female of your species, and—?"

"That isn't how it's done. No Bed Monster shares territory. I have to find someone who isn't yet committed to a bed."

"Where would that be?"

The big ugly hand made a gesture of ignorance. "I have no idea. I suppose I just have to travel about until somewhere I find her."

"Well, I plan to travel," Grundy said. "If you will be my steed, you'd get to cover quite a bit of the country."

"Sounds good," Snortimer agreed. "I'll be your steed—but only till I find romance."

Grundy realized that that could get him stranded somewhere far away, perhaps in the midst of Uncommitted Monster Country. But half a loaf was better than none. "Agreed. Let's start right away. Come on out of there."

"I can't," Snortimer said.

"But you said—"

"I said I'd be your steed; I didn't say I'd do the impossible. I can't come out until dark."

"But I was planning on traveling in the daytime!"

"Not with me, you're not! Light would destroy me instantly. Why do you think we Bed Monsters never climb up on *top* of the bed to grab at ankles? We're confined to the deepest shadows." He pondered a moment. "Which is unfortunate. There's a lot more than ankles up there."

"Why don't you go up and grab when the lights are out?"

The hand spread in a what-can-you-do? gesture. "Against the rules. There has to be some limitation, or all the Bed Monsters would take over the uppersides and put the children underneath. We can't bother anything we can't grab when the light's on."

"But you can travel from your bed, at night?"

"Some. As long as I don't bother anyone."

"I see. But why don't you go out and look for romance at night, on your own, then?"

"I wouldn't dare do it alone! Suppose I got trapped by a sudden light, and couldn't make it back to my bed before dawn?"

"What happens if you get caught away from your bed?"

"Extinction!" Snortimer replied with deepest dread.

"But then how can you be my steed and travel to the farthest reaches of Xanth in quest of romance?"

"I hadn't thought of that," the monster said.

Baffled, Grundy returned to Ivy. He explained the problem. "But there must be a way," he concluded, "or the Good Magician wouldn't have told me to do it."

"I'll ask Hugo," she said. She had evidently become reconciled to the temporary loss of her monster. Grundy suspected that little girls didn't really *like* having their ankles grabbed when they went to bed, whatever they might say to the contrary. "C'mon."

They went to the Magic Mirror and Ivy summoned Hugo, the Good Magician's son. Hugo was becoming a halfway handsome boy of thirteen. He listened to the problem and, at Ivy's urging, came up with the solution: "He'll just have to take the bed along."

Ivy turned to Grundy. "See? Easy as pie. Just take—" Then she did a doubletake. "Hey, that's *my* bed!"

"We all have to make sacrifices," Grundy said, suppressing an obnoxious smile.

But Ivy surprised him with another change of attitude. "Oh, I was tired of that bed anyway! You can take it with you. I'll sleep on cushions. They're comfortabler."

Grundy doubted that, but did not see fit to argue. Perhaps, for Ivy, it would become true.

He returned to Snortimer. "Problem solved," he announced. "We'll just take the bed along."

"How?" the monster asked.

Good question! Obviously if Snortimer were to be his steed, he couldn't also carry a bed, assuming he could move it at all. But Ivy had disappeared on some other errand, and Grundy knew he couldn't make Hugo answer questions the way Ivy could, if only because the boy was usually rather stupid. He would have to figure out something on his own.

"I think we'll have to get help," Grundy said. This was certainly becoming complicated!

"Let me know when you do," Snortimer said. "Meanwhile I'll snooze." In a moment there was the sound of snoring from the shadow.

Grundy wandered around Castle Roogna, trying to decide on a suitable person to ask for help. It had to be someone big and strong enough to carry the bed, and stupid enough not to ask why. Someone like Smash Ogre. But Smash was married now, and his wife Tandy kept him on a short leash; no hope there.

Well, maybe someone not stupid, but not important, either. Someone who had nothing better to do than carry beds around the countryside. Who would that be?

Suddenly he had a bright answer. He knew just the person!

Thus it was that he came to talk with Ivy's other grandfather, Bink. Bink had little to do with the activities of Castle Roogna and every month, when his wife Chameleon got smart and ugly, he tended to make excursions around Xanth on his own. Maybe he'd be willing to take a bed along.

"Why not?" Bink inquired amiably. He was about sixty years old now, but still hearty, and a pretty solid man. "But even a small bed would get heavy soon enough; I'll ask my friend Chester to help."

"But I'm not sure we should make a big production of this," Grundy said. "I was thinking of a quiet Quest."

Bink looked at him, smiling. "If I know my granddaughter, she's into mischief, and if I know you, you're trying to keep her out of it—and you're not allowed to tell."

"Something like that," Grundy agreed uncomfortably.

"Well, then, we won't tell. No one will miss us anyway."

"You're very understanding, sir," Grundy said. Bink might not seem like much, but he was a former King of Xanth, which meant he had Magician-class magic, though that wasn't evident. It seemed to Grundy that he had once known more about it, but he seemed to have forgotten.

"It's been a long time since Chester and I have had a decent adventure," Bink said.

That evening Bink and Chester showed up at the Castle. "Our wives aren't too keen on this," Bink confessed. "They're letting us go, but only for two weeks. That means one week out and one week back. Do you think you can complete your Quest in that time?"

"I hope so," Grundy said. He had no idea how long it would take to reach the Ivory Tower, especially since he didn't know where it was. "I haven't had a lot of experience with Quests, you know."

"Well, let's get on with it," Bink said. He carried a hefty coil of rope. Chester waited outside, while Bink marched in and upstairs, Grundy on his shoulder.

It seemed to Grundy that someone should have shown up to inquire what in Xanth they were doing, such as Ivy's mother Irene, who normally had supersensitive hearing and curiosity to match. But luckily no one was disturbed, and they reached Ivy's room undetected.

Ivy was awake, of course, though in her nightie. She almost flew to Bink's arms. "Ooo, Grandpa Bink, how exciting!" she exclaimed. "Are you going to steal my bed now?"

"That's right, sweetie," Bink agreed. And methodically he opened the largest window wide, tied his rope to the bed, and lifted it up.

Snortimer scooted away, startled. "Not so fast, monster!" Grundy said, dropping down. "You're my steed, remember?"

It was dark in the room, so he really couldn't see Snortimer very well, but the monster seemed to consist of five or six big hairy arms and hands and nothing else. Somewhat diffidently, Grundy climbed aboard, and found a fairly comfortable seat at the juncture of the arms. Snortimer was not a large monster, for he had to fit under the small bed, but he was a good size for Grundy.

Bink heaved the bed out through the window and let it down with the rope. It swung and bumped against the stones of the wall, generating an awful clatter, but still no one seemed to notice. What phenomenal luck!

When the bed scraped its way to the base, Chester Centaur caught hold of it with his powerful arms and set it on his back. They had rigged a harness for him so that he could carry it without having to use his hands, and its weight was no problem at all for him.

They bade farewell to Ivy, who remained thrilled at this secret adventure and perhaps a little jealous that she wasn't going along, but she knew as well as they did that there was no way her mother would let her get involved in something like this. And of course it was for the best of causes: the rescue of Stanley Steamer.

They went down and out, still without stirring up any commotion in the castle, and rejoined Chester. Quietly they walked away from the wall and crossed the moat and entered the main orchard. The trees rustled their branches, wondering what was going on, but did not interfere.

They wended their way on through the darkness, unspeaking. Grundy was able to see very little, but Snortimer had no trouble. The monster was of course a creature of the dark, completely at home in it. Grundy began to appreciate the wisdom of selecting a steed like this, though he remained uncertain whether the Good Magician's advice was good for the long term. He still had no idea where to find the Ivory Tower.

They came to a spot in the forest that Chester knew, where several great trees clustered to form a leafy bower. They stopped. "We can talk here," Chester said. "No one will overhear us. Where do we go from here?"

"I don't know," Grundy confessed. "I'm supposed to go to the Ivory Tower, but the Good Magician didn't tell me where it is. If one of you happens to know—"

"Not me," Chester said, and Bink agreed.

Grundy sighed. "I suppose we'll just have to search for it. I can ask the plants and things as we go along."

"The Good Magician must have had a reason to have you ride the Bed Monster," Bink said. "Maybe you had better just give the monster its head and see where it takes you."

"I suppose so." Then Grundy thought of something else. "I thought no adults could see the monster, or believe in it."

"We haven't seen it yet," Chester growled. "It's dark."

"But people become more childlike as they grow older," Bink said. "Maybe there comes a time when they believe in that particular monster again."

"Okay, Snortimer," Grundy said. "Go where you have a mind, and let's see if it's the Ivory Tower."

"I have no idea where to go either," Snortimer protested. Grundy could understand him perfectly, but the others could not speak the language, so couldn't participate.

"Isn't that great!" Grundy exclaimed. "Four of us here—and not one of us has any notion how to proceed!"

"Perhaps we should ask someone, then," Bink suggested mildly.

"Who would possibly know?" Grundy demanded dispiritedly.

"The female Gap Dragon," Chester suggested. "At least she has a motive to find Stanley."

"But she would gobble us up in a moment!" Grundy protested.

"Not if you presented our case clearly," Bink said. "I'm sure it will work out."

The man was certainly a fool! But Chester agreed with him, and Grundy was dependent on them to carry the bed. He had no choice. "I guess that's what we'll do, then," he agreed reluctantly.

"First let's get a good night's sleep," Bink said. "We'll have some heavy traveling coming up."

"But we have to travel by night!" Grundy protested.

"That's true," Bink agreed. "I had forgotten. Well, let's get a good night and day's sleep, and be fresh for tomorrow night."

Grundy chafed at the delay. Then he remembered Stella Steamer, the lady Gap Dragon, and decided that delay was no bad thing. What a bad beginning for this Quest!

Grundy worried that someone from Castle Roogna would discover them, as they were not very far from it, but still their luck held. That was gratifying, of course, yet still he felt out of sorts. This was supposed to be *his* Quest, but the others seemed to be running things pretty much their way. He was still just a golem, the least consequential of creatures.

The following evening, well-rested, they started off. Grundy rode Snortimer, and had to admit that the monster got around quite well. The only problem was the wan moonlight; Snortimer would not venture into even that dim illumination, and plowed through the densest brush to avoid it. Since the magic path tended to be open, quite a lot of it was moonlighted, so Grundy spent half his time off the path. However, Snortimer's big hairy hands grasped the brush with sure grips and seemed unbothered by even the thickest tangles, and soon Grundy stopped being concerned.

After an hour or so, they came to a surprise: a detour. A dark sign blocked the path. Grundy approached it until he was able to make out the print, even in the shadow. It said:

"CONSTRUCTION: D-Tails @ Shopping Centaur."

"That's odd," Bink remarked. "I hadn't heard about work on the magic paths."

"Well, we might as well go learn the details," Chester said. "They seem to be at a good place."

He was a centaur; naturally he saw nothing odd about the location. But Grundy didn't like this.

They took the indicated side trail. They had been proceeding north, toward the Gap Chasm; the detour took them east. The path seemed all right, but Grundy remained uneasy. He had never heard of a magic path being closed off for construction.

Soon they came to the shopping centaur. This turned out to be not a place but a creature: a lady centaur carrying a huge shopping bag. She carried a lamp, which made Snortimer scurry to cover in the shadows off-trail, so that Grundy did not hear her dialogue with Bink and Chester.

In a moment she continued on her way, and Grundy was able to rejoin the others. "She says the tails belong to the Bulls and Bears, and to be careful," Bink said. "The Bulls always go up, while the Bears go down, and it can get violent."

"What are Bulls and Bears?" Grundy asked.

"Mundane animals. Some must have strayed." Bink evidently wasn't worried.

They moved on. The detour continued roughly east, evincing no intention of turning north. Grundy's discomfort increased. He wasn't eager to encounter the Gap Dragoness, but this eastward drift was only wasting time and effort.

As the first wan light of dawn threatened ahead of them, Snortimer got nervous, and they had to make camp. They found an open field, and Chester pitched the bed there, and the Bed Monster scooted under it just before the light brightened.

Chester and Bink went foraging for food. Grundy, tired, simply lay down on the bed and slept. That aspect was very convenient; he would always have a comfortable place to retire.

Grundy woke abruptly. The sun was shining down slantingly, and creatures were all around him. At first he thought Bink and Chester had returned, but this was not the case; instead, a herd of huge four-footed, hooved creatures were milling around the bed. They seemed to be heedless of the bed's presence, and Grundy was afraid they would knock it over and thus expose Snortimer's retreat to the direct sunshine. That would be disaster!

"Hey!" he cried. "Watch where you're going!"

Still they ignored him, pressing heedlessly closer. Each creature had a shaggy coat and two stout horns on its head. One of them pressed in close to the bed, almost brushing it.

"What's up, anyway?" Grundy demanded, standing on the bed.

"Up?" Several nearby creatures swung their heads, for the first time taking note of him. They crowded in closer.

"Or down," Grundy cried. "What are you—"

"Down!" several creatures cried, horrified. A kind of stampede developed, momentarily abating the press of bodies about the bed.

But this turned out to be no improvement, for now a new kind of creature showed up. This was a hairy, muscular entity who lacked horns but had large teeth. Several of these surged toward the bed.

"Who are you?" Grundy cried, newly alarmed.

"We are the Bulls," the horned creatures lowed.

"We are the Bears," the toothed ones growled.

Now Grundy remembered: the creatures the tails belonged to, who always went up or down. He didn't like either—but he was stuck in their midst.

A Bear scraped by the bed, shoving it to one side. Grundy tumbled, almost falling off. "Hey, watch it!" he yelled, grabbing on to the bar at the foot of it.

But the Bears ignored him as determinedly as the Bulls had. "Down! Down!" they growled, and indeed they seemed to be traveling downward, for the field was tilted.

Grundy realized that this situation was beyond him. Where were Bink and Chester? He had to get the bed out of the field before these animals overturned it, and he couldn't do that by himself. But there was no sign of his friends.

More Bears surged down, gaining momentum. The Bulls were almost out of sight. Grundy knew he couldn't affect these blindly charging creatures physically, but remembered that he had made a slight impression with his words. They seemed to be very sensitive to references about direction. "Up! Down!" he yelled.

The nearest Bears hesitated, falling back for a moment. But then they resumed their charge, and the bed bumped across the field as their heedless imperative jostled it. It started to tip over, then plumped back.

He heard a whimper from Snortimer, underneath; naturally the monster was terrified.

"East! West!" Grundy yelled, but this had no discernable impression. "North! South!"

The charge continued. The bed moved some more, and a leg hung up in a hole. Again it started to tilt. "We're in trouble!" Grundy cried.

A passing Bear paused. "Who's in trouble?" it demanded.

"This bed's in trouble!" Grundy replied. "If you'd just stop shoving—"

"Oh," the Bear said, disappointed. It lost interest and resumed its downward charge.

"Thanks a lot, hairsnout!" Grundy screamed after it. "May a green hornet buzz up your—"

"Up?" another Bear asked, dismayed. "What's going up?"

"My blood pressure!" Grundy retorted. "What's *with* you beasts?"

But this Bear, like the other, had lost interest and resumed its charge.

So words had some effect, but not a reliable one. Maybe he would do better yelling randomly. "Pink moons in the lake!" he called.

It seemed to work. "What stock?" the nearest passing Bear asked.

"Purple comets in the soup!" Grundy responded.

More Bears paused. "That sounds bad," another said.

"It's terrible!" Grundy agreed, pleased with his progress.

But at that they all took off running, faster than before, threatening to sweep the bed right down out of the field, threatening to flip it over several times on the way.

"Red planets taking a bath!" he screamed.

The charge slowed. "Sell Red Planet!" a Bear growled. Then the motion resumed.

"Consolidated Nonesuch is going nowhere!" Grundy cried.

"Yes! Yes!" the Bears agreed, and accelerated.

"You stupes!" Grundy raged. "Just where do you think nowhere is?"

"Bad news, bad news!" the Bears cried, and pressed on.

Grundy tried again. "Amalgamated Parrot-Ox is buying out Con-Pewter!" *That* nonsense should make them take notice.

It did. "That's bullish for Con-Pewter!" a Bear groaned.

"Buy Pewter!" a Bull lowed. And now there was a resurgence among the Bulls.

"It's a crock!" a Bear protested, but the tide had turned. The Bulls surged back on the strength of the Pewter con. The Bulls retreated in confusion. The Con-Pewter age had arrived!

This was too much success! The charge of the Bulls was just as dangerous as that of the Bears. The bed was getting rocked.

"Kissimmee River is telling!" Grundy screamed.

"Telling?" a Bull snorted, dismayed. "That's not supposed to happen!"

"Well, it is!" Grundy said.

Evidently the notion of anything telling dismayed the Bulls. They milled about uncertainly, and the Bears began to reform their formation. This did little good for the bed, though; it got nudged right up against a tree.

"Yo!" a voice came faintly. "Grundy!"

Grundy looked. There was Bink, riding Chester! They were back! "Over here!" he cried. "By the tree!"

But the field was filled with milling Bulls and Bears, and it was obvious that Chester would have difficulty getting through.

A Bull crashed against the bed, and the bed slammed into the trunk of the tree, and a fruit plopped into the center of the bed, just missing Grundy. The fruit was as big as he was, and shaped like a giant light bulb; it would have flattened him had it caught him. "Watch what you're dropping!" Grundy yelled at the tree.

"It's your fault!" the tree retorted in plant language. "You stirred up the stockyard!"

"Who are you to blame anything on me?" Grundy demanded belligerently.

"I am a power plant," the tree replied proudly.

Suddenly Grundy saw a solution to his problem. "Give me a bite of that!" he said, pouncing on the fruit. It had split slightly from the impact of the fall; had it not landed on the bed, it would have broken right apart. Grundy snatched out a juicy seed and chewed on it.

In a moment he felt its effect. Power rippled through him. He did not become larger or more muscular; he merely developed a lot more strength in what he had. That was of course the nature of the fruit of the power plant: it made the eater strong. For a little while.

Grundy took advantage of the moment. He jumped down to the ground and took hold of a leg of the bed. "We're getting out of here!" he told Snortimer, who was huddled under the center, shaking with fear. "Just stay centered, so the light doesn't touch you."

Then he hauled on the leg. The bed moved. He strode forward, hauling the bed along. He moved it around the tree and on into the forest, out of the press of Bulls and Bears. By the time the strength lent by the power plant abated, he had brought the bed to safety in a thicker part of the forest.

Bink and Chester rejoined him. "We feasted on loquats, middlequats and highquats," Bink explained. "When we started back, we encountered traveling nickelpedes and had to skirt widely around them. Then we heard a commotion in the field, but we couldn't get to it quickly."

"We were trapped amid rampaging Bulls and Bears!" Grundy exclaimed. "Those are the craziest animals I ever saw! All they do is charge up and down, up and down! Luckily I found a power plant at the last minute."

"Yes, a fortunate coincidence," Bink agreed, smiling obscurely. Grundy wondered what he was thinking of, but wasn't in a mood to inquire.

"Let's get some sleep," Chester said gruffly. He lay down, letting his head and shoulders rest on a hummock. It was strange to see a centaur in that position, but of course Chester was no longer as young as he once had been and had to rest in whatever fashion was best for him.

Bink settled down against a tree. "Shouldn't we post a guard?" Grundy asked.

"Not necessary," Bink said, and closed his eyes.

How could the man be so sure of that? They weren't that far from the stockyard where the animals ranged, after all; suppose a stray Bull or Bear crashed through here? But Grundy was quite tired in the aftermath of his exercise with the power plant strength; one problem with that sort of thing was that there was a corresponding period of weakness to make up for the temporary power. He flopped on the bed and slept.

Bink's optimism seemed valid, for they rested undisturbed until nightfall. Then they roused, ate some quats that Chester had saved from breakfast, and resumed their travel.

As they wended along the path, which still bore determinedly east, they found themselves entering a more equine region. There were horseflies sleeping on the trunks of horse chestnuts, and night mares seemed to prowl.

They came to a fork in the path. They paused, uncertain which one to take, as neither went north. While they hesitated, two actual horses showed up. Horses were very rare in Xanth, being mainly mundane in their original form, but of course if Bulls and Bears could stray here, so could horses.

"Say, you horses," Grundy called. "We want to get back to the magic path going north. Which trail should we take?"

The horses paused, one in each fork. "Gee!" neighed the one at the right. "Haw!" neighed the one on the left. Then they galloped on down their respective paths.

"They're just horsing around," Bink said philosophically. "I suppose we'd better gamble on the more northerly path."

That was a decision Grundy himself should have made, the Golem thought, troubled. But who paid attention to him, even on his own Quest? They took the more northerly trail.

In due course they came upon a woman and a small equine creature. The woman had a little notebook, in which she was busily making notes by the light of the moon. She looked up, startled, as they approached. "And who are you?" she inquired, her pencil poised.

"I am Grundy Golem, on a Quest," Grundy said importantly from just outside the beam of moonlight. "These are Chester Centaur, Bink, and Snortimer. Who are you?"

"Snortimer?" she asked. "I don't see that one."

"He's the Monster Under the Bed. Most adults can't see him. It's your turn to answer, toots."

"How interesting," she said. "The Monster Under the Bed. I thought those were just fantasies."

"Look, cutie-pie," Grundy said sneeringly. "Are you going to answer a simple question, or have you forgotten your name?"

"Oh, yes," she said, finishing her note. "I'm EmJay, and this is my Ass."

"I can see where—oh, you mean that animal?"

"He's no common animal!" she said indignantly. "He's MiKe, my right-hand Ass, and he helps me a lot."

Grundy studied the shaggy beast. "Helps you with what?"

"Helps me make my notes. I couldn't get the job done without him."

"What are you making notes about?"

"About everything in Xanth, for my Lexicon."

"What good is that?"

"Well, I hope it will be useful for those who want to know about anything in a hurry."

"Like who?"

That seemed to stump her. "Well, *somebody* must be interested in Xanth!"

"The only one I can think of is Good Magician Humfrey, and he already knows everything he wants to."

"Maybe the Mundanes—" she said uncertainly.

"Mundanes! What do *they* know?"

"Very little," she said. "That's why they need a Lexicon."

"Female logic," Grundy said disparagingly. "Now get out of our way so we can get where we're going."

EmJay looked a little annoyed for some reason, but she rallied. "You said you were going on a Quest. What Quest?"

"What business is it of yours?"

"I want to list it in the Lexicon, of course."

Grundy considered. Probably there was no harm in telling her. "I'm going to the Ivory Tower to rescue Stanley Steamer."

"Oh, the little dragon!" she exclaimed, checking the entry in her notes. "May I come along?"

"Listen, sister," Grundy said angrily. "This is *my* Quest, not yours! I don't need any strange woman and her Ass messing it up!"

"You *are* a diplomatic one, aren't you!" she exclaimed. "What makes you think I would mess up your precious Quest?"

"You're a woman!" Grundy reminded her. "Of course you'd mess it up!"

She looked as if she wanted to argue, but thought the better of it. "Well, suppose we tag along a little way, and if we mess anything up, then we'll leave you alone?"

Grudgingly, Grundy agreed. Bink and Chester, both married to women, had maintained a remarkable silence.

They resumed their trek, with EmJay and Ass falling in behind. They made respectable progress for a couple of hours—until they encountered another woman.

This one was young and sultry. "Well, now!" she breathed. "What have we here?"

"We don't need another woman!" Grundy snapped.

"I am not exactly a woman," the new one murmured.

"You sure *look* like a woman! What are you, then—a monster?"

"In my fashion," she agreed. "I am a succubus, on the prowl for business."

"Uh-oh," Chester said.

"We aren't your business," Bink said firmly.

"Are you sure?" she asked archly. She shimmered, and suddenly she looked exactly like Bink's wife Chameleon, in her prettiest phase.

"We're sure," Chester said.

The succubus shimmered again, and there stood Chester's mate, Cherie, in her most fetching pose. "I do a lot of business with married males," she said.

"Not with these ones," Grundy said. "Go away, you slut."

"Maybe I'll just tag along a while," the succubus said. "In case someone changes his mind."

She was magical; they couldn't do anything about her. But Grundy had another irritation. The succubus had tried to tempt both Bink and Chester, but hadn't even bothered with Grundy himself. That showed how *he* rated. Of course he would have told her to go away—but he felt insulted that she hadn't tried. Not even the most corrupt creature thought him worth noticing.

"Succubus," EmJay murmured, making a note.

Chester nudged Bink. "We're okay for now—but what about when we sleep? That's when a creature like that gets you."

"There won't be any problem," Bink said.

No problem? There would be an awful row when the wives heard about it, Grundy knew.

But as dawn loomed, and they set about making camp for the day, the solution to the problem of the succubus appeared. "Oh, I can't face the light!" she exclaimed, and hurried away.

The fact that they were now sleeping by day gave them security from this threat. Had Bink known, or was it just a lucky break?

3

Con-Pewter

In the evening the succubus was gone, but EmJay and her Ass remained. Grundy muttered something about half a loaf being better than none, and mounted Snortimer. Maybe if they moved along rapidly, they'd leave the Lexicographers behind.

The path wended its idle way along, teasing them, now north, now east. They paused in alarm as a huge shape passed overhead, but it was no dragon, only a big house fly. The thing has disproportionately small wings, and an unstreamlined roof, so that its flight was erratic; it seemed about to crash at any moment, but somehow it bumbled on. They paused to pluck some succulent fruit to eat, until EmJay's Ass brayed.

"What're you talking about, you asinine creature?" Grundy asked it.

"Well, if you *want* to eat passion fruit . . ." the Ass replied in braytalk.

"Passion fruit?" Grundy asked, dismayed.

"Sure," the Ass brayed. "We Lexed that yesterday. That's why the succubus hangs out here. Once a man chomps into that fruit—"

They decided to pass the fruit by. Grundy heard a muffled curse from the side, and realized that the succubus had been watching from hiding. He was tempted to make an obscene gesture in her direction, but knew she'd take it as a compliment.

They found some innocent breadfruits and a fresh babbling brook further along, so were able to eat and drink safely. The brook talked incessantly, of course, but that was the nature of its kind. Actually, it had quite a bit of gossip to babble, about the nefarious doings of the local creatures, that Grundy found interesting.

Then, abruptly, the brook went silent. Grundy looked at it in surprise. "What's the matter, wetback?"

"The—the giant!" the brook babbled briefly, then froze up. A thin film of ice formed on its surface. It was stiff with fright.

Grundy looked around. "Giant? I don't see any giant."

Bink and Chester and the Ass all peered about. Nothing was visible. "That brook's got water on the brain," the centaur muttered. "There's no giant around here!"

Then they heard a distant crash, as of a boulder smashing through brush, and felt the ground shudder. Stray fruits and nuts were jostled from trees. After a pause, there was another crash, slightly louder, with more insistent shuddering.

"That's either a remarkable coincidence—two boulders falling out of nowhere—" Bink began.

There was a third crash and shudder, louder yet.

"Or the footfalls of a giant," Chester finished.

Another crash. "And the brook saw it first, because it flows in that direction," Grundy added.

"It's coming this way," EmJay said, alarmed.

Chester shaded his eyes with his hand, peering in that direction. "I may be getting older, but my eyesight shouldn't be that bad. I don't see any giant."

They all looked. The crashing footfalls continued, getting closer, but none of them could see any giant. "This is crazy," Grundy said. "There's *got* to be something there!"

Then, on a hill visible some distance away, they saw the brush and small trees crunch down as if pressed by an invisible foot. The sound came again.

"Do you know," Bink said, "I remember long ago, when Magician Trent and I fought the wiggles, and Chester's uncle Herman gave his life—"

"Uncle Herman!" Chester exclaimed respectfully.

"The creatures came from all around," Bink continued. "Large and small, natural friends and natural enemies, all united in that effort of extermination—"

"It happened again," Grundy said, "when little Ivy spied another wiggle nest five years ago."

"And one of the creatures was an invisible giant—a big, big man. We couldn't see him at all, but we could hear him and, ah, smell him. He was a hero too; he gave his life—"

"Invisible giant!" EmJay said, making a note.

Grundy caught on. "Could he have left an offspring?"

"It seems likely. Most creatures do. Of course it would have taken several decades for a creature to grow that large."

"And now it is several decades later," Chester said, as the approaching crashings almost drowned him out. "Are those giants friendly?"

"Does it matter?" Bink asked. "We can't see him, and he probably doesn't see us. But if he steps on us—"

Now they smelled the giant. The odor was appalling. "I guess no lake's big enough for him to take a bath in," Grundy said, wrinkling his nose.

"I don't know about you folk," the Ass brayed, "but I'm getting my tail out of here!" He galloped off.

"Wait for me, you coward!" EmJay cried, running after him.

There was yet another crash, closer yet. "Sounds like good advice!" Bink said.

"Pile on!" Chester said. "I can move faster than you can."

Bink jumped on the bed strapped to the centaur's back, and Grundy scrambled onto Snortimer. The centaur was already in motion. He galloped down the path in the opposite direction to that taken by EmJay and Ass, for which Grundy blessed him.

But the terrible footfalls continued to come closer. It seemed that the invisible giant was going the same way they were! Maybe the centaur hadn't been so smart after all. Being free of pesky company wouldn't be all that satisfying, if they got squished flat under the heedless foot of the giant.

Chester put on more speed as he encountered a straightaway, and for a while seemed to be drawing ahead. Then the path curved again, and he had to slow to make the turns, and the giant's feet crashed closer. Yet Grundy saw that they couldn't take off to the side, because the jungle here was impenetrable; they could be squished by the edge of a foot before they got far enough away.

Then Grundy spied a cave. "Look there!" he yelled in Chester's ear. "Maybe he won't step on a mountain!"

Chester saw the cave and veered to enter it. As he did, the trees immediately behind them bent down and snapped like twigs, and the ground shook with force like that of a quake. For an instant the centaur's hooves left the ground; then he landed and charged at full velocity into the cave.

There was light inside. Perceiving that, Snortimer made a desperate leap to the safety of the shadow under the bed on the centaur's back. Grundy had to let go and catch hold of Chester's human torso. The light was not necessarily a good sign, because that suggested that it was inhabited, and creatures like ogres and dragons were partial to caves. But the ground quaked again, and rocks plunged down from the ceiling; a stalactite speared past Chester's nose. They weren't safe yet!

The cave tunnel led directly into the mountain, and it was wide and straight; Chester made excellent progress despite his burden. The crashing fell behind. They had gotten far enough inside to be out of range of the heedless giant; or perhaps the giant had simply passed by the mountain, proceeding to whatever mission moved him. Chester slowed to a trot, then a walk, and finally a standstill.

They were in a large, bright cave whose walls were smooth and polished. Before them stood a metallic box with a series of buttons at the front, and a pane of glass at the top.

GREETINGS, the pane of glass printed.

Bink and Grundy dismounted. "And greetings to you, you rusty box," Grundy said facetiously.

YOUR VOICE SOUNDS FAMILIAR, the screen printed. WHAT IS YOUR IDENTITY?

"It communicates!" Grundy exclaimed, surprised. Usually the inanimate communicated only in the presence of King Dor, whose magic talent stimulated it. Grundy could talk to anything alive, but this was obviously not alive.

ANSWER THE QUESTION, the screen printed.

"I'm Grundy Golem," Grundy snapped. "And who are you, printface?"

GRUNDY GOLEM, the screen printed. THE ONE WHO STATED THAT AMALGAMATED PARADOX WAS BUYING OUT COM-PEWTER?

"Yeah, I guess so. What's it to you, metal-brain?"

THAT WAS A LIBEL. AS SUCH, IT IS ACTIONABLE.

"I don't like this," Chester murmured. "This thing is eerie."

"What are you talking about, glassy-eye?" Grundy demanded.

I AM COM-PEWTER. I WILL ACCEPT YOUR RETRACTION AND APOLOGY NOW.

"Apology!" Grundy exclaimed indignantly. "Why should I apologize to a grouchy metal box with a glass top for making up a nonsense sentence to distract the Bulls and Bears?"

BECAUSE YOU LIBELED ME, the screen printed. NO ONE HAS BOUGHT ME OUT.

"Uh, Grundy," Bink murmured. "It might be better to—"

But the golem's dander was up. "You simple sheet! Shut your print before I break your face!" And he made as if to kick at the glass.

Print flowed very rapidly across the screen. GOLEM LIFTS FOOT, SLIPS ON GREASE SPOT, LANDS ON POSTERIOR.

Grundy's non-kicking foot slipped on a grease spot, and skidded out from under him, and he landed hard on his bottom. "Youch!" he exclaimed. "What happened?"

I REVISED THE SCRIPT, the screen printed.

Grundy climbed to his feet, rubbing his rear. The jolt of falling had cleared his head on one detail: he now remembered that he had said *Con*-Pewter, not *Com*-Pewter. So he had been talking about something else, and had not insulted this thing. But his ire had been aroused, and he was not about to tell it that. "I think you're a lying hunk of metal!" he exclaimed.

OBNOXIOUS GOLEM SUFFERS TEMPORARY MOUTHFUL OF SOAP, the screen printed.

Suddenly Grundy's mouth was full of foul-tasting substance. "Hwash hth helth?" he spluttered, trying to spit it out.

Bink had a flask of water; he held this carefully so that Grundy could slurp from it and rinse out his mouth. The flask was about as tall as Grundy himself; the difference between his physical stature and that of normal human beings became more obvious at times like this.

Meanwhile, the screen blithely printed: IT IS NOT HELL, AS YOU SO QUAINTLY PUT IT, BUT SIMPLE JUSTICE.

"Simple justice!" Grundy exclaimed as he got his mouth clear. "You metallic claptrap—"

"Ixnay," Bink murmured again. But again he was too late; the machine had heard.

FOUL-MOUTHED GOLEM TRIPS OVER OWN FLAT FEET AND FALLS IN MUD PUDDLE, the screen printed.

And Grundy tripped and splatted into a puddle of mud that he was sure hadn't been there a moment before.

"That thing is changing reality!" Chester exclaimed. "Everything it prints, happens!"

ARE YOU READY TO APOLOGIZE, WOODHEAD? the screen inquired as Grundy hauled himself out of the puddle.

"Grundy, I really think it would be better to—" Bink began.

"Apologize?" Grundy demanded furiously. "To a tin box with a dirty screen? What do you think I am?"

I THINK YOU ARE A LOUD-MOUTHED, SWELL-HEADED, SELF-IMPORTANT IGNORANT EXCUSE FOR A FACSIMILE OF A LIVING CREATURE, the screen printed.

"Apt description," Chester muttered, thinking Grundy would not overhear.

Unfortunately, Grundy *did* overhear. His rage magnified. "And you're a glass-eyed, button-nosed excuse for dead garbage!" he yelled at the screen. "If you were alive, I'd challenge you to—"

TO WHAT? the screen demanded.

"Grundy, I think we'd better not aggravate—" Bink murmured.

Grundy had broken off because he had been unable to think of anything horrendous enough. Bink's attempt to caution him only gave him evil inspiration.

"To prove you're smarter than I am, junk-for-brains!" he cried. "You just sit there doing nothing, trying to mess up those of us who have something important to do. How great does that make you?"

THAT IS AN INTERESTING CHALLENGE, the screen said. LET ME CONSIDER IT. And the screen dimmed, while the word CONSIDERING appeared faintly.

"The golem didn't mean it," Bink said quickly. "We don't need to challenge you. We came in here by accident."

The screen brightened. YOU CAME IN HERE BECAUSE THE INVISIBLE GIANT HERDED YOU HERE, it printed. At the top of the screen the word CONSIDERING remained in smaller print; evidently it was able to converse while considering.

Now Bink was interested. "You wanted us to come here? What are you?"

THAT IS NOT IMPORTANT, the Com-Pewter printed.

"Why certainly it is," Bink persisted. "If we are to engage in a challenge with you, we have a right to know what you are and how you operate."

THAT DOES NOT CALCULATE, the screen protested.

"Yes it does," Bink said. "We may have no quarrel with you at all. We have to know you better to ascertain this."

The screen blinked. Evidently it was having trouble concentrating on Bink's point while also CONSIDERING Grundy's challenge. Its metallic mind was divided, and therefore less efficient. Bink evidently understood this, and was taking advantage of it. Grundy realized this, and decided that it was better to leave this in Bink's hands. The old man was not entirely stupid.

"Exactly how did you manage to get us here, if you can't leave this cave?" Bink asked.

The screen hesitated, then printed: I ARRANGED TO PLACE A D-TOUR ILLUSION ON THE ENCHANTED PATH, TO DIVERT TRAVELERS HERE. ONCE SECURELY COMMITTED TO D-TOUR, THEY WERE TO BE HERDED HERE BY THE INVISIBLE GIANT.

Grundy slapped his forehead with the heel of a hand. They had fallen for an illusion! There was no true detour!

"And why did you want to bring travelers here?" Bink asked.

Again the screen hesitated, as if the machine did not really want to answer, but remained confused by the split thinking effort. I AM CONFINED TO THIS AIR-CONDITIONED CAVE. IT GETS BORING. IT IS INTERESTING TO PLAY WITH INDEPENDENT ENTITIES.

So there was the motive. The Pewter was looking for entertainment, and they were it. That pleased Grundy no more than the rest of the situation did.

"You can't act directly, beyond this cave?" Bink asked.

Again the hesitation. I CAN NOT. I HAVE NO POWER OF PERSONAL MOTION, AND THE EXTERNAL EXTREMES OF TEMPERATURE AND HUMIDITY WOULD DAMAGE MY CIRCUITS. I MUST ACT THROUGH OTHERS, OUTSIDE.

"But inside this cave, you control reality?" Bink asked.

I CAN REWRITE THE SCRIPT HERE, it agreed.

"How did you come to have such fantastic power?" Bink asked.

I WAS MADE BY THE MUSES OF PARNASSUS TO ASSIST THEIR WORK, the screen printed reluctantly.

"Then why are you not with the Muses?"

THEY MISDESIGNED ME. THEY WISHED TO RECORD REALITY, NOT REMAKE IT. SO THEY FILED ME OUT OF THE WAY, IN CASE THEY SHOULD EVER NEED ME AGAIN.

So here was this powerful, bored Pewter, locked in this isolated cave, trying to entertain itself. Grundy would have felt sorry for it, if he weren't already so mad at it. He was caked with mud, and his mouth still tasted of soap.

"So your concern is not really with a stray remark Grundy may have made among the Bulls and—" Bink was saying, when the screen changed.

CONSIDERATION COMPLETED, it printed. CHALLENGE ACCEPTED. HERE ARE THE TERMS.

"Hey, wait!" Grundy protested, no longer eager to contest with a device that could change reality simply by printing it on its screen. Had he known more about the Pewter, he would have been more careful about his language. "I change my mind!"

THE CONTEST WILL OCCUR IN THIS CAVE, the screen continued. THE FOUR LIVING ENTITIES VS. THE DEAD ENTITY. THE FOUR WILL ATTEMPT TO LEAVE THE CAVE. SUCCESS WILL BRING FREEDOM. FAILURE WILL BRING ETERNAL CONFINEMENT HERE.

All four of them started. Snortimer remained hiding under the bed on

Chester's back, but the bed shuddered with his reaction. Eternal confinement?

"Now we didn't agree to that—" Bink said.

MAN PROTESTS, BUT THEN REMEMBERS THAT HE DID AGREE, the screen printed.

"Now I remember," Bink said. "We *did* agree!"

EXCELLENT, the screen printed. THE CONTEST COMMENCES IMMEDIATELY.

Bink and Chester and Grundy exchanged glances. They had been trapped by the Pewter's revision of reality! If any of them tried to protest again, the machine would simply revise the situation to make them conform to its script. Its attention was no longer divided; it was now in command.

"But we're not clear on the rules!" Bink protested.

SIMPLY STATE <ENTER>, the screen printed. THEN GIVE YOUR INTERPRETATION. THEN STATE <EXECUTE>. TURNS WILL ALTERNATE.

"Enter *what?*" Grundy demanded.

YOU MAY HAVE THE FIRST TURN, the screen printed, then went blank. The machine had told them all it was going to.

"I think I understand," Bink said. "We shall take turns establishing our versions of reality. Whichever version proves to be more compelling will prevail. It's a contest of wits. If we are to escape, we must prove we are smarter than Pewter is. If we aren't smart enough to escape, then it will have proved itself to be smarter than we are. But we had better establish some rules of procedure, so we don't mess ourselves up."

"Rules of procedure?" Chester asked, perplexed.

"We can't all enter statements at once; we would be working against each other. We need to be united. I think the machine will play fair; we just have to maintain our discipline and make our best choices. I remember once long ago, when I was down in the cave of the—but never mind. We should choose one of our number to make the entries."

"But that machine can be tearing us up, while we discuss it among ourselves!" Chester pointed out.

"I don't think so. Machines don't have the same awareness of time that living creatures do. Until we make an entry, it will simply wait, and until we execute, nothing will happen."

"Who makes the entries?" Grundy asked suspiciously.

"Why, the leader of the party, of course."

"And who is that?" Grundy was annoyed all over again, because obviously Bink had preempted his Quest.

"I should think that would be the one who is on Quest," Bink said.

"But that's *me!*" Grundy said.

"Why so it is. Then you should make the entries."

Grundy could hardly believe it. "What will the rest of you do?"

"We shall discuss the choices and offer advice," Bink said. He turned to Chester. "Don't you agree?"

Chester looked uncertain, but went along with his friend. "I guess so."

Suddenly Grundy liked Bink much better. "Okay. What's your advice?"

"I think we need to devise a strategy of escape. Perhaps we can have a door open in the wall, that leads outside."

"Great!" Grundy exclaimed. He faced the screen: "Enter: A door to the outside opens in the cave wall. Execute."

Immediately a door opened where there had been none before. Could it really be that easy? Grundy took a step toward it.

But now print appeared on the screen. UNFORTUNATELY, THE EXIT IS GUARDED BY FEROCIOUS LIFE-EATING PLANTS, it showed.

Grundy stopped still. Now the passage was wreathed by horrendous green plants that had large cup-shaped leaves that drooled bright sap. Tendrils cast about, as if seeking something to clutch. Some of the leaf-cups seemed to have teeth.

"I don't think we want to walk there," Chester said, shuddering.

"I wish we had some Agent Orange!" Grundy muttered. "That would wilt those plants right off the wall!"

"Why not?" Bink asked. "All you have to do is Enter it."

So he did! Grundy faced the screen again. "Enter: We find Agent Orange before us! Execute."

Agent Orange appeared before them.

BUT AGENT ORANGE HAS THE SAME EFFECT ON ANIMALS AS ON PLANTS, the screen printed.

"Can that be true?" Chester asked, concerned. "If we use it on those plants and then walk through, we'll be destroying ourselves."

"It it wasn't true before, it is now," Bink said. "It seems that neither side can reverse the reality of the other, but can modify what the other has. We don't dare use Agent Orange now."

Grundy agreed. He wasn't sure what counted as animals, but it certainly included Snortimer, and probably Chester and Grundy himself, and might even include Bink. "We'll have to try a new ploy," he decided. "One that can't be reversed like that."

"When I was in Mundania," Bink said thoughtfully, "I found that in some regions they required a document to let a person travel. It was called a passport. I wonder whether that would work here?"

"How does it work?" Grundy asked.

"It's a little book, and you write in it where you're going, and they check it to make sure you really go there."

"That wouldn't work quite the same in Xanth," Chester remarked.

"No, it wouldn't," Bink agreed.

Grundy thought about that. Obviously a device to facilitate going somewhere would do it magically in Xanth, and unmagically in Mundania. If they had a magic book that conducted them outside—

"Enter," he told the screen. "The travelers find four passports, one for each of them."

Four small books appeared. Bink picked them up and passed them around. Grundy could hardly hold his, as it weighed half as much as he did.

Bink carefully wrote in his: *Gap Chasm*. The others followed his example. Since no destination had been spoken, they hoped the Pewter wouldn't catch on.

Then they saw the print on the screen: RED TAPE PREVENTS THE USE OF THE PASSPORTS.

Now they saw the red tape. Festoons of it were floating down from the ceiling. Streamers settled about them, and soon they were buried in the stuff. It didn't hurt them; it merely entangled them so that they could hardly move. It was difficult even to see their passports, because of the crisscrossing strands of ribbon.

"Evidently Pewter has learned something about Mundania," Bink muttered, disgruntled.

They struggled to free themselves of the tape. The stuff tore readily, but by the time they got it all clear, the passports had been lost in the shuffle.

"Let's find another passage out," Chester said. "One too broad to be blocked by plants."

"Enter," Grundy said. "They find a broad, clean passage, clear of plants and all other barriers. Execute."

The passage manifested on the other side. Of course this one led further into the mountain, but it was broad and nice.

But the screen printed: THEY HEAR AN AWFUL ROAR, AND REALIZE THAT A FIRE-BREATHING DRAGON IS COMING DOWN IT.

The ensuing roar was indeed awful! "We can't go up *that* passage!" Grundy said.

"Unless we find a way to deal with the dragon," Bink pointed out.

"What would scare off a dragon?" Grundy asked.

"A basilisk," Chester said.

Good idea! "Enter," Grundy said. "A basilisk walks up the passage toward the dragon, glaring about. Execute."

The little reptile appeared. The direct glare of a basilisk could kill another creature, even a dragon.

BUT THE BASILISK CHANGES ITS MIND AND STARTS BACK TOWARD THE GROUP, the screen said.

"Oopsy!" Grundy breathed. "Enter: The basilisk remembers where it was going, and heads back up the passage, tuning out all distractions. Execute."

The others relaxed as the nasty little reptile resumed its progress; surely Pewter couldn't change *that.*

AS IT ROUNDS THE FIRST TURN, the screen printed, IT ENCOUNTERS A MIRROR, AND STARES ITSELF IN THE FACE.

Naturally when that happened, the little monster fell dead, for no basilisk was proof against its own fatal stare.

"Nevertheless," Bink murmured, "we now have the initiative, because we retain the tunnel."

There was another roar. "And the tunnel retains the dragon," Chester said, touching his bow nervously.

"Ah, but we also have the mirror," Bink pointed out. "Pick it up, turn it around, and it will confound the dragon the same way it confounded the basilisk."

"We can try it, certainly," Grundy agreed. "Enter: The centaur picks up the mirror, turns it about, and proceeds up the tunnel. When the dragon sees its reflection in the mirror, it will think that is another dragon, and will back off."

They watched the screen to see whether they had finally foiled the machine. They had not.

THERE IS THE SOUND OF RUSHING WATER, the screen printed. A RIVER IS DRAINING INTO THE PASSAGE, AND WILL WASH EVERYTHING OUT BEFORE IT.

They weren't getting anywhere. Every time they made a move, Pewter countered it. Yet Bink seemed positive.

"You know," he said conversationally, "they have some worse monsters in Mundania than in Xanth. Some of the birds, especially. We have ogres and ogresses, and dragons and dragonesses, and the like. But I remember one there called the egret, that had a long yellow beak. If we could get one of those on our side—"

"What good would that do?" Grundy asked. "The machine would just counter it. We need to get out of here, not play with birds!"

"I suppose so," Bink agreed. "And you never can tell what those birds will do. The female of the species is twice as bad as the male; if we ever encountered a female egret we'd be lost."

What was he getting at? Of course they wouldn't summon a female egret! "Let's just try to open another door out—one that can't be blocked by plants or dragons or water," Grundy said.

"Yes, I suppose that's best," Bink agreed. "Let's protect it against plants and dragons and water."

"And egrets," Chester put in.

"And egrets," Bink agreed.

"Enter," Grundy said. "They discover a new passage, with no bad plants, no dragons, no water and no egrets. It leads straight outside. Execute."

The new passage appeared. It looked perfect.

But the screen was ready. AND THERE, it printed dramatically, IS AN EGRESS!

And a big bird with a swordlike yellow beak appeared. It took one menacing step toward them.

"Oops," Grundy said, dismayed. "I forgot to exclude the female of the species!"

"But the female is not an egress," Bink said smugly. "Pewter just assumed that, applying logic to the name. An egress is actually a form of exit."

"A form of exit?" Grundy asked. "But there's the bird!"

"Egrets, male or female, are harmless," Bink said. "We won't take our turn to abolish it. All we have to do is walk out the true egress." And he led the way.

The Pewter was helpless, for it could not act until they made another entry and gave it its turn. They simply marched physically out the egress, ignoring the bird.

A roll of confused symbols crossed the screen. /\/\ <<>>±±^^XX¿¿. Then it got its mechanism straight. CURSES, the screen printed. FOILED AGAIN!

They had escaped—but somehow Grundy wasn't completely satisfied. Bink had found the way out. Bink was the true hero of this episode. He, Grundy, had failed again; he remained a nonentity. He had suffered almost as bad a setback as Pewter had.

4

Mystery of the Voles

They camped for the day in the thick of the jungle. Bink still seemed unconcerned about predators, and felt no need for a watch for the night. Grundy was glad not to have to stay awake, but felt obliged to grouch about it anyway. "What makes you so sure there's no danger?" he demanded. "We almost got stuck forever in that cave!"

"No we didn't," Bink said. "We got out readily enough."

"That was a lucky break! If Com-Pewter hadn't gotten confused about the female egret—"

"There would have been something else. We would have gotten out one way or another, unharmed. Meanwhile, we had an interesting experience and learned something about another entity of Xanth. I think that was worthwhile."

Grundy shook his head, bemused. Bink seemed to be living in a fool's paradise, trusting to coincidence to rescue him from his own folly. It was true that the man did seem to have phenomenal luck, but luck could turn at any time. It might be best not to associate with him longer than he had to, because eventually they were bound to find themselves in a situation they could not escape.

But he needed Bink and Chester to carry the bed. Grundy was not happy with the present arrangement, for several reasons, but he was unable to change it. He sighed, and slept.

At night they ate and headed north. They had lost the path; perhaps it had not gone beyond the Com-Pewter's mountain anyway, as the machine had set it up to bring in entertaining people. They didn't want to retrace their steps; not only would that waste an extra day or more, it would take them through the stockyard of the Bulls & Bears and the haunt of the succubus and the invisible giant; they might even encounter EmJay and Ass again. Once was enough for all of those!

So they plowed through the dense vegetation, going toward the Gap Chasm, which they were sure could not be far distant. The geography of Xanth seemed to change every time a person went out in it, like the Good Magician's castle, but the Gap was eternal. It sliced across Xanth, separating it into northern and southern halves, and now that the remnants of the forget-spell on it had finally dissipated, many folk remembered where it was. Of course there were still pockets of forget here and there, and probably some of the mysteries associated with the Gap would never be unraveled, but certainly they would find the Gap if they just kept going north.

Chester paused, listening. Now Grundy heard it—an ominous rattle, as of a poisonous snake or a ghost. Trouble?

"Friend," Snortimer said in monster language.

"You're sure?" Grundy asked.

"I recognize the rattle. It's one of Ivy's friends."

"Well, if you're sure—"

Snortimer took off at a lope, his hands drawing him rapidly along through the brush. Grundy had to admit that in this terrain the Bed Monster was better than any conventional steed would have been, for Bink and Chester were quickly left behind.

Soon they burst upon—a horse. A rather shaggy stallion, with several bands of chain around his barrel. These were what rattled. "That's Pook, the ghost horse," Snortimer said.

Naturally Snortimer could not speak the equine language, and the ghost horse did not understand Bed Monster language. That was Grundy's talent. It had been some time since he had seen Pook, so he might not have recognized him without Snortimer's assistance. "Pook, I presume?" he inquired of the horse.

"Oh, I wanted to scare you!" Pook complained.

"I can't be scared right now," Grundy explained. "I'm on a Quest."

"A Quest! I haven't been on one of those for centuries! Not since Jordan the Barbarian tamed me."

"Jordan! Is he here?"

"No. It wasn't safe for Threnody to be too close to Castle Roogna, you know, because of the curse, so they moved away. But we stayed halfway near, because Puck likes to visit Ivy."

Puck was the foal of Pook and Peek. They were a family of ghost horses, and the foal had remained young for centuries, because ghosts changed slowly. Since Grundy liked the Pooka family better than he liked Jordan and Threnody, he was satisfied with this encounter. "We're heading for the Gap. How far do we have to go?"

"Not far," Pook said. "But the route is devious. There are several hungry dragons and a monster or two in the way."

"We don't have forever," Grundy said. "Is there a good, fast way there that avoids the hazards?"

"Sure. We can lead you through it, if you like."

That was exactly what Grundy would like. "Thanks!"

Now Peek and Puck showed up. Peek was a beautiful shaggy mare with similar chains, and Puck was a frolicsome young creature whose chains threatened to fly loose when he leaped. They peered curiously at Snortimer, for though they knew what he was, they had never actually seen him before. It was unusual for Bed Monsters to stray far from their beds.

Bink and Chester crashed up to join them. There were introductions; then the ghost horses showed the route.

It was as if a path appeared where none had existed before. Suddenly it was much easier to penetrate the wilderness, though their route was now quite curvacious. Nobody complained, because everyone knew that this was necessary to avoid the lurking dragons and monsters. Actually, it had been a lucky thing to encounter Pook; this help would save them a great deal of time and trouble. Grundy knew that Bink took such luck for granted, but certainly it was with them at the moment.

As dawn neared, the terrain grew rougher. There were numerous crevises in the ground near the Gap Chasm, as if fragmented from it. They decided to camp, as they could not quite reach the Gap before day. The ghost horses could go abroad by night or day, but preferred the night, so they were satisfied. Puck trotted about, locating fruits and nuts and water; Chester, who had the appetite of a horse, really appreciated that.

Snortimer disappeared under his bed, but the others remained up for a while, talking. Grundy was happy to translate; it made him feel important.

"Do you really want to go to the Gap," Pook asked, "or do you need to cross it?"

"Neither," Grundy explained. "We're going down into it, to meet the Gap Dragoness."

"Oh, then you don't need to go to the brink! I know of a tunnel that leads down into it. Jordan and I used it to get out, four hundred years ago, and I'm sure it's still there."

"Great!" Grundy exclaimed, and translated for Bink and Chester.

"Who made the tunnel?" Bink inquired, interested.

"We don't know. It's just there."

Just there. Perhaps that was enough of an answer for a horse, but Grundy was unsatisfied. Someone had to have made that tunnel, and now he was quite curious who. After the experience with the path leading to the Com-Pewter cave, Grundy was more cautious about simply using what was there. If the tunnel had been there for centuries, probably it was safe; but if it connected to Com-Pewter's cave. . . .

"I think we ought to find out more about this tunnel before we commit ourselves all the way to it," Chester said. "It's a long way down to the bottom of the Gap Chasm, and if anything happened—"

"My thought exactly!" Grundy agreed. "Let's find out who made it, then we can use it. Some things wait for a long time to catch the unwary."

They slept. At night the ghost horses showed them to the tunnel. It opened from the base of a small north-south chasm, as if it had been there before the chasm opened. Sure enough, when they explored the opposite side of the cleft, there, hidden under a fall of debris, was another tunnel: the evident continuation of the other. Since the first tunnel proceeded down into the Gap, this other must go elsewhere, and should be safer to explore.

Grundy took charge. "Let's send one party down into it, while another watches from outside," he said. "Maybe we can call back and forth, and trace it from the surface."

Grundy rode Snortimer into the tunnel, while Bink and Chester stayed outside. Little Puck followed Grundy in, planning to act as liaison between the two parties. Since the three of them were of small size, it was easier for them to explore without disturbing anything.

There was a little fungus glow on the walls. Puck and Snortimer didn't need it, but that wan light helped Grundy a great deal.

The tunnel wound along like a worm, remaining approximately level, which meant that the surface of the ground was not too far above. But their hope of maintaining voice contact was vain; nothing could be heard. Puck could have returned to inform his parents where Grundy was, but that would have meant a long trot, and he might have trouble finding Grundy when he came back. Nothing was working out quite as planned.

They came to a fork in the tunnel. Grundy took the one to the right, as it was slightly larger and cleaner. But soon there was another fork, and another. In fact, a labyrinth was developing! Grundy was worried about getting lost, but Snortimer assured him that he could retrace his course anytime.

Then there was a rumble, and suddenly part of the tunnel collapsed behind them. Snortimer leaped forward, avoiding the stones and sliding dirt, and Puck practically sailed ahead. Apparently their passage had shaken the old structure enough to start the shakedown.

They were unharmed—but now their return route was blocked. Snortimer might be good at retracing his route, but he could no longer do that. They could be in trouble.

Grundy urged his steed on, trusting that he would be able to find a way back around the blocked passage. They had passed so many intersections that there had to be a connection. Meanwhile, he wanted to finish the job he had come to do and get out of here before anything else happened.

The labyrinth of passages began to assume a form. This seemed to be a series of concentric circles, with the inner circles larger than the outer ones, as if closer to the center of things. Whatever there was that was worth finding, would surely be found in that center!

There was another shudder, and they heard more stones falling, to the side. This time it couldn't be the fault of the three of them, they had been stepping very lightly. Was something else causing it?

They went on, more nervously. Grundy had never been bothered by tunnels or tight squeezes; his size and agility had always enabled him to get clear. Now he was beginning to be bothered. It was obvious that neither Snortimer nor Puck felt any more at ease than he did.

The going got easier as the tunnels became larger. These ones were in better repair; their walls were turning smooth, and their floors were firmer. The fungus glow brightened. Snortimer began to grow nervous, not liking the light, but did not actually balk. Probably this glow would seem like deepest darkness in daylight, so the monster was able to tolerate it.

Finally the tunnels became so large and so close together that the spaces between them were more like walls. Then the walls disappeared, and what remained was a fair-sized chamber: the center of the labyrinth.

In the very center of that chamber was a small, ornate chest. Could it be a treasure?

Excited, now, Grundy went to it. But what might be small to a man was large for him; he was unable to lift its heavy lid.

"Let me do it," Snortimer said. He reached forth with a huge hairy hand and grasped the lid, hauling it off.

Grundy grasped the edge, hauled himself up, and peered into the open chest. He saw gleams of reflected light, such as might come from jewels or glossy metal, but couldn't quite make out what the objects were.

Snortimer reached in and drew out a handful. They seemed to be objects made of metal—curving spikes, hollow inside. Grundy took one, and found it heavy. It was about a third his own length, shaped like a very long, thin drinking horn, all of bright metal.

"Jewelry?" he asked. Neither Snortimer nor Puck could answer; they had never seen anything quite like this.

"Well, let's take one out with us," Grundy decided. "Maybe one of the others will recognize it." He was disappointed that the chest had not contained treasure, though he really had no use for treasure anyway. It was mostly human beings and dragons who placed value on treasure, so others tended to copy that attitude.

Snortimer fastened one of the objects to Puck's band of chains, so that the little ghost horse could carry it back conveniently. It was little enough, as treasures went.

He was disappointed on another score: here he had penetrated to the center of the labyrinth, and unveiled its secret—and found nothing worthwhile. Certainly no living creatures had been here for centuries, and there seemed to be no traps. It was probably safe to use the other tunnel down into the Gap Chasm, if it didn't collapse on them.

"Let's get out of here," he said.

The others were happy to go. They started back—and heard another rumbling. There was going to be another collapse!

Suddenly Grundy recognized a pattern. "Chester—those are his heavy footfalls!" he exclaimed. "He's trotting around up there, looking for us—and knocking the stones down! That's why tunnels keep collapsing!"

That did indeed seem to be the reason. "Chester, slow down!" Grundy called—but when he raised his voice, the sound echoed as if he were a giant, and dirt sifted down from the ceiling of the chamber. He could bring it down on himself!

Silently, they hurried back. Chester's erratic trotting continued to shake the chamber, making them increasingly nervous.

They reached the point of the first cave-in. Now they had to figure a way around it, intersecting their original tunnel on the other side. That shouldn't be difficult—but Grundy felt a tightening apprehension.

He guided Snortimer to the left, hoping to cut back right. But though the passage soon forked, neither fork bore back the way they wanted. This was like the detour in the forest, that had refused to return to the magic path. The perversity of the inanimate! If he had Dor's talent, he could simply ask the passages where to go, and they would answer. For that matter, he could have asked the metal thing what it was, and solved the mystery. But that of course was why Dor was rated a Magician, and was now King: his magic talent was more versatile than Grundy's. Anyone could talk to living things, if he knew how; only Dor could talk to the inanimate.

The tunnel forked again, and again neither fork went where they wanted it to go. Grundy was about to turn back and try the other direction—when there was another rumble, and the passage behind them collapsed.

"Chester, you hoofbrained horse's rump!" Grundy wailed impotently. "You're destroying us down here!"

Now they had to go on, and none of them knew the best way through this maze. They just had to keep going and guessing—

Before long, Grundy knew they were lost. The passages went on and on, dividing and merging, and there was no way to tell which way was out, or whether any way remained open. They were trapped.

Grundy thought of something else to try. "Maybe if we knock on the ceiling, they'll hear us, and can come in from the other side."

Snortimer used one of his hairy hands to pick up a rock, scrambled up the side, and banged on the ceiling. Some pebbles were dislodged, but there was no collapse. He tapped in a pattern: KNOCK-KNOCK, KNOCK-KNOCK, KNOCK-KNOCK BANG!

It worked! The earth shuddered as the centaur trotted over, orienting on the sound.

In fact, it shuddered too much. "Another collapse!" Grundy screamed, and they dived out of the way as the ceiling sagged and then fell. They had almost brought disaster on themselves!

They choked on the clouds of dust in the air, as the rocks settled. They would never get out this way!

Then sharp-eyed Puck saw something. He neighed and started forward, scrambling over the rocks. "Watch out!" Grundy cried. "You'll bring another fall down on your head!"

"Yo!" Chester called. "You okay, down there?"

The collapse had opened up a new way out! That was the night sky up there!

Grundy mounted Snortimer again, and they scrambled nimbly up to the surface. It was a tremendous relief to be free!

Once he was far from the hole in the ground, Grundy described his adventure, embellishing it only slightly, and showed them the metal spike Puck had brought out. "What do you think it is?" he asked.

Neither Bink nor Chester had any idea. "Not treasure, certainly," Bink concluded.

"More like a tool," Chester said. "But it has no handle."

They decided to camp one more day, then take the tunnel down into the Gap. Obviously the tunnel represented no trap, as long as they were careful not to trigger a collapse.

But as the day brightened, Grundy remained unsatisfied. There were too many unanswered questions! Who—or what—had made all those tunnels, that network of passages surrounding the central chamber? What had happened to those creatures? Why had they left a treasure chest full of hollow metal spikes? He hated to remain in ignorance.

At last he got up and walked alone to the entrance of the tunnel to the Gap. He stood there and stared at it. "If only I knew who made you!" he exclaimed.

There was the rustle of leaves. A giant ancient acorn tree grew at the brink of the cleft; some of its roots had been exposed, but it had survived. "I can tell you that, golem," it rustled.

The tree! It had to be many centuries old! It had been here when the tunnel was new! "Tell me!" Grundy cried.

"It was the voles," the tree rustled.

"The what?"

"The voles. Human folk call them by other names, but they haven't appreciated the real voles."

"What other names?" Grundy asked, perplexed.

"Wiggles and squiggles and diggles."

"Wiggles!" Grundy exclaimed, appalled. "Are they swarming again?"

"Of course not, golem," the tree rustled, chuckling in its fashion. "But they're related. The wiggles are the smallest and worst, and the diggles are the largest and best, and in between are the squiggles. They're all related."

"I know that, barkface! What about the voles?"

"The voles are the true name for that extensive family of tunnelers. They were once more common than they are now; you hardly see any of their family branches anymore. But the greatest of them were the civilized voles, bigger than the squiggles but just as tunnelsome. It was here they had their main camp, a thousand years ago. I was just a sprout when they left, but I remember."

"They departed a thousand years ago?" Grundy asked, amazed.

"Give or take a century; I lose track. My memory rings aren't what they used to be. Before the dominance of the goblins and harpies, anyway."

"The harpies and goblins haven't been dominant since the days of King Roogna!"

"Just so," the tree agreed.

"These voles—just what were they like?"

"They were fairly big—bigger than the squiggles of today, but smaller than the diggles. Big enough to make these tunnels."

"Centaur-sized, then!" Grundy said.

"Maybe a little smaller. They didn't like to be crowded, so they made their tunnels with some clearance. It's hard for me to judge, because I was so much smaller then."

"These voles—they were just big squiggles, just tunneling everywhere?"

"They tunneled, but they weren't just squiggles!" the tree rustled. "They did things, there underground. They had conventions, or something, they made plans—and then they went away."

"Where did they go?"

"That I don't know. They just went, leaving their tunnels behind."

So the tree really didn't know much. But Grundy tried again: "We found some sort of metal thing, a chest full of them, like hollow spikes, only slightly curved. Do you know what those would be?"

"Oh, yes, of course. I saw those being used. They are artificial claws."

"What?"

"The voles dug so much, they wore off their natural claws. So they put on artificial ones, made of metal, very strong. Then they could dig twice as fast, and not get as tired. Those claws were their most prized possession."

Of course! Hollow claws, put on over the natural ones, like gauntlets. That would greatly enhance the ability of a digging creature. Mystery solved.

But as Grundy returned to the bed, he realized that the greater mystery remained. Where had those voles gone, and why? It was evident that nothing had hurt them, for there were no skeletons and there was no damage, other than that done by Chester's hooves. They must have gone of their own volition—their own vole-ition—to some place of their choosing. Perhaps they were there today, digging even better labyrinths.

But probably he would never know where or why. It was a frustrating frustration.

5

Stella Steamer

In the evening they proceeded to the tunnel and entered it. The ghost horses, satisfied that all was well, did not accompany them; they preferred to graze on the surface. Again the dim illumination of the fungus helped them, without bothering Snortimer unduly; it was almost as if the voles had had Bed Monsters in mind. Or maybe such fungus was part of the natural habitat of nocturnal monsters. It was, at any rate, another fortunate coincidence.

Grundy led the way, because Snortimer was most at home in a dark passage like this and was very sure-handed here. Chester and Bink had to be more careful, with their big clumsy feet. Once again Grundy appreciated the Good Magician's wisdom in specifying this particular steed. Often Humfrey's prescriptions made a good deal more sense than they seemed to at first.

The tunnel wound down and around, tantalizing them with a seeming descent to the bottom, only to rise again. Obviously the voles had not considered directness to be a virtue! This was probably their scenic route, though all there was to see was round walls.

Then an aperture appeared, into which a stray beam of moonlight probed. Snortimer shrunk away; moonlight wasn't deadly to him, but he distrusted it on principle. Chester paused to peer out—and whistled. Grundy dismounted and went over to look, climbing up to the centaur's shoulder in order to reach the elevation of the hole.

Now he saw it. Above, the pale moon squatted on an unruly cloud. Below, the awesome precipice of the Chasm opened. Grundy felt suddenly dizzy, as if falling into that terrible Chasm. Chester's big hand caught him before he fell. "You need all four feet on the ground before you lean out that window," the centaur murmured.

True words! Grundy scrambled back down and away from the hole; he had had more than enough of it!

Travel resumed. Progress seemed swift enough, but was actually slower than it would have been on level ground, because they were constantly stepping over stones and clearing cobwebs from their way.

Somewhere around midnight they heard something, and paused. It was a low whistling or moaning, coming from somewhere ahead, in the tunnel. "Something's there!" Grundy exclaimed, horrified.

"I'm sure it's all right," Bink said nonchalantly.

"How can you be so sure things will be all right, all the time?" Grundy demanded.

But Bink only smiled and shrugged. Obviously he knew something Grundy didn't, and that annoyed Grundy inordinately.

They waited, for there really was not much else they could do. The noises approached, and in due course a dark shape loomed in the tunnel. Grundy shrank back, and Chester drew his sword, but Bink remained unconcerned.

It seemed to be an animal, smaller than the centaur, but massive. It had front feet with enormous claws. It moved along, and it was evident that there was not room for it to pass them in the narrow tunnel. Yet it did not pause; it just moved on at them.

"Just let the vole pass," Bink said. "It's harmless."

"A *vole?*" Grundy asked.

"The ghost of one," Bink said.

With that, the creature moved right through Chester, through Bink, and brushed by Grundy with no impact. It was indeed a ghost.

It proceeded on up the tunnel, going its mysterious way, paying the living party no attention.

"I daresay the civilized voles could be nervous about an apparition like that, just as we tend to be about human ghosts," Bink remarked.

Chester resheathed his sword. His hand was shaking. "I daresay they could," the centaur agreed, relaxing.

Grundy understood Chester's embarrassment perfectly. He had been on the verge of terrified, yet obviously there had been no danger. Naturally voles had ghosts; every species did. But for a moment it had certainly seemed like a monster!

They resumed their trek down. Grundy pondered again what he had learned about the civilized voles. It made sense that their ghosts could not accompany them; most ghosts were locked to the regions of their deaths. But where had the living voles gone, and why? There was still no answer.

As dawn neared, they reached the bottom of the Chasm. They simply set up the bed in the comfortable darkness of the tunnel, then went out to forage for food. "But if you hear the dragon coming," Chester warned Grundy, "get over to us quickly, because you're the only one who can talk with it."

Grundy smiled. That was true enough; without him, there could be a most awkward misunderstanding! He felt more important.

The bottom of the Gap Chasm was a fairly nice place, at least in this region. There were small trees and bushes, and fruits were abundant. The only thing that was missing was animal life. That was because the Gap Dragoness ate all of that.

For a long time people had considered the Gap Dragon a terrible scourge, serving no useful purpose. Now it was known that the combination of Gap and Dragon served, historically, to protect Xanth from the worse scourges of the Mundane Waves of invasion. That had become clear when the so-called Nextwave (now the new Lastwave) surged through; the Gap had become a major line of defense. Grundy wondered how many other seemingly evil things of Xanth actually had good purposes, when understood. There was a lot more to Xanth than met the casual eye.

They finished their meal and slept. Around noon the ground shuddered, somewhat the way it had when the invisible giant had stridden toward them but less so. This was the familiar whomp! whomp! of the Gap Dragon.

Suddenly the whole party was alert. Grundy stood before the tunnel exit, ready to meet the dragon first. This was his moment of power.

She whomped into view: a long, low, six-legged dragoness, moving with surprising velocity. Steam belched from her mouth and nostrils, adding to the splendor of her approach. There was hardly a more impressive figure than the Gap Dragon—or Dragoness—in full charge!

"Halt!" Grundy cried, holding his little hand aloft. "We come in friendship!"

The dragoness whomped on, her gaze fixed on Chester.

"Hey!" Grundy said. "Slow down! I told you—"

She steamed right by him, her jaws opening. Chester, no coward, had his sword in hand, ready to defend himself—but no ordinary centaur was a match for such a dragon, and Chester was no longer in his prime.

Grundy realized that the dragoness was so intent on her presumed prey that she hadn't heard him at all. Dragons generally had limited intellects, and could truly concentrate on only one thing at a time. How could he get through to her before disaster?

He saw a shadow in the sky. A roc was wheeling, perhaps curious about the proceedings. Grundy had a notion.

"Hey, brothers!" he squawked in roc-talk. "Let's go down and haul on that dragon's tail!"

Stella Steamer skidded to a halt, blowing out a vast cloud of steam. "You try it, and you'll get such a chomp—!" she hissed in dragon-language. Then she paused, for the rocs were nowhere close.

"It's me, Stella," Grundy cried. "Grundy Golem! We're here on business!"

"I'm not Stella," she steamed. "I'm Stacey!"

Oops—he had forgotten. "Sorry. I misremembered."

"But I like Stella better," she decided.

"Anything you like," he agreed, as one does when facing a dragon. Now at least he had her attention.

"You're not strays?" she growled.

"Not strays," he informed her firmly. "We came to see you about Stanley."

"Stanley! You found him?" She had of course been advised of the disappearance of the little dragon.

"No. I'm on a Quest to find him. Bink and Chester helped me travel here. I must ride the Monster Under the Bed to the Ivory Tower. But I don't know where the Ivory Tower is. I was hoping you had heard something."

"Nothing," she said with deep regret, exhaling another cloud of steam. "Of course I don't get much chance to talk to most passing creatures before I eat them, and the rocs won't give me the time of day."

"Of course not," Grundy agreed. "They've got stone for brains."

"But even if Stanley wasn't lost, he'd still be too young," she growled, discouraged. She was patrolling the Gap only temporarily; it was normally Stanley's job.

"Not necessarily," he said. "There's been a technological breakthrough. Reverse-wood and Youth Elixir. He can be any age, instantly."

"Any age!" she steamed, delighted. "We've *got* to find him!"

"But if you have no notion, then—"

"Maybe the Monster of the Sea would know!" she hissed eagerly. "He came from Mundania thousands of years ago, and knows an awful lot about the hiding places of monsters of all types. If anyone would know, where the Ivory Tower is, he would!"

"I'll be glad to ask him. Where is he?"

"He skulks off the east coast, foraging up and down the length of Xanth, looking for maidens to eat, or something." She licked her chops.

"The east coast!" Grundy exclaimed. "My friends have to return home; we couldn't possibly get that far in the time they have!"

"I will take you there!" she said, animated by the prospect of finding and maturing Stanley.

"You don't understand, Stace—uh, Stella. I'm riding Snortimer, the Monster Under the Bed, and the centaur is carrying the bed."

She nodded. "Those Bed Monsters are sadly limited. Still, I could tote that bed, if that's the only problem."

Grundy realized that this was another lucky break. He could go on without the man and the centaur!

He switched to man-tongue and explained. "Good enough," Bink agreed. "We were about to have to turn back anyway. It's been a fine mini-adventure, but the wives—"

"I'm never going to get married!" Grundy said. "Wives are a terror."

Chester waggled a warning finger at him. "You won't have a choice, if some golem damsel sets her cap for you."

Some golem damsel. That sobered Grundy. There *was* no such creature; he was the only one of his kind.

"Chameleon should be very pretty by the time I get back," Bink murmured, mostly to himself. Grundy realized that there had been method in Bink's generosity; he had been adventuring during the period when his wife was least attractive, and would return when she was most attractive. Even in old age, Chameleon in her pretty phase was something special. Grundy would have settled for a Golem damsel of that nature.

It was agreed. Bink and Chester returned up the tunnel, after tying the bed to Stella's back. At the moment of parting, Bink turned seriously to Grundy. "Be careful," he cautioned, just as if he had paid any attention to that before. Then the Gap Dragoness whomped forward, and Grundy had to cling desperately to the bed to prevent himself from flying off at each whomp. He hoped Snortimer wasn't getting motion sick. It was a long way across Xanth, especially by whomp-travel, and they were only partway along by nightfall. Grundy had managed to get some sleep during the day, but now Stella needed to rest. They discussed it, and decided that Grundy and Snortimer would go on ahead, and Stella would catch up to them the next day, hauling the bed. She was able to crawl out of the harness so that she could hunt, and the truth was that Grundy was happy to be elsewhere while she was hunting.

Snortimer started out somewhat wobbly, but got unkinked after a while and moved along well enough. They made good progress along the valley of the Gap, keeping mostly to the shadows where the moonbeams couldn't reach. But after a while a cloud blotted out the moon. That suited Snortimer just fine, but Grundy was annoyed. "Who do you think you are, cutting off my light?" he demanded in human tongue. It was rhetorical; only King Dor could talk to the inanimate and have it answer.

The cloud only intensified, sealing off the last vestige of light, so that Grundy could not see at all. He was all right, as Snortimer remained perfectly sure-handed in the dark, but still it bothered him. "You fog-faced puff of dirty mist!" he railed at the cloud. "If you were a living creature I'd prick your mangy balloon!"

There was a rumble of thunder. Oh, no—it was fixing to rain! "What noise is this?" Grundy demanded. "You think you're pretty big stuff, sounding off, don't you! Well, you're nothing but hot air!"

There was a louder peal of thunder. Could the cloud hear him, or understand him? Grundy remembered something Ivy had said about a mean little cloud called Cumulo Fracto Nimbus who thought it was a king. Maybe this was that one. If so, he knew how to insult it—and he was in just the mood to do it.

"You bag of wind," he yelled. "You call yourself a king? You stink to high heaven!"

Now there was no doubt the cloud heard him. There was a gust of wind and a roll of thunder that traversed the Chasm.

Grundy was beginning to enjoy this. He realized that he would get wet, but he could handle that. There wasn't much else the cloud could do, because it couldn't see him in the dark, and he was constantly moving. "You sound like a stink-horn!" he yelled. "Smell like it, too!"

A bolt of lightning struck the ground where he had been. Oh, that cloud was angry! Obviously it could understand the human language, and it had a bad-weather temper. Ivy had described it perfectly: a grandiose stormcloud with delusions of grandeur.

But now dawn was approaching. That meant they would have to stop and camp for the day—and be a sitting target for the lightning. Grundy hadn't thought that far ahead. What was he to do now? And, to his horror, Grundy realized he had made another oversight: traveling without Snortimer's bed. Now the Bed Monster had no bed to hide under, as the dangerous light came. If the storm didn't get them, the daylight would.

They would simply have to find a place dark enough to protect Snortimer until the dragoness caught up with the bed. "Look for a cave!" Grundy directed his steed in monster-tongue.

Fortunately the Gap was riddled with crevices and caves. Snortimer swerved to the side and up the sheer cliff, surprising him; Grundy hadn't realized how well the monster could climb. Some distance up the side there was an opening, and they crawled in. Inside there was a fairly comfortable cave chamber, quite suitable for their purpose. It had enough curvature to guarantee that no beam of light could strike Snortimer as long as he remained away from the entrance.

Grundy, however, didn't need to stay back. He dismounted and stood at the front. "Nyah, nyah, you flatulent cloud!" he yelled. "Your lightning bolts are too dull to stick in the ground!"

Furious, the cloud hurled a bolt at him. But it missed; the broad surface of the cliff provided nothing for a bolt to fix on. The bolt bounced off the stone above, and clattered to the base, where it lay dented and harmless, slowly dulling from white-hot to red-hot. In time it would become cold iron gray, and eventually rust away. A spent bolt was a sad thing.

"You call yourself a storm?" Grundy yelled. "I call you Cumulo-Fracto-Numbskull!"

Oh, the cloud was mad! Lightning flashed across it, revealing a puffy cloud-face surmounted by a foggy crown. This was Fracto, all right!

"I can see you're a real dunderhead!" Grundy called, taking off on the "thunderhead" he knew the cloud preferred to be called. "I'll bet even *I* can make water better than you can!"

That did it. Fracto set about making water. Rain poured down, splattering across the cliff. Some splashed in, but promptly seeped out again; this cave was not only secure from light, it was safe from flooding too.

Meanwhile, day was arriving; even the full fury of the storm could not blank out all the light of the sun. "You'll dry up any minute now, mist-for-brains!" Grundy shouted.

The rain poured down with doubled intensity. Water sheeted along the cliff and crashed in a torrent into the ground below. Puddles developed and expanded. It was, Grundy had to admit to himself, an impressive effort.

But of course that wasn't what he told Fracto. "If that's the best you can do, Cumulo-Fatso, you'd better retire to some greener pasture and sprinkle their flowers. A baby could dribble better than you can!"

It wasn't possible for the storm to get any angrier, but it succeeded anyway. A deluge came down while Grundy continued to hurl up insults. He hadn't had a name-calling workout like this in years!

The puddles expanded to ponds, and to little lakes. Still the water poured down. The liquid had no ready egress (Grundy smiled as that word came to him, thinking of birds and pewter) from the Gap, so it piled up. The bottom was becoming a single expanse of water, like an inlet from the sea. "Is that the best you can do, you cumbersome fractious nincompoop kinky clown of a cloud?" he demanded.

The king-cloud was so enraged that jags of lightning shot out of its posterior, illuminating the whole Chasm. Thunder crashed continuously, wind whipped violently about, and rain came down in bucketfuls. The water level rose, creeping up toward Grundy's cave.

Now, belatedly, he realized what could happen. If the rainfall continued unabated, it could flood the cave, forcing Snortimer out into the light, wiping him out.

Then, faintly over the constant noise of the rain, he heard splashing. He peered, and saw a distant cloud of steam. Stella Steamer was caught in the water, and by the look of it she couldn't swim. She was being carried along by the flow of it, thrashing about, trying to keep her head above the surface.

"Enough!" he cried. "I'll stop insulting you, Feculo!"

But now the cloud had the advantage, and had no intention of letting it go. The water descended without pause, deepening the lake. Fracto didn't care if Stella drowned, as long as he got Grundy too!

"Stella!" Grundy screamed in dragon-tongue. "Find something to hang on to!"

But there was nothing to anchor her. Slowly she was carried on past his cave, having increasing difficulty as the water deepened. The bed was tied to her back, hampering her. She was surely going to drown!

Grundy scrambled back inside the cave. "Snortimer, the water's rising, the dragon's drowning, and we'll drown too if we don't get out of here!" he exclaimed.

"I can take care of that," Snortimer said.

"You can? How?"

"I'll just pull the plug."

"The what?"

"Let's go!" Snortimer said. "But you'll have to shield me from the light!"

Grundy jumped on, spreading his body as well as he could to intercept what dim light there was, and the monster scrambled out of the cave. Snortimer winced as the palest light surrounded him; then he dropped into the water and sank below. Grundy held his breath and hung on, not knowing what was happening.

Snortimer scrambled rapidly hand over hand down under the water, moving along the bottom of what was now a deep lake. In a moment he came to a large circular plate set in the ground. He braced two arms against the ground, grabbed the edge of the disk with two more, and used another to steady himself. He hauled on the disk.

Slowly the disk came up. Then it was out of its hole, and water was pouring through. Snortimer hauled it to the side and let it go; it snagged in a crack and hung there, letting the current go by.

Now the water was sucking rapidly through the hole left by the disk. Snortimer clung to the ground, and Grundy clung to Snortimer, and the water rushed by them with increasing force. Grundy didn't know how long he could hold his breath, but he had no choice. If he stopped holding it, he would drown.

Surprisingly swiftly, the water sucked down through the hole, and the lake in the Chasm drained. Soon there was nothing remaining but puddles.

Already Snortimer was scrambling in the direction the dragon had gone. "My bed!" he gasped.

His bed, of course! He had to get under cover before the cloud cleared up!

They found Stella downstream, shaking herself. Snortimer dived under the bed that was still strapped to her back. The bed was soaking, but it represented security for the monster.

Just in time! Cumulo Fracto Nimbus, seeing the drop in the level of water, was giving it up as a bad job. Grundy was tempted to call, "Good riddance!" at the cloud, but refrained; his mouth had caused enough trouble already.

Where had all the water gone, he wondered? There had been so much of it—and now it was all belowground. Was it rushing through endless caverns, down to some sunless sea? Were there people down there, or monsters, and if so, how were they handling all that water? Probably it would not be smart to stay around long enough to find out; they might not be entirely pleased by the abrupt deluge.

Stella seemed all right; the water had drained in time, and she was of a tough species. Grundy settled on top of the squishy bed and relaxed as she whomped on.

Fracto, his rage spent, floated away, and the sun reappeared. Slowly the bed dried out. By nightfall it no longer squished.

This night Grundy and Snortimer did not range far ahead; they decided to wait until the dragoness was ready to move in the morning. After all, there might not be another plug, ahead.

6

Monster Tales

On the third day they arrived at the eastern coast. The Gap extended into the ocean, and an island was offshore. That had once been known as the Isle of Illusion, for Queen Iris had resided there, clothing the region with illusion. Today it was occupied by no one of consequence. "Every so often someone sends up a firebird or something," Stella remarked. "I don't know what they're up to; maybe they just like to watch the flames from the tail."

That was probably it. "Where is the Monster of the Sea?" Grundy asked.

"He can be anywhere along the coast," she growled. "You'll have to summon him."

"How do I do that?"

"He only comes for damsels in distress. If you catch a damsel and chain her to a post by the shore—"

"I can't do that!" Grundy protested.

She considered. "I suppose you can't. You're too small."

That wasn't the way Grundy had meant it, but he stifled his smart remark. "What other way?"

"Maybe if you *pretend* there's a damsel in distress—"

That seemed possible. "We'll fashion a dummy, and I'll imitate her voice," Grundy decided.

"Good luck," Stella growled. "I've got to go back on patrol." She whomped back down the Chasm.

At night, Snortimer came out and foraged for the makings of a dummy. He gathered driftwood that was bent into shapely configurations, and tied it together with vine. He was really pretty handy—which wasn't surprising, considering that he was mostly made of arms and hands.

Grundy, searching for food, suddenly felt his foot go cold. It was as if he had stepped in deep snow—but there was no snow. He checked, and discovered that he had stepped on a burr. No wonder! Those things were impossibly chilly.

They set up the dummy at the shore. Then Grundy imitated its voice. "Oh, help!" he wailed in the most distraught femalish tone. "I'm in horrible distress!"

Nothing happened. But of course it could take the monster time to arrive. Grundy repeated the call every hour or so, hoping it would be heard.

Dawn came, and they retreated to the bed. The night had been quiet, but the day was otherwise.

First, a little roc swooped down, evidently taking the bed for a tidbit. Too late, Grundy realized that they should have concealed it. The roc would simply lift it up and carry it away, and he dreaded to think what would happen to Snortimer.

Grundy dashed across the sand to the spot where he had stepped on the burr. It was still there. He picked it up, though it chilled his hand to the bone, and charged back just as the roc arrived. The bird was just extending its claws toward the bed as Grundy hurled the burr at its head.

The roc, with an automatic reflex, snapped the burr out of the air and swallowed it. Then the bird froze, not quite literally. It forgot the bed and pumped its wings, flying up—but there was a rather strange expression on its beak, and ice was forming on the outside of its craw. It flew away somewhat erratically.

Grundy smiled. It was a young roc, still inexperienced. A mature one would have known better than to eat the burr. Next time, *this* one would know better. He had just contributed to its growing pains, so to speak.

He settled down to rest, as there was nothing he could do about the bed right now. At night he could get Snortimer to haul it across the sand to cover, for Grundy himself lacked the strength. But he remained halfway alert.

In the late afternoon he was roused by a distant scraping or brushing sound. He jumped up and looked—and was dismayed. A beachcomber was coming down the beach. This was a giant comb with enormous teeth, advancing across the sand, combing out all debris. Behind it the sand was level and clean; the debris piled up in front of it, to be moved to some dumping site. Obviously the bed would be dumped along with the rest of the trash.

Desperately Grundy looked around. He remembered seeing something that might—yes! There was a small pumpkin growing at the fringe. He dashed across to it, used a sharp shell-fragment to saw it free of its vine, and shoved with all his might. The pumpkin weighed more than he did, but the beach was slightly inclined, and he was able to start it rolling just as the beachcomber arrived.

The comb caught the pumpkin and tumbled it about. The pumpkin burst, getting its innards all over the comb's teeth. That was exactly what Grundy had hoped for.

The teeth absorbed the juices of the pumpkin. Then the magic of the pumpkin acted on them. They were pumped up, swelling like balloons. In moments, the comb ground to a halt, unable to push its own fat teeth through the sand. The bed had been saved, again.

When evening came, they moved the bed to safety under a mys-tree, where any intruder would have great difficulty figuring things out. Grundy continued to imitate the calls and pleas of the dummy-damsel, though he had some private reservations about seeking the aid of a monster that preferred to feed on this sort of prey.

Next day, about noon, the Monster of the Sea arrived. First a ripple developed in the water, then a wake; finally a grotesque head poked up. The Monster had a flexible pink snout, bulging nostrils, cauliflower ears and two enormous ivory tusks. His eyes seemed beady, but as he came closer Grundy realized that they were more like bloodshot saucers; it was the size of the creature that made them seem small.

Grundy glanced down and discovered that his knees hadn't changed to jelly; they merely felt that way. Did he really want to continue this mission? "That's the ugliest puss I've ever seen!" he breathed.

The Monster honked. Grundy jumped; naturally he understood the honk, and what it signified was this: "And you're the least significant twerp *I've* ever seen!"

Those big, convoluted ears were good at hearing! "I'm on a Quest," Grundy replied defensively in honky.

"Aren't we all!" the Monster agreed.

"You? What's your Quest?"

"I liberate damsels in distress." The Monster waded through the shallow surf toward the dummy. He had huge flippers and a serpentine tail, and he was even bigger than he had seemed. Strings of seaweed were festooned across his scales. He smelled of ill fish.

"Um, about that particular damsel—" Grundy began.

"Be with you in a moment, mini-pint," the Monster honked as he heaved himself out of the water and hauled his blubbery body somewhat awkwardly across the sand. "First things first."

"But you see that's not really a—"

"I came to liberate her, and liberate her I shall!"

"She's a dummy. She—"

"Don't call any damsel a dummy!" the Monster chided him, continuing forward.

"But this one is *really* a—" Grundy said.

The Monster halted abruptly, eyes on the dummy. "That's no damsel!" he honked.

"It's a dummy, dummy!" Grundy exclaimed. "I've been trying to tell you!"

"A mock-damsel!" the Monster honked, amazed. "Who would do a thing like that?"

"Well, you see—"

"Here I swam half the length of Xanth at top velocity to reach the poor damsel before she expired, and all for nothing?"

"What good would it have done her, anyway?" Grundy exclaimed. "She'd be as well off dying of exposure, as being gobbled by you!"

"What?" the Monster honked, perplexed.

"Why euphemize? You may call it liberation, but it's their lives and your hunger you are liberating!"

"My dear insignificant golem!" the Monster honked. "Whatever gave you that idea?"

"It's true, isn't it? You consume only damsels in distress?"

"I consume only plankton," the Monster honked, affronted. "Do you think there would be enough damsels in all Xanth to feed me, if your heinous charge were true?"

Grundy contemplated the enormous bulk of the creature, and realized it was true. A thousand damsels would not sustain that mountain of flesh. "Plankton?"

"It's a magic food found only in the sea. Very tasty. I strain it through my teeth."

"But those tusks—"

"Are for self-defense, of course. There are some pretty bad creatures out there."

"Uh, I guess I was led astray by your reputation," Grundy said, embarrassed.

"You shouldn't credit hearsay," the Monster reproved him. "Now why is this mock-damsel here?"

"I set it up," Grundy confessed. "It was the only way to summon you."

"*You* perpetrated this indignity?" The saucer-eyes reddened alarmingly.

"I need your help! It isn't only damsels that get in distress, you know."

The Monster considered. "I suppose that could be true," he said, relenting. On a scale of ten, his orbs declined from a bloodshot factor of eight to six. "In what manner?"

"I need to get to the Ivory Tower."

"The Ivory Tower!" the beast honked, his eyes shooting up to nine. "I never go near that accursed device!"

"Oh? What do you have against it?"

"Look at these tusks!" the Monster honked, waving them in the golem's direction alarmingly. "Of what do you suppose they are made?"

"Uh—ivory?"

"Precisely. And that Tower—"

"I see your point. Someone wants your tusks for that tower."

The orbs ameliorated. "Actually, no. The Tower has been complete for centuries. But it was fashioned of the ivory of many innocent monsters like me, and every time I hear about it I think of the sacrifice of those poor creatures to the greed of the Sea Hag."

"The Sea Hag?"

"She who crafted the Tower. A horrendous witch, the scourge of the sea."

"I'm not sure I like this," Grundy said. "I have to ride the Monster Under the Bed to the Ivory Tower, if I am to rescue a banished dragon."

"A dragon-damsel in distress?" the Monster inquired, intrigued.

"No, this is Stanley Steamer, a male dragon, formerly of the Gap Chasm."

"Oh, *that* dragon! I wondered why he had been replaced by a female, recently. Still, if he's locked in the Ivory Tower—"

"I'm not sure that's the case," Grundy confessed. "I understand that Rapunzel is actually at the Tower, and maybe she will know where Stanley is."

"There's a damsel in that Tower? She must be in distress!"

"Well, I don't know anything about her, except that she corresponds with Ivy, the daughter of the human King."

"If she's in that Tower, she's captive to the Sea Hag, and she's certainly in distress!"

Grundy realized that this could be a useful interpretation. "That might be the case. Perhaps she needs rescuing."

"I hate the Ivory Tower, and I hate the Sea Hag," the Monster honked passionately. "I shall have to rescue that damsel!"

"Well, since I need to go there anyway—"

"Yes, yes, to be sure," the Monster agreed. "We must be instantly on our way. There's no telling what horrors the Sea Hag visits upon that damsel daily!"

"To be honest, Ivy didn't say anything about horrors," Grundy said. "Ivy sends boxes of junk to Rapunzel, and Rapunzel sends boxes of puns. I don't think it's an even exchange, but I wouldn't exactly call it horror, either."

"Are they good puns or bad puns?"

"Is there such a thing as a good pun?"

"Of course not! They must be bad puns. If that's all she has to send, she must be living in horror."

Grundy nodded. "I hadn't thought of it that way. You're right, of course. We'll have to rescue her. But we can't start till evening, because I have to bring Snortimer along, and his bed."

"Impossible!" the Monster honked.

Grundy thought fast. "A night start would be better, to fool the Sea Hag."

The Monster considered. His blubber paled. "We'll wait."

Grundy had won his point. Somehow he did not feel reassured. What was there about the Sea Hag that put such a tremendous monster in fear, when she wasn't even looking for ivory anymore?

Grundy wanted to return to the bed and continue his daytime nap, but was afraid the Monster would change his mind and depart without them if he gave him too much leisure. So he decided to keep the Monster's mind occupied. The best way to do that, he knew, was to get him talking about himself.

"Where did you get the reputation for consuming damsels in distress?" he asked.

"Now that's a long and sad story, replete with irony," the Monster honked, trundling down to the water.

That was exactly what Grundy wanted: a story that would distract the creature for a significant period. "I'm interested in learning the truth," Grundy said encouragingly.

"Well, let me get settled comfortably, and I'll tell you." The Monster completed his trundle to the water, excavated sand with his flippers, formed a comfortable cavity, and commenced his narration:

It all started (the Monster narrated), back in Mundania perhaps five thousand years ago, give or take a few hundred. It seems there had been a number of storms in the region of a land called Ethiopia (Mundanes have strange place names) and the superstitious natives believed that, if they sacrificed their King's daughter to the sea, the storms would stop. That was nonsense, of course; any self-respecting storm would simply take the damsel and continue unabated. So they chained the beautiful virgin named An-dro-meda to a rock by the sea and left her there.

Now it was sheer happenstance that I was in the area, and heard about it from the local fish. They said that this truly luscious morsel of mortal distaff pulchritude was exposed near the shore, with no one to help her. That bothered me; I don't have any particular brief for land creatures, and less for those of the human persuasion; but, though the males can be troublemakers, the females can be rather innocent. They should have chained out a man in armor, not a harmless damsel. There wasn't even any storm in the area at the moment. So I went to look— and do you know, she was indeed a luscious creature, ripe and succulent and fully packed. The tide was rising, and a peculiar Mundane fish called a shark (I warned you about those names!) was circling, waiting for the water to rise enough to enable it to swim to her and tear off some of that tender flesh. Even if the fish didn't eat her, the rising water would drown her, so she was obviously doomed.

Well, I decided to do something about it. I wasn't limited to the water the way the fish was, though I do prefer it; it offers a useful support, for one thing. So I hauled myself out and approached her. Oh, she was a lovely creature! If I had any taste for flesh, I would have slavered over her attributes. She had more meat on her rib-cage than I had seen in decades, and her hams were plush indeed!

She saw me and ululated, I presume with pleasure, for it was obvious that I had come to help her. I inserted a tusk into a link of the chain that bound her hind foot and wedged it out of the stone. That freed her —but I knew it would be useless to return her to the savage folk who had chained her so cruelly here. I tried to tell her that if she would just climb on my back, I would carry her safely to some more equitable culture, but of course I could not speak her language. So I tried to signify my intent by gestures, and I think she was beginning to understand.

Then this idiot wearing winged slippers came flying by. He had a sword in his right front appendage and a circular shield on his left, and without waiting to ascertain any part of the situation he dropped down and pricked me in the snoot with his weapon. Now my snoot is very tender, and he happened to strike a vein; blood welled out and spread across my face, splattering into my eyes. Had I realized his intent, I would never have permitted him to approach; I could readily have knocked him out of the air with a tusk. But I have ever been slow to appreciate the malice of strangers, until too late.

Temporarily blinded by blood, and still unwilling to appreciate the magnitude of his calumny, I plunged into deeper water to wash off my snoot. That was effective, and the cut closed in a moment, for we monsters are of hardy stock.

But in that time, the light-footed man, whose name was something stupid like "Per-see-us," made off with the maiden. He just carried her away! I dread to think of her fate at the hands (if that is the correct term) of that lecherous brute. But I could do nothing; they were already airborne when I broke the surface again.

I learned later that Per-see-us had vilely slandered me, telling the damsel that I had come to consume her, and that he had killed me. He was of course wrong on both counts; I had come to rescue her, and the story of my demise was greatly exaggerated. It was only a pinprick, after all, and a treacherous and lucky one at that. But the credulous humans thereafter chose to believe that *I* was the villain of the episode. I, who had broken the chain that bound her to the sea! I had a lower regard for the human kind after that, you may be sure!

Still, I perceived that there was a need to protect other such maidens from similar atrocities, so I constantly patrolled the shores, ready to rescue any that I spied. This led to certain altercations with other idiots of the Per-see-us stripe, as you may imagine. I remember one of them, called Ja-son; he had some foolish notion of locating the Golden Fleas that resided on a dragon. What right he thought he had to such elegant fleas I'll never know, but he got himself a boat called the Arrgh or some such and came pestering me. Evidently he presumed I was the dragon. Only the very stupidest of idiots could fail to perceive the distinction between a dragon and a sea monster, but he fitted the description. He stabbed at me with his pinpricker. Annoyed, I simply gulped him down whole.

Now I am not a flesh eater, and this carrion had a foul taste. Revolted, I soon regurgitated him, but the damage was done: the foul taste remained in my mouth for weeks. I understand the fool finally found the right dragon and stole the fleas from it, carrying them on a motley yellow sheepskin. There seems to be very little justice in Mundania!

Disgusted by episodes like these, I finally migrated to Xanth. Unfortunately, the calumny of Per-see-us pursued me, and folk here, too, believed that I was looking for damsels to harm rather than to help. But I refuse to be dissuaded by ungratefulness; still I range the coast seeking damsels who require aid. And that is my sad story, and the reason for the misunderstanding that surrounds me.

The Monster fell silent, his tale done. Grundy wasn't quite sure whether to believe him, but decided the more expedient course was to accept the Monster's version of historical events as factual. "I'm certainly glad to get the story straight," he said.

"It's good to get my side of it spread about," the Monster honked. And, strangely, he no longer seemed as ugly as he had. His appearance was the same, but Grundy just didn't perceive it as unpleasant.

"This Sea Hag," he asked. "Just how bad is she?"

"Ah, the Sea Hag," the Monster sighed. "I really wish she weren't involved in this! I don't like the notion of tangling with her one bit!"

"But you're a Monster, the scourge of the sea!" Grundy protested. "What have you to fear from her?"

"Let me tell you about her," the Monster said. "She is a Sorceress, and no mortal creature can oppose magic of that level except another of that level."

"A Sorceress? There are only three in all Xanth today," Grundy protested. "Iris, Irene, and Ivy. The Sorceresses of Illusion, Growing, and Enhancement. There aren't any more."

"There aren't any more living *in Xanth,*" the Monster honked. "But the Sea Hag is *off* Xanth, and she's not exactly living. That may be why she has escaped your notice."

"But the Good Magician knows everything!" Grundy said. "He would have told us, if—"

"I have heard of your Good Magician," the Monster honked. "Does he provide information for the asking?"

"Not exactly," Grundy admitted.

"And is he in full command of his faculties today? I understand he is getting old."

"He's young, not old—or was when I saw him last."

"Young? How can that be?"

"He's been sneaking nips of Youth Elixir. He OD'd."

"Youth Elixir! Wouldn't the Hag be a terror if she got hold of that!"

"No one but the Good Magician knows where the Fountain of Youth is," Grundy explained. "And he's not about to share his secret with anyone else."

"I hope not! It's just about the only thing that could make the Hag more dangerous than she is."

"Just what is her talent?"

"Immortality."

"But you said she wasn't exactly alive!"

"Precisely. She occupies a body and lives till she tires of it. Then she kills it and takes a new body, usually a younger one. A fairer one. Of course it doesn't stay young or beautiful after she's used it a few years; her Haggish nature gradually transforms it to hideousness. That doesn't bother her; she can always change it for another."

"But how—?"

"It's her talent. When her body dies, she is a ghost for a few hours—I don't know how long she can remain discorporate, but it isn't long—and then invests a new host, which she controls until its death. She can do this as often as she wishes, and she can invest any host."

"*Any* host?" Grundy asked, appalled.

"Any host that agrees to let her in," the Monster qualified.

"But who would do that?"

"No one—in his right mind. But she has ways of clouding minds. That's why I'm afraid of her; she might trick *me* into accepting her."

"Trick you? How could she do that?"

"You can never be sure what her form will be, because she can take over any living creature who lets her. She's had centuries to practice her nefarious wiles. She could be a damsel in distress . . ."

Oh. And when the Monster of the Sea agreed to liberate her, the agreement might constitute more than intended. Grundy appreciated the danger. But he had another concern. "Why would she keep someone locked up in the Ivory Tower?"

"You haven't perceived that?" the Monster honked.

"Why would I ask, if I had?"

"The Hag has been in this vicinity—the eastern coast of Xanth—for centuries. People are catching on. Mothers warn daughters about her. I'm sure it's getting harder for her to take over healthy human hosts. Animals, too, may be alert, as I am. She can take over any creature, male or female, though I believe she prefers female for long-term use. That doesn't mean males are safe; it means she'll use them only temporarily, killing them off when she finds a better host. So it makes sense for her to cultivate a perfect host—some young woman who can't get away, and who doesn't even know what the Hag contemplates."

"But everyone in the area must know!" Grundy protested.

"Yes. Except a person raised in an isolated tower, who never talks to anyone else."

"Rapunzel!" Grundy exclaimed, finally catching the Monster's drift.

"That is why the Hag built the Ivory Tower," the Monster agreed. "To enable her to raise a girl, in each generation, who was completely innocent, yet healthy and intelligent and beautiful. In the Ivory Tower there is no chance to learn about the real world, yet that person can be quite intellectual. The Hag has fine taste in women, since she likes to have the most attractive and useful bodies. Inevitably those bodies age and uglify under her influence, but if they are outstandingly beautiful at the outset, that process takes longer."

"Obviously Rapunzel knows something," Grundy said. "That has to be the reason the Good Magician sent me to the Ivory Tower. But if she's completely shut off from the rest of Xanth, how *could* she know where the missing dragon is?"

"She would know anything the Hag told her," the Monster pointed out. "And the Hag would need her to know the general geography and cultures of Xanth, because once the Hag takes over that body, the Hag is restricted by the limitations of the host. Obviously she knows she's the Hag, and remembers what she's done, but her physical and mental abilities are defined by those of the host. That's another reason to have a substantial period of training. Just so long as the captive doesn't learn about the real nature of the Hag herself. So probably Rapunzel knows where just about everything is, so that the Hag can find it when she has that host."

"Yes, that makes sense," Grundy agreed. "From Ivy's description, Rapunzel is a nice person, and a pundit."

"Who sends her puns," the Monster agreed. "But she won't stay nice, once the Hag takes over."

"She is definitely a damsel in distress," Grundy concluded. "And we've got to rescue her."

"Agreed," the Monster honked. "But this will be no easy task. I believe others have tried to get into the Ivory Tower in prior centuries and all have come to grief."

"I can imagine," Grundy said glumly.

"It is an interesting coincidence that your Good Magician should send you on this mission just at this time, when the damsel surely needs rescuing."

"Not coincidence at all!" Grundy said, half angrily. "The Good Magician must know about the Sea Hag after all and has dispatched me to break up her foul mischief!"

"Undoubtedly the case," the Monster agreed.

Unfortunately, Grundy was not at all sure he was up to the challenge. He was, after all, only the height of the span of a human man's spread hand. He was definitely no hero!

Now it was dusk. It was time to fetch the bed and Snortimer, and start on their swim to the dread Ivory Tower.

7

Ivory Tower

They traveled south along the coast. The Monster was so big and steady in the water that he was like a floating island; the bed simply perched on the barnacled back without falling off, and Grundy and Snortimer perched on the bed. The Monster couldn't talk to them while swimming, because his snoot was mostly underwater, but that was all right; Grundy had had his fill of conversation for now.

Progress was slow, however; the Monster was no speed freak. The voyage required several days. At dawn they camped on an isolated promontory that the Monster assured them was safe; there was an inlet that was almost a cave, providing deep shade for the bed, which made Snortimer more comfortable. The Monster swam out to the deep ocean and fed on plankton, while Grundy found some edible lichen in assorted candy flavors. Snortimer had no trouble; he fed on the dust under the bed, as he always had. He had evolved from dust, and to dust he would return, when Ivy grew up and stopped believing in him. That was the tragedy of all Bed Monsters.

As they wended farther south, the complexion of the shore changed. The normal greens and browns of trees faded, to be replaced by tan, and then yellow, and finally bright gold. "What's with the land?" Grundy asked when the Monster paused.

"Didn't you know? This is the Gold Coast."

Oh. That didn't explain much, but Grundy didn't want to admit his further ignorance, so he did not inquire again.

At length they hove into view of the dread Ivory Tower. It was, Grundy discovered, a lighthouse. A yellow beam of light swung around from its apex, brightening the heaving surface of the sea and the projecting rocks of the coast. This was a lonely region, forbidding and unpretty. Mundanes might find golden land beautiful, but golems had better taste. Grundy would never have come here, had he not been on Quest.

They paused at a distance. Grundy knew that the Monster dared not approach too close, lest the Sea Hag spy him. The next phase of this adventure was up to Grundy himself.

It was possible, the Monster had assured him, to reach the base of the Tower from the land, by crossing the shoals at low tide. There would not be much time, because the moment the tide reversed, that section would fill in with water, returning the Tower to its island status. However, since Snortimer could climb a sheer cliff face, Grundy wasn't worried about that aspect. Of greater concern was the whereabouts of the Sea Hag. Was she in the Tower now, or elsewhere?

It was fairly high tide now. The Monster nudged in close to the golden shore and landed them near a golden grotto, lifting the bed into it with a flipper. It was an awkward operation, but successful; now Snortimer was secure under the bed in a deeply shadowed nook, just the way he liked it. Still, he complained: "I miss Ivy's cute little feet."

"The sooner we get this Quest done, the sooner she'll be using this bed again," Grundy reminded him. "If you don't find romance first."

"Um, to be sure," Snortimer muttered, as a splash of water drenched the bed. He did not sound entirely satisfied.

Grundy decided to wait and watch for a while. The Monster believed that the Hag made regular trips to and from the Tower, though he had never actually observed this, being too nervous to remain long enough to watch. In fact, the Monster was already gone, having swum to deeper waters to feed. He would be back in due course, to help rescue the damsel in distress—but Grundy realized that it was up to the Golem to work out the proper strategy.

He was in luck. On the afternoon of the first day he saw a rowboat coming around the Tower. Evidently the Hag had it moored by the door at the base, and was now heading to land for supplies. If she stayed away until low tide, Grundy could cross to the Tower and enter, and perhaps rescue Rapunzel, just like that. Probably the Hag locked the door from the outside so that the girl couldn't escape. If he could just find a way to unlock it—

He waited nervously as the day waned. The Hag did not return. He assumed it was the Hag, though he had not been able to get a clear view of the figure in the boat, because it could be no one else. Certainly

Rapunzel wouldn't be going shopping! But if the Hag had someone else to do her bidding—

No. It had to be her!

Meanwhile, the tide was going out. At dusk the bar was beginning to show; within another hour they would be able to cross. Still the boat did not return; maybe the Hag planned to return in the morning. That would be so convenient for Grundy that he hardly believed it.

As night became firmly established, he roused Snortimer. They had to leave the bed in the grotto; it was under cover and high enough so that high tide would not reach it. But of course they did not plan to remain long at the Tower; this deed was best done quickly.

As the water receded farther, they made the crossing. There were still inlets and puddles to hurdle, but Snortimer could handle them. Grundy judged that they would have no more than an hour; longer, and the tide would trap them.

It was a farther distance than it had seemed. The terrain of the bar was not even; it was rough and craggy. Even at ebb tide, the waves crashed against the rocks. To a regular man this might not have been too bad, but each wave was about nine times as high relative to Grundy. He could be swamped in water that was only knee-deep to a man. Once again he was reminded of his basic inadequacy as a hero; he simply lacked the stature!

It took twenty minutes to make it to the base of the tower. They scrambled around it—and were dismayed.

There was no door. The wall was a smooth cylinder throughout. How had the Hag gotten out?

Grundy peered up into the sky. The Tower seemed immensely tall from this vantage, poking up almost to the restless night clouds. The only aperture seemed to be at the top: a window not far below the rotating beam, facing seaward.

"She must have a ladder," Grundy concluded glumly. But then he remembered his steed's ability. "We'll just have to climb up it." The prospect scared him, for it looked to be a very long way up, but what alternative did they have?

He held on tight, and Snortimer took hold of the wall. The huge hairy hands scraped across the polished ivory—and found no resistance.

The ivory was simply too slippery for Snortimer to scale. The cliff of the Gap Chasm had been rough, with a network of little cracks and crevices that assured a grip; this wall had none. They could not get up that way.

"Oh, zombie-slush!" Grundy swore, frustrated.

There was a sound, far above, as of a window being opened. "Is that you, Mother Sweetness?" a gentle voice called.

Mother Sweetness? What nonsense was this?

"Why are you back early?" the voice called.

Grundy had to answer. "I—I am a visitor," he called. "May I come up and see you?"

There was a dulcet gasp. "Oh, I dare not talk to strangers!"

Naturally the Hag had warned this innocent young thing against strangers! "But I have come a long way just to talk with you!" Grundy called.

"No, Mother Sweetness is very firm about that. No strangers!" There was the sound of a window being closed.

Grundy thought desperately. "I'm not exactly a stranger!" he called. "I'm from Ivy!"

"Ivy!" The window reopened. "My pun-pal!"

"The same! I'm on a Quest for her, and I must talk with you! It's very important!"

She hesitated. "Well, I suppose for a moment—"

"But I don't know how to get in," Grundy called. "I can't find the door."

There was a tinkle of laughter. "Silly! There *is* no door! Ivory Towers don't have accesses to the real world."

"But then how does anyone get in?"

"Just a moment while I let down my hair."

"Rapunzel, this is no time to do your hair!" Grundy cried.

Again her laughter tinkled down upon them. She seemed to be a merry soul. "It's for you, of course. That's how Mother Sweetness comes up."

Then a hank of fiber fell down to dangle just shy of the ground, startling them. Grundy reached out to touch it, and found it composed of fine silken fibers. It was her hair!

He stared up. The tower seemed to be hundreds of feet tall, and the hair dangled all the way down it. What amazing tresses she possessed! But though he could climb well enough for a few feet, he knew this was beyond him; his arms would give out before he was more than a fraction of the way up, and he would fall back to the rocky base. If the Sea Hag could readily climb that distance, she had to be one tough old creature!

Then Snortimer took hold. He, naturally, had no trouble; he could climb anything, once he got a grip on it. Grundy mounted, and up they swarmed, virtually running up the side of the Tower. In a few minutes they were near the top.

Belatedly, it occurred to Grundy that the sight of Snortimer might alarm the girl. After all, Snortimer *was* the Monster Under the Bed, a figure of terror for most young folk. "Close your eyes as we come in!" he called.

"Close my eyes?" she asked, perplexed. "But—"

How could he explain? But then he realized that they had another problem. Her chamber was lighted; Snortimer could not enter! "Or turn out the light," he said. "It—it's blinding me."

"Oh." In a moment the light went out; evidently she had the lamp within reach.

Snortimer scrambled on up in the dark, and into the window. The absence of light solved both problems neatly!

But once they were inside, Rapunzel wanted to light the lamp again. "If I turn it low, your eyes will be able to adjust," she said reasonably.

"Wait!" Grundy cried. "The truth is, I didn't come alone. My friend —he can't face the light."

"Your friend?" she asked. "Who is he?"

"He is known as the—well, he lives under the bed."

"Nobody lives under *my* bed," she said.

"Under Ivy's bed," Grundy explained somewhat lamely. "He—he's my steed. He can climb better than I can, because he's got more hands."

"Ivy's bed?"

"She's a child, and all children have—things under their beds."

"Oh, you must mean Snortimer!" Rapunzel exclaimed. "Now I remember; she's mentioned him."

"But he can't come out into the light, and we couldn't bring the bed up here, so—"

"He can borrow *my* bed," she said warmly. "I've always wanted a Monster Under the Bed!"

"I don't know—" Grundy said. "I think he can only live under Ivy's bed."

"Nonsense. I'm her pun-pal. That makes my bed just as good." She moved about in the darkness. "Where are you, Snortimer? Let me show you my bed."

"I don't think—" Snortimer said to Grundy in Monster-tongue.

"Now I'll be most unhappy if you don't try my bed," Rapunzel said, beginning to sound unhappy. "I've never had a Monster Under my Bed, even to visit; Mother Sweetness never would allow it. Whatever will I do, if you refuse?"

"Better at least try it, Snort," Grundy mumbled, feeling awkward. This was the last kind of discussion he had anticipated. But when Rapunzel sounded happy, she sounded very very happy, and when she sounded unhappy, it was awful.

Grudgingly, Snortimer moved across the dark chamber to where she indicated her bed was. A surprised snort followed. "I can use it!" Snortimer exclaimed. "It's comfortable! Grade-A dust!"

"In that case, perhaps we can light the lamp," Grundy said. "He's safe, under the bed."

In a moment, the light came on; evidently she had a magic match. At first it was indeed blinding; then he adapted.

Beautiful was hardly the word to describe Rapunzel; it was inadequate. She was as lovely a creature as he had encountered. She seemed to be about twenty years old, with eyes that shifted colors in the angles of the shadows, and hair like endless silk, ranging in shade from almost black at her head to bleached white at the end of the tresses. She wore an old-fashioned Mundanian skirt and bodice, with velvet slippers. A series of stout combs buckled her tresses in place; she was busy hauling them in and fastening them in place, hank by hank. Grundy wondered that the weight of it didn't drag her head down to the floor. But her hair seemed to compact as it curled against her head, so that no matter how much of it she piled on, it remained of only ordinary volume. Obviously her magic talent was her hair; it was both infinite and finite.

"Oh—I thought you'd be larger," she said.

"I guess I forgot to tell you," Grundy said. "I'm a golem."

"A golem?"

"I was fashioned of wood and rag and string," he explained. "Several decades ago. Later I managed to become alive, but my size didn't change."

"That's all right," she said. "I like you the way you are."

"You do?" This, too, caught him by surprise.

"Of course. There are advantages to being the right size." And abruptly she was his size.

Grundy stared. Where a full-sized human girl had been, there now stood one slightly smaller than he was. She was identical in every respect, and every bit as lovely, only smaller. "How—?" he asked, dazed.

"I'm of mixed elfin/human stock," she explained. "It all started four centuries ago, when my great-to-the-nth-degree grandmother Bluebell Elf met this handsome human barbarian warrior and used adaptation magic on him, for a tryst. Ever since, their descendants have been able to shift from her size to his, and in between, and beyond. So I can be anywhere from your size, which is smaller than an elf, to giant size, which is larger than human, though that's about the limit. Some of my ancestors have married elves, and some human folk, depending on their tastes, but the magic has carried through. Size really doesn't make much difference to me, but I've tended to stick to human size because that's the way Mother Sweetness is. Also, my hair might not reach all the way down, if I were too small, though I'm not sure about that; it does keep growing, and I haven't tried it in that size recently."

"Bluebell Elf," Grundy repeated, remembering something. "I know a human man from about that time, named Jordan. He says he—"

"Yes, he's the one!" she exclaimed, clapping her little hands enthusiastically. "I always wondered what became of him, after he left the Elven tree. Because my first female ancestor was elven, she never knew more about the man, because he was the roving kind, as barbarians are."

"That I can tell you," Grundy said, pleased. He liked this woman very well. "But there is something more serious I need to tell you first. I'm afraid it will be very difficult for you to accept."

"Oh, I don't think so!" she said cheerily. She came to sit by him on the floor, as the furniture was too large for either of them, now. Her proximity had an electric effect on him, for not only was she the loveliest creature of his size he had encountered, she was treating him exactly like a person. "It's so delightful to have company—I've never had a visitor before, you know—and even a Monster Under my Bed, even if it's only a borrowed one. It does get lonely, being alone all the time, when Mother Sweetness isn't here. Of course I do correspond, and exchange things with Ivy, though I don't have anything very good to send her compared to the wonderful things she sends me—"

"The wonderful—?"

She jumped up, even prettier in her lithe activity than she had been when sitting. "See, I have them here on a table. Here, I'll have to change to reach it." She shifted to human size, reached down her hand, and picked Grundy up, setting him gently on the table. Her fingers were soft and fine and smelled faintly of bubblebath. "Now hold my hand," she said, extending one finger.

Grundy took hold of the finger—even the nail was smooth and sweetly shaped—and suddenly she was small again, and with him, holding hands. "I can't do it by myself," she explained. "I have to stand where I change, if you see what I mean. I can get down by jumping and changing in midair, but it's hard to get *up* without breaking the table." She smiled brilliantly. "But with another person, then I can be with that person—and so here I am, on the table, with you."

Indeed she was, and Grundy was mightily impressed. He had never been with a creature like this before, and he liked it very well. His whole limited life seemed to assume more significance, just because of her presence.

They faced a substantial collection of oddments: bits of string, pebbles, sand, flower petals, fragments of pottery, a paperclip, a Mundane penny, a fragment of colored glass, and so on. These were the ordinary things that Ivy had sent in exchange for all the beautiful puns Rapunzel had sent. Yet the woman seemed to be quite pleased with them.

"I'm not sure that what you send her is inferior to what you have here," he said cautiously.

"But these are things of the real world!" she exclaimed happily. "All I have to send are used puns, and they're very cheap. See, there's some piled up in the corner." She gestured, and Grundy saw assorted knick-knacks there. One was a green bottle; another a branch of a tree, and another was a ball formed of fingers and hands.

"What are they?" he asked.

"Oh, one's a club soda; I haven't sent her that because I don't want her to get clubbed. That branch is an evergreen; it turns anything it touches green—you can see how the floor has become green there. And a handball, and tail-lights—"

"I understand," Grundy said, seeing the lighted tails.

"Pun-things hardly relate to the real world," Rapunzel continued. "But these artifacts Ivy sends—each a little bit of her reality—how I wish I could go there! I want so much to join the real world."

"I would like to take you there," Grundy said, hardly believing that it could be so easy.

"Oh, I can't go," she said, frowning, and it was as though a cloud passed over the lamp, dimming the room. "I have to mind the lamp."

"The lamp," he asked, looking at it as the fog about it dissipated.

"This is a lighthouse. The beam has to keep swinging around and around, so that the Monster of the Sea doesn't crash against the rocks in the dark."

Oh, the *big* lamp! "But the Monster of the Sea doesn't come here!" Grundy exclaimed. "He's afraid of the Sea Hag."

"The what?"

"The Sea Hag. She—"

"What is this word "hag?""

Was she teasing him? "That's what I have to tell you, that you may not like. Maybe you'd better sit down for this."

"Very well," she agreed readily enough. "Hold my hand."

He held her hand, no great chore, and they walked to the edge of the table. Then she jumped off—and changed to human size in midair. She landed solidly, but Grundy was still clasping one of her fingers. Then she lifted him down, and across to the couch, where she reversed the process. Now the two of them were sitting on the couch, quite comfortable.

Grundy remained somewhat awed by the facility with which she shifted size without sacrificing any of her daintyness, but he forced himself to focus on the subject. "It's about the one you call 'Mother Sweetness,' " he said. "She—may not be quite what you believe."

"But I've known her all my life!" Rapunzel exclaimed.

"How did you come to be here in the Ivory Tower?" he asked, hoping to find a way to say what needed to be said without alienating her.

"Well, I don't remember it myself, but from what I have been told, my parents were in trouble, and Mother Sweetness arranged to help them, and so they gave their next child to her to raise, and that was me. And I really have no right to complain, for Mother Sweetness has been very good to me, but sometimes—"

There wasn't going to be any easy way. "Outside, she is known as the Sea Hag," he said. "She takes young women and—and uses their bodies."

"I don't understand," Rapunzel said, her brow furrowing prettily.

"She—takes over their bodies. Makes them hers. I don't know what happens to the—the original owners. So instead of being an old hag, suddenly she's young and beautiful. Then she arranges for a new body, for when she gets old again and needs it. That way, she's immortal—only not with her own body."

Rapunzel stiffened. "I can't believe that!"

"I was afraid you wouldn't," Grundy said. "But if you don't believe it, you may be doomed to a fate worse than death."

"But Mother Sweetness has always treated me so well."

"And never let you leave the Ivory Tower."

"I explained about that. The light—the Monster—"

"And I explained that the Monster never comes this way, except this time, to help rescue you. He knows the Sea Hag of old."

She shook her head. "You seem like such a nice person! How can you say such a mean thing about Mother Sweetness?"

She refused to believe him. For that he could hardly blame her—yet somehow he had to convince her. "Well, I understand that she can't take over a person's body unless that person gives permission. So if you don't give permission, then maybe you'll be safe, even if you don't believe. You don't want your body taken over by another person, do you?"

Rapunzel shuddered fetchingly. "No, of course not! But I just can't believe that Mother Hag—I mean, Mother Sweetness would ever do such a thing! She's taken such good care of me!"

"Because the Sea Sweetness—I mean, the Sea Hag wants to have the best possible body to use! She has prepared you exactly for her purpose, telling you only what she wants you to know, preventing you from ever learning the truth. Does she know you've been corresponding with Ivy?"

"Of course. I was afraid she would be vexed, but when she learned that Ivy was only a child she decided that it was all right. Children don't know very much. But I'm not allowed any other pun-pals."

"Because she doesn't want you to learn anything about the real world! Not until it's too late!"

Rapunzel shook her head. "I just can't believe—"

There was a voice from outside. "Rapunzel, Rapunzel, let down your long hair!"

"Oh, she's back!" the girl exclaimed, her hand flying to her mouth in alarm. "She mustn't find you here!"

Grundy felt the same. But he was trapped; he and Snortimer couldn't escape, with the Hag waiting below. What was he to do now?

8

The Sea Hag

"Rapunzel!" the Hag called more peremptorily from below.

"Oh, I must let her in!" the girl said, jumping off the couch and becoming human-sized.

"You mustn't!" Grundy cried. "She and I are natural enemies!"

"I don't know what to do!" Rapunzel exclaimed, distraught.

"Whatever you do, don't let her in!" Grundy said. "She is an evil creature."

"Rapunzel!" the Hag called again.

"I just can't believe what you say about Mother Sweetness!" Rapunzel said, going to the window.

Grundy realized that the more he tried to condemn the Hag, the more it damaged his own credibility in the damsel's eyes. He would have to face the Hag directly. He dreaded the prospect, but saw no alternative. "Then let her in," he said with resignation.

Rapunzel was already taking the combs out of her hair and letting it drop down outside the Tower. Then she braced herself as the Hag took hold below.

Grundy saw how the slack went out of her hair and how it jerked as it was hauled on. But this did not seem to discomfit the girl as it might have; her head moved only marginally as the hair took the weight of the climber. He realized that this was part of its magic: not only did it add no particular volume or weight to her head, it nullified the weight of what touched it, as far as Rapunzel was concerned. She really seemed to be a creature of two magic talents—but he knew that the magic of heredity didn't count as a talent, so her size-changes weren't a talent.

The rules of magic could seem devious at times, but they were reasonably consistent.

What was he going to say to the dread Sea Hag? He was horrified by the prospect of this confrontation. *She doesn't have any other magic!* he reminded himself desperately. *All she can do is kill herself and take over the body of whoever lets her. I don't need to be afraid of that!* But he was afraid. He wished he could have avoided this scene. If only he had left before the Hag returned!

All too soon the Hag reached the window and scrambled in. She was indeed an ugly creature. She wore a black cloak and black cap with a dangerous-looking hatpin, and black high-heeled boots and black gloves; even had she been beautiful, her aspect would have seemed sinister. Her facial features were not physically deformed; in a picture they might have seemed ordinary, considering her evident age. But evil animated them, causing her mouth to be lined with cruelty, her nose to project snoopiness, her ears to be attuned to slanderous sounds, and her eyes to focus on all that was ugliest in the situation. Grundy hated her instantly and thoroughly—but he was also sickly afraid of her.

"Mother Sweetness!" Rapunzel exclaimed, embracing the Hag. That appalled Grundy, but he dared not protest.

The old woman glared about, her nose sniffing. "I smell intruder!" she snapped. Then her mean old eyes fastened on Grundy.

"I—I have a visitor—" Rapunzel explained faintly.

"That's no visitor—that's a wretched golem!" the Hag hissed.

"You aren't any great beauty yourself, picklesnoot," Grundy retorted automatically, before he realized what he was going to do. His terror of the Hag reduced him to his most fundamental nature: the smart mouth.

"I'll get rid of it!" the Hag exclaimed. She strode to a closet and fetched out a broom.

"Whatcha going to do with that, witch—ride it?" Grundy demanded.

"I'm going to sweep you right out of this Tower!" she exclaimed, coming at him with the broom.

"Oh!" Rapunzel exclaimed, appalled by this violence.

Suddenly Grundy realized that this could be a way to convince the damsel of the truth about the Hag. Let the evil witch show her nature! "You couldn't sweep the dust out of your ears, old snoop!" he taunted her, dodging nimbly to the side as the deadly broom swept across.

"Stand still, you runt, and I'll flatten you!" the Hag grunted, smashing the broom down at him.

But Grundy had had decades of experience dodging just such attacks, and readily avoided the blow. However, he paced himself so as to be just a little way clear, so that the Hag would not know how clumsy her attack was.

This had an unanticipated effect. It fooled Rapunzel too, and she screamed as the broom landed. "Ooo, you'll squish him!" she cried, horrified.

Grundy was quick to take advantage of the situation. He scrambled to the damsel and hauled himself up her skirt and to her pretty shoulder. "Don't let her squish me!" he pleaded in her fair ear.

The Hag, enraged, raised the broom like a club and charged forward —only to discover where Grundy had gone. She paused, broom threatening.

"What are you doing, Mother Sweetness?" Rapunzel cried, distraught. "I've never seen you like this!"

The Hag lowered the broom and composed herself, not wishing to disillusion the damsel. After all, if Rapunzel ever got the notion that the Hag was evil, she would not cooperate by yielding her body for the Hag's use.

This, Grundy realized, was the true confrontation: the question of whether Hag or Golem was telling the truth. If he could win that, he would be able to rescue the damsel; if he could not, then all was lost.

The Hag forced a smile to her malevolent face. "I am only trying to rid this chamber of this rodent," she explained.

"Ask her why she keeps you prisoner here," Grundy suggested.

"But you are not a prisoner, my dear!" the Hag protested before Rapunzel could speak. "This is your home."

"Ask her why you never get to go out," Grundy prompted.

"But someone must remain to supervise the lighthouse lamp," the Hag said. "It operates independently, but sometimes it glitches, and then it must be promptly attended to. You know that, my dear. Now just let me remove this vermin—" She extended her gloved hand.

"Ask her why *she* doesn't tend the lamp while *you* go out," Grundy said quickly.

"But you don't know the outside world," the Hag said.

"Yes I do, Mother Sweetness," Rapunzel said. "You have taught me all about Xanth, haven't you?"

This made the Hag pause. She had of course taught the damsel only what she felt it was safe for the damsel to know and that would also be useful after she took over the body herself. Naturally a lot had been omitted, but it would be awkward to admit that.

"Has she told you about the way the Monster of the Sea never uses the lighthouse beam?" Grundy asked the damsel.

"But the Monster *does* use it," the Hag protested as innocently as she could pretend.

"How odd that the Monster told me the opposite," Grundy remarked.

"Rapunzel, are you going to believe this little liar?" the Hag demanded.

Now Rapunzel hesitated. She really did not know whom to believe. "I—"

Grundy saw that straight dialogue was not going to do it. He would have to force the Hag's hand more directly—and that would be risky. "Maybe I'm wrong," he said to the Hag. "If I stop insulting you, will you let me alone?"

The sinister calculations passed almost visibly across the evil face. The Hag didn't know how much he might have told the damsel before the Hag's return, or how much of that the damsel believed. Certainly she didn't want him staying around to utter more truths to the damsel. She would try to eliminate him at the earliest opportunity. "Why of course, you little—creature," the Hag said with a semblance of sincerity.

So far, so good. "Then I'll just cross over to the bed and rest myself," Grundy said. He climbed down Rapunzel, who was a bit startled by the procedure, and scooted across the floor to the bed. He hiked himself up the leg of it. "Stay alert," he muttered to Snortimer as he passed.

He reached the top, and made himself comfortable. "How about something to eat, old crone?" he inquired politely.

The Hag stiffened. As he had suspected, she had not taught Rapunzel the meaning of terms like "crone." The damsel probably thought it was a respectful address, and the Hag dared not signify otherwise.

Then the Hag smiled, though it was as if she had to use hooks to stretch her grim mouth into the configuration. "Of course, Golem. I'll be right back." She trundled out to the kitchen.

"Mother Sweetness always speaks the truth to you?" Grundy asked in the moment that granted him. He knew the Hag was listening, and would zip right back if he tried to disillusion the damsel.

"Always," Rapunzel agreed.

"So if you ever found her deceiving you in one thing—"

"Here is your food," the Hag said, back already. She carried a chunk of hardbread almost as big as Grundy himself.

"That's great, old trot," he said with a smile. "Set it down right there." He gestured to the foot of the bed.

But the Hag was bringing it right to him. "I know this will do you good," she said between her clenched teeth.

"On your mark, Snort," he murmured, low-level.

Suddenly the Hag dropped the roll and grabbed Grundy. "Ha, I've got you, you little chunk of garbage!" she exclaimed.

"What are you going to do with me, grotesque Hag?" Grundy demanded loudly.

"I'm going to wring your stupid tiny sniveling neck, Golem!" she said.

"But you promised to leave me alone, snotface!"

"And you were fool enough to believe me, you bit of rag and bone!" she exclaimed with satisfaction.

"But that means you broke your word, prunebottom!" he said as if shocked.

"Oh!" Rapunzel cried with maidenly dismay.

The Hag glanced back at her. "Oh, shucks!" she muttered. "Well, I'll get her straightened around after I'm rid of you. She always listens to my side, when there's nothing else." And she took hold of Grundy's head and started to twist.

"Now, Snort!" he screamed.

A huge hairy hand reached out from under the bed and grasped the Hag's thin ankle. It squeezed and yanked.

The Hag let out a truly grotesque shriek and dropped Grundy. Simultaneously there was a snort of deep disgust: Snortimer's, because of the poor quality of the ankle he had had to grab.

Grundy was ready for this. Instead of falling, he clung to the witch's hand, scrambled to her arm, and up to her shoulder. There in her cap was the huge metal hatpin he had spied before. While she flailed with her arms, trying to catch her balance, he took hold of the round knob at the base of the pin and hauled the length of steel out of the hat. In a moment he had a fine sword.

The Hag finally managed to wrench her foot away from Snortimer's grasp. Grundy jumped down to the bed, holding his weapon. He bounced several times, as if on a Mundane trampoline, but kept his balance.

"What's a Monster doing under this bed?" the Hag screeched.

Grundy scrambled off the bed and dashed across to Rapunzel. "Are you satisfied now?" he called to her. "You saw her break her word!"

"There must be some misunderstanding," Rapunzel breathed, distraught. "She couldn't have meant to—"

"Hey, old bag!" Grundy called to the Hag. "What are you going to do with me when you catch me again?"

"I'm going to bite your troublesome little wooden head off, and spit it into the sea, Golem!" she called back. "Right after I hack this Bed Monster to pieces and cook it in the pot!"

"No misunderstanding, as you can see," Grundy said. "She's an evil old woman, who has deceived you all along. She cares nothing for you, only for your body—when she's ready to take it for herself."

"No, no!" Rapunzel cried, completely shocked. "That can't be true!"

"Hey, old dog, how old are you?" Grundy called to the Hag. "Is it true you were born yesterday?"

"I'm thousands of years old!" the Hag cried, stalking him again with the broom.

"That's impossible!" Grundy exclaimed. "You don't look a day over a century!"

"This *body* is only sixty years old," the Hag said, swinging the broom. "I took it forty years ago from the last girl I raised in this Tower."

"Just as you are going to take Rapunzel's body," Grundy said sneeringly as he dodged the swipe. "Of course nobody believes such nonsense."

"Nonsense?" she screeched. "I'm a Sorceress, you contraption of rag!"

"You mean to say you never cared for Rapunzel at all, old frump?"

The Hag, intent on stalking him, had grown heedless of the damsel's presence. "Of course not, Golem! No more than I cared for any of the fifty maidens I used before. They're all mere fodder for my longevity."

Grundy saw Rapunzel lean against the wall as if about to faint. She had had enough. "Snortimer!" he cried in Monster-tongue. "When I douse the light, you go tie the damsel's hair to the chair, get her out the window, and help her climb down. I'll distract the Sea Hag."

Snortimer snorted agreement from under the bed. Then Grundy lunged at the lamp with his weapon, running it through. The glass chimney shattered; the flame shot high, then puffed out. They were in darkness.

"Think that will save you, Golem?" the Hag cried, bashing at the spot with the broom.

"No, but maybe *this* will," he cried. He strode forward and plunged the hatpin where he judged one of her big feet was.

He scored. The pin stabbed into bony flesh. The Hag let out an ear-splitting screech and jumped back. She wasn't seriously damaged, for the leather of the boot protected her foot, but now she was twice as angry as before.

There was an exclamation from Rapunzel. "Go with Snortimer!"

Grundy cried to her. "Make yourself small, get on his back; he'll take you safely down!"

"But you—" she faltered.

Grundy lunged at the Hag's ankle, catching it a grazing blow. "I will follow, once you are safe!" He jumped back as the broom came at him again, telling its position more by sound than sight.

"You little piece of excrement," the Hag cried. "When I get through with you, you won't be more than a spot on the wall!" And the broom smashed down with such force that the wind almost blew him off his feet.

"You can't even catch me, you *big* piece of excrement!" Grundy responded.

"Just let me make another light!" the Hag said. She fumbled her way to the kitchen, where there was evidently another lamp.

"Going down," Snortimer called in monster-tongue.

"On your way!" Grundy replied. "I don't know how much longer I can distract her."

The Hag came back, carrying a new lamp. Light flooded the chamber. "Where's the damsel?" she screeched, abruptly realizing what had happened.

"She gone, old fang," Grundy informed her. "She has escaped your clutches at last."

The Hag dashed to the window. "She's descending her own hair!" she cried. "I'll cut it off!" She drew an immense carving knife she had evidently brought from the kitchen.

Oops! Grundy hadn't counted on this! One slash with that knife, and Rapunzel and Snortimer would both plunge to the rocks below.

He charged forward—but now the Hag could see him. She pointed the terrible blade at him. "Come within range, Golem, and I'll skewer you right through your big mouth!"

Grundy hesitated. Her threat was no bluff; she could and would do exactly that. He would not be able to do anyone much good if she wiped him out. Strangely, he felt no fear, now, just a wary frustration; how could he distract the Hag long enough to allow Rapunzel and Snortimer to reach the foot of the Tower?

The Hag reached behind her and caught the hank of hair that went out the window. It was securely knotted to the chair, and the chair was too big to fit through the window, so the anchorage was good. But now the Hag slowly brought the knife to the taut hair. "One cut, and poof!" she cackled, grinning.

Grundy thought fast. If he charged in, she would skewer him, then cut the hair. His hatpin was no match for her knife. If he threw the hatpin at her, it might distract her a moment, but couldn't really hurt her, and then he would be without any weapon. If he insulted her again, she would merely get even by cutting the hair. He had to find some other way.

He found it: logic. "If you cut that hair, Rapunzel will fall to her death—and you won't have a nice young body to take over. You'll be stuck up here with no way to get down and no body left to take but mine."

"Yuck!" she exclaimed. She looked at the knife, then withdrew it. "You're only half-right, Golem, but that's enough. I'm not limited to whatever's close at hand; when I become a ghost, I can travel any distance to seek a new host. But it is true that I don't enjoy pot luck; I'd much rather have the body I have so carefully prepared, young and beautiful and packed with exactly the information I have chosen. So I won't kill her." She grimaced. "But *you* I have no use for. You I can dispatch now."

She lunged for him, her blade sweeping through the place where he stood. But Grundy, alert for exactly this treachery, jumped straight up, came down after her hand passed, and stabbed a mighty stab of the hatpin into the back of her hand.

"Yowch!" she screeched, wrenching her hand away. The pin was caught in it; Grundy had to let go lest he be carried along. But he made good use of this new moment of distraction. He ran to the lamp and shoved at its base, trying to push it over. In darkness he would be relatively safe.

"Oh no you don't!" she exclaimed, recovering herself enough to snatch up the lamp. It had been too heavy for him to budge quickly enough; that play had failed.

Grundy scrambled for the window. He grabbed the hair and started to let himself down outside.

The hair was now slack below him; Snort and Rapunzel had reached the bottom! But now the Hag's head poked out the window. "I don't want her to die, but I'm happy to have *you* die, Golem!" she exclaimed, putting the knife to the hair again.

She had him this time! Grundy could neither let go nor stop her; his life was in her hands. But perhaps his wit could save him. "If you cut it, you'll still be trapped up here," he said. "You can kill yourself and seek another body—but right now Rapunzel won't accept you, so you'll be stuck with whatever else is handy, and then you'll have to die again to get to Rapunzel. You'll have to get her up here again, without her hair to climb on. That's an awful lot of trouble to get one silly golem."

"Confound it!" she swore. "I hadn't thought of that! I don't like to die any more times than I have to. It hurts, for one thing, and I'm disoriented for a while after I move into a new host. The girl would be apt to get away."

"Too bad, old wrinkle!" he agreed.

For a moment he thought he had overdone it, for her knife slashed at the hair. But then she stopped. "You'll not trick me that way, Golem! I will preserve my descent. But maybe I can still get rid of you!" And she took hold of the hair and started to shake it.

Grundy's grip on the hair was already tiring, for he was not used to sustained hanging. Now he was banged against the ivory wall. He was in worse trouble than ever; even if she stopped moving the hair, it would not be long before he fell on his own. It was a long way down!

But at least he had saved Rapunzel! If he had to die, this was the way to do it. He had at least done somebody some good.

"Get away, monster!" the Hag cried angrily. Grundy wondered at that, as his hands lost power; he was hardly a monster!

Then his grip slipped. His little hands tore free of the hair, and he fell into the night.

9

Escape

A big, hairy hand caught him and hauled him in. Grundy tried to fight, thinking it was the Hag—then realized it was Snortimer. "You caught me!" he exclaimed, dazed.

"Well, I was coming up to get you anyway," the Bed Monster replied gruffly in monster-tongue.

Grundy shut up. He was weak with relief. He had thought he was going to die, but was glad he had not. After all, he had not yet completed his Quest! It would have been very embarrassing.

Snortimer carried him down to the base, where Rapunzel waited in the pale moonlight. Apparently this emergency had caused the Bed Monster to become less shy of that light. Rapunzel was human-sized, and sitting in the Hag's rowboat, for the tide had come in and flooded the island. Grundy wondered whether she had remained that size while Snortimer carried her down the wall; she must have been very heavy. But if she had turned small, then what about her hair? That had remained full-sized. Well, it wasn't worth worrying about; they were all safely down, and they had the boat.

But Rapunzel's hair was tied to the chair at the top of the Ivory Tower; she could not travel from this spot! Unless—

The damsel drew out a pair of scissors. "Oh, I really hate to do this!" she exclaimed. "But—"

But what choice was there? They had to get moving before the dawn!

She handed the scissors to Snortimer. "You do it," she told the monster.

Snortimer took the scissors in one big hairy hand, and grabbed her hair with the other. Holding it firmly clear of her head, he hacked away with the scissors. In a moment Rapunzel's head of hair was short and wild, while the remainder of her tresses swung from the Tower. It was done.

Tentatively, she touched her head. "How do I look?"

"Awful!" Grundy said without thinking.

Rapunzel burst into tears. "My lovely hair!" she cried in anguish.

Snortimer, mortified, scuttled under the seat.

Grundy hated to see such a lovely creature in distress. Her hair was nightmarish, but Rapunzel herself remained beautiful. He had to reassure her.

"I meant—" he started.

"I know what you meant!" she wailed.

"But you were so brave to cut it off!" he said.

She brightened slightly. "Was I really?"

"So you think you've gotten away, do you?" the Hag called from above. "Well you haven't! I'm coming down."

"We've got to get away!" Grundy exclaimed. "Rapunzel, you're big enough to use the oars—"

"Don't you dare!" the Hag called. "You just sit right there, girl, until I come for you."

Rapunzel sat frozen.

"We have to move!" Grundy cried. "Take the oars and row!"

"I can't," Rapunzel said tearfully. "Mother Sweetness told me not to."

"But she's not your friend!" Grundy reminded her. "She only wants to use your body!"

"I know. But still, I can't directly oppose her. She's all I have known."

Grundy realized that he was up against a truly nice person. Rapunzel, even though she now knew the facts, simply could not bring herself to act in a contrary manner. She couldn't betray the person she had known all her life.

Meanwhile, the Hag was climbing out the window. Obviously she intended to climb down the hair, land in the boat, toss Grundy and Snortimer overboard, and carry the damsel back up to the chamber atop the Ivory Tower. With Rapunzel captive again, the Hag would have all the time she needed to persuade her that it was all a bad dream, and in the end she would have the body.

He had to do something! But what? It simply was not possible for him to man the big oars himself.

"Snortimer, can you—?"

But then the moonlight intensified, and the little monster scrambled farther under the seat. He was no help—not while the light was too strong.

Grundy looked about. Above the heaving sea a mean little cloud hovered. That was the one that had moved out of the way, allowing the moonlight to shine down on them unimpeded.

Was that coincidence? That cloud had a familiar look. Could it be Cumulo Fracto Nimbus? This was just the kind of thing that cloud would do, when it saw its opportunity!

But maybe Grundy could turn that malice to his advantage! He knew that Fracto had a bad temper and a lot of hot air. If he could make the cloud blow its cool—

"Hey, Fracto!" he called. "What are you doing so far from home? You'd better get back to land, where it's safe!"

The cloud huffed visibly. That was Fracto, all right!

Meanwhile, the Hag was starting down the hair. This was going to be close.

"Fracto, you're nothing but a windbag!" Grundy cried. "You used up all your power back in the Gap! You couldn't work up a decent storm now to save your foggy skin!"

The cloud puffed up ominously. An experimental bit of lightning flashed, and there was a rumble of thunder.

"Don't pull your fakery with *me,* foggybottom!" Grundy cried. "I know you're just a cottonpuff! All you can do is huff and puff and rattle around! You don't have enough power to blow at that Ivory Tower, even!"

The cloud huffed and puffed and blew at the Tower.

"Hey!" the Hag cried. "Watch what you're doing, you soggy mass of nothing!"

Affronted, Fracto blew harder. The Hag swung about on the hair, banging into the Tower. She was only a quarter of the way down, and couldn't move well while the wind was blowing.

"Leave my ugly friend alone!" Grundy yelled with sudden inspiration.

Naturally Fracto now concentrated on the Hag. The cloud moved nearer the Tower and began spitting rain at it.

"Get away from here, you vacuous piece of mist!" the Hag screamed, furious.

"Yeah, cauliflower-nimbus!" Grundy put in. "Do what she says!"

The cloud was really worked up, now. It had swelled to triple its prior size, and fairly glowed with contained lightning. It oriented more carefully on the Tower.

The Hag, perceiving this development, hastily scrambled back up the hair toward the safety of the chamber. She didn't want to get caught halfway down when that storm let loose.

Fracto, seeing her trying to escape, hastily sleeted on her. Tiny pellets of ice bounced off the Tower, but they weren't enough to make the hair slippery.

"See?" Grundy called nastily. "Your real name must be Cucumber-Fraction-Nimble!"

A jag of lightning fired out of the cloud to strike the Tower. But the Tower was impervious to influences from outside; it stood unaffected. The Hag clambered back into the chamber, then turned to lean out and shake her fist at the cloud. "I'll occupy a roc and flap you into oblivion!" she screeched.

The cloud had not only driven back the Hag, it had blotted out most of the moonlight. "Come on, Snortimer!" Grundy said.

Rapunzel clapped her hands. "That was very clever of you, Grundy!" she exclaimed.

Good—she had recovered from her stasis. Now if he could just get her safely away from the Tower before the Hag realized—

Snortimer grabbed the oars and began to row. But the boat was moored to the base of the Tower. "Untie it!" Grundy cried, for the knot was too massive for him to handle.

He had been speaking to Snortimer, but it was the damsel who did it. That was interesting—she answered to the voice of authority, wherever it might be.

They nudged out to sea. But now the storm was striking in earnest. Hailstones plopped into the water all around them. "Get under cover!" Grundy yelled, afraid the damsel would be struck.

Rapunzel changed to golem-size and ran under the seat. Snortimer shipped the oars and joined her. Grundy went there too, as the hailstones began scoring on the boat. The waves were getting so rough that it would have been useless to row anyway.

In fact, they were *too* rough. The boat rocked up and down, proceeding from apex to trough in horrendous fashion, and water began slopping inside. "Oh, we'll drown!" Rapunzel cried.

Grundy knew he had brought it upon them. He had used the storm to stop the Hag, but now it threatened to stop them too. "Maybe I can summon the Monster of the Sea," he said. "He's out here somewhere, and if we drift far enough from the Tower, he can pick us up." He climbed to the top of the seat.

"Oh, be careful!" the damsel cried.

"Got to be done," Grundy said grimly. He worked his way to the side.

"You're so brave!" Rapunzel said.

"Brave? I'm terrified!" he said. And he was. But he saw no other course.

He braced himself, stood up as tall as he could, and yelled: "Monster of the Sea! Monster of the Sea! Can you hear me!" There was no answer. He called again, and again, but either the noise of the storm was too great, or the Monster was too far away to hear, or both.

A larger wave washed over, knocking him down. One of Snortimer's hairy hands reached out and caught him before he tumbled to the bottom of the boat or, worse, overboard. He was getting to like hairy hands!

"What were you doing?" Rapunzel asked, frightened. "I thought you were going to call the Monster."

"I *was* calling the Monster!" Grundy snapped as he shook some of the water off his body.

"But you were honking! Were you blowing your nose?"

"That's Monster-talk."

"You mean you can talk their language?" she asked, amazed.

"Certainly. I'm the Golem of Communication. I can talk to any living thing."

"Oh, that's impressive!" she said. She was not being sarcastic, for there was not a sarcastic bone in her lovely body; she was really impressed.

Another wave smashed across the boat. "But he didn't answer," Grundy said gruffly. "And if we don't make contact with him soon—"

"Maybe if—" she began, hesitantly.

"Yes?" It was better to keep talking, so that the hopelessness of their situation would not be too apparent.

"If you can talk to anything—" Again she hesitated.

"I can, but—"

"Maybe if you asked a fish—"

Grundy knocked his head gently against the side of the boat. Of course! He could send a fish as a messenger to the Monster! "Good idea, Rapunzel!" he exclaimed, giving her a quick squeeze.

He scrambled back up to the seat and the edge, heedless of the waves, and yelled at the water: "Hey! Any good fish about?"

There was no answer. He realized that the fish, being underwater, couldn't hear him; he had to get into their medium. "Hey, Snort! Tie a line to my foot so I can dangle in the water!"

"No!" Rapunzel exclaimed, putting her fingers to her mouth in that maidenly way she had.

"Got to be done," Grundy said. "I have to talk to the fish in their medium."

Snortimer was good at handling cords and ropes, because of his several strong hands. In moments he had Grundy secured by the feet. "Pull me out after a moment, so I don't drown," Grundy told him, and jumped overboard.

The water caught him the moment he entered, hauling him back. He scraped along the outside of the boat before the slack was taken up. Then he called to the fish in fish-tongue: "Hey, your poor fish! My name is Grundy. I need a messenger!"

Now a fish swam up. It was a big bass. "My name is Tard; I need a meal," it said, and opened its big mouth wide.

Grundy scrambled to get away, but could not; the line held him fast. He kicked at the fish's nose. Then Snortimer hauled on the cord, and Grundy was drawn up and out of the water, escaping.

"Did you talk to one?" Rapunzel asked anxiously.

"Not exactly," Grundy spluttered. "I was almost eaten by a big bass, Tard."

"I've heard they'll eat anything," the damsel said disapprovingly.

"Got to try again," Grundy said, and jumped back into the water. "I need a messenger!" he called, alert for the bass.

A chunk of fish floated by. In a moment an aggressive, masculine fish arrived. "Did you see the rest of the cod I was eating?" it inquired.

Grundy decided not to aggravate this one. "The cod piece went that way," he said, pointing.

"Thanks, pal," the fish said, swimming after it. "I wouldn't want to lose that meat!"

Then Snortimer hauled him up again. "Not yet," Grundy reported.

On his third descent he spied a flying fish just getting ready to take off. "Hey, take a message to the Monster of the Sea," he called to it. "Tell him where we are!"

"Willco, Roger," the fish replied, and accelerated out of the water.

"I think we've got it," Grundy gasped as Snortimer hauled him up again. "I told a flying fish; they're very fast."

They retreated under the seat to ride out the storm until the Monster came. A fair amount of water was now sloshing around in the bottom of the boat, making things uncomfortable, but they were hopeful that they would soon be rescued.

Then a monstrous green tentacle flung itself over the boat. Rapunzel screamed. "What's that?"

"That's the tentacle of a kraken weed," Grundy said with horror. Then, to the kraken: "What are you doing here?"

"A flying fish told me there was food here," the monster replied in kraken-talk.

Grundy's hope sank out of sight. "The fish told the wrong monster!" he cried.

Another tentacle came over the boat, holding it fast. A third one came, snaking down under the seat, looking for prey. Rapunzel screamed again. Damsels were very good at screaming in emergencies, even those raised in Ivory Towers.

Snortimer grabbed the tentacle in a big hairy hand and squeezed it. "Ouch!" the kraken cried, and threw in three more tentacles. Snortimer grabbed two more of them, but more came in, too many for him to overcome. Slowly they dragged him from under the seat. Rapunzel's screaming was continuous.

Then the kraken grunted and let go. Its tentacles twisted and thrashed about. In a moment it was gone.

"What happened?" the damsel asked, uncertain whether it was all right to cease screaming.

Grundy looked out. A huge shape loomed beside the boat. *"Our* Monster's arrived!" he exclaimed, relieved.

"When I saw the weed going somewhere so fast, I was suspicious," the Monster said. "I thought a damsel might be in distress."

"You were right!" Grundy exclaimed. Then he translated for Rapunzel.

"Oh, I'm so happy to be rescued!" she exclaimed. She changed to human size, leaned over, and patted the Monster's nearest flipper. The Monster blushed pink with pleasure.

Now the storm was abating. Light returned—but not moonlight. "Dawn!" Grundy cried, appalled. "And we don't have the bed!"

"Just tell me where to go," the Monster said, picking the boat up by a flipper and setting it in his back. "There are a few minutes yet before the sun comes up."

"Back to the golden grotto!" Grundy cried. The Monster moved out, churning up a violent wake. It was the fastest he had ever moved.

Fracto, in the sky, spied them. The cloud darkened, then reconsidered, catching on to their problem. It started to lighten, to let more of the light of day past. The sky lightened, and Snortimer whimpered and wedged as far under the seat as he could.

They zoomed up to the rocky golden shore. But here the water was relatively shallow; the Monster could not go all the way, since the tide remained low. Still the light brightened, as the cloud malevolently dissolved its vapors.

Grundy realized that there was no time for finesse. "Throw the boat!" Grundy cried. "We'll hang on!"

The Monster picked the boat up again with a flipper, then heaved. The boat flew through the air, and splashed violently in the shallow water just beneath the rock-formation where the bed was hidden. It was an awful jolt, but Grundy couldn't afford to worry about that.

"Climb out!" he told Snortimer. "The bed's close!"

But it was already too bright. Snortimer huddled under the bench, petrified, unable to move out.

Rapunzel had gone to golem-size for the throw. "Get as big as you can!" Grundy told her. "Stand in the water!"

She jumped into the water, becoming full human-sized.

"Now reach in and grab Snortimer," Grundy directed. "He's not that big; just haul him out and toss him into that cave!"

She did as directed. The Bed Monster, paralyzed by the brightness developing around them, offered no resistance. In a moment he landed in the cave.

"You're there!" Grundy cried at him. "Get under the bed!"

But Snortimer was too far gone. He just lay there beside the bed.

"Stuff him under there!" Grundy cried to Rapunzel. "Quickly!"

She obeyed. The Monster was finally back where he belonged. But was it in time?

Rapunzel lifted Grundy up to the cave and set him on the bed. Then she held his hand and joined him there, golem-size again. "Is he all right?" she asked worriedly.

Grundy spread his hands. "I don't know. He had bad exposure. We'll just have to wait and see if he recovers."

"What's the situation?" the Monster of the Sea honked.

"He's under the bed—but hurt," Grundy reported. "We don't know how bad it is."

"Is the damsel all right?"

"She's all right," Grundy reassured him. "You liberated her."

"Then I must be going," the Monster of the Sea honked. "I can not long remain in this shallow water."

"Go, and welcome!" Grundy agreed. "You have done all that could have been asked." He had discovered, somewhere in the course of this Quest, that things tended to work better if he erred on the side of more credit for others rather than less. Insults had their place, of course, but so did compliments. It was an interesting discovery, whose ramifications he had yet to explore properly. "Take the boat with you, so the Hag can't use it; we've got her confined to the Ivory Tower."

The Monster drew on the trailing rope on the boat, and brought the craft to him. He set it on his back and pushed out to sea. "Good fortune, hero and damsel!" he honked in parting.

Grundy jumped. "What did he say?" Rapunzel asked, but Grundy was too embarrassed to tell her. Hero? *Him?* What a joke!

10

Coming to Terms

Tired from the rigors of the night, they lay on the bed and slept. There was plenty of room for both of them, as Rapunzel remained golem-sized. She slept at one end, and Grundy at the other.

At noon Grundy woke and got up. He peered under the bed. Snortimer still lay without moving. Yet he was not dead; Bed Monsters dissolved into dust when their ends came. There was still hope.

Grundy went outside the cave to forage for something to eat. He found a patch of sugar sand, and a puddle of reasonably fresh water. Those would have to do.

Rapunzel was up when he returned. He explained about the sand and water, apologetically. To his surprise, she seemed pleased. "I've never eaten directly from the real world," she said. "It will be a new experience."

Some experience! But he took her to the sand and puddle, and she ate and drank and expressed satisfaction. Then they returned to the cave and the bed.

"Is he going to get better?" she asked.

Grundy spread his hands. "I just don't know how bad it is," he confessed. "I'm hoping that rest is all he needs."

They returned to the cave, but Snortimer was no better. They sat on the bed and worried. "I promised to help him search for romance," Grundy said dispiritedly. "What have I brought him?"

"Romance?" she asked, combing her hair with a little silver comb she had with her. As she got her shorn hair in better order, it looked nicer; she was still the prettiest creature he had seen.

"He was lonely, under his bed. He wanted to find a female of his kind before he—well, you know that Bed Monsters usually don't survive after the children on their beds grow up and stop believing."

"Yes, of course. I was brought up to be rational, so I never had a real monster under my bed. I really missed that. But—"

"Wait," Grundy said, realizing. "You're not a child now. How is it that Snortimer was able to hide under your bed?"

"It's not age that decides it," she explained. "It's attitude. Most children think it's grown-up not to believe in Bed Monsters, so when they grow up, they don't. But since I didn't have a Bed Monster, I never had the experience of truly believing, and so never grew out of it. You have to experience something fully, before you can leave it behind. So I'm retarded in ways like that; I'm still ready to accept a Bed Monster, and my bed showed it."

"If you're retarded, I hope you never grow up!" Grundy exclaimed.

"I mean that I haven't had the experience of the real world," she explained. "I know about it, but I haven't experienced it. So I know a lot about Bed Monsters, but Snortimer is the first I have actually encountered. I'm so sorry he came all this way for nothing."

"For nothing?" Grundy asked blankly.

"He can't find romance. There *is* no female of his kind."

"What?" Grundy asked, appalled.

"Bed Monsters don't breed the way other creatures do. They don't reproduce. They form spontaneously from the dust under a child's bed, and they dissolve back into dust when the child stops being a child. Snortimer's the only one I know of who has traveled away from his bed."

"Well, actually we brought the bed along. But—"

"But his whole hope is vain," she concluded. "I suppose we'll have to tell him, if—"

"If he pulls through this crisis of light exposure," Grundy said morosely. "If I had known about this, I would never have—"

"Of course," she agreed quickly. "You are a nice person."

Grundy laughed ironically. "I'm neither nice nor a person. I'm a loud-mouthed golem."

"You certainly *are* a person!" she insisted. "And a brave one too! The way you fought Mother Sweetness—" But this brought her up short. "Oh, I wish I hadn't thought of that!"

"She really wasn't what you thought," Grundy said uncomfortably. "Naturally she didn't show her mean side to you."

"I realize that, now. I see that there were inconsistencies in the picture of Xanth she presented for me. If there were no things I didn't know about, why wouldn't she allow me to leave the Tower? Everything seemed to make sense, from the Tower; now that I'm away from it, I can see that reality isn't quite the same. Still, Mother Sweetness was the only person I knew, and it really hurts me to know that she—"

"I guess it's the same kind of shock for you that it will be for Snortimer, when he learns that—"

"You're very perceptive, Grundy."

"No I'm not. I just happen to know what it's like."

"What it's like?" she asked blankly.

"To have no female of your species."

"But golems can be made in any type!" she protested.

"But not *living* golems. When I was wood and rag, all I wanted was to become real. But when I became real, I discovered I was alone."

"I never thought of that! That's terrible, Grundy!"

"Anyway, that's not my Quest," he said uncomfortably. "I'm searching for Ivy's little dragon friend, Stanley Steamer. The Good Magician told me to ride the Bed Monster to the Ivory Tower, and now I've done that, but I still don't know where Stanley is."

"But I know that!" she cried, clapping her hands. "There's a young six-legged dragon with the Fauns and Nymphs."

"A steamer?" he asked, excited.

"Yes. He arrived there about three years ago, in a puff of smoke."

"He's all right?"

"So I understand."

"Then why didn't he go home to Ivy?"

"The Fauns and Nymphs won't let him go." Then her fair brow furrowed. "But that's strange, I realize now. The Fauns and Nymphs are supposed to be innocent folk who don't hurt any creature. How could they hold a dragon captive?"

"There must be a side to them that the Hag didn't tell you about," Grundy said grimly. "I know Stanley would have returned to Ivy, if he possibly could have."

She shook her head. "It must be so. The Fauns and Nymphs migrated south when the ogres migrated north; now the ogres are up by the Ogre-fen-Ogre Fen, and the Fauns and Nymphs are down below Lake Ogre-Chobee. It's really not a great distance from here, as the roc flies. I'm sure Stanley could have gone home, if permitted."

"Well, I'm going to rescue him and bring him home," Grundy said. "I have to, or Ivy will do something disastrous. She's a little Sorceress, you know."

"Yes, she's to be Queen of Xanth one day. I suppose when she grows up, she'll stop corresponding with me. Adults don't believe in pun-pals any more than they do in Bed Monsters." She dipped her gaze, sadly. "I wish I could have met her."

"But you can meet her!" Grundy said. "You're free of the Ivory Tower now!"

"Why, so I am!" she agreed, surprised. "But I'm not sure I could travel all that way alone. The fact that I know about the dragons and other creatures of Xanth doesn't mean I could handle them if I encountered them; in fact I'm sure I couldn't."

"You can travel with us," Grundy said. "We're going there, just as soon as we rescue Stanley."

"Why, so you are," she agreed, smiling gladly. "But I'm afraid I would only be in your way."

"I don't see why. Snortimer could carry both of us; he's strong enough." Then he remembered the Bed Monster's state. "Only—"

She sighed. "Only he's ill," she finished. "I had forgotten. What will you do, Grundy, if he—?"

Grundy shrugged. "I'll just have to go on alone."

"But then I could go with you!"

"On foot? I don't think you would like that."

She pondered. "Maybe you could talk to animals, and get a ride for us."

He nodded. "Yes, I could do that. But I'd rather go with Snortimer. He's been a good steed and a good friend, and—"

"Surely he will get better!" she said positively."

"Surely he will," Grundy agreed, but a big ugly doubt was hovering about him.

"Only—" she began.

"Yes?"

"What about the bed?"

Grundy sighed. "You're right. We have to take that along. But I should be able to get an animal to carry it."

Then Rapunzel screamed.

Grundy jumped up. "What? Where?"

"That!" she cried, pointing at the floor.

Grundy looked. His heart sank. "A nickelpede!" he exclaimed.

"That's right—they infest these caves. They like the gold, though they can't eat it. Some creatures are like that. Where there's one, there's hundreds!"

"It's searching for meat," Grundy said.

"Can it reach us, up here on the bed?"

"In time. But it's not after us. It's after Snortimer."

She put her hand to her mouth. "Oh!" she cried with new horror.

"We've got to stop it," he decided. "If it doesn't return to its nest, the others won't know Snortimer's here." He moved to the edge of the bed.

"But how can we stop it?" she asked, peering down.

"I'll need a weapon," he said. He looked wildly about. "I wish I'd saved that hatpin!"

"I have a fairly large pin," she said. "Of course it's small, now, because—"

"Change size and get it for me," he said urgently.

She changed to human size, reached into her dress, and brought out a large pin. She handed this to Grundy, then changed back to his size.

The pin made a good sword. Grundy held the shaft between his teeth, and climbed down the leg of the bed.

The nickelpede was now approaching one of Snortimer's limp hands. It was a roughly circular creature standing about knee-high to him, but it's two big claws reached up meanacingly. They seemed to be gold-plated; this was one rich little monster.

Grundy stabbed at the thing with his pin. The point was sharp, but it scraped off the metallic hide and did no harm. The nickelpede clicked its claws and advanced, forcing Grundy to jump back. Those pincers could gouge disk-shaped chunks out of metal; they could surely do worse to his flesh!

He circled around, seeking some vulnerable spot. Suppose he skewered an eye? That would set the thing back! There was only one problem: he couldn't find any eyes. The thing had feelers or antennae, and when he stabbed at them, they simply swayed aside.

How about the feet? The thing had six or eight little pedal extremities, and they couldn't be too heavily armored, or they would impede its walking. If he took out several feet, that might ground it.

He watched for an opening, then stabbed at a foot. He missed—but the nickelpede didn't; one of its claws whipped around and caught his pin. CRUNCH! Grundy was left holding half a pin.

Dismayed, he backed away. The nickelpede pursued, aware of its advantage.

Grundy tripped over a ridge in the stone floor, and fell on his back. The nickelpede clacked its mandibles and scuttled toward him.

Something huge came down. The nickelpede disappeared.

Startled, Grundy rubbed his eyes and looked again. The huge thing was Rapunzel, human-sized. She had stepped on the nickelpede.

"Ooo, ick!" she exclaimed, stepping away.

The nickelpede was done for; she had squished it. But in a moment she was back to golem-size, standing on the bed, her face in her hands.

Grundy climbed back up. "You saved me!" he exclaimed.

"I just couldn't let you get chomped!" She sobbed. "Ooo, I never did anything like that before!"

"I'm glad you did! I messed up, the way I usually do, and if you hadn't—"

"You were so brave! When I saw you fall—"

"I'm not brave!" he protested. "I was terrified!"

"Well, you *looked* brave!"

He wasn't used to this sort of compliment and didn't know how to handle it, so he changed the subject. "There are bound to be other nickelpedes coming. We need some better way to hold them off. Do you know of anything better than stomping?"

"If we could find a nickelodeon," she said uncertainly.

"A what?"

"They eat nickelpedes. There are supposed to be some along the Gold Coast but I don't know exactly where."

"I'll go out and find one!" he said.

"But what if another nickelpede comes before you get back?" she wailed.

"Stomp it!" he snapped, and scrambled down the leg of the bed and across the floor of the cave.

She didn't answer. He didn't like being gruff with her, but knew that if he didn't solve the problem of the nickelpedes soon, they would both suffer a lot more grief than hurt feelings. The other nickelpedes of the region would soon smell the blood of the first and converge, and when they did, no amount of stomping would stop them.

Above the grotto, he approached the first plant he spied. "Hey, leaftop—have you seen any nickelodeons hereabouts?"

To his surprise, the plant responded: "Certainly. One prowls this region all the time."

"Point in its direction!" he cried.

Soon he was on his way, tracing down the nickelodeon. He could hardly believe his fortune. Before long he reached its lair. The thing turned out to be a somewhat dumpy box with a slot in the side. It didn't look like much, but he had to trust Rapunzel's information. He hoped it was alive, so that he could talk to it.

"Are you alive?" he inquired cautiously in human tongue.

The box shook itself. "What a note!" it rumbled.

That enabled him to identify its language. "Are you hungry?" he asked the nickelodeon.

"I'm always hungry!" it responded. "But it's getting harder to catch my meals."

"If you come with me, I've got a place where nickelpedes are coming in on their own. If you wait quietly—"

"On my way!" the odd creature agreed, rising on a number of little legs and traveling along.

When they reached the grotto, they found Rapunzel distraught. She had trodden on three more nickelpedes, but remained terrified of them and appalled at herself. "Oh, I wish I had never left the Ivory Tower!" she cried, blowing her nose into a dainty hanky.

Already she was missing her captivity! How bad would it be if the Sea Hag got her alone and started in with the "Mother Sweetness" business?

"You crawl under the bed next to the Bed Monster and wait," Grundy told the nickelodeon. "Take only the ones that actually come under the bed, so as not to alert the others. Can you do that?"

"Trust me to know my business," the creature replied. It wedged under the bed.

Grundy clambered back to the top of the bed. "Come on up here," he called to Rapunzel. "Small-size."

In a moment she was with him, still sniffly. "It was horrible!" she said. "I don't know which I hate worse: those nickelpedes, or having to squish them!"

"We should be all right now," he said reassuringly. "I found a nickelodeon."

"Oh, wonderful!" she exclaimed, brightening immediately. If she reacted strongly to negatives, she reacted just as strongly to positives. Grundy was not used to associating with a person whose moods were this mercurial, but he found he rather liked it. Rapunzel had no affectation; she was honest in her responses, as a child was.

They waited and watched and soon spied another nickelpede slinking in from a shadow. These creatures, like Bed Monsters, could not stand much light, but of course Grundy could not afford to move Snortimer into the day, even if he had had the size and strength to do it.

The nickelpede moved under the bed. There was a kind of click and slurp. Then there was a strange sound.

Grundy and Rapunzel exchanged a glance. "That's a song!" she whispered.

Grundy peered over the edge of the bed. "Who's singing?" he asked in nickelodeon language.

"I am," the box replied. "I always sing when I eat."

Grundy shrugged, but didn't object. It took all kinds to make Xanth.

"Actually, it's rather pretty music," Rapunzel said.

"Just so long as it keeps every nickelpede away from Snortimer," Grundy muttered.

They waited, and the music continued as more nickelpedes arrived. What was going on below was horrific, but the music made it seem almost nice.

"Back on the boat," Rapunzel said after a while, "you did something. May I ask you why?"

"I was only trying to get us safely to land," he said.

"Oh, certainly, and an excellent job you did, too. But this was something else."

Grundy shrugged. "Tell me what I did, and I'll tell you why."

"You—you squeezed me."

"I did?" he asked, surprised.

"When I suggested you use a fish as a messenger. Why did you do that?"

Now he remembered. "I—in the distraction of the moment, I acted without thinking. I apologize for—"

"But I liked it," she said.

Grundy reconsidered. "It was such a good suggestion, I just—well, it was just my quick way of saying thank you."

"Why didn't you just say 'Thank you?' "

Grundy shrugged, embarrassed. "I should have, I guess. It just—it just seemed to be a better way, at the time."

"Mother Sweetness never squeezed me," she said.

"Of course not. She didn't really like you."

"Oh." She considered for a bit. Then: "Do you really like me, Grundy?"

"I think you're beautiful," he said.

"I don't think you answered my question."

"I don't know how to answer it," he admitted.

"Why?"

"Well, you're a beautiful woman, and I'm a golem."

"Does that mean you don't like me?"

"It means," he said with difficulty, "that I can't afford to."

"I don't understand."

He knew she was not being difficult. She had had no experience with the folk of the real world beyond the Ivory Tower. She knew *of* them and *about* them, but not how they interacted. She didn't realize how demeaning it was to be a Golem.

This would require some delicacy, and that was a thing he wasn't used to. He had always simply told off people, insulting them, making them react. He knew he couldn't do that with Rapunzel; it would be like treading a delicate flower underfoot.

"Suppose Snortimer met a female Bed Monster he really—could like," he said. "Then he realized that there are no females of his species, and that she was something else. That she only *looked* like his type of monster. Could he afford to—to like her?"

"Why not?" she asked, still perplexed.

"They would be of different species," he repeated.

"But isn't all right for creatures of different species to like each other? Don't you like Snortimer?"

"Yes, of course I do! But—"

She began to cloud up. "But you don't like me?"

"That's not the same! Snortimer and I are not—"

"Not what?"

"Not male and female." Was there no gentle way out of this?

"I'm female," she said. "Does that mean I can't like Snortimer?"

"No," he said, pained. "That's not it. Of course you can like him."

"Then is it all right if I like you?"

"Oh, certainly! But—"

"But you can't like me?"

He just wasn't getting through! He would have to be blunt, though it would shock her and perhaps alienate her. "You—right now you look just like a beautiful female golem, and if you were that, you would be the girl of my dreams, and I would want to—to have a relationship with you that—that might lead to—" He stalled out; it was impossible to be blunt with her.

But at last she caught on. "To mating with me!" she exclaimed.

Ouch! "I didn't mean—"

She looked disappointed. "You didn't?"

"Not—precisely," he said unhappily. "But it's academic, because you're *not* a golem girl, and—"

"But anybody can mate with anybody, in Xanth!" she said excitedly. "That's how all the crossbreeds came about. My ancestors were human and elven."

"Which means you have a future with either human or elven kind," he said. "Not with golem kind."

"Why not?"

He laughed bitterly. "Why would anyone who had the glorious worlds of human and elven kinds available ever settle for a golem?"

"Why *wouldn't* anyone?" she countered.

"Because a golem is nothing!" he exclaimed. "Nothing but wood and rag!"

"But you're not wood and rag anymore. You're flesh, just as I am."

"The principle remains. My body may have changed, but I'm still a golem."

She pondered. "So it's not really a failing in me, but a failing in you."

"Now you've got it," he agreed grimly.

"Thank you for explaining it to me. I really didn't understand."

"You're welcome," he said, halfway wishing he were wood and rag again. Then perhaps it wouldn't hurt so much.

"But would you do one thing for me, please?"

"Of course. I said I'd get to you to Castle Roogna, and—"

"Squeeze me again?"

"What?"

"As you did before. Instead of saying 'Thank you.' "

He was somewhat baffled, and somewhat dismayed. "Why?"

"I like it," she said simply.

Oh. He stood up on the bed, and she stood, and he put his arms around her and squeezed, diffidently.

"No, that doesn't seem the same," she said.

"Because it's not spontaneous."

"That makes a difference?"

"Of course it does! Things that are acted out are never as good as things that are natural. It's the difference between make-believe and reality."

"All my life has been make-believe," she said. Her face clouded up, and one big tear formed in her right eye.

"Don't feel that way!" Grundy exclaimed, squeezing her more tightly. "You have all reality ahead of you!"

"But I don't understand reality!" she protested.

"Give it time, girl! Once you get to Castle Roogna—"

"*Now* it feels the same," she murmured.

"What?"

"The squeeze."

"Oh." Hastily he turned her loose.

"Wasn't it supposed to?"

How could he explain? He went to the edge of the bed and peered over. He saw a nickelpede scuttling under. The nickelodeon put down its slot and sucked the creature in. More music played.

The nickelodeon spied him. "This is an excellent location," it said. "There should be even more nickels when night comes."

Probably true, Grundy realized. They would have to get out of here, because when the nickelodeon became sated, the nickelpedes would swarm, and that would be doom for any normally fleshed creatures.

Rapunzel joined him. "Is he all right?" she asked.

She meant Snortimer. "I don't know. I'd better go down and check."

"I'm sorry if I offended you," she said contritely. "I really don't know how to interact with real people."

"No fault in you!" he said, embarrassed again. He went to the leg of the bed and climbed down it.

"May I come too?" the damsel asked.

"There are nickelpedes down here," he reminded her.

She decided to remain above. He reached the floor, circled the nickel-odeon, and went to Snortimer. The hands remained limp on the floor—but was there a hint of animation? Snortimer didn't breathe or eat the same way other creatures did, but the big hairy hands did have normal flesh. Grundy touched a hand, and it was warm. That confirmed that he was alive. "Snort?" he asked, but there was no response.

He walked to the entrance of the grotto. The shadows were lengthening outside, causing the golden hue of the landscape to deepen. Dusk was coming—which meant more nickelpedes. If Snortimer didn't revive soon—

He turned back. Rapunzel was sitting on the edge of the bed, her pretty legs dangling down. "What are we going to do?" she asked.

Legs dangling down. Grundy thought of something. "Change to human size," he told her.

She started to stand up on the bed.

"No, stay sitting there," he said. "Just change—as you are."

Perplexed, she resumed her position, then changed to human size. Now her legs reached the floor.

One of Snortimer's big hairy hands quivered. Bed Monsters existed for no other purpose than to grab the ankles of children sitting on beds. Rapunzel was at times childlike in her innocence, and she had ankles that any creature would like to grab. Would they be enough to rouse the monster?

"Make a little scream," Grundy told her.

"What?"

"As if you're afraid something might grab your ankle."

She glanced down. "Eeek!" she said, starting to draw her legs out of the way.

That did it. Suddenly one of Snortimer's hands moved out and grabbed her ankle.

"EEEK!" Rapunzel screamed, wrenching her legs away.

Snortimer chuckled.

"He's back!" Grundy cried.

She clapped her hands. "Oh, how clever of you to figure that out!"

"You just had the right ankles to revive him," Grundy said. "Any creature who could resist them would be dead."

"But *you* never grabbed them," she pointed out.

"I'm not a Bed Monster." Grundy didn't care to admit that he would have dearly liked to grab one of her ankles, had there been any respectable pretext to do so.

He turned and went back to the grotto entrance. His gaze went out to the Ivory Tower, now a dark spike against the dim horizon.

Then he heard something. It was a faint scream from the region of the Tower, followed by a splash.

Seagulls had been patrolling the region. Now they veered, to circle around the Tower.

Then the lighthouse beam went out.

"Something strange," Grundy said, returning to the bed.

"I—felt it," Rapunzel said, putting one delicate hand to her heart. "Something awful."

"There was a scream and a splash from the Ivory Tower, then the beam went out."

"Oh, no!" she cried, horrified.

"Wht does it mean?"

"Mother Sweetness has died!"

"She—how can you know that?"

"I felt it, just now, but I didn't know what it was. But I know that there has to be a living person in the Tower, or the light goes out."

"She must have jumped!" Grundy exclaimed, his horror joining hers. "She didn't climb down the hair!"

"No point in that, once we took the boat," she said. "She can't swim."

"But the tide—when it recedes, it is possible to walk across to land. Didn't she know that?"

"Of course she knew that!"

"Then why didn't she wait for the tide?"

"She must—she must have wanted to die," Rapunzel said brokenly. "Oh, it is all my fault!"

"But she doesn't die," Grundy reminded her. "She just changes bodies."

"Yes." Then the damsel's lovely face twisted with new horror. "She's ready to take a new body now!"

And the body the Sea Hag wanted was Rapunzel's. Now, abruptly, her course made sense. Why wait for the tide, while Grundy and the damsel went off into the jungle where the Hag might never find them, when she could act more rapidly and effectively as a temporary ghost?

11

Siege

"We've got to get out of here!" Grundy said.

"No use. As a ghost, she can move much faster than we can. She's not limited to the region of her demise."

Grundy considered. "How long does she have to take over a new body—do you know?"

"She never told me anything about that," the damsel said tearfully.

Of course she wouldn't have! But Grundy remembered the Monster of the Sea saying something about twelve hours. Probably if the Hag did not succeed in taking over Rapunzel's body during this night, the threat would be over.

"Well, when we see her ghost coming, you be sure to tell her your body is your own."

"Her ghost may not be visible," she pointed out. "Most ghosts can't be seen unless they want to be."

"Still, we'd better move," he decided. "We have to get clear of the nickelpede region."

"Whatever you say, Grundy," she said, frightened.

He went to the bed. "Snortimer, are you all right now?"

"All right," the Bed Monster agreed. "I thought it would be easier to dissolve into dust, but then I saw those ankles—"

"We'll have to move out the moment the darkness is complete." Then Grundy saw another problem. "The bed! How will we move the bed?"

"I can carry one end," the damsel volunteered.

"That's no work for a girl like you!" Grundy protested. "It's a long trek."

She shrugged. "Maybe you can ask a monster."

"I'll go out and see what I can find."

"I'll go with you!" she said anxiously.

"But suppose too many nickelpedes come? We may need you to step on them."

"But I don't want to be alone!"

"Alone?"

"I mean, with no human company. You see—"

"*I'm* not human company. I'm a golem."

"I mean—if she's coming to take my body—"

There was that. Snortimer might not know the difference, but probably he, Grundy, would. "She can't take your body unless you let her. Do you plan to let her?"

"No!"

"Then you should be safe from that, regardless of the company you're with."

"I don't think so. If she talks to me—"

And the Hag had run the damsel's life for two decades. Rapunzel wasn't very good at saying no to things. "You're right. We'd better stay together."

It was dark now, and Snortimer was fully operational. "Can you carry one end of the bed?" Grundy asked the monster.

"Sure."

"Then we'll haul it to regular ground, where I can see what suitable monster I can find to carry it."

Snortimer lifted one end, and Rapunzel, in human-size, lifted the other. Grundy led the way out of the grotto.

It was a short but difficult climb to the level land, and the damsel was panting, her bosom heaving in the manner that only that kind of bosom could, but they completed the chore in good order. On one side was the Golden Coast and the sea while on the other was sand and the onset of the jungle. In the dim moonlight that jungle looked forbidding indeed.

Grundy stood on the bed and called to the nearest tree in tree language: "Are there any good-sized monsters around here?"

"There's the Gold Bug," the tree responded.

"What's that like?"

"It marches up and down the coast, gold-plating everything."

"Does it ever go inland, to Lake Ogre-Chobee?"

"Never."

"Scratch that," Grundy muttered.

"What did it say?" the damsel asked.

"There's a Gold Bug, but it stays strictly on the Gold Coast."

"I knew that," she said.

"So do you have a better suggestion?"

"Since we need to go to Lake Ogre-Chobee, maybe we should find an ogre. Not all of them migrated north."

Grundy brightened. That *was* a better suggestion. He moved as if to squeeze her, but this time thought the better of it. For one thing, she remained human-sized at the moment. "Any ogres around here?" he asked a different tree.

"That depends on your definition of ogre," the tree replied.

"Say, what kind of a tree are you?" Grundy demanded suspiciously.

"I am a casuis-tree."

That figured. It was almost impossible to get any useful information from a casuis-tree, because all it would do was argue about fine points and make hair-splitting distinctions. He returned to the first one. "Any ogres here?"

"There's an ogress who prowls by almost every day."

Good enough! "Hey, Ogress!" Grundy yelled in ogre-grunts. "We have mess!"

She heard him. "Hey great! Won't be late!" she bellowed in reply, and began crashing toward them. By the sound of it she was proceeding in normal ogre fashion, knocking trees out of the way instead of going around them.

Rapunzel was frightened. "I just thought—" she said timidly.

"I'll make her some kind of deal," Grundy said reassuringly. "We'll be there in no time."

"But suppose—suppose Mother Sweetness takes over the ogress?"

That stopped Grundy cold. If the ghost of the Sea Hag took over the ogress, they would be in her power. That would mean doom for Grundy and Snortimer, and the Tower for Rapunzel. There seemed little doubt the Hag *could* take over the ogress, for such monsters were notoriously stupid.

The crashing came nearer. "Hey, old shoe!" the ogress called. "Where is you?"

But now Grundy did not dare answer. The risk was too great.

They waited nervously, hoping the ogress would not be able to find them. The crashing approached, then drifted astray; without directions, she had lost them. "Me pound head, make he dead!" Grundy heard the angry ogress mutter in mild frustration as she moved away.

So much for enlisting the aid of a monster! No monster could be trusted. Not while the ghost of the Sea Hag hovered near.

"We'll just have to tote it ourselves," Grundy said regretfully. "This is apt to be a long, hard trek."

"I don't mind," Rapunzel said. "I'm not in a hurry to get to Castle Roogna anyway."

Grundy was surprised. "But that's where the human beings are!"

"Yes," she agreed.

"You don't want to join them?"

"I like being with you," she said simply.

He couldn't answer that. "Might as well start off. I'll get directions from the local foliage."

Rapunzel, in human size, picked up her half of the bed, and Snortimer took his end. They carried the bed slowly along, while Grundy selected the best route with the advice of the plants.

Several hours later, they were marginally closer to Lake Ogre-Chobee, and both Bed Monster and damsel were tired. "We'll have to rest," Grundy decided. "This is going to be a *very* long trek."

Snortimer crawled under the bed, and Rapunzel flopped atop it, not bothering to change to smaller size. Grundy considered staying awake to stand guard, but he was tired too, as he had walked the full distance himself, and what was slow for the other two was a running pace for him. He might have ridden on the bed, as his weight would hardly have made a difference to them, but he had felt too guilty to do that.

"Alert me if any monsters approach," he told the surrounding brush, and the brush agreed. Plants were generally accommodating things, when asked politely.

He settled down beside Snortimer under the bed, as there was no room on top of it. He remained uneasy, but he slept.

Some time later a hand came down to pick him up. "Oh, Rapunzel," he said sleepily. "What's on your mind?"

"You have caused me a good deal of trouble, Golem," she said, frowning as she sat up and held him near her face.

"I regret that," he said. "But there didn't seem to be any better way."

"You could have stayed entirely out of my life," she said, her even teeth showing in a way that was not completely attractive. "What business did you have at the Ivory Tower anyway?"

"You know that," he reminded her. "It was the only way to complete my Quest to rescue Stanley Steamer."

"A mere dragon!" she exclaimed derisively. "A troublesome monster! Hardly worth the ivory in its tusks!"

"Stanley has no ivory," he protested.

"Then it was for nothing at all," she said. "You messed up my schedule something awful. Now I have to get back to the coast and the Tower, through all this stupid jungle."

"But you don't want to go back there!" he protested. "The Sea Hag is there!"

"The Sea Hag!" She sneered. Then she cackled. "Whom the hell do you think you're talking to, wretch?"

Now at last he realized what had happened. The ghost of the Hag had come while they slept, and taken over Rapunzel's body! Disaster had come upon them.

He struggled to escape, but the grip was tight. "How would you like me to squeeze you?" the Hag asked through the sweet lips of the damsel. Already the lovely features were assuming an unlovely cast. The slender fingers closed more tightly about him. The witch might have the body of a fair young woman, but that hand had a lot more power than existed in all of Grundy's body, and the force was terrible.

He bared his teeth, leaned forward as far as he could, and bit the uppermost finger. His relatively tiny teeth sank into the massive flesh. He could not do lethal damage, but the bite had to hurt.

"Wretch," the Hag screeched, dropping him. "I'll twist your head off!"

Grundy scrambled under the bed, but the hag hauled the bed out of the way, exposing Snortimer, who whimpered. "I'll destroy both of you!" the Hag cried, snatching for Grundy again.

He tried to run away, but she caught him and lifted him up. "I'll bite your face off!" She opened her once-sweet mouth, where the teeth already resembled fangs.

Grundy flailed desperately, though he knew that everything was lost. "No! No!" he cried.

"Grundy! What's the matter?" she asked.

He was on the ground again, scrambling to avoid her hand. "No! No!"

"But I don't know what to do!" she protested, the tears starting.

Slowly it penetrated: he had been dreaming! It hadn't happened. Rapunzel's body had not been taken over by the witch.

"It's nothing," he said, shaken. "I just had a nightmare." Indeed, now he saw the hoofprint of the mare. What a dream she had brought him.

"A nightmare?" Rapunzel asked.

"You haven't met them before?"

"Well, I know what they are, of course. But Mother Sweetness never allowed them in the Ivory Tower."

"That figures." He straightened himself around, shaking dirt and twigs out.

"Let me bring you up to the bed," she said anxiously, reaching for him again.

Grundy looked at the approaching hand. He saw a mark on the index finger. "No!" he cried in panic.

"What?"

"How did you get that mark?" he demanded, pointing.

She looked. She rubbed her finger. Dirt smudged off. Her finger had no injury.

He relaxed. "All right—bring me up," he agreed. "Then change to my size." He knew he couldn't afford to let a bad dream cause him to distrust her.

She brought him up, and changed. Grundy described his bad dream, and she was sympathetic. "Oh, no wonder you shied away from me!" she said. "You thought I was—"

"I should have known better," he said ruefully. "But some of those nightmares are realistic."

"Let me squeeze you," she said.

"No!" Then he had to laugh. "Sorry. The dream—"

"Of course," she agreed, hurt.

"No, I really am sorry. Here." He leaned over and kissed her.

Several things occurred at this point. He hadn't realized he was going to do that; it was indeed spontaneous. She, not quite realizing what he was up to, turned simultaneously to face him. Thus instead of kissing her cheek, he scored on her lips. This changed the effect. Her lips were the softest, sweetest things he had ever touched.

After an eternal moment, they broke. "I know what that was!" she exclaimed, delighted. "That was a kiss!"

Grundy could only nod, privately overwhelmed by the impact of it. It was obviously the first such experience for her; it was also the first for him. And, he thought ruefully, it had better be the last.

"How did I do?"

"What?"

"Did I kiss well?"

Well? He felt as if his feet had not yet regained the ground. But how could he tell her that? The act had not been intended as any test of her prowess! But if he told her no, she would be hurt. "Uh, yes."

"Do people usually kiss when they're sorry?" she asked brightly.

"Not exactly," he mumbled.

"Good. I'm not sorry. Let *me* try it now."

"You don't understand—" he protested, drawing away.

"But I'm really *trying* to understand," she said. "I want to know how things are in the real world." She leaned toward him, lips pursed.

He drew further away, not knowing what to say. As a result, they both lost their balance and fell on the bed, she on top of him. "Like this?" she asked, putting her lips to his.

Grundy was pretty sure he would regret this, but for a moment he gave up the fight. He wrapped his arms about her and held her tight while they kissed.

After a much longer eternal moment, she lifted her head, smiling. "Oh, my, this *is* fun!" she exclaimed. "I never knew what I was missing, in the Ivory Tower!"

And he, Grundy, had never truly known what *he* was missing, all of his life! But he couldn't tell her that. She had what he lacked: a future with the human or elven kind.

"Dawn is coming," he said somewhat gruffly. "We had better get the bed to cover."

"Oh, my, yes!" she agreed. She sat up carefully, shifted to human-size, and helped Snortimer carry the bed to the deep shade of a stout umbrella tree. Then, remaining that size, she moved about the area, locating and plucking some fruits that she brought back to the bed. Then she changed back to golem-size, and they chewed into the huge fruit.

Now the sun was up and bright. "I think the ghost is gone, now," Grundy said. "She must have had to take some other form. So we can relax."

"Just the same," she said, "stay close by me."

Again, he knew he would be sorry, for the closer he stayed by her, the more he liked her, and not just as a friend. When she found her own place with her own kind, whichever kind that might be, he would be twice as lonely as before. But at least there was this moment—this moment of the journey. Now he, like she, was not in any great hurry to complete it.

They settled on the bed, lying side by side. She took and held his hand, and he did not protest. Her little intimicies were so innocent, for her, and so significant for him—but he didn't want to point that out to her. Her naïveté was part of her appeal.

They slept again, and this time no night mare visited. But a pesky fly did. It was a fast-buzzing, biting kind, and it settled on Grundy's leg and took a chomp. To a human-sized person it would have been a nuisance; to Grundy it was a jolt that wrenched him brutally from his repose.

The fly was clumsy. He reached down and grabbed it by the wings. It buzzed furiously, but he held it tight. "You bit me!" he exclaimed, in fly-talk, looking at the welt rising around the fang marks on his leg.

"I'll do more than that to you, wretched golem!" it responded.

"Yeah?" He looked about. Above them was a large spider's web. "Do you want this fly?" he called out in spider-talk.

The spider came out. "Certainly, if you're not going to eat it yourself."

Grundy stood, then heaved the fly into the web. "Catch!"

The spider caught. In a moment the fly was tied up in webbing. Then the spider chomped off the fly's head.

"So much for that," Grundy said, slightly nauseated. He wiped his hand off on the mattress of the bed. What had possessed that fly to attack him like that?

"Ooo!" Rapunzel exclaimed.

Grundy looked. Now a bee was coming at him, in a bee-line. He threw himself out of the way, and the bee plunged into the mattress and stung it before realizing that it had missed its target. "Curses!" the bee buzzed in bee-talk. "Foiled again!"

Unfortunately for the bee, it was one of the type that die after stinging. In a moment the bee rolled over, dead. Grundy took hold of it by a wing and hauled it to the edge of the bed and over, so that it dropped to the ground.

"Why did it do that?" Rapunzel asked, amazed.

"I wish I knew!" Grundy said. "The insects of this region don't seem to like me."

"Not only the insects!" the damsel exclaimed. "Look!"

A hummingbird was approaching. The humming became loud as it hurled itself at Grundy. He leaped out of the way, and it missed him and smacked into the trunk of the umbrella tree. The shock was so great that it dropped to the ground, dead.

"This is most curious," Grundy said. "All these creatures attacking so blindly, and dying so quickly!"

There was a commotion in the brush. A rat scurried toward them, its little red eyes gleaming, its needle-sharp teeth showing. "I'm going to chomp your legs off, then your arms, then your head!" it snarled in rat-talk. "Then I'll get mean."

"You can't fight that!" Rapunzel cried with alarm.

Indeed, he could not; the rat massed a good deal more than he did, and had natural weapons he could not match. It charged to the nearest leg of the bed and began to scramble up.

"Snortimer!" Grundy cried.

The leg of the bed was in shadow. A big, hairy hand came forth to grab the rat. It hurled the rodent into the trunk of a tree.

The rat squeaked as it struck, and fell to the ground, dead.

Grundy relaxed somewhat. "Something about this doesn't add up," he said. "These creatures don't even know me, yet—"

There was another disturbance. A Mundane hound came into sight. Now that the border to Mundania was open, Mundane creatures had migrated to Xanth in increasing numbers. Many fell prey to the magic predators, but some survived nicely—and the hounds were among the latter group.

This one slavered as it charged directly toward Grundy. Rapunzel screamed and jumped off the bed, assuming her human size. She scrambled into the brush.

The hound leaped for the bed. Grundy threw himself to the side, and the hound missed, landing on the far side. It rolled and turned, growling. "Grundy Golem, you will be dead meat!" Then it leaped again, jaws gaping.

Again, Grundy threw himself to the side, and the hound was unable to correct course because it was in midair. But again it reoriented. Grundy knew that he could not avoid it much longer. But what could he do? He didn't have time to get to a tree so that he could climb out of its reach; he had to remain where he was, precarious as that might be.

The hound leaped a third time, sailing over the bed—and a club crashed down in its head, killing it.

Amazed, Grundy looked up. There was Rapunzel, holding a heavy dead branch. "Oh, I never killed a real animal before!" she cried. "But I *had* to! It was going to eat you!"

"You had to," Grundy agreed weakly. Had Xanth gone mad? All these completely unprovoked attacks!

"What did it growl at you?" she asked.

"It called me by name," Grundy said, remembering.

"But how could it know your name?"

Then the truth dawned: "The Sea Hag!" he exclaimed. "She's assuming new forms!"

"*She* hates you," the damsel agreed.

There was a roar. "Oh, no!" Grundy cried. "That's a chimaera!"

"We can't fight that!" she said.

"We never thought of what she would do if she didn't get your body!" Grundy said. "She's more dangerous this way than she was as either Hag or ghost!"

The chimaera stalked toward them. It had the head of a lion, the tail of a serpent, and a second head of a Mundane goat growing out of its back. It was one of the most ferocious of Xanthly creatures.

"So, stupid golem, you come to your ridiculous end!" the goathead bleated in caprine talk. "How could you ever have thought you could oppose one of my ilk?"

"What's she saying?" Rapunzel asked, shaking with terror.

"I'll tell you what I'm saying!" the lionhead roared in feline tongue. "Golem, I'm going to consume you and that Bed Monster, piece by bloody piece, unless—"

"She's making a deal!" Grundy whispered, amazed all over again.

"What kind of deal?" the damsel asked, perplexed despite her terror.

"Tell her this, Golem," the goathead bleated. "I will destroy you and the Bed Monster, unless the damsel returns to me."

Suddenly the nature of the campaign came clear! The Sea Hag had not given up on Rapunzel; she wanted the damsel back under control, in the Ivory Tower. That would have only one end.

"I won't tell her that!" Grundy said.

"Tell her!" the lionhead roared. "Or I'll destroy her too!"

And that, too, made sense. If the Sea Hag couldn't have her captive back, there would be nothing left for her except revenge. Certainly she would never let Rapunzel go free to live her own life! Wouldn't it be better at least to let the damsel live?

"I know what she wants!" Rapunzel cried. "Oh, I'd rather die!"

"Then die you shall!" the lionhead roared. "But first you will watch what I do to your foolish friends, just in case you should be moved to change your mind." The monster stalked forward.

But now there was a new commotion—and Grundy knew it couldn't be another incarnation of the Hag, because the last one hadn't died.

In a moment it came into view: two people, a handsome young man and a pretty young woman. "Jordan! Threnody!" Grundy cried with enormous relief.

The chimaera glanced back with one of its heads. "Nobody can save you, Golem!" it snarled. "I will destroy them too!"

Grundy wondered what impossible coincidence had brought his friends here at this moment. But he didn't stop to ponder. "I'm in trouble!" he called.

Jordan drew his sword. "Not anymore," he said confidently. He advanced on the monster. He was a fine figure of a barbarian warrior.

"Very well, fool!" the lionhead snarled. No ordinary man could stand up to a chimaera, and the Hag knew it.

Jordan, however, was not an ordinary man. He had been a ghost for several hundred years, and now was alive again. He had been just about fearless in his first life, and now he was more so. He had a special talent that the Hag might not know about.

The chimaera pounced. Jordan slashed so quickly and hard with his sword that the monster's lionhead was lopped off.

Surprised, the monster landed, turned, and surveyed the situation. Another creature might have died on the spot, but this one was made of sterner stuff. Then the goathead opened its mouth and spewed forth a stream of fire.

Jordan tried to duck, but wasn't quick enough. The fire caught the upper part of his head, burning off his hair, one ear, and an eyeball or two. Rapunzel screamed.

Now the chimaera stepped up, the goathead guiding the lionclaws. It raised a foot, about to disembowel the still-standing man.

"Right before you!" Threnody called. "Now!"

With one mighty heave of his sword, Jordan cut off the goathead. This was too much even for the chimaera. It fell down and died.

"But the man!" Rapunzel cried with horror. "His eyes!"

"Yes, I'm afraid they're pretty well cooked," Threnody said, cocking her head as she studied Jordan. "But don't be concerned; he heals quickly."

"He—?"

"His talent," Grundy explained. "He can't be permanently hurt. You'll see."

Threnody took Jordan by the hand and guided him to the bed. "Sit down," she told him. "Danger's over."

Grundy wasn't at all sure of that, but he hoped there would be a while before the Hag found another monster to occupy. "How did you come to be here?" he asked.

"We received a message from Bink," Threnody explained. "He told us that it would probably be a good thing if we traveled through this section of Xanth. So we did."

"Bink! But he didn't even know I'd be here, or what trouble I'd be in!"

"It must have been a lucky coincidence, then," she said.

A lucky coincidence. The kind that happened perpetually when Bink was around. Now it had been extended to the farthest shore of Xanth. What was there about the man?

Threnody glanced at Rapunzel. "I don't believe I know you."

"She's Rapunzel," Grundy said. "I'm rescuing her from the Sea Hag."

"The Sea Hag?"

"She's immortal. She occupies other folk's bodies, until they die. She was in this chimaera. Now she'll appear in some other form, and try to kill us again. We're under siege."

Threnody pursed her lips. "I see. Then I think we had better stay with you for a while." She glanced at Jordan. "Feeling better, dear?"

Jordan's head was already sprouting new hair. His scorched-off ear was growing back, and his eyes seemed to be uncooking. It was an amazing thing to watch. He nodded affirmatively; he was feeling better.

"You may have to fight again, soon," Threnody told him.

Jordan shrugged. Evidently the prospect didn't bother him.

"If no attack occurs within an hour, we should be all right," Threnody said. "What sort of form will this Hag assume next?"

"There's no telling," Grundy said. "We'll have to be suspicious of everything."

"Very well. I'll stand guard; the rest of you rest."

"I couldn't rest!" Rapunzel protested. "This has been so horrible!"

"Then let the menfolk rest," Threnody suggested. "You and I can chat."

Grundy sighed internally. Now the damsel would find out what real human beings were like. He had known it would happen, but had hoped he would have a few more days before then. Still, the arrival of Jordan and Threnody had been most timely, and he really couldn't protest. His relationship with Rapunzel would be over, but at least he had his life.

"Come on, Jordan," he said to the healing man. "Lie down here for an hour. I'll snooze on your chest, if you don't mind. That way, I'll know if anything approaches you."

Jordan lay down, and Grundy climbed onto the man's solid chest and lay down. He didn't really expect to sleep, but he surprised himself by doing so almost immediately.

12

Ever-Glades

They slept a good deal more than an hour; it was afternoon when Grundy woke. Jordan was just stirring; that was what had alerted him. The girls were nearby, putting the finishing touches on a pretty fancy repast.

Jordan sat up, and Grundy simply climbed to his shoulder. The man's head was entirely better now; his hair had regrown completely, and his eyes and ears were whole. There weren't even any scars; it was just as if he had never suffered injury. Grundy had known about the man's talent, but this still impressed him. Any other man would have been in very sad state, after such a battle with a chimaera.

"I'm hungry," Jordan exclaimed, stretching. "Let's eat."

They went to join the girls. There were fruits and nuts of many descriptions, and milk and bread and cookies and assorted other delicacies. "Where did you find all this?" Grundy demanded.

Threnody shrugged. "Oh, here and there," she said. "There are always good things to be found in Xanth, if you know where to look."

Evidently so. "But the Hag—"

"Never showed," Rapunzel said brightly. She was golem-size, and she had done something with her wild, shorn hair, because now it was pleasantly curly. Her clothing had been ragged and sweat-soaked after the trudge, but now it was neat and clean. She had been the prettiest young woman he had encountered; now she was more so.

"Maybe she was tired, after getting killed so many times," he said uncertainly.

"Come, sit down, eat," Rapunzel said, leading him to a chair fashioned from a fragment of wood and some straw. "What will you have?"

"We really should be under cover, in case she comes as a big bird, or a dragon—"

Rapunzel shook her head. "See those chips in a big circle around us, Grundy?" she asked, pointing.

He looked. "Yes, but—"

"That's reverse-wood. If she tries to pass that circle, it will reverse her magic."

"Reverse-wood!" he exclaimed. "I didn't realize that was here!"

"Threnody found it," she said. "She and Jordan have been traveling through the area, and they found a cache on the other side of Lake Ogre-Chobee, near the region of madness, so they brought some along. She carried it in her purse. Of course she couldn't stay too close to him when he fought, or when he was healing, but—"

"I'll say!" he agreed. "Reverse-wood reverses any magic in its vicinity! I remember when the Good Magician was near some, and his information became disinformation. But—"

"Its range is very short," she reassured him. "It doesn't affect us, as long as we don't go too close to the circle. But it kept Mother Swe—the Sea Hag away. She may be watching us now, but she doesn't dare come in, because, even if she flew over the circle, we could toss a chip at her."

"That's terrific!" he cried. "You're very smart!"

"Oh, no, Threnody figured it out. She's been in the wilderness a long time and is jungle-wise. She told me a lot."

Surely so! "So now you can see what the human state is like," he said, glad for her, but sad for himself.

"Actually, Threnody's a halfbreed, like me. She's a human/demon cross, while I'm human/elven. She married a straight human man."

"Say, I had forgotten it in the excitement!" Grundy exclaimed. "Jordan is your—"

She blushed fetchingly. "Yes. My ancestor."

"Your ancestor," he repeated. "I hope you find him satisfactory."

She laughed. "Silly! How can I pass judgment on him?"

"Still, he's a full human being, so you can get a notion what that is like."

"Not really. He's a barbarian from four hundred years ago; he has never been part of today's society, because he stays with Threnody, and she can't go to Castle Roogna."

Because the curse on her would cause Castle Roogna to fall. The girls had evidently been talking about various things. "Well, once we get you to the castle, you'll be able to see human society for yourself."

"True," she agreed, not sounding enthusiastic.

Meanwhile, Threnody had been talking with Jordan, who of course had not had a chance before to catch up on all the wrinkles of this situation. Now he looked across at Rapunzel. "Say," he said. "You remind me of—"

"Of her elfin ancestor, Bluebell," Threnody said firmly. She tweaked his restored ear. "Past history for you, barbarian."

He laughed. "Bluebell! She was certainly a fine—Yow!" For Threnody had converted her tweak into a fierce pinch.

"Do you see anything wrong with a man marrying a crossbreed?" Rapunzel asked Jordan.

He hesitated. Threnody gave his ear another pinch. "No, of course not," he said quickly. And everyone laughed.

The meal was wonderful. Rapunzel insisted on selecting delicacies for him, catering to his every whim. Soon Grundy was stuffed. He liked all of this very well—the food and the service. But he did not let himself forget that such pleasure would soon pass.

They rested again in the afternoon, preparing for the night. This time Grundy and Rapunzel had the bed and slept holding hands, though it was evident that there was no immediate threat. No night mare came; it was hard for the mares to reach a sleeper by day. Jordan and Threnody took a walk, scouting out the vicinity; they didn't seem to need as much rest as Grundy and Rapunzel did, perhaps being jungle-hardened.

At dusk Grundy stirred and found Rapunzel still asleep, still holding firmly to his hand. She was such a beautiful and nice creature, whether awake or asleep! If only she had been a Golem . . .

She woke. Her eyes opened and fastened on him, and she smiled. "Come here, Grundy," she said. "I want to do something spontaneous."

Against his better judgment he leaned down to her. She caught him in her arms, drew him close, and kissed him.

"You shouldn't be doing this," he told her when she let him go.

"Why?"

Those innocent, direct questions! How could he answer? But he was obliged to try, again. "You don't want to spoil your future with your own kind."

"Did Jordan spoil his future, when he dallied with Bluebell?"

She was the descendant of that union! Of course she saw no wrong in it. But did this mean that she saw him as Jordan had seen the elven maid? Someone to be loved and left?

He broke contact, got to his feet, and headed for the edge of the bed.

Rapunzel scrambled after him. "Grundy!" she cried. "Did I say something wrong? I'm sorry!"

No, of course she hadn't said anything wrong, by her definitions. *He* was the one who was being difficult. Why couldn't he just accept the way she was, enjoy her attention while it lasted, and be satisfied when it was over?

She caught his hand again. "I only want to please you, Grundy," she said, her eyes beginning to fill. They were shifting colors, as was their way; at the moment they were going from purple to blue. "What am I doing wrong?"

"Nothing," he said, realizing that part of this was Threnody's doing: advice on the practicing of wiles, an area in which the woman was surely expert. "But I'm not Bluebell."

"I don't understand!" she protested, her chin trembling.

What could he do? "Of course you don't," he said gently, and squeezed her hand.

They climbed down off the bed and checked on Snortimer. He was fine; the day's rest had done him a lot of good.

Now Jordan returned, leading a monster. It seemed to be a small sphinx: a creature with the head of a woman, the body of a lion, and large bird's wings. It towered over the man, for even a small sphinx was a giant among animals. The oddest thing was its face, for it resembled—

"Threnody!" Grundy exclaimed.

"Well, it is my talent," the sphinx replied. "We thought it would be easier traveling if we had some size."

Grundy remembered: her talent was the changing of form. This was similar to Prince Dolph's talent; but while he was a Magician, and could change instantly to any living thing, she was a demon crossbreed, and could do it only slowly and stage by stage. It must have taken her all afternoon to achieve the size, mass and form of this monster, and it would take her just as long to change back to her natural aspect.

But she was right: some size would be useful. Now she could carry the bed and the rest of them without difficulty, greatly facilitating the trek to Lake Ogre-Chobee. Even the Hag would hesitate to attack a monster like this!

Night closed in. Now they had a problem: what about the reverse-wood? Some of that ought to be brought along, but Threnody could no longer carry it, for it would seriously interfere with her magically achieved state. Anyone who carried it would have to travel apart from the rest of the group, and that would be awkward at best, and danger-ous at worst. The Hag might be waiting for just such a division of the party, so she could pick off outlying members.

"We'll have to leave it behind," Grundy decided with regret. "It's more dangerous to us than to the Hag, while we travel, because we can't just leave it in a circle. It will be a liability to whoever carries it."

"Maybe we could drag some along behind us, on a long lead," Jordan suggested.

That seemed worth trying. They got a vine, packed some chips in a bag, and tied it to the end of the vine. The other end of the vine they tied to the tail of the sphinx. It was an odd-looking arrangement, but it seemed to be the best way.

Jordan loaded the bed on Threnody's back and fastened it there. Then Snortimer climbed up, and helped Grundy and Rapunzel. Jordan preferred to travel under his own power, so he walked alongside.

The sphinx moved out. Each step was a giant one, and though the pace seemed slow, progress was fast. The brush and trees moved smartly to the rear.

Snortimer was intrigued. It was the first time he had traveled on top of the bed, instead of under it. He had no eyes or ears that showed, but he could evidently see and hear, and he made a thumbs-up gesture with a couple of hairy hands. Fortunately for him, the moon was dim this night, and out of position; there was not enough light to hurt him. Grundy knew that the green cheese that comprised the moon aged rapidly, so that it could not glow with full force after the first few days, and by the end of the month it would fade all the way to oblivion. Then, phoenixlike, it would regenerate for the next month.

Soon they left the jungle and emerged into a broad expanse of swamp or field. Tall grass ranged as far as the eye could see, even from this elevated perch; it was punctuated only by occasional islands of trees.

"Have you been here before?" Grundy asked the sphinx.

"No," she answered. "We came down from the north, after we crossed Xanth. I've never seen a field like this before."

"It's the Ever-Glades," Rapunzel said. "We have to cross it to reach Lake Ogre-Chobee from this direction. There's something funny about it, but I'm not sure what."

"Something the Hag didn't tell you?" Grundy asked.

"Maybe. She only told me what she thought I ought to know. Of course I never expected actually to be here."

The sphinx plowed on, leaving the grass swiftly behind. One tree island after another passed, but the overall terrain didn't change. The night passed, and morning came, but still the glades stretched out interminably.

A bird with a crown flew by. Suddenly it plunged into a patch of water, nabbing a fish. "Oh, that's a kingfisher!" Rapunzel exclaimed, clapping her hands.

"The king of birds?" Grundy asked.

"Not exactly. It fishes for kings among the fishes."

Farther along they spied a long green creature basking in the early sun. "What's that?" Grundy asked.

"That's an allegory," Rapunzel said. "They often associate with hypotenuses and relevants and parodies. They can be very dangerous if they catch a person offguard."

Grundy had heard about the other creatures. The hypotenuse was big and blubbery with a triangular-shaped orifice; the relevant was even larger, with a nose that dangled to the ground; and the parody was a bird that liked crackers. None of them were the sort he cared to encounter casually, but the allegory was the worst.

Indeed, the allegory was now swimming toward Jordan, climbing out on the muddy bank. But the barbarian simply drew his sword and braced himself, and the green monster changed its mind. It turned on fat little legs and returned to the shallow water. It seemed that not too many creatures cared to tangle with a barbarian warrior who was looking for a fight.

They snacked on the remnants of the prior day's feast, while the sphinx cruised on. Threnody was surely getting hungry, but she didn't complain; she probably wanted to get them all safely across this blank region before changing back to human form.

But the Glades went on and on, endlessly. Afternoon came, and then evening, and nothing seemed to have changed. "At this velocity, we should have been there by now," Rapunzel said, worried.

Now the sphinx paused. "I just remembered something," she said. "Sphinxes have excellent memories! The Glades are magic. They go on forever. That's why they are called 'Ever-Glades.'"

"Forever?" Grundy asked, horrified. "But then how do we get across them?"

"This is the kind of question that can send a person hurtling from a cliff to doom," the sphinx said.

"Maybe we can use the reverse-wood," Rapunzel suggested.

"How would that work?" Grundy asked. "It only reverses what's next to it, and the Glades are everywhere."

"Well, maybe one step at a time," she said uncertainly.

"Worth trying," Jordan said. "I'll fetch it in." He walked back.

But in a moment he said, "Oh-oh. Cord broke."

It was true. Somewhere along the way the cord had frayed and separated, and the reverse-wood had been lost.

"I can change to a bird and look around," Threnody offered. "That would take some time, however."

"There's no point in trudging on endlessly," Grundy said.

So they made camp where they were. There was an island of palm trees close by, their palms and fingers spreading out to provide shade, and some had cocoa-nuts filled with warm cocoa. It was a satisfactory place to visit, though they didn't want to stay there forever.

As night closed, Snortimer came out from under the bed; he had had to hide when day had come. Threnody commenced her change to bird-form. This was fascinating to see. First she gradually lost mass without changing size or shape, so that after an hour she was a ghostly sphinx that the others could walk through without hurting her. Then she changed to bird-size, with all her diminished mass solidifying. That took another hour. Finally she changed to bird-form, becoming a swift, which of course could fly high and fast.

"She's been working on that," Jordan said with pride. "It isn't easy to fly, just because you have the bird's form; you have to learn how. She still can't do it as well as a real bird can, but she's improving."

The swift spread her wings and took off. She was somewhat clumsy, and lurched a bit, but she got straightened out and ascended into the starry night sky. If Lake Ogre-Chobee were close by, she would surely spy it!

Then a larger shape appeared, flying after the swift. "That's a falcon!" Jordan exclaimed. "Get out of there, Renee!" It was a nickname he called her, dating from the time she had been a ghost.

The swift turned and dived, trying to get back to camp, but the falcon followed, cutting across to catch her. "Gotcha, you interfering wench!" the falcon squawked in bird-talk.

"That's the Sea Hag!" Grundy cried, appalled.

Jordan brought out his bow and nocked an arrow.

"You can't shoot!" Rapunzel protested. "It's dark, and they're moving; if you hit anything, it's likely to be the wrong one!"

But the barbarian squinted, and held his aim, and as the hawk dug her claws into the swift and spread her wings to ascend, he fired. The shaft sailed up—and transfixed the body of the hawk. Both birds fell—but the swift was alive, the hawk dead.

"What an amazing shot!" Rapunzel exclaimed.

"I'm a barbarian," Jordan said shortly, putting away his bow. He strode out to recover the swift.

She was injured. The Hag-hawk's talons had punctured her body, damaging muscles and tissues. She was not in critical condition, but she would not be flying again this night.

Jordan shook his head, pained. "She can't heal the way I do," he said. "I never meant for her to get hurt!"

"The Hag was just biding her time, waiting her chance," Grundy said. "She wanted to get rid of Threnody, because she was making it too easy for us to travel. I should have been alert for that."

"We none of us were thinking," Jordan said gruffly.

They stood a kind of vigil, while Threnody slowly returned to her normal form. It took half the night, because of her injuries, but at last she was lying in human guise, with puncture-wounds in her arms and body. Grundy wished they had some healing elixir, but that was precious stuff and no one had thought it necessary.

"Oh, it can be so ugly in real life," Rapunzel murmured. "Almost, I wish—"

"That's what the Hag wants," Grundy reminded her. "To make you so miserable that you'll be glad to go back to the Ivory Tower."

Her chin firmed. "I'll never go back there!" she exclaimed.

They rested for the rest of the night, as there was no point in trying to travel, especially with Threnody injured. Grundy and Rapunzel insisted that Threnody be given the bed to lie on, until she was better. "And if Snortimer grabs your ankle, don't be concerned," Rapunzel told her. "He means no harm."

"And he has good taste in ankles," Grundy added.

The two of them settled in a nest of tall grass they fashioned. Rapunzel had never once changed to her human-size, since the arrival of Jordan and Threnody. She stayed close to Grundy, and always held his hand when they settled down. He didn't dare confess how much he liked that.

"I wish the falcon hadn't been killed," he said morosely.

"I know what you mean. Now she's loose again."

"And we don't know when or where or in what form she'll strike."

"I wish there was some way to make her stop wanting my body!" Rapunzel said. "I don't really want harm to come to her, I just want her to leave me alone."

"Well, if we get you to Castle Roogna," he said, "I'm sure someone there will be able to help you."

She lay a while in silence. Then, with feminine shift of mood, she asked: "Why did you say you aren't Bluebell?"

He sighed. "It doesn't matter."

"Yes it does. I made you unhappy, and I didn't want to do that. Threnody gave me some advice on how to get along with a man, but it doesn't seem to be working very well."

"Because I'm not a man," he said.

"Well, you certainly aren't a woman! It's obvious you aren't Bluebell. So why did you have to say it?"

Regretfully, he explained. "Because she was just a temporary connection. He loved her and left her."

"But that was all it was ever supposed to be!" she protested. "Elves and men don't stay together."

"True."

"And I'm descended from them."

"True."

"So *why* aren't you Bluebell? I mean, of course you aren't, but—"

"I don't want to be loved and left."

"But nobody's leaving you!"

"You are. Once we get you to Castle Roogna, so you can join your own kind."

"I'm not even sure what my own kind is!"

"Human or elven," he said tiredly. "You'll be able to take your choice."

She considered. "Let me see if I have this straight, at last. You like me, but you know I'll leave you when I find out what my true heritage is, so you don't want to get too involved."

Grundy was startled. "That's it exactly!"

"And you're a Golem, a living Golem, and there's no one else exactly like you, male or female, so you know you have to be alone."

It was amazing how completely she understood his situation, now. "Yes."

"But if you ever did find someone else, you would never change your mind."

How tellingly and cruelly she put it, without understanding how it cut him. "I'm glad you finally have it clear."

"You don't *sound* glad."

"I'm glad you understand, not glad for me," he clarified.

"I may have it straight, but I don't understand."

"What?"

"Now you're confused," she said, satisfied. "Serves you right!" And she took his hand and settled down to sleep.

It took him somewhat longer.

Next day, while Threnody continued to lie on the bed and heal, now and then dangling a well-turned ankle down for Snortimer to grab at, the others tried to find some way out of the Ever-Glades. Since there was no end to the sealike grass, they explored the island of palm trees. But it was only an island; no matter which way they went through it, they came out on the opposite side and faced the expanse of grass again. The faint hope that the trees would banish the grass was dashed.

Grundy tried questioning the palms. "Do you know any way out of here?"

The hands clapped, applauding the question. "There *is* no way out of here! That's what so nice about the Ever-Glades."

An allegory swam up, checking them over. It looked just like the one they had seen before. "Do you know any way out of here?" he asked it.

"Well, speaking metaphorically," the creature began.

"Yes or no?"

The allergory smiled with its long and toothy snoot. "No." Then it tried to snap him up.

Grundy jumped back, ready for that move. Naturally such a predator wouldn't tell him of any way out.

"I guess," Jordan said at last, "we had better just plow on and hope we get somewhere. That's the barbarian way."

That did not appeal particularly to Grundy, but he had nothing better to offer. If they weren't going to get out of the Glades, they might as well do it with their best effort.

They decided to move out at nightfall, because Threnody pronounced herself well enough to travel. But she was obviously not completely healed, so the others refused to let her change to sphinx-form and carry them; she had to remain as herself.

Who would carry the bed? Rapunzel could change to human size and carry one end, but she seemed reluctant to do that. She had remained golem-sized the whole time they were in the Ever-Glades, and Grundy appreciated that without quite understanding her rationale. Certainly there were advantages to the human size! Threnody was too weak to do it, and Snortimer was likely to have trouble doing it here in the swamp; his hands tended to sink into the muck, making progress difficult unless he used all five of them cleverly. Grundy himself couldn't do it; he was far too small.

That left Jordan. "No problem," the barbarian said.

"But who will carry the other end?" Grundy asked.

"Just tie the bed to my back," Jordan said.

"But it's too heavy to—"

"Not for an uncivilized warrior," he said cheerfully. And indeed he was correct; they bound the bed to his back, and he heaved it up, leaned forward somewhat, and strode forth.

The others followed. Threnody was second, and Grundy and Rapunzel mounted Snortimer and brought up the rear. The Bed Monster was able to carry them without difficulty, because they were small and light and because he didn't need to use any hands to hold them in place, as he would have had to do for the bed. He picked his way across the tufts and hummocks of the swamp, and kept the pace handily.

But it was to no avail. They trudged along all night, and as dawn threatened they remained exactly where they had been: in the middle of the Glades. They found another copse of trees exactly like the first and set up the bed under a palm tree just like the first.

"Oh!" Rapunzel exclaimed.

Grundy rushed over, alarmed. "What?"

"This *is* the same place!" she exclaimed. "See, there are the dents of the four bed legs, and there's the place where we buried our—" here she pinkened a trifle—"refuse."

Sure enough: their toilet trench was there. Grundy alerted the others, and quickly they verified that every tree was the same, with the same cocoa-nut shells remaining. They had been here before.

"But we traveled in a straight line!" Jordan said, scratching his head. "I steered by the stars; I know I didn't make any circle!"

The others agreed. They had not drifted aimlessly. But this was the same place they had left.

"Let me check this," Jordan said. He stepped out toward the nearest other island of palms.

"Take me with you!" Grundy cried.

"Okay," the barbarian agreed, and reached down a hand for him. Grundy scrambled up to his shoulder.

They crossed rapidly to the other copse. At one point there was a stirring in the water, but Jordan put his hand on his sword and Grundy called out: "Keep your snoot clear, allegory!"

"Oh, you again," the allegory muttered from the shadow. "You'll never find your way out of here, you know."

It was the same allegory! Grundy felt a chill, for he knew the creature could not have followed them all that way on its fat little legs.

The other island turned out to be identical to the first, cocoa-nut shards and all, and—there were the others of their party!

"What are you doing here?" Grundy demanded.

"What are *you* doing here?" Rapunzel responded. She was now sitting on Threnody's shoulder, emulating Grundy's style. "We just watched you enter the other copse!"

"We did," Grundy said. "This *is* the other copse!"

"No, this is the original one," she insisted. "We never moved."

"Something mighty peculiar here," Jordan said.

With that they all agreed. But Rapunzel was more thoughtful than the others. "I wonder—I wasn't told much about the Ever-Glades, but there is something—they're not as big as they seem."

"That doesn't make much difference," Grundy said, "if we can't get out."

"I think we should experiment," she said. "You see, we watched you go northwest, but you came up behind us, from the southeast. Maybe if we had watched the other way—"

"Say, yes," Grundy agreed. "Let's try it again, only this time you watch both ways."

And so they did. He and Jordan headed northwest toward the other copse, while Rapunzel dismounted and watched them go, and Threnody went to the opposite side of the island and watched for what might occur there.

About halfway across, Grundy's sharp eyes spied something. "There's someone there!" he said.

Jordan peered ahead. "That's Renee!" he said.

Grundy turned to look back. Because he knew exactly where to look, he was able to spot little Rapunzel. "They're both places," he said.

They proceeded on past the allegory and reached the new copse. "You never left, right?" Jordan asked Threnody.

"Correct," she agreed. "I simply crossed, and saw you coming from the other island."

Now it was definite: it was all the same place, no matter how they moved. Grundy crossed over to the northwest side, leaving Jordan and Threnody where they were, joined Rapunzel, and looked across to the other copse. There he was able to spy two figures, male and female, standing at its southeast edge.

"We are all here—and there—and everywhere," Grundy said, amazed.

"Now I think I remember," Rapunzel said. "It's a—a little universe in itself. We simply go round and round it, never escaping."

"And all our long treks—were simply round and round," Grundy agreed. "We should have saved our energy."

Jordan and Threnody came up. "How the blank are we going to get out of here?" Jordan asked, bewildered.

The others shrugged. They had no idea. It seemed that they really were stuck in the Ever-Glades forever.

13

Fauns & Nymphs

They ate and rested, as they were all tired and there seemed to be nothing better to do at the moment. Grundy and Rapunzel slept on the bed, while Jordan and Threnody settled elsewhere in the copse.

In early afternoon they woke. Rather, Grundy woke; the damsel was already awake, because she was kissing him.

"I suppose this is a silly question," he began when she was through. "But—"

"I was just thinking," she said, addressing his question skew-fashion. "Here we are, lost in the Ever-Glades because we just can't seem to find out how to get anywhere. And here we are too, you and I, for the same reason."

"The same—?"

"If I knew how to get anywhere with you, I'd do it. But I can't figure out how."

"Rapunzel, you don't need to get anywhere with me!" he protested. "You have two whole futures to choose from!"

"Because I just can't make you *listen*. And I wish I could."

"But—"

"So I kissed you," she concluded simply.

Evidently that made sense to her. Grundy sighed and got up.

"Suppose we never do find our way out of here?" she inquired after a moment. "Would that be so bad? I mean, I was trapped in the Ivory Tower for most of my life, and I got along all right, and so I'm used to it, only now I have company, and maybe in time you would accept it too."

To be sealed away forever, with plenty of food, and her for company? No, it wouldn't be bad! But he knew he had no right to want that. "I have a Quest," he reminded her. "I promised to rescue Stanley Steamer."

"Yes, of course," she agreed. "You're very conscientious."

They foraged for another meal. "I wonder where that Hag of yours is?" Jordan said.

"She must be trapped here too," Grundy conjectured. "Unless she knows some way out."

"I don't think she would have come here, if she didn't know a way out," Rapunzel said. "I'm sure she knew the nature of the Ever-Glades."

The allegory nosed up to the island. "I certainly did," it said in reptile-talk.

Grundy jumped. "You!" he exclaimed.

"You mean that's the Sea Hag, now?" Threnody asked.

"Yes," Grundy agreed heavily. "It seems she took over that body, after the hawk died."

"I'll kill it!" Jordan said grimly.

"No, that will only free her for another form," Grundy warned. "Better to keep her in the form we know."

"But it's a dangerous form," Threnody said nervously.

"*Any* form is dangerous, when it's the Sea Hag," Grundy said.

"Yeah, I guess so," he agreed, looking at Threnody. She continued to heal, but the marks remained on her body. It was evident that Jordan was more upset by the injuries she had received from the Hag than the far worse ones he had received. Considering his own talent, this was understandable.

The allegory was listening to them, evidently understanding human speech though it could only talk in reptilian. "And I know the way out of here," it hissed. "If you want to escape the Glades, I can tell you how."

"Fat chance!" Grundy hissed back.

"You know what I want, Golem," it said.

"What's she saying?" Rapunzel asked, worried.

"You know what she's saying," Grundy said.

"Oh." Again her hand went to her mouth, in that maidenly alarm he found so attractive.

"Don't worry," he reassured her. "That's one deal we'll never make."

"But if she can get you free—"

"No!"

"Yes," the reptile hissed. "Not today, not this week perhaps. But after a month, a year of idleness, of boredom, however long it takes, you will be ready to deal. Send her back to the Ivory Tower, and I will show you the way out of the Glades."

"Jordan," Grundy said sharply. "I've changed my mind. I think this creature should be killed."

Jordan smiled. He drew his sword. But the allegory moved with surprising swiftness, splashing back into the water and zipping away, out of reach.

"At least we know there *is* a way," Grundy said.

"There is a way," Rapunzel agreed, gazing at him.

In the later afternoon Threnody approached Grundy. "I'm getting better," she said. "I could change to a form that could go after that allegory, and—"

"To what point?" he asked. "We really shouldn't kill it, and it certainly won't tell us what we want to know. Not without a deal I won't make."

"I was thinking more deviously," she said. "I'm not the nicest of women, down inside. I've done some pretty bad things in my time, in a cause I believed was right. I know I can do what I have to do."

Now he was curious. "What's that?"

"I can catch her and make her hurt until she tells us how to get out of here."

"Torture her?" he asked, shocked.

"I told you I wasn't all that nice. If I turned into a water dragon and went after her, I could chew on her bit by bit, one leg at a time, and she would—"

Grundy felt sick. "I don't think I like that way. Anyway, I think she would rather die than tell us, because she *can't* die."

She nodded. "You're probably right. But I just thought I'd mention it. We're not entirely helpless."

"Are all females like you, underneath?" he asked, grimly intrigued.

"Of course not. Most are relatively innocent, and some are truly nice creatures, like Rapunzel."

"She is, isn't she?" he agreed with relief.

"But even that kind can go after what she wants. I remember when I decided that Jordan was the man for me . . ." She sighed and shook her head.

"But Rapunzel hasn't met any men yet, except for Jordan."

"I think she has," Threnody murmured, smiling in that obscure way women had.

"Oh? Where?"

She laughed. "Never mind. I'm sure everything will work out, in its fashion." She moved away.

Grundy shook his head, perplexed. Then Rapunzel rejoined him, and he forgot whatever he had been trying to be bothered about.

Next day Grundy climbed a tall tree and looked about. All around were the little islands of palm trees, all of which he knew had golems looking about, because all were the same. What a hopeless situation!

Then he spied something else. He squinted at it, trying to make quite sure it wasn't an illusion. But soon he was sure! "Centaur ho!" he cried, scrambling down the tree.

In a moment everyone was looking. It was definitely a centaur forging toward them through the marsh. In due course Grundy was able to recognize him: "Arnolde!"

Indeed it was Arnolde, the only nonhuman creature ever to have been the human King of Xanth. He sloshed to the copse and raised a hand in greeting. "I'm glad to find you well," he said. He was old, and his coat was turning gray, but he remained reasonably spry. He wore Mundane spectacles to shore up his declining eyesight.

"But we're trapped!" Grundy exclaimed. "And now you are, too!"

"Not so," Arnolde said cheerily.

"You don't understand. These are the Ever-Glades. There is no way out."

"And I am a Magician," the centaur reminded him. "My magic can handle this."

"But your magic only works outside of Xanth! It's an aisle of magic. Here it makes no difference."

"Allow me to explain. I have been experimenting with reverse-wood."

"We had some of that, but—"

"It reverses the thrust of any magic in its vicinity. Thus, when I carry it, it causes me to generate a Mundane aisle in Xanth. Now you might not feel this is a useful function; however—"

Suddenly Grundy caught on. "It's magic that holds us here in the Glades!" he cried. "If that is nullified—"

"We can get out of here!" Jordan finished.

"That was my supposition," Arnolde agreed. "So if you are ready to travel with me—"

"But how did you happen to come here?" Grundy asked, still hardly believing this good fortune.

"My friend Bink suggested that the Ever-Glades might be the ideal place to test out the Mundane Effect," Arnolde said. "And I constrained to agree with him. If I did not get lost there, I should not get lost anywhere."

"Bink!" Grundy exclaimed. "I should have known! He's been sending people after me!"

"I'm sure he meant no harm," the centaur said. "His talent is very special."

"What *is* his talent? I can't remember."

Arnolde looked thoughtful. "Oh. Well, in that case perhaps I shouldn't have mentioned it."

"But you *did* mention it! That guy seems to be crazy careless and crazy lucky. Does his magic have something to do with it?"

"I would say that is a fair assessment," the centaur agreed. And that was all he would say on that subject; instead he deftly turned the dialogue to the group's own situation.

They explained about Grundy's Quest, and the manner he had rescued Rapunzel from the Ivory Tower, and how the Sea Hag was following them and trying to get Rapunzel to return to her power. "She was giving them some trouble, when we arrived," Jordan said. "Just in the nick of time."

"When Bink is involved, such coincidences do occur," the centaur said knowingly.

"But now we're stuck in the Ever-Glades," Grundy concluded. "Or were, until you showed up. Are you sure your Mundane aisle can get us out?"

"We shall certainly find out," Arnolde said. "Where are you going from here?"

"To Lake Ogre-Chobee, where the Fauns and Nymphs are. They're holding Stanley Steamer."

"Very well, we shall go there." The centaur stretched. "Tomorrow morning, if that is all right with you. I am not as youthful as I once was, and the day is becoming advanced."

Of course they agreed. Arnolde joined them in a meal of cocoa and nuts, and found a comfortable spot to stand and sleep.

But in the night there was a commotion. The allegory was on the island, scrambling away from Arnolde. "Oh my gracious!" the centaur exclaimed. "That animal has absconded with the reverse-wood!"

Grundy knew instantly that that was potential disaster. Without that wood, Arnolde would be trapped with the rest of them. He leaped onto Snortimer. "We've got to recover it!" he cried.

The Bed Monster was able to function well in the darkness. He scrambled after the allegory, catching it at the edge of the copse. Now, by the dim light of what remained of the moon, Grundy saw that the creature was hauling the wood along on a string, much as the sphinx had with the prior wood. But as Snortimer pounced on the wood, the allegory jumped forward and snatched at it. The two arrived at the same time, and one of Snortimer's hands banged into the allegory's long green nose.

"Get the wood! Get the wood!" Grundy cried.

Snortimer tried, but as he reached for it, the allegory snapped at his hand and he had to whip it back out of the way. The reptile reached for it with its snout, but Snortimer made two big hairy fists and punched a one-two combination on that snout.

Now Jordan arrived. "Back off!" he called. "I'll take care of that critter!"

That seemed best. But as Snortimer retreated and Jordan advanced, the allegory lunged at the chip of wood and caught it in its mouth. Before they could act, the creature swallowed the wood and started to scramble for the water, where Grundy knew it would be almost impossible to catch it.

But then the reptile stiffened. In a moment it collapsed and lay still. Jordan, ready to swing at it with his sword, hesitated.

Grundy realized what had happened. "It's dead," he said. "It was magically animated by the Hag, and when it swallowed the wood, it reversed. Now it's magically *un*animated—and so it is dead."

"Well, that solves that problem then," Jordan said. He chopped down with the sword, cutting the body in half. Then he fished out the chip of wood and rinsed it in the nearest water.

For a moment Grundy wondered why the wood didn't hurt the barbarian, but then realized that Jordan had long-since healed and was not using his magic talent now. In effect, he was an ordinary man, and so the wood had no effect on him.

They had recovered the wood, and that was good. But now the Hag was a ghost again, and that was bad. Had they been able to leave her as the allegory, she might not have been able to pursue them, for it would have been very difficult for her to kill herself in that form.

"I will hold it right in my hand, hereafter!" Arnolde said as they returned the chip to him. "I had set it beside me, because the magic frame really is more comfortable than the Mundane, but I see in retrospect that that was a miscalculation." And he clamped his hand firmly around it.

They returned to sleep, though in Grundy's case it was not the easiest thing to do. But Rapunzel whispered to him how brave he had been and held his hand, and that was very pleasant. He almost regretted that they were about to escape this trap.

In the morning they ate again and started off. Threnody had changed to golem-size, to Grundy's surprise; suddenly there were two women in his range. The three of them got on the bed, which Jordan had tied to Arnolde's back, and rode along in style. Snortimer was squeezed under it, since this was day, and Jordan walked along beside.

"Do your changes in shape and size bother Jordan?" Rapunzel asked Threnody as they moved out.

"No," the woman said with a laugh. "I'm always the right size for him, when he wants me to be. We all have different talents, and each of us can do things the other can't."

"But you can become much larger than he can," Rapunzel persisted. "Doesn't he get afraid, when you're huge?"

"Never. It's not the size that counts, it's the relationship. I love him. He could slay me with one sweep of his sword, and I could not recover, but I know he wouldn't, because he loves me."

"The relationship," Rapunzel agreed. "That makes everything all right."

Grundy listened without commenting. It might be true that the relationship was more important than the size—but she had relationships yet to form with her human and/or elven kinfolk. He knew, if she did not, that no golem was a part of either society. How he wished it could be otherwise!

Here in the Mundane aisle, in the light of day, the scene was strange indeed. The nearest palm tree no longer had hands and fingers; instead it had funny large green leaves, each deeply serrated to resemble hundreds of thick blades of grass. It was singularly uninteresting. When they passed by a cocoa-nut tree, the big nut was not chocolaty at all, but a big, crude capsule of fiber that it would have been impossible to eat. When they stepped into the sea of grass, however, it was—a sea of grass.

With a difference. This was not a true swamp, but what seemed to be an imitation swamp set up on a barren surface. It was as if someone had dumped some globs of mud and splashed some water and set out some tufts of grass, so that, from a distance, it would look like a real swamp, and left it there. But a short distance away, beyond the aisle, the swamp returned in its full force, the grass being thick and green. It was easy to see where the aisle left off, because of the poverty of the scenery that commenced at its edge.

They proceeded to the next copse of trees—and the terrain changed. The grass fell behind, and ordinary Xanth vegetation returned.

Arnolde came to a halt. "The Mundane aisle is not kind to normal things," he said. "I think you will travel more pleasantly if I leave you now. I believe the camp of the Fauns is immediately ahead."

Grundy knew he was right. Fauns and Nymphs were fundamentally magical creatures, and reverse-wood would not make them comfortable at all. Arnolde had done his job, and they were duly grateful. All of them told him so emphatically, which embarrassed him. Perhaps the fact that Rapunzel and Threnody climbed up and kissed his right and left ears, respectively, had something to do with it. He was after all a rather self-effacing scholar, not given to heroism.

Arnolde departed, his ears still blushing, to pursue his further experiments with Mundane-aisle Effects, and the rest of them went on to the Faun camp.

"I'll carry the bed again," Jordan said. "Just tie it on my back, same as before."

"But it's day," Grundy protested. "Snortimer needs it."

"Why? He's standing in daylight now okay."

Astonished, they all looked at the Bed Monster. There he was, in full light, suffering no harm.

"How—?" Grundy asked.

"Arnolde gave me a sliver of the reverse-wood," Snortimer explained in Bed-Monster tongue. "He thought that if it reversed all magic, including his, it should reverse mine. So I tried it."

"That's one smart centaur!" Jordan said.

"We could have done that before," Grundy exclaimed. "When we had the other reverse-wood! We never thought of it."

"Because we're not smart centaurs," Threnody said.

So they tied the bed to Jordan's back. Now three of them rode on Snortimer, but their combined weight was so slight it didn't matter. Grundy realized that this gave Threnody the chance to continue resting and healing while traveling. "You know, this is a nice enough size," she remarked. "I should use it more often."

"It certainly seems adequate to me," Rapunzel agreed.

Grundy said nothing. He had no choice; this was the only size he had ever known.

The approach to the Faun & Nymph Retreat was a single, fairly narrow path that wound about through a gully that soon became a chasm. Sheer cliffs rose up on either side, peaking in a jagged mountain range that hadn't been visible from a distance. It was evident that this path was the only way anyone could enter the premises. It was pleasant enough, however, and there were no signs of danger.

It opened on a truly delightful scene. There was a fine blue lake beside a lovely little mountain, with a thick green forest filling in around them both. The whole was enclosed by the jagged ring of mountains.

In a moment the residents showed up. They appeared to be as harmless as the scenery: they were dancing Fauns and Nymphs. The Fauns were roughly human in form, but with hoofed feet, shaggy legs, and little horns on their heads. The Nymphs were naked, youthful women, each prettier than the others. They swung their tresses engagingly about as they danced. "Oh," Rapunzel said, putting a hand to her shorn hair.

"You are beautiful with or without your hair," Grundy told her seriously.

"Oh!" she repeated, brightening.

The Fauns and Nymphs swarmed up. From close range, they appeared to be of several different types, but all were smiling and friendly. "It's so interesting to see them in person," Rapunzel said. "Dryads and Dryfauns, Oreads and Orefauns, Naiads and Naifauns—"

"What, what, and what?" Grundy asked.

"The different species of Nymphs and Fauns," she explained. "The Drys live in the trees, the Ores in the mountains, and the Nais in the lake. Each adapts to its environment—"

But now the residents were crowding around. "What strange creatures!" they exclaimed. "The one wears a bed and the others are little folk on a monster!" For the Fauns and Nymphs were far larger than golems, though not large by human standards.

"We're looking for a little dragon," Grundy said. "We understand he's here. His name is Stanley Steamer."

"Stanley!" they exclaimed. "Yes! Yes!"

Now Stanley himself appeared—and Grundy was amazed. The dragon was no longer little and cute; he had in the intervening years become a formidable middle-sized monster. He looked perfectly healthy and happy.

"Stanley!" Grundy called in dragon-talk. "My how you've grown!"

The dragon whomped up to join them, exhaling cheerful clouds of steam. "But *you* haven't!" he replied, recognizing Grundy. "And who are those two golem girls?"

"This is Threnody," Grundy said, indicating her. "You've met her before, she's usually larger. And this is Rapunzel, Ivy's pun-pal. I rescued her from the Ivory Tower, on the way to rescuing you."

"Me? I don't need rescuing!" Stanley protested.

"What is he saying?" Jordan asked.

"He says he doesn't need rescuing," Grundy said. He returned to dragon-talk. "Then why didn't you return to Ivy?"

Now Stanley looked sad. "I would like to. But I can't."

"Are the Fauns and Nymphs holding you?"

"Not exactly."

"Then you are free to go, aren't you?"

"No."

Grundy turned to the others. "He says they aren't holding him captive, but he's not free to go."

"That doesn't make sense," Jordan said.

But now the Fauns and Nymphs were swarming over Stanley, hugging him and kissing him and teasing him, and his attention was distracted; there was no point in trying to question him further at the moment.

Threnody's eyes narrowed. "I think I begin to get a glimmer why he isn't eager to leave," she said.

Grundy nodded. "Who would!"

"Oh, you like that sort of treatment?" Rapunzel inquired.

"Well—"

"I thought maybe you didn't."

"We have to figure out how to get Stanley to go home," he said gruffly.

But the more they saw of the Faun & Nymph Retreat, the less likely their mission seemed to be to succeed. These creatures seemed to spend all day in innocent pleasures, swimming, playing, eating, laughing and chatting merrily. There was never a cross word, never a scowl; everything was optimistic. They did not exclude the visitors; Grundy and his party were welcomed into water, mountain and trees.

Threnody noted Jordan watching half a dozen green-haired Dryads playing tag in the spreading branches of a great old acorn tree. The Nymphs screamed shrilly with joy as they chased one another about, and their arms and legs flashed prettily, and their bare bosoms heaved, and their tresses flung about with abandon. "I think I'd better get back to human-size," she muttered darkly.

Meanwhile a party of Orefauns was scaling the central mountain, linked together by ropes. There really wasn't anywhere to go, and there wasn't much challenge, as it was a very small mountain, but they seemed happy in their activity. It was as if they had never done this before. Their hooves were good for this kind of work.

The Naiads and Naifauns were playing water polo, flinging a ball about, splashing and ducking each other and having, if possible, an even better time than the others.

Then there was a stir back at the entrance to the Retreat. A party of goblins had showed up, armed with spears and clubs. "Round up the juiciest ones," the goblin chief cried. "We'll feast tonight."

The nearest Nymphs screamed as they were grabbed. Stanley's ears perked up. He had settled down under a tree for a snooze, but now he was alert. He huffed up a head of steam and whomped toward the goblins.

"Dragon!" the chief cried in terror.

The goblins dropped the struggling Nymphs and fled back down the path. Stanley whomped after them, toasting their rears with fierce steam. In a moment the goblins were gone.

The Nymphs returned to their play, seemingly unconcerned about their near escape.

Grundy shook his head. "Now I think I understand why he can't leave," he said. "These Fauns and Nymphs are helpless before any predator. They don't know how to fight. They can't organize. They forget any bad thing as soon as it is past. If Stanley weren't here, they would soon be decimated by the goblins and anything else that came by."

"And if we take him away," Rapunzel said, "it would be at great cost to them."

"But I promised to bring him back to Castle Roogna," Grundy said. "It's my Quest, and I have to fulfill it if I possibly can."

"Even at such a cost?" she asked.

"I don't know." Indeed, he discovered himself at the crossroads of the most difficult choice he had yet faced. He couldn't give up his Quest —yet it would be wrong to deprive this community of its only protection from the hazards of the region.

Evening was coming, and the Fauns brought down fruits from the trees and fresh berries from the mountain and sea biscuits from the water and formed a feast. The visitors were invited, of course, and the food was very good. But Grundy remained pensive, not seeing any proper course.

As the shadows lengthened, Snortimer scrambled away. "That shadow!" he cried in monster-tongue. "It's reaching for me!"

"But you're a creature of shadow," Grundy reminded him. "You live in darkness."

"I'm afraid of the dark!"

"Afraid of the dark!" Grundy was astonished. "What's the matter with you?"

"I don't know," the Bed Monster confessed. "But now I love the sunshine and can't stand the dark."

"But it's dark under your bed."

"The bed!" Snortimer exclaimed with horror. "Don't let it get me!"

"What's the matter?" Rapunzel asked.

"Snortimer's afraid of the dark, and doesn't want to go back under his bed," Grundy said, baffled.

She laughed. "Silly! It's the reverse-wood."

Of course! "Get rid of that sliver of reverse-wood," Grundy told the Bed Monster.

Snortimer tossed aside the sliver—and suddenly dived under the bed. He had reverted to normal, and could no longer stand the light. One mystery solved.

"Just let me make sure he's all right," Rapunzel said. She went to the bed, climbed up on it, then changed to human-size. She dangled her pretty ankles down toward the ground.

Snortimer grabbed. Rapunzel screamed and yanked her legs away. "He's all right," she pronounced.

But the Nymphs had noted this action. "Ooo, let me try!" an Oread exclaimed. She ran to the bed, plumped down on it, and dangled her legs.

Naturally Snortimer grabbed. "Eeeeek! " the Nymph screamed happily, yanking her legs away.

Suddenly they were all doing it. The evening resounded with their joyous shrieks, squeals and giggles. One Naiad, being less agile on land, lost her balance when grabbed and tumbled under the bed. "Eeek!" she screamed. "He's all hands!" There followed a sound suspiciously like kissing, and she rolled out and into the water, a broad smile on her face.

The Bed Monster, it seemed, was a success. But Grundy looked across to where Stanley lay, supposedly snoozing, and saw that the dragon looked a trifle greener than usual. For three years he had been the center of attention; now there was competition.

Grundy ambled over to the dragon. "Not that this is relevant," he said in dragon-talk, "but there's a little girl at Castle Roogna who only has eyes for one dragon."

Stanley sighed steamily. "Actually, I'd like to see Castle Roogna again. But what would happen to these nice Fauns and Nymphs?"

To that Grundy had no answer. He returned to the bed, where the Nymphs were finally tiring of their sport.

"It's getting too dark," one explained. "We have to go to sleep."

And, shortly, all of the Nymphs and Fauns were sleeping in their various habitats, the boundless energy of their day becoming the easy repose of their night. Stanley positioned himself across the entrance path so that he could intercept any intruders, and slept himself.

Jordan and Threnody settled down under an acorn tree. She was changing back to human-size; at the moment she was in the diffuse, ghostlike stage, having increased her size but not yet her mass; in another hour she would be solid again.

That left the bed for Grundy and Rapunzel. She had shifted back to golem-size. Her changes were instant, unlike Threnody's, but she had no other forms. There generally did seem to be a tradeoff, in magic; few people had it all, and those were Magicians or Sorceresses. Little Dolph could change instantly to any form, and therefore he was a Magician, destined to be King of Xanth if Ivy didn't want it.

"Hey, Grundy," Snortimer called from under the bed.

"Here," Grundy said.

"You know, we've found your dragon, but we haven't found romance for me. That was part of the deal, you know."

Grundy looked at Rapunzel, stricken. What could he say?

"Is he asking what I think he's asking?" Rapunzel asked.

"Yes. And I don't know what to tell him."

"Why, tell him the truth," she said. "He deserves to know, you know."

"But—"

Rapunzel said it for him. "Snortimer, it grieves me to tell you this, but there are no females of your species."

"I suspected that," the Bed Monster muttered, and Grundy translated. Snortimer could understand human-talk, as many monsters could, though he couldn't speak it.

"But I'm sure your life can be worthwhile," Rapunzel said. "Those Nymphs seemed to like you very well."

"But I can't stay here," Snortimer replied glumly. "It's Stanley's territory."

And so there was a dragon who would return to Castle Roogna, but could not, and a Bed Monster who would remain here, but could not. Xanth was full of ironies.

"Somehow, there's an answer for everything," Rapunzel said consolingly. "I just know it."

She was somewhat nymphlike in her positive attitude. Grundy wished he could share it, but he could not. Being on a Quest was not as simple as he had imagined.

Then Rapunzel took his hand again, and almost he was able to believe that things were better than they were.

14

A Bonnet of Bees

In the morning the Fauns and Nymphs roused, and flocked to see the visitors, just as if they didn't remember them. Stanley whomped over. "Every day is new for them," he explained in dragon-talk. "They don't remember overnight. That's why the goblins and ogres and things can raid; the Fauns and Nymphs never learn and take no precautions."

"They *really* need protection," Grundy agreed, perceiving the larger picture. Of course it wouldn't be right to deprive the community of its only protection. But how could he return to Castle Roogna with his Quest unfulfilled?

The Nymphs rediscovered the Bed Monster, and shrieked with delight as Snortimer grabbed at their attractive ankles. Stanley turned a darker shade of green, but made no comment. The Fauns fetched in the morning feast of fruits and biscuits. Everyone was happy—except the visitors, who were cursed with memories longer than a day.

"If there is no solution," Rapunzel murmured, "maybe this would be a good place to stay."

"No!" Grundy said. "I have a Quest to fulfill, and you need to be restored to your own kind, whichever that is. There has to be a way."

"Of course," she said, somewhat sadly.

But in midmorning things abruptly changed.

There was an ominous humming from the entrance-trail. Soon it manifested as a swarm of B's, and by the sound of it, they meant no good.

They were huge B's, similar to bees but larger and more magical. Each was a quarter the size of Grundy, and they had horrendous stingers. They spread out and dive-bombed the hapless Fauns and Nymphs. The attacked creatures screamed—then acted very strangely. One insisted on running out in front of all the others and staying there no matter what; another went to the rear of the group and would not be budged. A third started peering about, looking and looking as if he could not see enough. Another cried, "I have seen the light!" over and over. Another got down on the ground and tried to tunnel into it. All of them were doing such peculiar things that the others could not figure it out—until getting stung themselves and taking off on their own peculiarities.

Jordan glared about, sword in hand, but this wasn't much good against the B's. "What does it mean?" Threnody asked.

"I think those are B's from a Have," Rapunzel said. "I have learned about them, but never seen them until this moment."

"A B-hive?" Grundy asked. "But all B's live in hives!"

"A B-Have," she said. "That's a very special kind. When they sting, the victim be-haves in the manner dictated by the sting. It looks to me as if there are several types of B's here—a B-fore, a B-hind, a B-lieve, a B-neath, a B-hold—"

"Oh!" Grundy exclaimed. "The one who's trying to go before everyone, and the one going behind, and the one who sees the light, and the one trying to get down beneath—"

"And the one looking all about," Threnody put in. "That's the one stung by the B-hold!"

"And I see a B-seech, a B-side, a B-stir, a B-reave—" Jordan added.

"And a B-siege, a B-set, a B-tween—" Grundy added.

"And a number of B-wilders and B-wails," Rapunzel concluded. "But why are they attacking the innocent folk?"

But now one of the insects was making a B-line for Grundy. "Have you had enough, golem?" it buzzed in B-talk.

"The Sea Hag!" he cried, catching on.

"Oh, no!" Rapunzel exclaimed in maidenly dismay. "She's still after me!"

"You can't have her, Hag!" Grundy cried.

"I am not the Queen B," the B buzzed. "I am merely her messenger. She says the Fauns and Nymphs will suffer excruciatingly until the girl is returned to her."

"What's she saying?" Rapunzel asked, distraught.

"This is only a messenger with an ultimatum," Grundy said. "The Hag wants the usual. It seems she has taken over the Queen B, so these B's obey her."

"And they're going to harass the innocent creatures until she gets her way," Threnody said. "I know how she thinks. We've got to nullify her."

"This is my job," Grundy said. "I'll go to the B-Have and settle with her once and for all."

"We'll all go," Jordan said, touching his sword.

"You men are so headstrong and foolish," Threnody said. "If everyone goes, the B's will simply swarm in and sting us, and we'll spend all our time in weird activity and never get there. No, this has to be a covert operation, accomplished while most of the swarm is away from the Have. Probably Grundy could do it alone, if he could sneak away—"

"No! It's too dangerous!" Rapunzel cried.

"It's too dangerous *not* to try it!" Grundy said grimly. "Snortimer, can you get me out of here without being spotted by the B's?"

Snortimer didn't answer. It was day, and he was huddled under the bed.

Grundy went and got the loose sliver of reverse-wood. He tossed it under the bed. The Bed Monster caught it automatically—and came sailing out, suddenly afraid of the shadows. "I can do it!" he cried.

"Good enough!" Grundy mounted. "Keep them distracted," he called to the others.

"But you'll have to do it by nightfall," Threnody called back. "Because then they'll return to their Have anyway—"

"By nightfall," he agreed. Then he hung on, as Snortimer scurried for the ring of mountains.

They climbed the rough-hewn slope, Snortimer's hands readily grasping the crevices. Because they were off the path, the B's did not spot them. They circled around until they could intersect the path out of sight of the swarm, then proceeded rapidly along it.

As they left the Retreat, Grundy began calling to the surrounding vegetation. "Where is the B-Have?"

"South," the vegetation agreed.

They bore south through increasingly rough terrain, dodged around a tangle tree, and came into sight of it: a huge hive in the shape of a lady's bonnet, hanging from a big branch. They stopped short, for a number of guardian B's buzzed around it. "I'll have trouble getting at the B in that bonnet," Grundy muttered.

"I could climb up the tree and rip it down," Snortimer suggested.

"And get hopelessly stung," Grundy retorted. "That's no good. I need to sneak in, seal it off, and then go after the Queen. I can fit inside; you can't."

"It's dangerous," Snortimer reminded him.

"Set me on the branch," Grundy said. "Then when I sneak in, you leap up and jam something in the entrance. Then get out of there before the B's catch you."

"You fools," another voice said. "That'll never work."

Grundy looked around. There was a tremendous spider, with a circular web that spanned from tree to ground.

"You know these B's?" Grundy asked in spider-talk.

"I feed on them," the spider said. "But they're getting pretty canny, and now they avoid my web no matter how carefully I conceal it."

"Then how do you figure you know so well how to handle them?" Grundy demanded.

"I didn't say I knew how to handle them," the spider said. "I just know what won't work."

"That's not much help," Grundy said sourly.

"Why should I help you, anyway?"

"Because I could make it worth your while."

"How?"

"I could call some B's here, so you would have a season's feast."

The spider's mandibles watered. "Ah, maybe I could help you . . ."

"How?"

"I could give you some silk to let yourself down to the entrance to the B-Have."

Grundy considered. "Not worth it. I'd just get stung when I got there."

"I could give you a web-net to put across the entrance, so that you could prevent any B's from passing in and out; they can't handle that stuff. It tangles up their wings."

Grundy wavered. "So that once I got in, I could seal it off behind me. That does sound good. But I'd still have to deal with the ones remaining inside."

"I can give you another web-net, that you could sling over a B, incapacitating it long enough for you to stab it with your sword."

"Done!" Grundy cried.

And it was done. The spider made him a line, an entrance-cover web, and a throw-net. In return, he positioned himself behind the big web and sounded off in B-talk:

"Help! I'm a succulent flower just bursting with pollen, and I haven't seen a B in just *ages!*"

Immediately several B's buzzed at him—and were caught in the web. In a moment the spider had caught them and trussed them up.

Grundy realized that this could be a good thing for him, too. The more B's the spider caught, the fewer would remain to attack him.

But not all the B's around the bonnet had charged in. The ones remaining seemed to be the warriors, who didn't fetch nectar from flowers. How could he lure them in?

Grundy smiled. His usual weapon was his best. "Hey, you horses' B-hinds!" he yelled. "You couldn't hurt an intruder if your hides depended on it!"

That aroused several. They buzzed angrily at him—and were trapped by the spider.

He tried again. "I think your stingers are dull! You're nothing but useless drones!"

That roused several more. But two or three remained, too dull or too canny to respond.

Grundy had a flashbulb of an idea. "Help: I'm in trouble!" he screamed in the voice of a Queen B.

That got them. Without pausing to reason why, they zoomed to him —and were caught.

"That seems to be all that are presently available; are you satisfied?" he asked the spider.

"Definitely," the spider agreed, selecting a succulent B to suck dry. Grundy turned away; he really didn't enjoy watching the way a spider fed.

Now Snortimer carried him up the tree and to the branch above the nest. "If I don't come out before the swarm returns, get out of here," Grundy told the Bed Monster. "Go back to the others and tell them they'll have to get along without me."

"You're brave," Snortimer said.

Grundy laughed. "Brave? I'm terrified!" Then he let himself down on the silken line, and swung to the entrance to the bonnet. After a couple of tries he was able to catch on to the rim and scramble in. It was a tight squeeze, for he was larger than the average B, but that made it easier for him to wedge himself in without falling.

Inside, he took out the first net and carefully applied it to the rim of the hole. The webbing was light but very strong, and sticky at the edge; the spider had told him how to use it, and though he was clumsy, not having as many legs as a spider did, the web fastened very firmly. No B would readily pass in or out of this!

Now came the bad part. He knew there were other B's inside; he could hear them humming as they worked. He held his pin-sword in one hand, and his web-net in the other, and worked his way upward.

The bonnet, inside, was constructed of many thick layers of cardboard, arranged in rings. Several passages opened out to the sides, slanting upward. He had thought the bonnet would be dark inside, but it was not; the B's had set small glowing fungi at the intersections. That made it easier for him to travel, but also made him more visible. Well, they could probably tell he was here by the smell, anyway, once they were alerted. So far the B's seemed to be minding their own B's wax, fortunately.

This was a huge, three-dimensional labyrinth, seeming much larger from the inside than it had from outside. Perhaps the B's B-witched the bonnet to make its inner dimensions magically greater. But there was no intentional confusion; the passages were straightforward, and it was easy enough to proceed directly toward the center.

Up to a point. When he reached what he presumed to be the central chamber, where the Queen B should be, the passage was blocked by the sturdy gray cardboard building material. This was evidently a restricted area.

He tried to poke a hole in it, to push through, but it was surprisingly tough stuff; his pin could poke into it, but only with such difficulty that it wasn't worth the effort. He needed a fast way in.

So he took a side passage. This was easier at first, because it was level, but he had to walk hunched over. The diameter of it was too small for his comfort, and he didn't know where it was leading. He kept his pin and net ready.

In due course the passage debouched into an impressive chamber. There were hundreds of cells, hexagonal in cross section, each filled with amber substance and sealed with translucent wax. This was evidently the honeycomb—the food storage depot of the Have. Grundy liked honey, but he wasn't hungry for this right now. He just wanted to get his job done and get out of here before the swarm returned. He didn't know how much time he had; the controlled lighting made this place seem timeless.

A worker-B was at one of the hex chambers. It spied Grundy. "Hey —you're not supposed to B here!" it buzzed in B-talk, alarmed.

"I'm the honey inspector," Grundy said, hoping to keep things quiet.

"I'm going to fetch the supe b-fore I get in trouble!" the B buzzed, scrambling toward an exit.

Grundy ran after it, stabbing with his pin. He hated to do it, but he couldn't afford to have the supe on his case! But the B scrambled out just ahead of him, getting away.

In moments several B's buzzed in. One was evidently the supe-B. "That's no inspector, that's an intruder," it buzzed. "Sting it!"

Three B's charged him. Grundy backed up against the wall of hexchambers, pin and net ready. But more B's were entering the chamber, and he knew he would soon be overwhelmed.

Then he had another lightbulb notion. He reversed his pin and stabbed into one of the wax seals behind him. The point penetrated and stuck; he wrenched it out sideways, and the whole wax cap pulled off with a slurpy sucking sound. The thick honey oozed out.

"Save that honey!" the supe buzzed, horrified.

The nearest worker batted its faceted eyes. "I didn't know you cared, Supe."

"*That* honey, stingerface!" The supe buzzed angrily, pointing two legs at it. The worker, chastened, got to work.

Grundy moved over and wedged out another cap and then a third. When a worker charged him, he put away his pin for a moment and used his hand to scoop out a glob of honey. He hurled it at the B. It didn't hurl very well, but a good part of it got on the B's wing, and got the creature in serious trouble. It forgot him in its effort to get the gooey stuff off and back into the leaking chamber.

Soon Grundy was able to leave the honey-pot chamber unmolested.

But he still hadn't found a way into the central cavity. Instead he came to a quiet, dim chamber lined with cells that did not hold honey. He peered closely at one—and discovered that there was a monstrous grub in it. A developing B! This was the nursery.

A nurse-B was approaching. Grundy didn't have the heart to wreak mayhem here, so he hastily exited by the nearest side passage. This took him on around the Have and upward. In due course he came to a new, smaller chamber that had cardboard tapestries on the walls.

A young and astonishingly pretty female B angled her antennae at him as he entered. "Well now, a visitor," she buzzed dulcetly.

"Uh, yes," Grundy said, uncertain what was going on here. "I'm, uh, looking for the Queen."

"Oh, really," she buzzed. "I didn't think you were the type. You look more like a golem than a drone."

"I *am* a golem," he confessed, surprised by the way she accepted him. She was much larger than the worker-B's, and could have caused him some alarm if she had attacked, but she seemed quite friendly. "And you—"

"I am Princess B-Nign," she buzzed. "Soon I will take my maiden flight and mate with the worthiest drone, and then start my own bonnet."

"B-nine?" he asked, mishearing her buzz. "There are eight others?"

"Of course not," she buzzed cheerfully. "I was one of the first two out of incubation, so I fought and killed the other, B-Twelve, despite all the vitamins she had taken, and then cut off the heads of all the remaining prospects, B-One through B-Twenty. There are no other Princess B's but me, now. Isn't it romantic?"

"But you seem like such a nice creature!" Grundy blurted.

"I *am* a nice creature," she buzzed. "I simply did what had to be done. A Have cannot support two Queens."

"Well, the Queen for *this* Have has been taken over by an evil mind," he told her. "I have come here to capture her and take her away."

"That so?" she buzzed, interested. "I *thought* she was acting peculiar recently. Sending almost the whole swarm out to bother the Fauns— we've always been at peace with the Fauns before. But when the Queen commands, all obey."

A new notion surfaced. "Suppose I took the Queen away—what would happen to this Have?"

"Why, I would have to take it over, of course. That wouldn't bother me; it's always better to start with a well-established situation if one can. I'm not truly looking forward to starting my own; I understand there are all manner of dangers out there, such as birds and insectivores and pitcher plants."

"There are," Grundy agreed.

She wiggled her fair antennae at him. "Do you suppose—"

"If you'll just tell me how to get into the Queen's chamber, I'll do my best to take her out. I won't kill her."

"You won't?" she buzzed, disappointed.

"If I did that, her spirit would simply take over another creature, probably you."

"Mercy is best," she agreed. "But you won't let her go?"

"Never," he agreed.

"Take the third passage to your right," she said, indicating a tunnel.

Grundy headed along the tunnel. He passed straight through the first intersection, and the second, and turned right at the third. This led directly into the huge central chamber.

He entered, and dropped to the curving floor, his pin and net ready. There was the Queen B. She was enormous, massing as much as Grundy, and she had big sturdy claws and a phenomenal stinger. "So you have come, Golem," she buzzed.

"I had to come," he agreed, trying to choke back the fear that welled up in him. How could he overcome this ferocious creature?

"And now I shall finally be rid of you," she buzzed. She stood, stretched her wings, and moved slowly toward him. "Do you know what I shall do to you?"

"I don't think I care to," Grundy said, watching her warily, trying to figure out her most likely mode of attack.

"I will sting you just hard enough to render you helpless but alive and conscious," she said, seeming to relish her own words. "Then I will use your flesh to feed my new crop of warriors. It will give them a healthy taste for blood."

Grundy quailed. That was just as bad as having one's mind taken over by the Hag! "But first you have to score on me," he said with whatever poor façade of bravery it was possible to manage.

"And after that, I'll have all your stupid friends stung into submission too," the Queen Hag continued, stalking him. "Until at last Rapunzel is ready to do anything to spare them further humiliation and agony. Anything at all!"

"You are the haggiest Hag I've ever met," he told her, trying to judge whether he could catch her in the web-net with a single heave. She was so big!

"And after I have her young and tender body, naturally I'll put it through its paces," she continued. "That barbarian's a fairly handsome lout; maybe before I have him dispatched, I'll—"

The thought of Rapunzel's body being used in that way so upset Grundy that he lunged at the B. This was what she had wanted; she buzzed straight up out of his way, so that he stumbled and lost his balance, expecting a resistance that he did not encounter.

Before he recovered, she dive-bombed him from behind. He heard her coming and threw himself flat, so that she zoomed over him. It was a close call; the blast from her wings struck all about him. He rolled over, sat up—and saw her coming at him again.

He hurled up the web-net, but it missed, blown away by that same wing-blast. He had to roll desperately aside to avoid her aerial charge, and the tip of a wing struck him as she passed. The wings looked gossamer-thin, but that was one smart rap!

He scrambled to his feet before she could reorient. He retained the pin, but he had lost the net. That was half of disaster, for though he might be able to kill her, he could not capture her. If he killed her to protect himself, that would only free her spirit to take another form—and he didn't want that!

The Hag gave him no time to consider. She looped about and came at him again. This time she moved slowly, almost hovering in place, watching for her opportunity. He held the pin, ready to stab her, knowing that that was no answer. She had maneuvered him into a position of kill or be killed, which was exactly what he didn't want.

Suddenly she moved. Automatically, he stabbed with the pin—and missed, for she veered away. It had been a feint. But she spun about and came back at him before he could recover, much more swiftly than she had before, and buffeted his sword arm. The pin was knocked away as he stumbled forward.

He turned to face her, but she was already on him, clutching him with her rough B legs, bearing him down under her weight and the thrust of her wings. He fell back, and clunked his head on the floor. It wasn't a hard floor, but he felt dizzy for a moment, unable to resist effectively.

"Now I've got you, Golem!" she buzzed. "I'm going to sting you into submission, not enough to kill you, just enough to paralyze you." And she maneuvered to bring her big sharp stinger into position.

"But you'll die if you sting me!" he protested.

"No I won't, Golem. There are B's and B's, and this kind stings with impunity. Now let me see; I want the flesh to be properly tender, so I think I'll sting you in the stomach. Brace yourself; this will hurt, and keep on hurting, as you swell up like a balloon. What joy!"

The terrible stinger was descending toward him, and he could neither throw her off nor roll out of the way; she held him too firmly, braced by her own buzzing wings. He reached wildly for the pin, but couldn't find it; it had probably rolled well clear. All his questing hand found was a loose length of line.

Line? That was the end of the net!

The stinger touched his clothing, as she maneuvered to sting him just the right amount—a more delicate matter than merely stinging to death. Now or never!

Grundy lifted his arm and flung the net up. It lifted, spread, and settled down over the B's wings. It clung to them stickily, for this was what it had been crafted to do—to be neutral to inanimate substance, but to catch wings firmly.

"Yeeech!" the B-Hag buzzed, jumping up and trying to free herself. But Grundy pulled on the line, and the net settled more firmly about her. A B with its wings entangled was a B largely helpless, as the spider had shown. Now he had her!

It was a struggle, for she was very strong, and tried to catch him with her stinger, but he continued hauling the net about, getting her snugly wrapped. He recovered his pin-sword and tucked it back through his belt. Then he hauled on his line, sliding her along. All was secure.

But the exit from this chamber was above, and he was sure he would not be able to haul her body up there. She was sure, too: "You haven't got me yet, Golem; the moment my swarm returns, you'll be stingbait!"

Surely true! What was he to do?

"And I hear them coming now, Golem!" she buzzed.

True again; he could hear the muted distant hum.

Then he figured it out. "Princess B-Nign!" he called. "I've got her! But I need an exit!"

There was a buzz at the hole. "Why so you do," B-Nign agreed.

"Sting this miscreant!" the Queen B buzzed imperiously.

"I can't do that," B-Nign replied.

"What? How dare you! *Why* can't you do that?"

"Because a Queen can't take orders; she can only give them."

"But I am the Queen!"

"You *were* the Queen. Now *I* am the Queen." And B-Nign flew down to the bottom of the chamber, landed, braced herself, and used her sharp B claws to cut open the sealed main entrance. Soon the hole opened up.

"Thank you, your Majesty," Grundy said, and shoved the deposed Queen into the hole. She fell straight down to the net covering the bottom of the Have.

Grundy followed, more carefully. But as he reached the main entrance, the hum of the returning swarm loomed loud. It was coming into sight! Feverishly he yanked away the net-supports, so that the Hag-B could drop to the ground below.

"Swarm!" the bundled Queen Hag buzzed. "Sting that golem! Kill the usurper Queen!"

B-Nign appeared at the entrance. "Ignore that trash," she buzzed. "*I am your Queen now.*"

Grundy hung by the edge of the hole, not daring to drop that distance, while the swarm approached. Which Queen would they obey?

Snortimer scrambled out below. "Drop: I'll catch you!" he cried.

Grundy dropped. The Bed Monster caught him. "Get me and that bundle out of here in a hurry!" Grundy cried.

Snortimer set Grundy on his back, picked up the bundle by the line, and scrambled away just as the swarm arrived.

"Help! Help!" the Queen Hag buzzed. But B-Nign was buzzing louder, and, after a moment's hesitation, the swarm oriented on her. Grundy had won this round!

The Queen buzzed again, more stridently: "B-Foul! B-Wilder! B-Devil! Here to me, my loyal minions!"

Three B's, summoned by name, hesitated; then they broke from the swarm and flew toward the Queen.

"You go to her?" B-Nign buzzed, imperiously enraged. "Then you are banished from this Have, miscreants! If you or she ever show your antennae in these parts again, you will be executed! I have buzzed!"

Grundy could tell by the way the three hesitated in flight that the sentence bothered them; it was terrible to be banished from the Have.

Obviously she could make it stick, because the rest of the swarm stayed with her. These three and the Hag were through here.

But now they had nothing to lose. "Vengeance!" the Hag buzzed. "Sting this golem! Free me!"

"Get out of here, Snort!" Grundy cried. The Bed Monster accelerated, scrambling for the path to the Retreat. In moments they were well away from the bonnet.

But the three grim minions of the Hag pursued them. Snortimer plunged through the thickest brush, to hide from them and confuse them, and this was working—but there was a snag. Abruptly he veered away from the deepest, most shadowed region.

"What's the matter, Snort?" Grundy cried, seeing the three B's hovering overhead, looking for them.

"I'm afraid of the dark!" the Bed Monster said.

"Oh, that. Of course. Just give me the reverse-wood."

Snortimer handed it up to him. It was no more than a splinter, but its potency remained.

But this pause gave the Hag her chance. She buzzed loudly, evidently calling again to her three loyal B's.

One of them heard her and zoomed in to the target. Snortimer dived under the brush and dodged to the side, and the B had to veer off. But every time they passed through a clearing, the Hag buzzed again, and the B reoriented. As they emerged to the regular path, the B could no longer be denied. It zoomed in, closed its wings, and shot at Grundy so swiftly that he knew the only way he could avoid getting stung was to jump off Snortimer's back—in which case Snortimer would be the one stung, and B-Foul would have time to free the Hag before Grundy could catch up. So Grundy didn't jump; he braced himself and took the terrible sting.

The B caught him on the right arm. It hurt, but only for a moment. Then the B was gone, its sting expended, and Grundy shook himself— and discovered he was unharmed. In fact, the dirt and grime and bits of spiderweb that adhered to him fell away, leaving him amazingly clean. What had happened?

But he had no time to ponder that, for the Hag buzzed again, and a second minion heard her and oriented on them. Snortimer, now on the clear path, doubled his effort and charged into the gloom of dusk. But, fast as he was, the B was faster. Slowly it gained, and as they shot through the gap in the ring of mountains, it caught up. Again Grundy had to remain and take the sting, rather than jump clear. Again he was tagged on an arm, painfully. Then the B left and Grundy took stock of himself again.

He seemed to be all right. In fact, he now seemed, despite the fatigue of his effort, to be marvelously clear-headed. There was no longer any confusion about his situation.

"Rapunzel!" he exclaimed. "She's a crossbreed, who has been raised alone. She can relate properly to neither the human nor the elven culture. I am doing her no favor by requiring her to make a choice between them. There is only one creature who can truly appreciate her nature, as the only creature of her kind—the one who is the only one of *his* kind!"

The Hag buzzed again. Now the third and final B heard her and responded. It zoomed in.

"Hurry, Snort!" Grundy cried. "We're almost there!" But the Bed Monster continued as if he hadn't heard Grundy, and the B gained on them.

"Try dodging!" Grundy advised. But again his friend ignored him.

Now they burst into the Retreat. There were the Fauns and Nymphs, and Jordan and Threnody, with little Rapunzel perched on her shoulder, Golem-style. Rapunzel smiled and clapped her hands. "XXXXX!" she exclaimed.

"What?" Grundy asked.

"YYY YYY YYYYYYY YYYY," Jordan explained.

Now the final B came down, so swiftly that there was no stopping it. It was aiming for Snortimer, evidently thinking that if it took out Grundy's steed, Grundy would be helpless.

Grundy leaped toward it at the last moment, intercepting the terrible sting. He was caught in the shoulder and spun about, and again it hurt. He fell to the ground, and the sliver of reverse-wood fell from his hand. The B flew unsteadily away.

Rapunzel was down on the ground and running toward him. "Oh, Grundy!" she cried. "Are you hurt? That was the bravest thing I ever saw!"

She was making sense, now! And abruptly he realized why: he had let go of the reverse-wood. That had been reversing his talent, so that instead of speaking and understanding all languages, he had spoken and understood none. No wonder Snortimer hadn't responded—Grundy had been spouting gibberish.

"Oh, Grundy, you're an angel!" Rapunzel exclaimed. "You even have a halo!"

Grundy glanced up, startled. There was a little circlet of light floating just above him.

Then his clear mind provided the answer. That last B that had stung him must have been B-Devil—but the reverse-wood had reversed the effect of the sting, making him angelic instead of devilish. The effect would only last a few minutes or hours, depending on the intensity of the sting.

And the prior B must have been B-Wilder, whose sting, reversed, gave him this uncommon clarity of mind. And the first sting must have been by B-Foul, the reverse effect making him uncommonly clean.

He had been brave, perhaps—but he had also been very lucky!

Now, while his mind was clear, he needed to act. "Rapunzel, I love you," he said.

"Why of course you do," she agreed, kissing him. "I thought you'd never realize!"

"Well, I—"

He broke off, for in their brief distraction the Queen Hag had finally worked her way out of the web-net. Now she buzzed up, hovering nearby.

"So, Golem!" she said in B-talk. "You thought to neutralize me, did you? Well, know that *my* sting is now set on max, instantly fatal to the victim."

Grundy experienced another cold wash of fear. "Instantly fatal," he echoed in human-talk.

"And do you know what I am going to do, wretched Golem?"

"I know," Grundy agreed, pushing Rapunzel aside so that there would be no danger of her getting stung too.

"I'm going to sting you to death," she buzzed anyway. "Then I'm going to sting your wretched friends. When Rapunzel sees them all die, and knows she is alone forever, she will be too distraught to oppose me any longer. Then I will take over her body immediately and use it as brutally as I can imagine. What do you think of that, Golem?"

Grundy drew his pin-sword. "You'll *have* to kill me, Hag, for I will never let you have Rapunzel while I live."

She buzzed so hard with laughter she wobbled in place. "You think to oppose me with that, Golem? Even if you managed to kill me as I kill you, it would make no difference, because I'll simply come back in another form. Even if you should kill me without getting stung, you'll still lose in the end. I have defeated you, Golem!"

Then she charged in. Grundy stood to take the assault, having no other choice, though he knew he had no chance.

Suddenly a huge hand swept between them. It caught the B and swept it away.

It was Rapunzel, in giant-form. She held the B in her hand. "I've got you, Hag!" she cried. "Sting me if you dare! Then you'll have nothing!"

The B buzzed angrily in her closed hand, but did not sting—because indeed that would be pointless. The one body the Hag couldn't afford to kill was Rapunzel's.

"And I wouldn't need to kill you," Rapunzel continued, "even if I could. Because you have no further power over me, Hag. I know you for what you are, and you will never have my body, for I will never consent, no matter what other mischief you do. If you deprive me of my friends, I'll simply kill myself." Then she opened her hand and let the B fly out, unharmed. "Now why don't you call my bluff?" she challenged.

The B hesitated, then flew toward the lake. It dived in, and a fish leaped up to swallow it. Rapunzel had finally faced down the Sea Hag, and was effectively free of her.

Rapunzel changed back to golem-size. Grundy went up and took her in his arms. "And you were calling what *I* did brave!" he told her.

"Well, she was attacking you," she said.

"Is she alive or dead, now?" Jordan asked.

"Probably dead, for the moment," Grundy said. "But her ghost will take over another body. Now I think she'll leave us alone, because she knows there is no way she'll take Rapunzel alive."

"So all you have left to worry about is your Quest," Threnody said. "And though I hate to say it, I fear that—"

There was a roar from the entrance to the Retreat. The remaining Fauns and Nymphs screamed and scattered into the dusk.

It was a giant, tiger-headed man. "Aha!" the tigerhead growled in tigerhead-tongue. "Delicious, juicy prey! I'll massacre them all!" He strode forward confidently.

But as he passed the bed, a big hairy hand shot out and grabbed his ankle. There was a horrendous roar.

The tigerhead was so startled he leaped high into the air, then turned tail and fled.

The Nymphs rushed back to the bed. "Snortimer saved us," they cried, dangling their fair legs down and laughing as he grabbed. "He's a hero!"

Stanley Steamer, who had just roused himself, ready to fight the intruder, made a low growl of disgust.

"Unless—" Jordan said.

Grundy jumped at the notion. He hurried over to the bed. "Snort, how would you like to stay here and protect the Fauns and Nymphs from molestation?" he asked. "With that sliver of reverse-wood, you could operate by day or night, and at other times you could just, uh, grab at pretty legs. I think that might be pretty, uh, romantic."

"Romance!" Snortimer agreed blissfully. "I have found it at last!"

Grundy turned to Stanley. "Which means that you can finally return to Castle Roogna and make Ivy happy, knowing the Fauns and Nymphs are safe."

Stanley brightened. He liked that notion.

"We'll go together, the three of us," Rapunzel said. "Now I think it won't bother me to meet the human community there."

15

Elf Quest

They had declared their love, but Grundy's doubts returned as his mind reverted to normal. Rapunzel thought she loved him—but she still hadn't been exposed to the elven or human cultures. Was it fair to have her make her decision on the basis of ignorance?

They were traveling on Stanley's back toward Castle Roogna, charting a course between Parnassus and Lake Ogre-Chobee, hoping to avoid the hazards of either region. It was not easy to hold on as the dragon whomped along, but they were doing it by using vines looped about Stanley's body. Perhaps this jogging about caused some of Grundy's doubts to fly loose, for Rapunzel picked them up. "You're thinking again!" she accused him.

"Well, suppose we get married, and then you discover it's a mistake?" he asked. "That you really belong in the elven society, for example, with an elven male?"

"It's not a mistake!" she insisted.

"But you have no direct experience with the elves! How can you be sure?"

She pondered. "Well, why don't we stop at an Elf Elm, then, and see? That should satisfy you."

She assumed that she would not be moved by the elves. He was not at all so sure. But her suggestion was good. If she was going to go to the elves, this was the time to find out. It was already too late for him, for his heart was lost, but perhaps not too late for her. He loved her and wanted her to be happy—in whatever way was best for her. "Yes. I will ask about."

He did so. The local trees did not know of any nearby Elf Elms. Grundy was half-relieved. Suppose there were no elves along their route? Then—No. He could not afford to take Rapunzel by default. She had to meet the elves and decide for herself and then meet the human community and decide again. Only then would it be all right.

They camped for the night and foraged for food and drink. They had no fear of predators, because Stanley was now a fairly formidable dragon. Hardly anyone bothered a dragon; those foolish enough to try had been culled out of the realm of the living in the course of many centuries. They made a nest of pillows to sleep on, and Stanley formed a circle around them, nose to tail, gently steaming. They were safe enough.

Rapunzel took his hand, as she always did. "I know you're trying to do the right thing, Grundy," she said.

"Trying," he agreed.

"I understand that men are mostly logical, and women are mostly feeling."

"I suppose."

"I've got the feeling this is a mistake."

"But you were the one who suggested that—"

"Now I've had time to change my mind."

"Change your—?"

"That's easier to do, now that my hair is short."

Grundy suspected that would not make an awful lot of sense to him if he reflected on it too long. Still, much of her magic had been tied up in her lovely long hair, and perhaps the length of it did contribute to the length of her determination. "But it just wouldn't be right to—"

"To love me without giving me a proper chance to explore my other avenues," she said. "I understand. But still, I wish I could avoid this process."

"I can't say I like it much myself," he said. "But suppose I—you—we—and then—"

"Suppose we gave ourselves to each other, and then discovered it was a mistake," she said, as usual phrasing his thought better than he could.

"Yes. And—"

"And so we would be sorry and very sad for our foolishness." She sounded so calm and rational!

"Yes."

She turned to him. "Oh, Grundy—let's do it!"

"What?"

"Oh, don't play the innocent with me!" she said reprovingly. *"I'm* the innocent, not you! Let's be foolish and see if we're sorry later."

Temptation tore at him. That would certainly be a way to settle it! His doubt was about to be overwhelmed. With no more than a semblance of sincerity, he temporized: "You can't mean that!"

She sighed. "Of course I don't mean it, Grundy," she agreed. "I knew you'd be noble."

Noble! His words had mocked his intent—but she had accepted the words, and now he was committed to them. He was not only insignificant in body, he was insignificant in spirit. He felt worse than ever.

"It was wrong of me to try to be a temptress," she continued. "I'm not good at it, because I don't have any experience."

"You're not good at it because you're a truly beautiful person," he corrected her.

"No, just inexperienced. You're the beautiful one, because you know what's right and wrong and choose the right."

"No! I'm nothing of the kind! When you said—I wanted to—I only—"

"I think you have an inferiority complex, Grundy. You don't even believe in your own good motives."

And she *did* believe—in his good motives. She was too good even to recognize the evil in another person's mind.

"Inferiority," he agreed.

"Still," she said, "I have a deep misgiving about this elf matter. I fear some nameless evil that is not of our making."

"If you really don't want to—"

"Oh, no, I'm sure you are correct. I should meet the elves. But I'll be very glad and relieved when it's over and we're back on the way to Castle Roogna. I'm not as worried about the human community, now, since I met Jordan and Threnody. They were all right. I can get along with their kind."

"Then maybe—"

"But I don't *love* their kind," she concluded. "I love *you,* Grundy. And if this elf business finally satisfies you, then it will be worth it."

Then it would be worth it . . . He held her hand, and drifted into a somewhat troubled sleep.

Next day they threaded the separation between lake and mountain and ferreted their way through the thickening jungle. Tangle trees were more common here, and others that seemed equally menacing, but when any started inching their foliage toward the travelers, Stanley jetted steam, and they withdrew.

Then Grundy picked up news of an Elf Elm. He sighed, inwardly; how convenient it would have been if there had been none! But now they had to go to it—a prospect he dreaded, though for no intuitive reason. He simply feared that Rapunzel would like the elves too well and would conclude that her proper home was there. But he had to provide her that chance.

They zeroed in on it, but the elven demesnes were extensive, and they did not reach the Elm by nightfall. So they camped and foraged and settled down.

"Oh, I feel it worse!" Rapunzel lamented.

"The elves won't hurt us," he reassured her. "Not when we explain. They are sensible folk."

"I know. It is not precisely their motives I fear."

But she didn't know exactly what she did fear. So she kissed him and held his hand tightly and slept, and in due course he slept too.

In the morning the elves were there.

"And what be ye doing in these our demesnes?" their leader inquired sternly in the human-tongue. He carried a hefty wooden mallet.

Grundy jumped up. "I can explain!"

"Ye'd better!"

"We were coming to see you, honored Elf," he said quickly. "Because one of our number is of elven derivation."

"That were not lightly claimed," the elf said, grimacing.

Grundy brought Rapunzel forward. She was busily brushing out her short hair, making herself presentable in the female manner on an emergency basis. "This is Rapunzel, who—"

"She be not elven-size."

"Show them," Grundy told her.

Rapunzel was abruptly elven-size, still trying to comb a tangle from her hacked hair.

The leader squinted at her. "Aye, she be fair enough! But size change be magic, no proof of origin."

"But her magic is in her hair, that—" Grundy realized that he could not prove anything by her hair, as she had lost her phenomenal tresses.

"My ancestors were Jordan the Barbarian and Bluebell Elf, of the tribe of Flower Elves," Rapunzel said, finally getting the tangle out.

There was a stir. "You claim good lineage, girl."

"The best," she agreed.

"And you?" the elf asked of Grundy.

"I am a golem. My talent is linguistics. And this is Stanley Steamer, formerly the Gap Dragon." Stanley puffed a ring of steam.

"A tame dragon?" the elf's brow arched.

"He is Princess Ivy's companion, in the human realm. We are returning him to her."

"Do ye several folk stand by your statements?" the elf asked gravely.

"Of course we do!" Rapunzel exclaimed indignantly. "What do you think we are?"

"Then we shall take ye to our tree for confirmation. If ye be confirmed, ye'll have no fear of us."

And if not? Grundy wondered, but didn't ask.

"We be of the Tool Tribe," the elf said. "I be Mallet, and these be Chisel—" Here he indicated an elf with a chisel. "—and Hoe and Wrench and Awl." He continued around the circle, each elf made obvious by his tool. But it was evident that those tools could quite readily serve as weapons.

Then the elves escorted the party to the Elf Elm. This was an enormous tree, its crown of foliage seeming small because it was so far away.

They halted a moderate distance away. "You who claim elven descent," Mallet said. "Carry that rock."

Startled, Rapunzel obeyed. She remained elven-size, so the indicated rock was larger than Grundy could have handled, but it was no easy thing for her to carry. She staggered forward with it toward the tree. Then, oddly, the burden seemed to grow lighter, and she carried it with less distress. As the others paced her, she relaxed, finally setting the rock on her shoulder so as to free one hand. "It's not as heavy as I thought," she confessed.

"Enough," Mallet said. "Your claim is verified."

"But you haven't examined your records!" she protested.

"Know, crossbreed, that the strength of elves varies inversely with our distance from the Elm," he explained. "Your strength be not as great here as ours, but the effect be manifest. You are of elven descent, whatever your other lineage."

She set down the rock. "I was not told of this!" She seemed pleased.

Grundy scowled inwardly. Naturally the Sea Hag had not educated her about this aspect of the elven culture; it might have made her eager to experience it. It also augured unfortunately well for her acceptance here and her possible decision to remain.

More elves descended from the high foliage, on thin lines, seeming to have no trouble holding on. The first to land on the ground was a handsome male elf whose beard was not yet full. "What have we here?" this one demanded.

"We have a girl of elven descent, Prince Gimlet," Mallet said. "With her entourage of golem and dragon."

Prince Gimlet oriented on Rapunzel. "And a fair creature she is, indeed, may I say!" he exclaimed, taking her hand and kissing it. She blushed, flattered.

Grundy kept his expression fixed on neutral.

Prince Gimlet's gaze passed over Grundy and Stanley. "Feed her companions, while I show our visitor our Tree," he said, making an offhand gesture.

"Oh, but I don't want to be separated from—" Rapunzel began.

"Obviously a dragon can not ascend a tree," the Prince told her. "He will be here when you return." And he put his arm about her slender waist and hauled her up, climbing the line with feet and a single hand. It was an amazing feat, even allowing for the elven strength near the tree.

"But—" Grundy cried, and Stanley steamed. But the other elves closed in about them, their expressions turning grim, their hands going to their tools, and Grundy realized that this was not the best occasion to make an issue. After all, he wanted Rapunzel to experience the elven culture, didn't he?

"Here be food," Mallet said, indicating the carcass of some kind of beast near the base of the tree.

Stanley went over, sniffed, and started chewing on it. But Grundy, following, saw some dead ants by the carcass. "What's this?" he asked in grass-talk.

"Poisoned meat," the grass replied. "They use it to get rid of pests."

"Stanley!" Grundy cried. "Don't—"

But it was too late. The dragon stiffened, his eyes assuming a glazed look; then he sank to the ground.

Grundy turned on the elves. "You—this is not—"

"Prince's orders," Mallet said. "Strange ones, I admit; we never poisoned a tame creature before. But he's the Prince."

Grundy started to run. But an elf reached down and caught him, and hefted him up overhead with one hideously powerful arm. He was helpless.

He was carried around the tree. The elf bent to touch the ground, and found a ring set there; he hauled on it, and a turf-covered slab came up. Beneath was a ramp going down. The elf dropped Grundy in and let the heavy slab fall back into place.

Grundy tumbled on down through the darkness, fetching up against a packed-earth wall. He was bruised and disoriented, but not hurt. He realized that he had abruptly been made a prisoner.

For a while he simply sat in the dank dark, sorting things out. Something was calamitously wrong—but exactly what was it? He had had little contact with elves, but he was absolutely sure they did not deal treacherously with visitors. They were resolute in opposition and loyal in support and always made their orientation clear at the outset. To challenge a visiting party, then accept it, then betray it—this was simply not the elven way. Yet it had happened. Grundy knew that he would be able to do nothing positive until he understood why. Certainly he could not pound on the exit panel and demand to be released; they would not release him without reason, and might simply dispatch him as they had the dragon to shut him up.

The dragon! They had poisoned Stanley! That was the most appalling thing of all! Without Stanley, his Quest was dead—not to mention the horror of losing a loyal friend.

He calmed himself. Stanley was not just another dragon, he was the Gap Dragon, just about the toughest breed there was, accustomed to eating anything. He was young and vigorous now. If any creature could survive poison, Stanley could. He hadn't eaten very much of the carcass before being affected. Probably he was merely stunned and would throw off the effect after a while. After all, in the past, as an adult, he had consumed zombies and cherry bombs and, once, a basilisk. If he had survived those, surely he could survive a little poison!

Perhaps he could check on that. Grundy ran his hands across the clammy earth until he found a worm hole. Then he put his mouth to the hole and murmured in worm-talk: "Hey, you worm! Where are you?"

Startled, the worm replied. "Who calls me from below?"

"It is I, Grundy Golem, friend to all insignificant creatures. I need your help."

"For a friend to insignificant creatures, I will help."

Grundy smiled in the dark. He had rather thought that would be the case. There was magic of a special nature in language. "There is a dragon above. Can you tell me whether he is alive or dead?"

"By the time I got there, he would surely be dead," the worm pointed out. "But I know a tunnelbug who is very fast; he can check this for you."

"That would be much appreciated, noble Worm."

In a moment the tunnelbug had gone to the surface and returned. "The dragon is ill, but not dead."

Grundy sagged in relief. "Will you carry a message to him? I must give it in dragon-talk, so he will understand, but you might carry it."

"I will try," the tunnelbug said bravely.

"Thank you so much, noble Tunnelbug! Here is the message, to be whispered in his ear." And Grundy then said carefully in dragon-talk: {DRAGON PLAY POSSUM TILL FULLY RECOVERED—GRUNDY} He repeated it several times until the tunnelbug had it straight, for dragon-talk was difficult for a bug.

In due course the bug departed. Now Grundy tried for something more ambitious. "Is there a squiggle in the region?" he called in squiggle-tongue.

He was in luck. A squiggle answered. It showed up in the cell with an explosion of dirt. "Eh, what? What?" it asked, perplexed.

"Oh honored Vole," Grundy said, remembering what he had learned in the vole-tunnels. "I am trapped here and need an escape. Will you make me a passage out, that exits well away from the tree, so the elves will not see me?"

The squiggle-vole was flattered. No one had considered it important enough for such a request, before. "Certainly, Golem. But wouldn't you rather explore the tree itself?"

"I would—but the elves would treat me badly. They have taken my friend up in the foliage, and I fear for her safety."

"The reason I asked," the squiggle continued, "is that it is a very short distance to the tree, and there is a shaft inside it that only we voles remember. If you would like to go there—"

What phenomenal luck! "Yes, honored Vole! That would be perfect! Except—is there a way out of it at the top? I can not help my friend if I can not get out of the trunk."

"There are crevices you could squeeze through," the creature agreed. "We use them to peer out at the elves, they unknowing, for we are very curious creatures."

"Most curious," Grundy agreed warmly. "I would be deeply grateful for such aid."

"Glad to help," the squiggle said, still flattered. It proceeded to dig in the fashion only its kind could, in moments making a short tunnel to the root of the tree. Sure enough, there was a cavity in the wood that Grundy found with his hands, for there was no light here. To make it even better, there were the handholds of an old ladder leading up, evidently intended for elves. The elf ancestors must have crafted this as a secret exit, then forgotten it.

He thanked the squiggle, then started to climb. Because the elves were twice his height, the rungs were more widely spaced than was convenient for him, but he was able to manage. He climbed through the darkness with fair dispatch, counting rungs as he went, so as to be able to judge the height. He figured that four hundred rungs should put him at the level of the foliage.

It turned out that that was a considerable climb. Each single rung was an effort, and soon he was tiring. At fifty rungs he paused, panting. One eighth of the way up? How could he ever make it!

The answer was, he *had* to make it. He knew that a tribe that would betray a welcome, poison a friendly dragon, and throw a Golem in a dank cell could not have anything very wonderful in mind for a young woman. Rapunzel was, in effect, confined in another tower. He would have to get her out.

He mounted another fifty rungs, and paused again. One quarter of the way up—and three-quarters of his strength had been expended, by the feel of it. But what was there to do, except continue?

He hauled himself on up. The 134th rung gave way when he drew on it, dropping his body while his heart remained at the prior level. His hands caught the next one down, so that he only dropped a third of his body-length, but it was an ugly sensation. He hung there, his fright overriding his fatigue. What a jolt!

Then he resumed the climb, somewhat more carefully. He tested each new rung before trusting his full weight to it. Naturally the rungs got old and weak with age, and their anchorages rotted away. He should have expected that. But it didn't make him feel better.

By the time he reached the 200th rung, the lift provided by his fright from the near-fall had faded, and his arms and legs were more tired than ever. Halfway—and now it would be almost as bad to descend as to ascend. He was stuck—rather, fully committed. But he still hardly believed he could make it the rest of the way up.

He ground on, one rung at a time, each one a worse torment than the one before. His hands were blistering from the friction, and his feet were hurting from the narrow support. Then the blisters burst, and each new grip was painful. He had to hold on more tightly, because of the slipperyness caused by his own leaking hands, but his strength was ebbing so that this was horrendously difficult.

Two hundred and twenty-five rungs—or was it two hundred and thirty-five? He was no longer certain of the count. Did it matter? The top was where it was, regardless of the count.

His left hand lost its grip, and his right was too fatigued to make a sudden grasp. But his feet slipped through the ladder, and brought him painfully short. He had not fallen—but that was accident as much as luck.

Wouldn't it be easier simply to let go? He would be down very quickly, his problems over.

Then he remembered Stanley Steamer, waiting below—for what? If Grundy did not return to him, would the dragon make it home to Ivy on his own?

Grundy resumed his climb, heedless of the agony of his hands. But now that agony was fading, for they were growing numb. He had to test his grip on each rung, not just to verify the soundness of the rung, but to be sure his grip would hold.

Up, up, eternally. He was no longer counting; that required too much energy. He just went.

Somewhere around 300 he stalled. His numbed muscles simply would no longer respond. His last vestige of strength was spent. All he could do now was hang there, until he dropped off.

But his mind had not been deadened as far as his body had. He thought of Rapunzel, at the dubious mercy of Prince Gimlet. Why had the Prince welcomed her, while treating her companions in such dastardly fashion?

The question brought the answer: Rapunzel was a beautiful and innocent woman. The very kind an unscrupulous man could sweep off her feet and use. Surely the Prince cared nothing for her personally; it was her naïveté he was after. So he had, literally, swept her off her feet, and given orders to dispatch her companions. This was the way a powerful and cynical person was. Grundy simply had not expected it among the elves, whom he supposed were superior to the human society in this respect. Live and learn!

The thought of what Prince Gimlet might even now be doing to Rapunzel spurred Grundy to renewed activity. His arms were numb, but he moved them, hooking clawed hands over the rungs and hoisting himself up and up. He had to be getting close! He was already farther than he had thought possible, at fifty rungs.

Above him a crevice of light showed. It was really very faint, but he had been in darkness so long that his eyes made the illumination seem strong. The squiggle had spoken truly!

Grundy no longer really felt his arms and legs; they seemed to have disconnected from his body. But his body continued to rise, until he was at the crevice. He peered through.

It was the elven kitchen. It had a stove and counters, and an elf cook was working. The crevice was behind the stove, perhaps caused by the drying effect of the heat. The stove appeared to be made of wood, which made Grundy marvel; what would such a stove burn, and how would it remain intact? It evidently worked satisfactorily. The walls of the chamber were leafy, and the workers were careful to step on the solid branches below, rather than on the twigs or leaves, lest they fall through. There was a lot more in an Elf Elm than outsiders knew!

He moved on up, feeling somewhat restored now that the desolate climb had rewarded him with this access. He didn't want the kitchen, he wanted the Prince's chambers. What he would do once he found them he didn't know, but that was not his immediate problem.

Farther up, on the other side, he found another crevice. This one overlooked the nursery, for there were elven babies sleeping in leafy cradles. Gusts of wind rocked those cradles, which were on smaller branches that bent with the light force of it. It seemed to be a convenient arrangement.

At a higher level was the sewing room. Elven maidens were working at a table, sewing garments and chatting merrily. Grundy paused to listen.

". . . and the dragon was tame," one was saying. "They rode on it. But Prince Gimlet ordered it put away."

"That's strange," another said. "We never harmed a friendly creature before."

"Have you noticed?" the first said. "The Prince has been acting strangely this past day. You know how he always puts his hands on us, pretending it's an accident?"

"That's because he's not supposed to fool with common girls," the third said. "But until he finds a suitable royal bride from another Elm—"

The second rubbed her rear. "Some day I'm going to 'accidentally' drop a plate of glop on his foot!"

"That's what I'm saying," the first said. "Late last night when I replaced the candles in his chamber, I thought sure he'd try to grab me the way he usually does, but he just sort of stared at me, seeming confused. I asked him if he was all right, but he just told me gruffly to get on about my business. He sounded strange. I thought maybe he had some royal indisposition, but I was just glad to get out of there without a struggle. Now, after this dragon business, I wonder."

"He grabs, but he's nice," the third said. "I never heard of him harming a friendly creature, before."

Then an elven matron entered the chamber, and the three shut up and concentrated on their sewing. Grundy moved on up, though he was sure no one suspected his presence.

So the Prince was acting strangely. But his action with Rapunzel was not strange. Obviously he had found a better woman to pinch. Grundy burned at the notion and kept climbing.

The shaft narrowed and finally debouched at what had once been a broken branch. A door cunningly crafted to resemble healed-over wood opened onto a network of branches clothed with leaves.

Grundy stood there, looking about, trying to decide what to do next. He remained almost dead tired and hadn't located the Princely chambers. Had all this been for nothing?

Then he heard voices below. He was *above* a chamber. He squatted down, then lay flat, parting the leaves with his hands, carefully. The voices became clearer—and now he recognized them. Rapunzel and Prince Gimlet!

He managed to arrange the leaves so that he could see them, without being seen. He hated to imagine it, but if Rapunzel liked the Prince's attentions, then she was not being forced, and it would be Grundy's duty to let her be. He could descend quietly, rejoin Stanley, and return to Castle Roogna to complete his Quest. The fact that his love would be lost would have no bearing on the matter. It wouldn't count at all—to anyone but him. But he had to be fair.

He hoped she hated the Prince.

As it happened, nothing much was happening. They were evidently completing a meal, a fairly sumptuous repast. Rapunzel, for all her dainty figure, had a good appetite. The smell of the food reminded Grundy that he had not eaten today. How he would like to have some of those leftover scraps!

"My dear, I like you," the Prince said, wiping his mouth with a fancy napkin. "I think I'll marry you."

"But I don't love you!" Rapunzel protested, amazed.

"What does love have to do with it? I am in need of a proper consort, who can not be from this Tree, and I believe you will do."

"But I love another!"

His gaze narrowed. "Oh? Who?"

"Grundy Golem," she confessed.

"But he is not of elven stock. You must marry within your culture."

"Why?" she asked, with that delightful innocence she had.

"Because that's the way it is. Now I'll just declare that you are to be my bride, and the elven banns will be published, and then in a couple of weeks—"

"No!" she cried.

"You prefer to marry the golem?" he asked incredulously.

"Yes."

Grundy's delight at this assertion was nullified by Gimlet's next words. "Then know, oh damsel, that the golem is even now our prisoner, and if you do not acquiesce with proper grace to this union, I will have him killed."

"Oh, no!" she wailed.

"Oh, yes," he said grimly. "Do you agree to marry me now?"

This was too much for Grundy. "No she doesn't!" he yelled.

"Grundy!" Rapunzel cried, delighted.

"How did you get up here?" Gimlet demanded, furious. He drew his weapon, which was a steel rod, with a handle set across the end like the horizontal stroke of a T, and a twisted point that looked wicked indeed.

He strode across the chamber and rammed the gimlet up, trying to spear Grundy.

Rapunzel screamed. Grundy, surprised, slipped off his branch and fell down through the ceiling. But he grabbed the Prince's raised arm as he dropped, and clung to it, trying to wrest away the weapon.

Immediately he knew he was in trouble. Not only was he still very tired, but the Prince had the elven strength, strongest here within the foliage of the Elm. He held his arm aloft, Grundy upon it, and caught the Golem by the scruff of the neck with his other hand. He ripped Grundy free as if he were a rag doll—as perhaps he once had been. Grundy was helpless.

The Prince readied the gimlet. "Now I shall run you through, as I should have done before," he said.

"No!" Rapunzel cried.

"No?" the Prince inquired, holding the point near Grundy's stomach. "And why should I desist, damsel?"

Rapunzel was stricken, knowing what he wanted. But if she gave him that, she would lose Grundy in another sense.

Grundy could not urge her to either course. She would lose him either way. She had to make her own decision.

"Spare him," she said brokenly. "And I will—will m-marry you." Then she sank to the floor, sobbing.

The Prince smiled. "So it seems you are some use to me after all, Golem. I never thought that would be the case, when I fought you in the Tower. But of course I was not using you properly. Why kill you and have the damsel kill herself, when I can have complete control over her merely by threatening you? So you shall live, but you shall not be free." He turned to face the entrance, which was a hole in the center of the floor. "Guards!"

Tower? Suddenly Grundy suffered a horrendous realization. "The Sea Hag!" he cried.

The Prince grimaced. "Curses! I shouldn't have let that slip. Well, it makes no difference. Once I marry her, I'll suicide this body and she will be Queen of the Elves, and I will assume her body."

"She'll never agree to that!" Grundy cried.

"Won't she—with your life still at stake?"

Grundy realized that Rapunzel would indeed give in again—to save him. Her love was true, and that was her undoing. He had been a fool to believe that the Hag had given up, merely because she had not been willing to sting Rapunzel to death when she had been a Queen B. She had merely sought another avenue—and now she had found it.

The guards arrived. "Confine this wretch in a cage," the Hag commanded. "This time watch him. See that he does not escape."

"Don't do it!" Grundy cried. "This isn't your Prince! It's the Sea Hag!"

"He's crazy as well as scrawny," the Hag said. "As you can see, I am unchanged."

"He's changed! He's changed!" Grundy cried. "You know how he's changed in the last day—since the Hag took over his body. This is an imposter, not your Prince at all!"

The guards hesitated. Obviously they had heard the gossip, and knew the Prince was different. But they weren't ready to defy him. They came toward Grundy.

"Would your Prince ever have poisoned a friendly dragon?" Grundy demanded.

At this, Rapunzel's head came up. "What?"

"They poisoned Stanley!" Grundy told her. "And threw me in a dank cell!"

"Oh, I must flee this place!" she cried, in her distress changing to human-size. In this form she seemed practically to fill the chamber, and her weight bore the branches of the floor down somewhat.

"You do, and he dies," Prince Hag said evenly, touching Grundy's belly with the point of the gimlet.

"Oh!" she repeated, horrified anew. She reverted to elf-size.

"Don't yield to the Hag!" Grundy yelled at her. "She'll kill me anyway, once she has your body! Go now, save yourself. Go down to Stanley and ride back to Castle Roogna! He knows the way!"

But this logic was too cruel for her maidenly heart to bear. She sank again to the floor, swooning.

"Now lock him up," the Hag told the guards. "I will see to the damsel."

"But that's not your Prince!" Grundy cried desperately. "Ask anybody! Ask the serving girls! You know he's changed. No elf acts the way he does, threatening innocent folk with death!"

Again the guards hesitated, knowing that he had a point. They had known the Prince a long time and recognized the change in him; now Grundy was providing an explanation.

"Obey," the Hag told them, "or I'll run *you* through!"

"That does it," one guard said. "I think the golem's right."

"Wretch!" the Hag cried, aiming the gimlet at him.

But the guards drew their weapons, which were a screwdriver and a trowel. Metal gleamed. They were as strong as the Prince, here. "The issue is in doubt," the other guard said. "We must schedule a trial."

"Over my dead body!" the Hag screamed, and now the Prince's face did in a way resemble that of the Hag of the Ivory Tower.

The two guards stood unflinching, weapons ready, not responding. It was evident that the elves were an independent breed who did not tolerate what they knew to be wrong, even when it seemed that their Prince ordered it. They had had time to ponder the business of poisoning a tame dragon and violating a sanctuary after it had been granted, and they were not having any more of it.

The Hag saw that she had overstepped her bounds and was only getting herself into trouble. She was not a natural elf and could not long fool true elves once their suspicion was aroused. She would lose all credibility if this continued.

"Then let there be a trial," she said, assuming an aspect of abrupt reasonableness. "A trial of right by strength—the golem and I. The survivor gets the girl."

The guards nodded. "That seems the best way," Trowel agreed. "We will schedule it for tomorrow—you against the golem."

Grundy could not protest, because his alternative was to get killed outright, here. But how could he hope to beat the horrible strength of the Hag in elven-form? He feared that he had only postponed the reckoning.

But Rapunzel brightened. "Oh, Grundy, I just know you can do it! Then everything will be all right!"

Or all wrong. But at least it gave her a night of hope, and that was worth something.

16

Trial

In the morning Grundy found himself stiff from the prior day's exertion and still somewhat tired. They had locked him in a leafy chamber for the night, alone, but the elven maidens had brought him food and a chamber pot and had rubbed healing salve into his blistered hands. He couldn't complain; if he seemed like a prisoner, still it protected him from the malice of the Hag, who was similarly isolated. He knew that Rapunzel was protected from contact with either litigant, until the decision was reached. The elves were, indeed, fair, in their rigorous fashion.

A guard, called Lathe, came to conduct him to the site of the trial. "Golem, you are not of our culture," Lathe said, touching the instrument that gave him his name. It was a kind of wooden framework with wheels mounted on it, used to rotate things that were being evenly shaped. Evidently he liked to be sure that a situation was properly shaped, too. "Do you understand the rules of the trial?"

"No."

"You have challenged the Prince's identity, and the Prince denies your charge. As we are unable to judge the merits of the case objectively, we are submitting it to trial by combat. Because you made the charge against the Prince, he has the choice of type of contest. He has chosen Lines and Boxes."

"Lines and Boxes?" Grundy demanded incredulously. He remembered the game he had played with the ant lion, back at the Good Magician's castle. But that was no duel-to-the-death! Well—not from the game itself. The consequence of losing, however, was death.

"You swing on the lines to the boxes, and cut the lines behind you. When you trap your opponent in a box, you dump him into the loop."

Evidently this was not the game he had played, though it seemed to have some similarities. Could similar strategies be followed? "I don't think I have done that before," Grundy said cautiously.

"Naturally not. It's an elven specialty that negates differentials in size and strength. You do, however, need to be agile, and some cleverness helps."

This was sounding better. "What is this loop you mention?"

"It is an ancient artifact we have had in our Elm for centuries. Anything that passes through it, never returns, unless it is attached to something on this side, so that it can be drawn back quickly."

"Sounds like the Void," Grundy said, shuddering.

"The what?"

It seemed that the elves of this tree did not know about the geography of Northern Xanth. "A black hole that never yields what it takes in."

"Perhaps so," Lathe agreed. "Certainly whichever one of you falls through the loop will not return."

So this was, indeed, a duel to the death, or the equivalent. Whoever passed through the loop would be finished, certainly. If he dumped the Hag through, Rapunzel would be forever free of that terrible threat. If, on the other hand, the Hag dumped *him* through . . .

Lathe conducted him to the site of the trial. This was outside the Elm; in fact, right beside it. A number of thin lines descended from the foliage, dangling down to near the ground. A smaller number of platforms were perched on poles rising from the ground. The poles were slender, and reached about halfway up the trunk of the tree, so that the little platforms swayed gently in the breeze. Grundy saw that there was a framework of slats about each platform, so that a person standing on one could have handholds. Still, it looked precarious. He would prefer to trust himself to a line, assuming that his abraded hands remained strong enough to hold on. The salve had done a marvelous job, so that the skin was now intact, but scars remained.

He peered to the ground, a dizzying distance below. There, within the ring of poles, was a large funnel that glistened; probably it had been greased. In the center was a small dark hole: the loop.

Lathe handed him a knife. It was small, suitable for his hand, and the blade was honed to a feather edge on either side. "One slash will sever a line," the elf explained. "Several slashes will be required to cut through a pole. However, either action takes time, and therefore sacrifices mobility."

Why was he saying that? Grundy shrugged, studying the layout to see whether any strategy suggested itself.

There were six boxes, and four lines dangled near the corners of each. The circle of boxes was tight enough so that it looked possible to swing from any one of them to any other; but they were still far enough apart so that any attempt to jump between them was bound to be futile. His challenge was to isolate the Hag in a box, and then dump her into that funnel below. Could he do it? He *had* to!

Now Rapunzel appeared, surrounded by elven maids. She remained elf-sized, but was still phenomenally beautiful despite her brief hair. She had to remain on a branch separate from the arena, where she could watch without interfering.

"Oh, Grundy!" she cried. "My premonition has come true! I wish we had not come to this place!"

He wished so too! His effort to provide her fair exposure to the elven culture had proven disastrous. But now she was apt to become a part of it, in the worst way.

And Prince Gimlet arrived. He was in brief athletic clothes and had exchanged his gimlet for a double-edged knife like Grundy's, only larger. The Prince had the advantage of size and strength, but those would not count for much as long as the two contestants did not touch each other, and might even be to his disadvantage on the precarious boxes. So this might indeed be a fair trial.

"Are the litigants ready?" one of the elves inquired.

"Ready," the Hag said with confidence.

"Uh, yes," Grundy mumbled. He hoped he was!

"Begin."

The Prince caught hold of the line closest to him and swung in to the nearest platform. Grundy found a line just within his reach, and did the same. He felt the stiffness in his arms anew, but had no real trouble. The contest was on!

The Prince took another line, and launched himself directly across the circle. Grundy hadn't expected this and stood and stared for a moment. Then he realized that the Prince's blade was aimed right at him, as the elf swung one-handed. He could be dispatched by the knife directly, then tossed into the loop! What difference did it make how he died?

He grabbed almost blindly at a line to the side and jumped off. His aim was bad, and he missed the adjacent platform. He swung erratically across to the one beyond—but already the elf was pursuing him, knife still extended.

This time Grundy got more of his wits about him. He hung onto the line he had, set his feet against the edge of the box, and shoved violently off. He sailed across the circle to the opposite platform, landed on it, then quickly cut the line he had used so that it would not swing back to the elf. He was learning!

But the elf merely took another line, and came after him again. Grundy didn't dare go across the center, when the elf was doing it; they would meet, and Grundy would be the one stabbed, for the elf's reach was twice his own. He had to move off to the side.

The elf pursued him in this manner all about the circle, and as they moved more of the lines were cut, until Grundy discovered that there had been a pattern in the pursuit. He was now trapped on a platform from which all the lines had been lost—but he had let go of his incoming line before realizing that. He couldn't get away!

He turned and braced himself, expecting the elf to come at him blade-first, but that wasn't the case. That would have meant a suggestion of a fighting chance. Instead, the elf handed himself down the line and swung down below, catching at the pole on which Grundy's box was perched. Then he sawed at it with the knife.

That had to be stopped! Grundy leaped out desperately, catching the upper section of the line that was supporting the elf. He couldn't swing it anywhere, because it was now anchored below, but he hoped to jerk it out of the elf's grasp and strand him on the pole.

It didn't work. The elf was far stronger than he was, and easily retained control of the line while continuing to saw at the pole. If Grundy slid down the rope, that knife would finish him; if he did not, his pole would soon fall, and he would be stuck right here, waiting for the elf to climb up and get him.

Then he had a desperate notion. If he could exert a sudden, hard shock to the line—

He reached up and sliced through the line above him. Suddenly he was falling. He hung on to his severed segment of the line, knowing that his weight would jerk at the elf when the slack was taken up.

Abruptly, it happened. The elf screamed as he was wrenched off the pole, and he fell toward the funnel.

Then the flaw in his plan occurred to Grundy. *He* was falling too! Somehow he had overlooked that when the seemingly brilliant strategy came to him. They were *both* descending to their doom!

Grundy's feet struck the funnel first, and he flipped involuntarily, absorbing the shock, and rolled toward the center. The elf landed more heavily, but there was some give in the funnel, and no bones were broken. Both of them slid down the greased slope to the loop.

Grundy heard Rapunzel's scream of horror. It had probably been issued some time ago, and was only just now catching up with him. Then he plunged through the dark hole of the loop.

He seemed to be in an opaque tunnel, falling yet floating. Then he found himself standing on a cavern floor, unharmed. In a moment the Hag landed beside him.

"Wretch!" she screamed. "Look what you've done!"

"I took you with me," Grundy said with a certain satisfaction. "Now you won't get Rapunzel's body."

The Hag looked around. "We'll see. The Brain Coral sometimes releases its acquisitions, if they have something to offer in exchange."

"The Brain Coral?"

"Didn't you recognize the loop, Golem? It's one of the entrances to the realm of the Coral. Nothing returns because the Coral keeps what it gets, until it decides to release it."

Now Grundy remembered. Long ago, he had been in the nether region of Xanth, with Bink and Chester Centaur and Crombie the Soldier and Good Magician Humfrey. Horrendous things had happened. They had encountered the Demon X(A/N)th, who was the source of magic, and for a time there had been no magic in Xanth. He didn't care to go through that again! He had been a true golem, then, and when the magic had departed, so had his animation, leaving him as a tangle of cloth and wood. Only when the magic returned had he revived—with one awful headache.

But the residence of the Brain Coral was under a black lake whose water slowly pickled anything in it and stored creatures in a half-dead state indefinitely. There was no water here. Instead there was a spacious dry chamber whose far wall was—

"Oh-oh," Grundy murmured, shivering.

"Maybe if I give you to the Brain Coral, it will let me go," the Hag said. "Or I might give it this elf-prince body, and take yours, and return to claim Rapunzel. She would do anything for you, without even questioning it. Then—"

"This isn't the Brain Coral's residence," Grundy said.

"Of course it is! I told you, I recognized the loop. I've never been here before, of course, but I know about the Brain Coral from way back. It's always ready to deal."

"Maybe once the loop led to the Brain Coral," Grundy said. "But this time it glitched. This is—" He found himself unable to say the dread words.

"If you're trying to talk your way out of this, Golem, it won't work. I will simply haul you in." And the Prince's hand reached out and grabbed Grundy by the collar.

Grundy pulled away—and the elf's hand could not retain the grasp. "You aren't near the Elf Elm any more, Hag," he said. "That body is no longer enhanced by magic strength. Also—"

The Hag dived for him. "I'll haul you in anyway, Golem!"

Grundy dodged aside, and the body of the elf stumbled past him. Then it stiffened. The aristocratic mouth opened and the eyes stared.

The body's impetus carried it forward another step, and animation returned. "What—?"

"You stepped into a Thought," Grundy said.

"A what?"

"A Thought. They exist here in bands, invisible, and when you step into one—"

"A hemale and a shemale were—it was grotesque!"

"You should talk, Hag! Here you are in a male body—"

"And an itmale looking on, seeking to—to—"

"And you thought you were experienced," Grundy said wryly. "Well, go step into another Thought vortex, and get some *real* experience!"

"But—"

"This isn't the cave of the Brain Coral," Grundy said. "It's the cave of the Demon X(A/N)th. And if we wake him—"

"It can't be!" She took a step toward him. "You're just saying that, Golem, to get out of—"

"Don't move about too much, Hag, or you'll—"

The elf's face froze again. Too late—she was already in another Thought vortex.

Grundy backed away—and stepped into one himself. It was the Demon S(I/R)ius, in Anonymale aspect, seeking a blood sacrifice for the autumn festival. *Canicula, here is the fawn-colored doggie for thy—*

Grundy emerged from the vortex, shaking. He didn't want to be the canine sacrifice for that festival!

The Hag had also emerged. "Unspeakable!" she spat. "I must get out of here!"

"Don't charge blindly about!" Grundy warned.

Again he was too late. She charged blindly toward the far wall, stiffened and stumbled as she tore through a Thought, righted herself, lumbered into another vortex, and finally crashed into the wall.

"Trouble!" Grundy muttered.

For that was no ordinary wall. It was in the form of a huge stone face, and she had just banged into its monstrous nose.

That did it. An enormous eye blinked. The Demon X(A/N)th was waking!

The whole cave shuddered as the face came alive. The Hag stood there before it, amazed. She might have existed for centuries, but she had had no experience with this entity! Grundy had—and knew that no matter how bad his situation had been a moment ago, it was now infinitely worse.

The phenomenal orifice of a mouth opened. "WHO COMES HERE?" it demanded.

The Hag didn't answer, so Grundy had to. "It's an accident, Demon!" he quavered.

"THEN I WILL DESTROY THAT ACCIDENT THAT DISTURBS MY REPOSE!"

That was exactly what Grundy had been afraid of. The Demon X(A/N)th cared nothing for the lives of ordinary creatures, and only wanted them to stay clear. There was supposed to be a magic shield to prevent anyone from blundering in, but apparently the loop had bypassed that. Now the Demon, the source of all this land's magic, was aroused and angry, ready to swat Grundy and perhaps the rest of Xanth out of existence as someone would an annoying fly.

What did he have to lose, now? "You wouldn't do that if you had any notion of the problems of real people!" Grundy cried.

The Demon paused. "It talks back?"

Grundy plowed on heedlessly. "You're omnipotent! You don't have any real problems! No wonder you don't care about ours! But if you were in my place for even one minute, you'd change your mind!"

The Demon considered. "Is this a wager?" he inquired mildly.

"Whatever you want to call it! You don't know a thing about real life!"

"Very well. We shall change places—for one minute."

Suddenly Grundy's consciousness was in the body and brain of the Demon. His gaze penetrated the rock of the physical realm as if it were mere haze and reached into the framework of the planets. He was in a foul mood, because he had been losing significance for several decades and seemed to be unable to reverse the trend. While it was true that he was omnipotent in the physical sense, he was not in the social sense, and the other Demons of the System were gaining on him. E<A/R>th now had progressed a notch in status, having <>'s, while X(A/N)th remained with ( )'s. That was humiliating, for that shemale was basically Mundanish in character. V{E/N}us had hoisted herself similarly, and was now considered to be a most *fatale femme*. Even distant P|L/U|to wasn't what he once had been, in local estimation. JU[P/I]ter was getting very big, and NE*P/T*une had acquired a virtual ocean of self-respect. And ··SA<<T/U>>RN·· was extremely fancy now. Everyone was progressing except X(A/N)th! If only he had some way to gain significance, some strategy of upsmanship to recover lost status!

Then the timeless minute was done, and Grundy was a golem again. His insignificant little mind was reeling. Truly, the Demon did have a problem! He would never have understood it, had he not been in the Demon's situation for that minute, for status was not a thing he had ever approached as a golem. Now he saw that the Demon was suffering in a manner that was, in its permuted essence, similar to his. Among omnipotent entities, the demon X(A/N)th was insignificant, and he didn't like it. Yes—now Grundy could understand. All that differed was the scale.

Meanwhile, the huge Demon face looked thoughtful. "I grasp your concern now, Golem," he said. "Your compass is infinitesimal, but your relative challenge is as great. Unlike me, you have a mechanism for solution."

"I do?" Grundy asked, surprised.

"All you require is the respect of a good woman—and you have that if you emerge from this situation."

Grundy realized that it was true. If he survived this, it would mean that he was victor in the trial—and he could lay claim to Rapunzel, who was eager to be claimed. The rapport with the elves had been hopelessly soured; she would never voluntarily join that society now. With her respect, he needed that of no other person.

If he survived. But that remained unlikely. The Demon had taken up his challenge to exchange places for a minute, for the Demon was a creature of challenge, but that did not signify any further commitment.

Unless—

"Let me make you another challenge!" Grundy cried. "You give me my ambition if I show you how to get yours!"

The Demon, being almost omniscient, was now slow to catch on. "Done, Golem!"

So he had the deal that would solve his problem. There was only one flaw. He had no idea how to solve the *Demon's* problem.

"Um, I'll need a little time to work it out . . ."

"I thought you might," the Demon agreed. "You shall have all the time you need, eternity if you wish. But one hour from now, if the deal has not been consummated, I will confine you to the storage of the Brain Coral, and send the Sea Hag back to the surface."

Ouch! That would mean that the elves and Rapunzel would believe the Hag had won the trial, and by the time Grundy returned, if ever, it would be too late; Rapunzel would be the Hag. The Demon certainly knew how to generate incentive!

The Hag caught on. It was obvious that the Demon was fully aware of her nature and didn't care. "Maybe I can make a deal, too—" she started.

"Better quit while you're ahead," the Demon advised her.

She shut up. Obviously she *was* ahead; all she had to do was wait one hour, and Grundy's default would send her to her victory.

Now the Demon's face became still, again resembling stone. But Grundy knew it would click back into animation in exactly one hour. He had to come up with his solution to the Demon's problem in that time. *Had* to!

His mind, naturally, was blank. How could he think of anything that the Demon had not thought of long before? His intellect was the merest fraction of the Demon's! He was really just a prisoner, as was the Hag, with a chance to gain an advantage if he proved useful to the captor. If he failed, the other prisoner would have the advantage. Should he not have tried at all, so that neither of them returned to the surface? Prisoner's dilemma!

Prisoner's dilemma . . . that reminded him of something. Bink had spent a lot of time in Mundania and brought back tidbits, and one of them was a riddle of two prisoners, very like this one. One prisoner could get better treatment if he gave evidence against the other—but if the other did the same, both would be treated more harshly than before. Both knew this. What, then, were they to do?

But enough of this distraction! He had a problem to work out. How could he help the Demon gain stature in the Demon society?

His mind went blank again. Then, idly, it returned to the prisoner's dilemma. If one prisoner knew the other would not give evidence, then he could afford to do it himself, and get better treatment without actually hurting the other. Still, if the other reasoned the same way—

Of course in this case the other prisoner was the Sea Hag, and he knew she would always do the most treacherous thing. He could safely assume that she would give evidence against him. So his choice would be whether to keep quiet, and let her have the advantage, or to give evidence, so as to bring her down with him, as he had during the Lines and Boxes Trial.

The trouble with that was, it didn't bring him a victory. What he really wanted was to leave her here, while he returned to Rapunzel. So he had to solve the Demon's problem.

Then it came to him: could there be a prisoner's dilemma type of solution that would help the Demon? For the Demon's situation was in its fashion similar to Grundy's: the Demon had to gain an advantage over his rival Demons, while they were trying to gain advantage over him. If there were a solution to the prisoner problem, it just might apply also to the Demon problem.

Well, suppose there were a strategy of play that would prevail, no matter what the other party did. One that the other party could catch on to and still not beat.

Suppose the moon *weren't* made of green cheese! He was dreaming of the impossible.

Yet, almost, he thought there could be something. After all, there had been a winning strategy in the original lines and boxes game with the ant lion. That had required a surprise move, a sort of sacrifice, that changed the complex of the configuration. Something that seemed non-sensical, yet in retrospect made absolute sense.

Look at it this way, he told himself: if there was such a strategy, Grundy Golem could achieve his heart's desire. If not, he couldn't. So —there *had* to be such a strategy. All he needed to do was work it out.

He got to it, scratching lines and boxes and figures on the cavern floor. But no matter how he figured it, he couldn't see how he could get ahead of the Hag, who would never give him the slightest break. It simply wasn't there; the best he could do was to bring her down with him, so that both of them lost. Except that they wouldn't; she would be granted the victory by default.

But then he realized that the Demon's situation differed from his in one important respect: there were more than two participants. Was it possible that the dynamics of several differed from the dynamics of two? So that what might be a losing strategy when going one-on-one could be a winning one when going one-on-several?

But each deal the Demon X(A/N)th made, Grundy remembered from his minute in the Demon's place, was one-on-one. First he inter-acted with one other Demon, then with another. Sometimes he gained a little against one, but then he lost more against another. So it reduced to one-on-one, and the loss continued, for it seemed that the other De-mons were more cynical and rapacious than X(A/N)th, and nice guys finished last.

If only nice guys could finish first!

But maybe they could—

Then it burst upon him. Neither the nice-guy nor the nasty-guy strat-egy was best, because others took advantage of the first and were out to get the second. What was needed was a tough-but-fair strategy that rewarded the nice guys and punished the nasty guys—and that the others know it.

Grundy scribbled some more. Suppose he tried Tough-But-Fair (TBF) against all other types? The always-nice would wash out quickly and drop out of the game, but how about the always-nasty? Could TBF beat the Nasties? It seemed to him that it was possible, if—

"Time," the Demon announced.

So soon! It had seemed like only a few minutes, but Grundy knew it really had been an hour, not a piece of a second more or less. "I—"

"Have you the answer?"

"I, uh, think so, but I need to test it—"

"Certainly I wouldn't want to use an untested strategy," the Demon agreed wryly. "Test it now."

"I, uh, need several people, like me and the Hag—"

"How many of each?" the Demon asked.

"Well, a minimum of two. You see, the types—"

Abruptly there were four people where there had been two. Grundy and the Hag each had a double. That wasn't exactly what Grundy had meant, but he was afraid that if he protested, the Demon would conclude he was stalling, and that could finish him. "Uh, yes, thank you. Now the rules—"

"You presume to dictate rules to me?" the Demon demanded.

"There have to be rules, to show how the game works, so that the strategy can operate," Grundy explained.

"Proceed."

"I think it's easiest if we use a point-scoring system. The complexities of Demon status are beyond human understanding, so—"

"True," the Demon agreed.

"So we can use simple-folk-minded numbers. But it will illustrate the underlying strategy—"

"Get on with it!"

"Uh, yes. Now the object is to score points. The one who scores the most points overall is the winner. So if my strategy always produces a winner—"

"You couldn't win anything, Golem!" one of the Prince Gimlet elves put in. "Everybody knows that!"

"Shut your puss, Hag!" the other Grundy snapped. "If everybody were here, they'd see you get your bottom booted!"

Grundy discovered that he rather liked his double; the golem had a good way of expressing himself. But he wasn't certain whose bottom would get booted. "Uh—"

"Then let everybody see," the Demon decided.

Suddenly everybody was present. It was as if the cave had become a monstrous theater, with themselves in the center. In the front row sat King Dor and Queen Irene and little Ivy and Dolph and King Emeritus Trent and Queen Emeritus Iris and Bink and Chameleon and Chester and Cherie Centaur and Arnolde Centaur and everyone else who was anyone in Xanth, and in the rows behind sat Jordan and Threnody and Stanley Steamer and Snortimer and everyone else who wasn't anyone, and farther back were all the other people and creatures who weren't quite classified yet. At the very most rear floated the glowering cloud Fracto. Most of them looked a bit startled, but none protested. All watched what had become the stage, and waited for Grundy's demonstration.

It had never occurred to Grundy to doubt the awesome power of the Demon X(A/N)th. But if it had, that doubt would have been obliterated in this instant. All the Magicians and Sorceresses and creatures and things of Xanth, summoned here in the blink of an eye—and the Demon hadn't even blinked. All watching Grundy. Waiting for him to perform.

Suddenly he suffered a siege of stage fright. His tongue seemed to swell up and fill his mouth, and his jaws crystallized. *All Xanth was watching!*

"Hey, snap out of it!" his double whispered, nudging him. "You've got to show the winning strategy."

But Grundy stood frozen, overwhelmed by the enormity of it.

"He has no strategy!" an Elf-Hag said to the Demon. "Dump him in the Brain Coral's pool and send me back to the surface!"

"Send *whom* to the surface?" the other Elf-Prince demanded.

"Who asked you to butt in?" the first replied.

Still Grundy was mute, conscious only of all those eyes upon him. He knew he was about to default his case and cost himself everything, but he just couldn't move or speak while he was the cynosure of this immense and important gathering.

Then a new voice cut through his self-immolation. "Oh, Grundy!"

Rapunzel! She was here too—and when he failed, she would pay the penalty as much as he!

His tongue shrank and his body unfroze. There was no way he could allow her to suffer like that!

"The object of this demonstration contest is to score points," he said. "The points vary according to the combination of decisions by the participants. Let's say that each person gives evidence against the other: in that case each will score one point."

"One point," one of the Hags said, suddenly paying close attention. She wanted to be sure that he had no case that would satisfy the Demon.

"Now let's say that each person does not give evidence against the other," Grundy continued. "In that case each will score three points. They remain even, no advantage to either."

"Three points," the other Hag said.

"But suppose one prisoner gives evidence, and the other does not," Grundy concluded. "Then the one who gives it gets five points—and the other gets no points."

"Definitely!" both Hags agreed, licking their Princely lips. It was obvious that both intended to score five points.

"I have been losing points," the Demon murmured. "But that is merely the situation, not the solution. What is your strategy?"

"Let me show you," Grundy said. "Each of the four of us—two Golems and two Hags—will match off against the others. The Hags will of course give nothing away to anyone—"

"Naturally," the Hags agreed.

"While the other Golem will follow my strategy," he said. He glanced at the other. "You do know it?"

"Oh, sure. I'm your clone; I know everything you do."

"Good. Now let's do this one at a time, so the Demon can see clearly what happens. There will be several rounds to each match, to allow the strategy to manifest as something other than chance. I will start off."

Grundy approached one of the Hags. He paused. "Oh—we'll need pieces of paper, and pencils, for—"

Again the Demon didn't blink. Little pads of paper appeared in each of their hands, and pencils in each of their other hands.

There was a small stir in the vast audience, and Grundy saw that each member of it also had a little pad and a pencil, except for Rapunzel, who had a puncil. Everyone was keeping score.

Grundy was shaken by another doubt. He had not had time to work this out thoroughly in his mind. Suppose his insight was not sound, and his strategy did not produce victory? Not only would he be confined forever in the storage lake of the Brain Coral and the Hag be given access to Rapunzel's body—*everyone in Xanth would know.* His humiliation would be complete and eternal. The golem in the gears, who had the chance to make things right, and fouled it up.

The very notion made him shiver and sweat. He had the apprehension of the inevitable, knowing that if anything good were to occur here, it could not be by the agency of anything as insignificant as a mere golem with a big mouth. Why was he even trying?

Then he saw Rapunzel watching him. She smiled and blew him a kiss. She believed in him.

She believed in him.

He might fail himself and fail others, as he had so often before. But how could he fail her?

"Now each of us will make a mark on our sheets," he told the Hag. "We shall make a smiley-face for Nice, meaning that we do not give evidence against the other prisoner, or a scowl-face for Nasty, meaning that we do the selfish thing and give the evidence. We each know that we will both be better off if neither is Nasty, but that one of us can get way ahead if that one is Nasty when the other is Nice. But we don't know how the other will choose. We won't know until we show our faces."

"Get on with it, Wretch," the Hag said.

"I am." Grundy marked a big smiley-face on his top sheet, so that the Hag couldn't see it. Meanwhile she marked what was surely a scowl-face on hers.

"Now we shall show our faces," Grundy said. He turned his around and held it up so that everyone could see it. More grudgingly, the Hag showed hers.

It was exactly as he had anticipated. Hers was a scowl.

"Now the Sea Hag has chosen to give evidence," he said. "I did not. Therefore the Hag scores five points, and I score none."

There was a muted sigh in the audience. Evidently they had wanted the Hag to lose.

But the game had just begun. If his strategy was valid . . .

"Now we shall go to the second round," he said. "We shall each mark our sheets again."

They did so. Grundy marked a scowl-face.

When they showed their sheets, both of them had scowls. "This time we match," Grundy said. "Both acted selfishly, so each of us receives just one point."

"But I'm still ahead of you, Golem!" the Hag said with satisfaction.

"So it would seem," he agreed. "Now the third round."

They marked their sheets again, and showed them. Both were scowls. "Another point for each," Grundy said.

"Seven to two, my favor," the Hag gloated. "You aren't getting anywhere, wretch!"

"Fourth round," Grundy said.

Again they marked their sheets, and showed them. Again both were scowls. "Eight to three," the Hag cackled. "Your stupid strategy is just digging you in deeper, Golem!"

"Fifth round," Grundy announced grimly. They marked and showed again, with the same result, making the score nine to four.

"Sixth and final round," Grundy said. His preliminary calculation had suggested that this was the crucial point. He had to trust it.

They marked and showed—two scowls. "Ten to five—I win!" The Hag chortled.

"You win," Grundy agreed grimly. The audience was deathly quiet. The Demon's lips twitched.

"But the trial is not over yet!" Grundy exclaimed. "This is only the first match."

"My matches proceed for eternity," the Demon grumbled.

"Precisely," Grundy agreed. "One match is nothing; it is the totality that counts."

Now he went to the other Hag. "I will now repeat the encounter with the next opponent," he announced. "Each of us will mark our faces—" They paused to do so. "And show them." They did.

The result was the same as before: his smiley-face against her scowl-face. He was behind by five points.

They played out the remaining five rounds, with similar effect. The final score was 10-5, Hag's favor. "I *like* your strategy, Golem!" She cackled.

"I have now had two matches," Grundy announced. "I have a total of ten points, while my opponents have twenty."

The massed score-keepers in the audience nodded somberly. Their calculations agreed. Only Fracto seemed pleased, though of course the cloud had no brief for the Hag.

But Rapunzel still smiled at him, showing her confidence. She, perhaps alone, retained her faith in him. He hoped it was justified.

He went to his third and final opponent, the other golem. Both marked their sheets, and showed them. There were two smiley-faces.

"Each of us has chosen to be Nice," Grundy announced. "Therefore neither has the advantage. Each gets three points."

They proceeded to the second round. The result was the same. Then the remaining rounds. In each case, each scored three points.

"The result of this match is a draw," Grundy announced. "Eighteen to eighteen. I now have twenty-eight points total, while my opponents have accumulated thirty-eight."

"So you are out of it," one of the Hags exulted. "One of us will win!"

"Perhaps," Grundy said. Now they were coming to the next critical point. If the others acted true to form—

"Let's finish this," the other golem said. "I have still to match the two Hags."

"Yes," Grundy agreed. "But stick to the strategy."

"Gotcha." The golem went to one Hag and went through the match

—with exactly the same result Grundy had had, losing ten to five. The wicked glee of the Hags could scarcely be contained, and the audience was glum indeed. The Demon looked bored, which was a bad sign.

Now it was time for the final match: Hag *vs* Hag. Each had twenty points, from her tromping of the two golems.

"Now if you'll just let me have some points—" one Hag said to the other.

Grundy kept his face straight, but inside he was almost unbearably tight. His fortune depended on his analysis of the nature of the Hag. This was the final critical point. If he had misjudged—

"Like Hades, you old witch!" the other snapped. *"I'm* looking out for Number One!"

"Well, if you feel that way, wartsnoot!" the other responded. "See what you get from me!"

Grundy relaxed. He had judged correctly.

They marked and showed—and naturally each face was a scowl. One point for each.

Both angered by the seeming betrayal by the other, they went to the second round—and scowl met scowl again. One more point for each.

So it continued. When the match was done, the Hags were tied, six to six.

"Now note the cumulative scores," Grundy said. "Each Hag has twenty-six, while each Golem has twenty-eight. The Golems are ahead."

There was a stir of astonishment through the audience, as the folk checked their scoresheets. Many had not been keeping them up to date, being certain that the issue was already decided. The two Hags made shrieks of indignation, and the Demon's sleepy eyes snapped back to full alertness. Rapunzel clapped her hands with maidenly delight, her faith vindicated.

"Note that neither Golem ever won a single match," Grundy said. "But the final victory must go to a Golem. The longer this trial continues, the more certain this becomes. In an eternal trial, this strategy must inevitably prevail."

The Demon was definitely interested. Curls of vapor rose from his countenance. "What is that strategy?"

"I call it Tough But Fair," Grundy said. "I start out positive, but after that I do back to my opponent whatever my opponent does to me. So when the Hag gave evidence against me in the first round, I did it back to her in the second—and continued until she changed. Since she never changed, we just kept on getting single points. When I matched against the other Golem, and he was Nice to me, I was Nice to him in the next round—and continued that way until he changed. Since he didn't change—"

"But you never won a match!" the Demon protested.

"And the Hags never lost a match," Grundy agreed. "But the victory does not go to the winner of matches, but to the scorer of the most total points, which is a different matter. I made more points tying with the other Golem than I lost losing to the Hags. Their selfish ways gave them short-term victories, but cost them the trial."

"A fluke!" a Hag screamed.

"No fluke," Grundy said. "You Hags can't cooperate with anyone, even your own kind, so you inevitably lose out to those of us who can. An enlightened cooperation is better, in the long run, than short-term selfishness." He turned to the Demon. "Now I realize this is just a simple game, hardly worthy of your notice. But the principle is sound. You should be able to apply the same strategy to your complex encounters with other Demons that are far beyond my understanding. You have been going for individual victories, and getting some, but like the Hags you have been losing overall. With this strategy you can lose matches, and the other Demons will think they are cleaning up, but inevitably as time passes—"

Slowly, the Demon smiled.

Then the cave was gone. Grundy was standing alone beside the Elf Elm. In the distance Stanley Steamer was lifting his head, getting wind of him.

And Rapunzel, golem-size, was swinging down on a line—no, it was her own hair, restored to its former length and splendor. The Demon X(A/N)th, eventually to be X[A/N]th or even ··X«A/N»th··, had added a bonus.

Rapunzel landed, and her lovely tresses floated down about her like a swirling halo as she did a little dance of joy. She was the most beautiful creature he could have imagined, and not just in her body. She laughed merrily as she ran to embrace him.

"Oh, Grundy!" she cried, and the two of them were lost amid the halo.

Puns have continued to come in, and I have used a number, but as I have warned in the last couple of Notes, the market for these is diminishing. Don't rush to send more; your effort is apt to be wasted. But here are the credits for those used in this novel, roughly in order of their appearance:

Greg Burris: the thesaurus; Stanley Cohen, M.D.: the snailboat and the Con-Pewter; Cathy Livoni (a novelist in her own right, author of *Element of Time):* the unicorn's taste for popcorn; Bryce Cockson: the secret of using reverse-wood with Youth Elixir; Mark Odegard: D-tails, shopping centaur, Kissimmee River, mys-tree, casuis-tree, Ever-Glades; Nicki Marino: going nowhere; Wm. Martin: parrot-ox; Robert Haight: power plant, handball, tail-lights, evergreen; Brent Edwards: lo, middle and hi quats, passion fruit; Rose Mary Scanlon: house fly; Dave Schwartz: babbling brook; Charles Puzio: passport; Ron Elam: burr; Jeff Sotland: pumpkin, club soda, evergreen (right: two people suggested it); Nick Jamilla: golden fleas; Chris Miller: reverse-wood used with the centaur aisle; Jennifer Davidson inquired whether I had ever based a novel on a limerick, and when I thought about it I concluded that maybe there was a limerick buried under the puns of *Golem;* you'll find it in the Lexicon under "Ass."

In addition, an insight by Steve Thaxton: a version of the hypnogourd exists in Mundania. It is called TV, and it causes folk to freeze in place while their minds get zonked, exactly as the gourd does. Perhaps this was obvious to everyone else all the time; I'm a little slow to catch on, is all. That, too, is in the Lexicon.

The concluding strategy for victory, here called Tough But Fair, was adapted from a Mundane program called Tit for Tat that is indeed a winner. The implications of that program are far-reaching, ranging from relations within a marriage (obviously Tat would be the male) to international dealings (if They bomb Us . . .), and are worth thinking about.

Meanwhile, there has been some leakage of Xanth magic into Mundania. Some of it is minor, so that only those who are paying close attention even notice. For example, the publisher took a ride in an airplane and was served a meal. All perfectly normal, you say? But she read the small print on a package of salad dressing and discovered that it contained Xanthan Gum. Now where do you suppose that came from? And who—or what—do you suppose was keeping an eye on her? Most Mundanes don't believe in magic, but sometimes they do wonder.

But the effects of the magic leakage don't have to be minor. Now—which is 1984 in my Mundane time—whole groves of Florida citrus trees may have to be deliberately burned up to control an infestation of a new form of deadly canker, that destroys the leaves and kills the trees. Florida citrus is in dire peril, because they don't even know where this canker disease came from, and have never seen this particular type before. It is as if it crossed magically from some other world. It is caused by a bacterium called Xanthomonas. That makes its origin clear to you and me—but naturally the citrus folk don't believe in magic. Sigh.

Sometimes fans send me gifts. I would rather that they did not, attractive as some of them are, because I can't send gifts to all my fans in return. I have had a lovely little Unicorn Plaque, a map of Castle Roogna, a pressed-flower portrait, pictures, books, bookmarks and so on. But one should be acknowledged here: a beautiful hand-embroidered map of Xanth by Wynn Hilty. I wonder if that type of work is what is called crewel?

I must remind you folk that though I have managed to answer my mail so far (except for those letters with no return address), it does take up to three months to reach me, so that by the time I do answer, the fan may have forgotten the matter. I once received a copy of one of my own novels, to be autographed for the birthday of a friend—three months after her birthday was past. I find that sort of thing very awkward. In that particular case I declared January 17 to be the 21¼ birthday of Miss LaRae Varty, and autographed the book for that occasion. But this matter of autographing copies by mail is a real nuisance and it does *not* please me to have to do it, because it takes more of my time than the book is worth, even when it isn't lost in the mail.

Another caution, while I'm in this area: please don't write to ask me for free copies of my novels. The publisher and I earn our livings by selling books, not by giving them away free. If you can't afford to buy a book, go to your friendly neighborhood library and check it out. If the library doesn't carry it, call the librarian discreetly aside and point out the error of her ways. If she doesn't see your point, you might try holding your breath until you turn purple, then foam at the mouth a bit, and perhaps she will see reason. However, I have been receiving reports that some libraries have stopped carrying my books, because they have been stolen. On occasion I have given autographed copies to a library—

and had them stolen. I have news for those who do that sort of thing: if you can read one of my novels and get the notion that stealing is all right, then I don't want you for a fan, because you don't understand my work at all. When you steal from the library, you are preventing anyone else from reading that book, and the very notion makes me want to drop you in the Void.

And a little story: Barry Aspengren was waiting in a line, reading an Anthony fantasy, when the young lady behind him inquired whether he was aware that the sequel was in print. This caused him to wrench his gaze from the page to focus on her. Her name was Ellen. That was their introduction: they had a common interest. Five months later they were married. Congratulations, folks!

Golem is the ninth novel in the original Xanth trilogy, and though I have other novels in this series in mind, there is also a good deal of other work to be done. For one thing, I turned fifty while writing *Golem,* and you may imagine how awkward it is to have an age like that sneak up on a person. For another, it was the first novel I composed on my new computer; my prior novels have been composed on the pencil, so it was quite a jump, and I'm still settling in. For a third thing, I have a number of other projects to work on, such as more *Adept* novels, as that trilogy is rather skimpy with only three volumes. So I plan to let Xanth rest for a while, and hope that you rabid Xanth fans will understand. In due course I expect to return to Xanth and find out what little Ivy has been up to. I understand there is quite a scandal when she gets into her teens and gets interested in a man from Mundania.

LEXICON OF XANTH

Compiled by M. J. Langley and Ass-ociates Michael and Keith

A

ADULT CONSPIRACY—The secret of summoning storks to deliver babies, kept by all grown-ups from all children.

AGENT ORANGE—A vaguely catlike, orange creature acting as an agent for the Catapult who returns his baskets to him. His talent is the killing of plants in the vicinity.

AIR—*See* ELEMENTS

ALLEGORY—A green creature with a long snout filled with teeth who lives in the water. It can turn a situation inside out without touching it.

AMORPHOUS MONSTERS—Creatures living in the hypnogourd with multiple hands and hungry snouts who are helpless against disdain.

ANCES-TREE—A tree whose trunk splits into two major branches, which in turn split to four, and so on, until at the fringe there are too many branches to track. The bark is corrugated to resemble words: the names of a person's parents, grandparents, and so on.

ARGUS—A sea monster described as having the body and tail of a fish, four stout legs terminating in flippers, with the tusked head of a boar (minus neck) and three eyes along the body (with the middle eye lower than the others).

ARMOR-DILLO—A metallic plant with a pickle smell. Although it grows the best armor, it stinks of the brine used to store it.

ARNOLDE—An Appaloosa bachelor centaur who wears spectacles and was keeper of the records at the centaur museum on Centaur Isle. His specialty is Alien Archaeology. It was discovered, after 90 years, that his talent is the formation of an aisle of magic wherever he goes. The aisle extends 15 paces to the front, and half that distance to the rear. When he uses reverse-wood, he generates a Mundane aisle in Xanth.

ARROW ELF—Member of the tribe of Flower Elves.

ARTIS-TREES—Many-splendored trees, with sculptured lines and multicolored leaves, marvels of symmetry.

ASS—An equine creature named MiKe who assisted in the preparation of this Lexicon. Possibly inspired by the limerick, anonymously authored: "There was a pert lass from Madras,/Who had a remarkable ass;/Not rounded and pink/As you probably think;/It was gray, had long ears, and ate grass."

AVARS—Mercenaries from a wild Mundane Turk tribe, the handpicked troops of King Oary, Usurper King of Onesti, Mundania.

AWL ELF—Member of the Tool Tribe.

B

B's—Larger and more magical than bees, living in a B-Have. They are of many types: B-hold, B-neath, B-wilder, B-foul and so on.

BAD DREAMS—These are generated within the hypnogourd from the raw materials of people's fundamental fears: loss, pain, death, shame, and the unknown. They aren't light fancies; there's a lot of evil in the world that needs recognition. It's a lot of work to craft each dream correctly and designate it for the right person at the right time. Such dreams are the realizations of the consequences of evil: a timely warning that all thinking creatures require. They are handled by night mares after the Night Stallion decides where they go.

BAG OF SPELLS—Given to Jordan by Magician Yin: seven inert spells in the form of little figurines, to be invoked at need: a compass, a shield, a monster, a skull, a stone, a doll, and a tangled vine. Each had a negative version lurking in wait.

BAOBAB TREE—A monstrous tree towering above the jungle, which grows upside down: the foliage is in the ground and the roots are up in the air. The space around it is clear, for it doesn't like to be crowded. A few baobabs can also be found in Mundania.

BARBARIAN—A Code of Conduct honored by all true barbarian warriors, requiring excellent coordination with weapons, closeness to nature, awkwardness with women, common sense, and completion of the mission.

BASEBALL DIAMOND—A glittering ball the size of Ivy's two fists, carved with many small facets. It is magically crystallized carbon, very hard, useful for games.

BASILISK—Called "Little King of the Reptiles," it emerges from a yokeless egg laid by a rooster and hatched by a toad in the warmth of a dung heap. Because few roosters lay eggs, the creature is rare. It looks like a small winged lizard with the head and claws of a chicken. Its breath is so bad it wilts vegetation, and its gaze causes death. Therefore it doesn't like mirrors. Periodically all the basilisks gather at the Land of the Basks to hold staring contests. Also called cockatrices, henatrices, and chickatrices.

BEARS AND BULLS—Strange Mundane stockyard animals who charge heedlessly up and down.

BEAUREGARD—A bespectacled demon, highly educated. He is working on his doctoral thesis, *Fallibilities of Other Intelligent Life in Xanth.*

BED MONSTER—*See* MONSTER UNDER THE BED

BEHEMOTH—A creature mostly mouth, who is the door to the Gateway Castle under Lake Ogre-Chobee.

BERRY-BERRIES—Doubled berries that taste good but slowly cause paralysis and wasting away. In Mundania a similar malady, beri-beri, derives from lack of B's.

BIANCA—Roland's wife and Bink's mother, whose magic talent is the Replay: the ability to jump back in time five seconds, in a small area.

BINK—The main character in the first two novels, who seems to have no magic, but is actually the most powerful Magician in Xanth because he cannot be harmed by magic.

BIRDLAND—Located in north central Xanth, where birds rule.

BLACK SWORD—A viciously enchanted sword.

BLOODROOT ELF—An elf of the Flower Tribe.

BLUE AGONY—A dark and mossy fungus. When eaten it turns the victim's body blue just before the body melts into a blue puddle that kills what it touches.

BLUEBELL—An elf maiden of the Flower Tribe who seduces Jordan the Barbarian (no difficult task). Ancestor to Rapunzel.

BLYTHE BRASSIE—A female inhabitant of the City of Brass, in the hypnogourd. Formerly called Blyght, she's a nice metal girl.

BOOK OF ANSWERS—One of the Good Magician's handy reference tomes.

BOOT REAR—A rare beverage distilled from the sap of the shoe-fly tree, it is a drink that has a real kick.

BRAIN CORAL—Living in a preservative fluid with stasis-magic, it operates through other agencies to accomplish its noble task. It cannot control a conscious, intelligent living entity, but rather operates through suggestions that seem like the creatures own notions. A number of creatures are stored in its preservative fluid, for eventual release.

BRASS CIRCLET—Worn by the werehorse on the left wrist/foreleg, it is a "short circuit" that can connect the gaze of the victim to a peephole in a hypnogourd, causing a serious problem.

BRASSIES—Residents of the City of Brass in the hypnogourd, they are made of brass. The males wear brassards, the females brassieres. They are activated to work on specific dreams, for their craftsmanship is excellent. To them, life is a fate worse than death, as they are not strictly alive.

BRONTES—A cyclops, a giant with a huge single eye. He and his brothers Steropes and Arges were once the Powers of the Air, but fell out of favor.

BUGBEAR—It has multiple bug legs, and wings and feelers and a huge horrible mask of a face, and specializes in scaring naughty children.

BUGHOUSE—A set in the gourd, crawling with all manner of bugs.

BURR—Makes whoever touches it very cold.

C

CACTUS CAT—One of the guardians at Good Magician Humfrey's castle. It has a feline face, but its fur is composed of large, stiff thorns, and it has knifelike blades of bone on the front legs.

CACTUS ELF—Of the tribe of Flower Elves.

CALLICANTZARI—Race of monsters, like transmogrified goblins, who live underground and undermine important trees. Their muscles may be attached backward and some bones are in the wrong places.

CANDY GARDEN—A set in the gourd: growing lollipops, licorice weeds, and a chocolate path. A sore temptation to children.

CASTLE ONESTI—An imposing fortress in Mundania.

CASTLE ROOGNA—Capital of the human folk, the castle's theme is harmony with man. Its gardens provide fruits, grains, vegetables, and small game. Although deserted for 400 years after the death of King Gromden, under King Trent it becomes the social and magical center of Xanth. Some of the trees and the zombies are guardians of the castle. Built by centaurs, it's approximately 100 feet on a side, roughly square, braced by a tower at each corner, with walls 30 feet above the moat.

CASTOR OIL—A lake of brownish fluid, used to lubricate rolling castors, the bane of all children.

CASUIS-TREE—An argumentative, hair-splitting plant.

CATALYST WATER—A substance that facilitates change and may give a person catarrh, catatonia or catalepsy.

CATAMOUNT—A large reddish feline who guards the Catwalk.

CATAPULT—A feline creature the size of a small sphinx, crouching in a clearing. For a dose of catnip, it will fling an object forward.

CATASTROPHE—A trophy of the posterior of a feline.

CATNIP—A pleasantly scented, mintlike plant with feline furry leaves, growing in a catacomb.

CATOBLEPAS—A creature with snakelike hair, reptilian scales, four cloven hooves, and a deadly stare.

C.B.P.—Circa Before Present—a useful concept when traveling to other times.

CEDRIC—A historical centaur of Xanth.

CENTAUR ISLE—The home of the centaurs of Xanth. An island off the southern tip of the peninsula where magic in centaurs is not tolerated.

CENTAURS—They date from C.B.P. 1800 when the first man and horse drank from a love spring. They have the body of a horse and the head and upper torso of a man or woman. They are superlative bowmen and spearmen, and are intelligent and honor-bound, but have a deep cultural aversion to magic, which they consider obscene in higher creatures. (Man is not a high enough creature to be considered obscene.)

CENTURY PLANT—Located in the center of the Date Palm, it has many bright leaves glittering in the sun like golden coins; in its very center is the Thyme plant.

CENTYCORE—One of the guardians of Good Magician Humfrey's castle, it is a creature without mercy. It has horse hooves, a monstrous mouth, and a branching antler of ten points projecting from the middle of its face, and the voice of a man.

CHAMELEON—Bink's wife, named after a shape-changing lizard, whose intelligence and appearance vary with the time of the month, as is the case with some Mundane women. At one time each of her aspects were named: Dee—normal; Wynn—pretty but stupid; Fanchon—ugly but smart. Dor's mother.

CHEM—A centaur, foal of Cherie and Chester: a pretty brown creature with flowing hair and tail and a slender, well-formed human torso. Her talent is that of map projection. It is her mission to map all of the peninsula of Xanth.

CHERIE—A centaur, Chester's wife and Chet and Chem's mother. Her specialty is humanoid history, and she served as Dor's tutor. Though it is difficult for her to realize it, she has the magic talent of beauty.

CHERRY TREE—Known for several kinds of cherries, depending on the variety, such as Chocolate or Bomb.

CHEST OF NUTS—Found on a chest-nut tree, it contains P-nuts, Q-nuts, blue, red, and hazel nuts, soft yellow butter nuts, sandy beach nuts, a cocoa nut, and several bolts and washers for good measure.

CHESTER—A centaur, Cherie's husband and nephew of Herman the Hermit. His rear is prettier than his face. He specializes in the study of horsepower and discovers he has a magic talent: the ability to conjure a silver flute that plays beautiful music.

CHET—A centaur, Chem's brother, whose magic talent is that of converting large boulders to pebbles by a process he calls calculus. It renders a stone into a calx, that can be used for calculating.

CHISEL ELF—Member of the tribe of Tool Elves.

CHOBEES—Mostly harmless and unrelated to other bees, they don't sting. They have long reptilian bodies with snouts and big, soft imitation teeth, and can be found in Lake Ogre-Chobee.

CLIO—The Muse of History. She lives on Mt. Parnassus, the home of the arts, sciences and history, and writes magic texts on Xanth.

CLOUDS—In Xanth, clouds are characters. The most common are the Cumulis, which are good-natured, especially Cumulis Humilis, very humble and fleecy. Some are floating dishes filled with water; when they get tilted, it rains. But some are bad-tempered Thunderheads, or funnel-shaped carnivorous clouds. Some make technicolor hailstorms, and some send down hail*stones* that are deadly. The worst cloud is Fracto, a perennial troublemaker.

COCKATRICE—*See* BASILISK

CON-PEWTER—A goblet that gives misleading information. Confused with *Com*-Pewter, a magical thinking machine.

COPYCAT—A creature like a Mundane cat, that sits on things and purrs and makes copies of them.

CORAL LAKE—The underground lake whose water is slowly poisonous yet doesn't kill—merely preserves and suspends creatures in its brine, alive. Presided over by the Brain Coral.

COWBOYS—Bullheaded men and cow-headed women, led by Ferdinand.

CRAVEN—A goblin, subchief of the Chasm Clan, father of Glory and Goldy Goblin.

CREWEL LYE—A magic mix used to clean the Tapestry.

CROMBIE—A soldier and woman-hater who finally found the one for him: Jewel the Nymph. Father of Tandy. His talent is Direction: he can point to anything. At one point he was changed to a griffin, in order to help seek the source of magic.

CRUEL LIE—Told by Threnody to Jordan the Barbarian: that she loved him. But the lie was a lie.

CRUNCH—A vegetarian ogre, father of Smash.

CURSE BURRS—Little balls of irritation that cling tenaciously to any part of the body contacted, and can only be removed by an original curse. Some have spread to Mundania, where they are called sand-spurs.

CURSE FIENDS—Basically of human stock, but all of them have the same magic talent: cursing. They live in Gateway Castle, under Lake Ogre-Chobee, and are expert Thespians.

CYRUS—Halfling son of the siren and the merman Morris. In water his legs become a tail.

D

D-TAILS—Posterior appendages of Bulls and Bears; Mundanes pay special attention to them.

D-TOUR—A tour that includes the Stock Market (to see the Bulls and Bears) and other oddities.

DARK HORSE—*See* NIGHT STALLION

DARK LANTERN—A lamp that emits impenetrable darkness.

DATE PALM—In the center of the Century Plant we find the Date Palm, whose fronds represent every day of the year. Each day a day-lily blooms.

DAY MARES—Counterpart to the night mares, these invisible equines bring pleasant daydreams to people.

DAY STALLION—Leader of the day mare herd: an invisible (to people) golden wingless flying horse.

DEADPANS—Creatures who live around cooking fires, associated with slinky copperheads. They are said to have the ugliest faces in nature.

DEE—*See* CHAMELEON

DEMONS—Beings who are eternal and live beneath Xanth's surface. Some are benign, some evil. Rarely, one will interbreed with a human being.

DEMON-STRIATION—Threnody's demonic talent of slow shape-changing, size-changing, and mass-changing.

DEMON X(A/N)TH—The source of magic. He lives in the deepest cavern, sealed off from intrusion, where he has been for a thousand or more years. His body has leaked a trace amount of magic into his surroundings, and this accounts for all the magic in Xanth. In return for a guarantee of privacy, he has bequeathed "Magician-caliber sorcery" to all Bink's descendents. He is frustrated by his inability to gain status on other Demons, such as E<A/R>th, V{E/N}us, P|L/U|to, JU[P/I]ter, NE*P/T*une or lovely ··SA≪T/U≫RN··.

DIGGLE—The largest member of the family of voles, which include also the squiggles and the wiggles. The diggle resembles a giant worm, moving by elongating and contracting his body. He will work for a song.

DIME—A Mundane silver coin, that causes things to stop on it. Dor once used it to stop Irene—maybe.

DIMEPEDES—*See* 'PEDES

DIPSAS—A little snake whose bite makes the victim unquenchably thirsty. There are few remedies, such as a draught from a healing spring or from the winespring of the wild women of Parnassus.

DOGWOOD ELF—Of the tribe of Flower Elves.

DOLLARPEDE—One hundred times the size of a centipede, but without much power, because it's made of green and gray paper. The face resembles that of a sphinx, while the backside suggests a bird waxing amorous with a shield. Some rare dollarpedes have silver backbones, and feed on things like Principal, Interest, Assets, Liabilities or Budgets.

DOLPH—The son of Dor and Irene, a Magician, whose talent is instant shape-changing.

DOR—The son of Bink and Chameleon, a Magician, later King of Xanth. His talent is conversing with the inanimate.

DRAGONFLIES—Insects that zoom around like little fighter planes jetting fire and strafing their targets. When hit themselves, they go down in smoke and explode as they crash into the ground.

DRAGON KING—An intelligent leader of dragons who understands the human language and believes it is impolite to toast Magicians. He has iridescent mirror-polished scales which overlap and are as supple as the best warrior's mail. His great front claws are burnished brass tapering to needlepoints. His snout is gold-plated and his eyes are like full moons. He likes the taste of Mundanes.

DRAGON LADY—A more recent leader, a regal queen of her kind, who reclines in her nest of glittering diamonds while reading *Monster Comics*.

DRAGONS—The most varied and dangerous life form in Xanth, with a number of types and subtypes. There are fire-breathers, smokers, steamers and some that are just dragons. There are small, medium and large. There are land, sea, air and tunnel dragons. In general, dragons are the standard against which all other viciousness is measured. Normally they don't attack men or centaurs because the numbers, weapons, organization and magic of such creatures make them formidable opponents, but it remains true that more men are eaten by dragons than vice versa.

DREAMS—Dreams don't just happen in Xanth; a great deal of effort and art is required for their crafting and delivery and presentation. Once presented, they aren't completely forgotten, but remain in the experience, influencing character. One of the many problems with Mundania is that its dreams lack sufficient authority.

DREAM EQUINE—*See* NIGHT MARE

DRYAD—A tree Nymph who ages with the tree she inhabits, beautiful and immortal as long as her tree survives. One aided in the preparation of this Lexicon.

DRYING STONE—A stone that emits a warming radiation. It's a cousin to the sharpening stone, which hones knives.

DUNE—Sand which preserves by cleaning and securing the bones of assorted creatures so they can be admired millennia hence. Their treasures are called fossils.

E

EARTH—*See* ELEMENTS

EBNEZ—Magician King responsible for developing Xanth's shield/shieldstone after the Lastwave invasion, for protection against future Mundane invasions.

ECLECTIC EEL—The eclectic way is to use anything handy, so it chooses things from everywhere and puts them together in bits and pieces, but does nothing original. It clears flotsam (parts of wrecked ships) and jetsam (things thrown overboard) and uses them for markers.

ELDERS—The Council of Elders is responsible for the Kingdom of Xanth during the absence of the King. The Elders take care of routine administrative chores and select a new King if anything happens. The Elders were responsible for the placement of Magician Trent as King, with certain conditions.

ELEMENTS—Air, Earth, Fire, Water and the Void—each has its special region in Xanth.

ELEVATOR—A magic chamber that rises or sinks when occupied. There is one at Gateway Castle, and some also exist in Mundania.

ELF ELM—The home of a tribe of elves, such as the Flower Elves or Tool Elves. The Elm gives strength to elves as they approach it, and in return they protect it. A blight eliminated such elms from Mundania, so that very few elves are now seen there.

ELSIE—Jordan's original girl friend, who had civilizing designs on him. Her talent was turning water to wine by touching it with her finger.

ELVES—Magical folk of humanoid stock who live in Elf Elms. Their strength varies inversely with their distance from their Elms. They are honorable and seldom interfere in the affairs of others. They stand about a quarter the height of human beings.

EMJAY—A woman who compiled the Lexicon of Xanth, with some ass-istance.

ENCHANTED PATHS—Paths used throughout Xanth, whose magic prevents harm from coming to those who use them.

ENSORCELMENT—A spell, such as that used by the Horseman on the Kings of Xanth, usually permanent until nullified.

EVER-GLADES—Marshes in southern Xanth that go on forever.

EXILE—At one time the penalty in Xanth for being without a defined magic talent. No untalented person was permitted to remain. King Trent abolished that.

EYE SCREAM—A cold, sweet, creamy confection, superior to eye smilk because the eyes of scream birds are fattier than those of smilks.

F

FANCHON—Chameleon in her smart-ugly phase.

FANTASY FANS—These may be made of bamboo, and when waved magically make a person think he is cooler than he is. Fans have an identity of their own; they gather periodically at fan conventions to shoot the breeze and blow hot air and decide who is the secret master of fandom. One is stored in the Castle Roogna arsenal.

FAUNS—Counterpart to Nymphs. They have little horns, shaggy legs and goat's feet, and like to play pipes, chase Nymphs, laugh, eat and sleep, in approximately that order. There are several varieties: DRYFAUNS associated with trees, NAIFAUNS associated with water (with flattened flipper-hooves and scales), and OREFAUNS associated with the mountains (with greenish hair and dark-brown fur). All are harmless, fun-loving creatures who have no memory of the past or concern for the future.

FAUX PASS—Pronounced "Fo Pa," meaning "giant misstep." Centuries ago, the giant Faux was tramping north and tripped on a mountain range obscured by clouds, creating a gap that ordinary creatures now use to get through. The term has spread to Mundania, where it is misspelled.

FEN VILLAGE—Jordan's original home, near the northeast border of Xanth, beside what is now known as the Ogre-fen-Ogre Fen.

FERDINAND—A noble bull of a man, leader of the Cowboys.

FETCH—Apparition of a living creature, seeming dead.

FIANT—A demon who works in a rum refinery, who dematerializes at will. He is large, muscular and fat, with squat horns and an unkempt beard and a barbed tail. He was at one time a great trial to Tandy, for when he looked at her his eyes glowed like smoky quartz shielding an internal lava flow.

FIRE—*See* ELEMENTS

FIREDRAKE—A small, ornate, winged fire-breathing dragon.

FIREOAK—A variety of acorn tree, protected by a hamadryad or tree Nymph. A magical effect called St. Elmo's Fire makes it stand out beautifully with the illusion of burning that discourages predatory bugs, except for fire ants.

FIREWALL—The wall of fire surrounding the elemental zone of Fire in northern Xanth.

FIREWATER—Water that burns. Some of it was used to guard the Good Magician's castle at one time. In Mundania they drink it.

FISH RIVER—Enchanted river whose water changes folk who drink it to fish.

FLASH LIGHT—Touch a button on its side, and you're there in a flash.

FLYING SNAKES—Airborne serpents, sometimes poisonous. They may be green, yellow or red, and bad-tempered.

FOAMING INSULATION—Material that foams up, then hardens in place to keep things warm or cold. It burns explosively.

FOOTBALL—A sphere formed of feet of all kinds, that tramples a path where it rolls.

FORGET SPELL—A powerful spell crafted by Magician Yang 400 years ago and detonated in the Gap Chasm 800 years ago, causing people to forget that the Gap exists. In the Time of No Magic it received a bad jolt and began breaking up, with serious consequences *(see* next entry). Today folk are able to remember the Gap, so it is beginning to appear on maps.

FORGET WHORLS—Fragments of the original Forget Spell, undetectable except by effect: any creature passing through one suffers amnesia. Most drifted south.

FOUNTAIN OF YOUTH—It looks like a regular spring or pool, but it causes any one who drinks its elixir to youthen. Good Magician Humfrey and the Gap Dragon OD'd on it and were rendered into babies.

FRACTO—The worst of clouds. He terms himself King Cumulo Fracto Nimbus, and has enormous vanity and a stormy temper, but in time he blows over.

FRIS-BEES—Shaped like little disks, they glide down to a flower, then spin away to the next.

FRUITFLIES—Winged fruits that fly aimlessly about.

FURIES—Three dog-faced old women, creatures of retribution. Their whips cause terrible agony, and their curses are devastating. They are: Alecto, of the sorrows; Megaera, of suffering; and Tisiphone, of guilt. They know the secret guilts of anyone they encounter, whether human or animal.

G

GAP CHASM—A monster crevice that separates Xanth into northern and southern segments, guarded by the Gap Dragon. For eight centuries it was concealed by the Forget Spell. There are several ways to pass it, but all are devious. The author of these volumes finally managed to purchase a tiny piece of the Gap Chasm's extension into Mundania, but the magic was gone.

GAP DRAGON—One of the most formidable monsters of Xanth. He is low-slung, with a triple pair of legs, and iridescent metallic scales. Though he has small wings, he is landbound, and travels by whomping along. He destroys all creatures unfortunate enough to blunder into the Gap. Accidently youthened to baby status, he was befriended by Ivy, who named him Stanley, because he is a steamer. During his second youth, his female counterpart, Stacey or Stella Steamer, patrols the Gap.

GATEWAY CASTLE—An underwater castle in Lake Ogre-Chobee, home of the curse fiends. It straddles the Vortex that drains into the nether region. Vigilant swordfish patrol a giant seaweed wall about it, and entrance is via the big mouth of a behemoth.

GEROME—A centaur, an Elder of Centaur Isle.

GERRYMANDER—A creature with an irregularly sinuous body, small wings, claws, tail, and a lizard head. It repeats: "I convolute, I divide, I conquer, I surround, I select, I cover whatever territory I need to hold power!" And it does. This monster also flourishes in Mundania, where it deprives common folk of their part in government.

GIMLET—Prince of the Tool Tribe of Elves.

GLASS MOUNTAIN—A mountain of glass, one of the guardians of the Good Magician's castle. It is brilliant, and lets Dor know it with bright repartee.

GLORY GOBLIN—A petite, stunningly beautiful goblin girl, daughter of Gorbage; Goldy's younger sister. Her friendship with Hardy Harpy almost generates war between the goblins and harpies.

GNOBODY GNOMES—A tribe of gnomes, near the Cowboys.

GNOMES—Humanoid folk a third the height of human beings, who reside underground and mine for gems. The males are surly, but the females, called gnomides, are nice.

GOBLINS—Related to elves, gnomes and such, and of modified human stock, goblin males are ugly and mean-spirited, while the females are lovely and sweet. Goblins once ruled much of Xanth, but a spell that caused the females to prefer the worst males caused them to decline in power over the centuries, and today they exist mainly underground or in mountain warrens. Their war with the harpies almost ruined the construction of Castle Roogna.

GOLD COAST—A region in southeastern Xanth where the shoreline is golden. The Ivory Tower is there.

GOLDEN FLEAS—The fabulous metallic fleas of an ancient Mundane dragon, sought by the idiot Ja-Son.

GOLDY GOBLIN—Eldest daughter of Gorbage, very pretty and nice. She traveled north to trap a male in the goblin fashion, aided by Smash Ogre, who obtained a magic wand for her.

GOOD MAGICIAN—*See* HUMFREY

GORBAGE GOBLIN—Chief of the North Slope Gap Goblins, ugly and unprincipled as expected, he nevertheless values his daughters and seeks the benefit of his kind.

GORGON—The personification of the promise/threat in woman. When she was young, the sight of her face stoned males; when she matured, her face stoned everyone, even animals. Sister to the Siren. Intrigued by Good Magician Humfrey, who made her face invisible so she could not accidently hurt others, she finally married him and had a son, Hugo.

GRIFFINS—One of the classier monsters, a griffin has the head and wings of an eagle and the body of a lion. There's hardly a better fighting animal, weight for weight, other than a dragon or an ogre. They are notoriously finicky, spending hours preening their feathers, and won't eat anything that's spoiled.

GROMDEN—Former King of Xanth, whose talent was to perceive the history of any object he touched. Old, bald and fat in his later life, he nevertheless had the guilt of a scandalous liaison with a demoness that resulted in Threnody, the object of Jordan's adventure.

GRUNDY GOLEM—A man-figure as tall as a spread human hand, he was fashioned from wood, clay, rags, and bits of other refuse, and animated. Later he learned to care and became alive or, as he calls it, real. His talent is the ability to converse with all living creatures. Cheap insults are his forte. *See also* RAPUNZEL.

H

HALF MEN—Human/animal crossbreeds, including centaurs, merfolk, Fauns, Nymphs, sphinxes, harpies, manticoras, werewolves and the Horseman. In Xanth such crossbreeding is acceptable and at times unavoidable, facilitated by unmarked love springs.

HAMADRYAD—A tree nymph. They inhabit and protect various trees in Xanth, and some in Mundania, though they are invisible and relatively powerless there.

HANDBALL—A ball formed of all manner of hands.

HARDY HARPY—One of the very few male harpies: young, clean, handsome, intelligent and with good personality. His liaison with Glory

Goblin almost touched off a renewal of the goblin harpy war, but also demonstrated that goblins and harpies share half-talents, which become whole talents when the two get together. He and Glory were able to become invisible, together.

HAROLD HARPY—An early prince of harpies, consort to Heavenly Helen Harpy.

HARPIES—Human/vulture crossbreeds: dirty birds with the head and breasts of women, and body of vulture. Most of them are raucous, ill-tempered, ugly old hens, but a few are young and nice, like Heavenly Helen. They have a centuries-long running feud with the goblins, because the goblin-girls lured the few male harpies away with their attractive legs. In return, the harpies put a spell on the goblins to make their women prefer bad men. This feud caused the power of both goblins and harpies to decline in Xanth, which was fortunate for human folk.

HASBINBAD—Punic leader of the Nextwave Mundanes who brought recruits from Iberia and Morocco. He had been transporting 1200 men and 9 elephants to Hannibal along with 50 horses. He was under the impression that this was Italy, Mundania.

HEADSTONE—A memorial marker that assumes the form of the head of whatever is buried near it.

HEALING SPRING—A source for healing elixir, that makes people and animals heal instantly. But it requires the beneficiaries to take no actions contrary to its interest, or the healing is voided.

HEAT WAVE—A spell for generating heat, in the shape of a wave, given to Smash Ogre by Joan/John the fairies.

HEAVENLY HELEN—Young and beautiful and pleasant harpy queen. Her punnish background is derived from Dante Gabriel Rossetti's poem *Troy Town,* which opens: "Heavenborn Helen, Sparta's queen,/(O Troy Town!)/Had two breasts of heavenly sheen,/The sun and the moon of the heart's desire:/All love's lordship lay between./(O Troy's down!/Tall Troy's on fire.)" Thus we have Heavenly Helen, Harpy's Queen, whose distinguishing feature is a pair of breasts, involved with the siege of Castle Roogna.

HELIOTROPE—A plant which mimics the sun's heat, dehydrating everything in its vicinity.

HEPHALUMPH—An elephantine creature inspired by one in the *Winnie the Pooh* series.

HERMAN THE HERMIT—A centaur, Chester's famous uncle, who helped save Xanth from a wiggle invasion. He was exiled from the centaur community because he had magic: the ability to communicate with the will-o'-the-wisps.

HERO DRAGON—A statue carved from genuine stone and set on a pedestal, resembling Stanley Steamer.

HERO'S CHALLENGE—The contest of magic in which Jordan seeks to fetch an object that turns out to be Threnody.

HIATUS—Son of Millie and the Zombie Master, and twin to Lacuna. His talent is growing organs—such as eyes, ears and noses on walls and books.

HIPPOCAMPUS—A monster with the head and forefeet of a horse and tail of a dolphin.

HIPPOGRYPH—A monster with the forepart of a griffin and body of a horse. It has golden feathers and a yellow tail. The steed of Xavier.

HOE ELF—Member of the Tool Tribe of Elves.

HOLEY COW—A big cow with a bumpy gait, as full of holes as any big cheese.

HOORAH BIRD—Derived from "Hoorah's nest"—a hodgepodge. A huge bird with bright but tasteless plumage, with patches of red, blue and yellow on the wings; a brown tail speckled with white, and a body streaked with shades of green. It collects things. When it spots something interesting, it cries "Hoo-rah!"

HORSEMAN—A werehorse, a human/equine crossbreed. Centaurs resulted from man-mare coupling, this one from stallion-woman at a love spring. He is handsome as either a white stallion or a man, but evil, using his Brass Circlet to ensorcel victims. He tries to take over the crown of Xanth, but is foiled by Mare Imbrium.

HORSES—There are really no true horses in Xanth, but a number of equine crossbreeds or variants, like sea horses, horseflies, centaurs, hippogryphs, unicorns, ghost horses, night mares and day mares.

HOUSE FLY—A flying house.

HUGO—The son of Humfrey (HU) and the Gorgon (GO), he is considered retarded because his talent of conjuring fruit doesn't work well. But under Ivy's influence he becomes remarkably intelligent and talented. Ivy considers him to be her Night in Shiny Armor.

HUMFREY—The Good Magician, whose talent is information. He is gnomelike, with enormous Mundane-type spectacles, and over 100 years old. He tends to be grouchy and to safeguard his privacy by establishing all manner of barriers to entry to his castle, but he always knows exactly what is going on. He typically charges one year's service as the fee for an Answer to a Question, and many people and creatures willingly pay that fee. When the Gorgon asked whether he would marry her, he made her serve a year before he Answered. This might seem extreme—but it gave her the chance to get to know him well enough to be sure, before committing herself. Humfrey is like that, being more rational and generous than is generally perceived.

HUMFREY'S CASTLE—Although the castle stays in the same place, it never appears the same twice. It was built on the same site as the prior castle of the Zombie Master, by centaurs who owed service to the Good Magician. Applicants for Answers must first struggle through three obstructions to gain entry.

HYDRA—A water dragon with a number of heads. When one is cut off, two more grow in its place.

HYPNOGOURD—A special vine grows the gourds, each of which has a peephole. Any creature who looks in is immediately trapped in the world inside, where bad dreams are fashioned. There are many types of residents therein, such as the metal Brassies, ifrits, paperfolk, walking skeletons and ghosts, but only the night mares can travel freely in and out, by night. The gourd's World of Night is, in allegory, the subconscious mind, and its power extends also to Mundania, though there are no peepholes there. However, there is a Mundane variant that makes similar idiots of viewers, called the TV.

HYPOTENUSE—A big, fat monster associated with triangles.

I

ICHABOD—A Mundane archivist discovered by Dor's party when it ventured past the Crimson Tide and into the Mundane realm of Montgomery *circa* 1950. He is a friend of Arnolde Centaur, and an excellent researcher on the magic of Xanth. He likes to look at (but not touch) nymphly legs.

IMBRI—*See* MARE IMBRIUM

IMPS—Very small humanoid creatures responsible for lenses for sunbeams and sparkles for morning dew. But the items work only once. The imps call it "planned obsolescence."

INANIMATE—In Xanth, as in Mundania, the Inanimate tends to be perverse. Dor is able to converse with it, and objects such as doors, tables, beds, stones, etc., evince a rather shallow sense of humor.

INJURE JAIL—A beverage concocted of incarcerated water, which forms a "jail" around the drinker.

INTERFACE—A spell in which two creatures are interconnected.

INVISIBLE BRIDGE—One way to cross the Gap Chasm, if you can see it.

INVISIBLE GIANT—A large, bad-smelling giant, impossible to see except by the trees and things crashing down.

IRENE—Daughter of Trent and Iris. Her talent is to make plants grow rapidly, so that in minutes one of them could complete a life cycle that would normally require years. She was first classified as of sub-Magician level talent, but later upgraded to full Sorceress. She has green hair and good legs (and that's not all), and no truck with sexism.

IRIS—One of the most potent Sorceresses in Xanth, her talent is illusion. She can make a nonexistent thing appear, or an existent thing disappear. Her Mundane form is frumpy, but she never shows that to the public; consequently she is glamorous. She married King Trent, and for a time was King herself, because Xanth has no reigning Queens.

IRON CURTAIN THREAD—Centaur artisans use it to weave material strongly resistant to penetration by foreign objects. It is very good for protective vests.

ISTHMUS—A narrow corridor of land leading to Mundania.

IVORY TOWER—A lighthouse on the Gold Coast, built by the Sea Hag, whose inhabitants may know a great deal, but are not in touch with the real world. Rapunzel was one of these.

IVY—Daughter of Dor and Irene, a Sorceress whose magic causes the qualities she perceives in those about her to intensify. She is a bright, insatiably curious and somewhat imperious girl. Wherever Ivy is, there is bound to be mischief.

J

JEWEL—A rock Nymph specializing in precious stones. It is her responsibility to see that all gems are properly planted in the ground, for others eventually to find. She rides a diggle, and her talent is Smells: how she smells is how she feels. She married Crombie the Soldier, and when there is a suggestion of his wandering, she smells of burning wild oats. But because she is a Nymph, she can not truly grasp anything evil, which is a problem for her daughter Tandy, when pursued by a lecherous demon.

JOAN—A male fairy, misnamed.

JOHN—The female fairy who got the name intended for the male, and vice versa. She is a pretty little female figure with sparkling mussed hair and thin iridescent wings with scenic patterns. She finally finds the one with her name, so they can exchange—and they fall in love.

JONATHAN—A zombie, an old friend of Millie the Ghost.

JORDAN—A barbarian adventurer, betrayed by a cruel lie, who becomes a ghost for 400 years before being reanimated. He is tall, broad-shouldered, hank-haired, big-footed, and naïve about women: in short, the very model of a modern fantasy hero.

JUMP-AT-A-BODY—A creature all hair and legs and glower, who came across from Mundania not too long ago when the Mundanes stopped believing. J-A-A-Bs don't have the courage to do anything bad; they just jump out to scare people, then run away.

JUMPER—A spider who inadvertently accompanies Dor in his Tapestry travels. Classified as *Phidipus Variegatus,* of the Family Salticide, he's a jumping spider. He has eight hairy legs, six green eyes scattered about his head, and sharp fangs projecting from his mouth parts. His fur is green, his legs gray. In short, he's a most handsome creature. His talent is the making of silk, and by using that he can suspend himself from high places, and even fly. He becomes a close friend and mentor to Dor. He is not, despite impressions, large; it just happens that when they meet, Dor is small, being in the adventure of the Tapestry.

JUSTIN TREE—A man who was transformed by Evil Magician Trent into a tree. His leaves are like flat hands and his trunk is the color of tanned flesh. His talent is voice projection, so he can converse with untransformed folk. Given the chance to change back to man-state, he elects to remain a tree.

K

KING—The King of Xanth must be a Magician. For a long time only men were Kings, until a loophole in the sexist wording of the law was discovered, and Sorceresses were allowed to become Kings too. At one extreme point Mare Imbri, a night mare, was King.

KINGFISHER—A bird that fishes for kingfish.

KISSIMMEE—A river that kisses and tells. It also exists in Mundania, where it doesn't tell.

KITTY-HAWK—A small winged feline with the feathers and tail of a raptor.

KNOCK-KNEED KNIGHTS—Figures in metal armor who reside in caverns adjacent to the pasture of the Cowboys and use the latter for their violent entertainment. They are from a far place called "Kon-Krete" where things are very hard, and without honor they are nothing.

KNOTWEED ELF—Member of the tribe of Flower Elves.

KRAKEN—A seaweed monster, always dangerous.

L

LACUNA—Twin sister of Hiatus, daughter of the Zombie Master and Millie. Her talent is to form print on anything, which she can change at will. She messed up the Humfrey-Gorgon wedding by changing "until death do you part" to "the few measly years you hang on before you croak." That sort of thing.

LAKE OGRE-CHOBEE—A big lake in southern Xanth where chobees and curse fiends live.

LASTWAVE—Occurring about 150 years ago, it was a Mundane invasion so savage that the people of Xanth decided to prevent any further invasions. King Ebnez adapted a magic stone of great potency to project a deadly shield that killed any creature passing through it. The Lastwave originated in A.D. 1231 Mundania, where Mongols thought they were invading the Korean peninsula. (There is no consistent ratio between time in Mundania and Xanth.)

LATHE ELF—A guard of the Tool Tribe of Elves.

LEXICON—Compiled by three curious Mundanes who wished to recall readily all the properly forgotten things of Xanth. They were aided by a dryad and a querulous Secretary Bird prone to lethargy spells.

LIGHTNING BOLTS—The weapon of storms. A fresh bolt is devastating, but after lying and cooling on the ground for a few hours it can be used to bolt walls together.

LINES AND BOXES—A game played in Xanth and Mundania, in several forms.

LOAN SHARKS—Big fish with colored fins, eager to make loans requiring the repayment of an arm and a leg.

LOOKOUT ROCK—It isn't very high, but its situational magic makes it seem elevated, so that much of Xanth can be viewed from it.

LOOP—An opening to the nether realms of Xanth.

LORD OF FLIES—The King of the Flies, currently reading a book called *The Sting* by Wasp.

LOVE BUG—An insect that exists in both Xanth and Mundania. Its major propensity needs no explaining.

LOVE SPRING—Any of a number of springs whose water causes the drinker to fall instantly in love with the first creature of the opposite sex encountered thereafter. Such springs have had considerable impact on evolution in Xanth.

LUTIN—A foul-tempered, shape-changing creature.

M

MAENADS—The Wild Women of Parnassus. Stay clear of them.

MAGIC COMPASS—A disk within which a needle of light shows, pointing to something. A variant exists in Mundania.

MAGIC DUST—Dust that is highly charged with magic that wells from the nether caverns of Xanth. Magical effects are especially strong in its presence, and its diffusion throughout Xanth helps account for the nature of this land. A village is near its main site; the villagers pulverize the magic rocks and employ a captive rocbird to blow the dust into the sky. The concentration of dust accounts for a region of madness there.

MAGIC SHIELD—*See* SHIELD

MAGIC SNIFFER—A creature with a long limber snout with snorts out flutelike music and smells magic. It feeds on magic berries, and is harmless.

MAGIC SPRINGS—Waterholes with various magical properties. Some are love springs, some have healing elixir, some bring forgetfulness, and one is the Fountain of Youth.

MAGIC STONES—Enchanted stones. In one case they cause water flowing over them to flow uphill, and even make a loop in air. In Mundania this effect is called anti-gravity, and is much sought after.

MAGIC TALENTS—Every human person in Xanth has one magic talent, and two are seldom the same. Talents range from minor, such as making a yellow spot on the wall, to Magician-caliber, such as transforming any creature instantly to any other creature.

MAGIC WAND—A stick that levitates the object it points at. Presently encoded to respond only for GG, or Goldy Goblin.

MALLET ELF—Member of the tribe of Tool Elves.

MANTICORA—A monster the size of a horse, with the head of a man, body of a lion, wings of a dragon and tail of a scorpion. Its more horrendous features include triple rows of teeth and blue eyes.

MARE IMBRIUM—A night mare who originally resided in the gourd and carried bad dreams to deserving sleepers. The "Sea of Rains" on the moon is named after her, and her hoofprint shows a moonscape with that feature highlighted. By special dispensation, she was able to go out in daylight, where she resembled a solid black horse, though she could still dematerialize in darkness. She communicates by projecting dreamlets to people that may show her as a young woman in black; in the dreams she can talk normally. She was a major figure in the defense of Xanth during the Nextwave invasion, and at one time was the Mare King, but gave her physical life in the effort. Now she is a day mare, bringing pleasant daydreams to people; she likes this job better than that of nightmaring. The author's daughter Penny has a horse that resembles Imbri, and the volume *Night Mare* is dedicated to her.

MELT SPELL—An old spell Ichabod found while cataloguing spells for Arnolde. It melts the Horseman's sword.

MERMAIDS—Female creatures with human upper parts and piscine tails, related to Naiads (freshwater Nymphs), Nereids (sea Nymphs) and Oceanids (Ocean Nymphs). The siren is related, being able to convert between Nymph and mermaid forms.

MERMEN—Male creatures, human above, fish below, also called Tritons. They carry wicked triple-tipped spears (tridents) and are related to Naifauns and Nereifauns.

MIDAS BUG—A Gold Bug: a fly with the talent of turning everything it touches into gold. Dangerous.

MIDNIGHT SUNSTONE—The rarest of all jewels, it shines only in the presence of magic. Dor gave it to Good King Omen of Onesti, in exchange for Irene.

MILLIE THE GHOST—Once a chambermaid at Castle Roogna, she was ensorceled by Vadne and became a ghost for 800 years. Her body was formed into a book titled *The Skeleton in the Closet*. She was restored in modern times, and married the Zombie Master. Her talent is Sex Appeal, which makes her popular with men, less so with women. Mother of Hiatus and Lacuna.

MINOTAUR—A hero of bovine past, who went to Mundania to seek his fortune, believed to have acquitted himself very well in labyrinth competition in Kon-Krete.

MOAT MONSTERS—A requisite for every respectable moat, guardians of castles. Huge serpentine creatures.

MONSTER OF THE SEA—A sadly maligned liberator of damsels in distress who once tried to rescue the Mundane maiden An-Dro-Meda, but was misunderstood.

MONSTER UNDER THE BED—*See* SNORTIMER

MORRIS—A merman who marries the siren. They have a son, Cyrus.

MOUTH ORGAN—A structure the size of a tree, made up of mouths. Big mouths blast out low notes, and small ones the high notes. It is a natural musical instrument, part plant, animal, and mineral. Its seeds sprout little mouth organs, some of which drift into Mundania and are frozen in that immature state, but can still make music.

MUNDANIA—The land beyond Xanth, largely devoid of magic, and of little interest. It is almost impossible for Mundanes to reach Xanth, while Xanthians can readily reach any time or place in Mundania via the Isthmus. Mundanes regard this as unfair. The Mundane State of Florida has a suspicious resemblance in outline to Xanth.

MURPHY—An old time Magician whose talent is making things go wrong. He lost the contest for the crown to Magician Roogna, but his power remains undiminished in Mundania, where it is known as Murphy's Law.

MUSES—The nine patrons of the arts and sciences, who reside on Mt. Parnassus. Clio, the Muse of History, seems like a sensible woman, though somehow her texts on Xanth keep leaking out to Mundania, where they are called fantasies. It's an insult to a careful scholar.

MYS-TREE—A tree that is difficult to figure out.

N

NEEDLE CACTUS—A plant with needles it can shoot at enemies. It tends to shoot first and ask questions later.

NEXTWAVE—The latest of the devastating Mundane invasions of Xanth. This one is composed of Carthaginian mercenaries, *circa* 500–1000 B.C., led by Hasbinbad.

NICKELODEON—A boxlike creature that sings as it consumes nickelpedes. Harmless, if you can stand the noise.

NICKELPEDES—Ferocious insects five times as big as centipedes, with pincers of nickel. They attack anything moving in shade or darkness, but can not function in direct sunlight.

NIGHT MARES—Dream equines who deliver bad dreams to deserving sleepers. They have a bad reputation, but are only doing a necessary job. They travel only at night, and their hoofprints are maps of the moon with the moon features associated with individual mares highlighted. Included in the herd are Mares Australe, Crisium, Frigoris, Humerium, Necaris, Nubium and Vapors. Mare Imbrium (Imbri) figures prominantly in Xanth history. Night mares can travel almost anywhere, and evidence of their presence has been noted in nocturnal Mundania.

NIGHT STALLION—The leader of the herd of night mares. He is a huge, wingless horse of midnight hue, also known as Trojan or the Dark Horse. He assigns the dreams to be delivered. He tried to warn King Trent about the dangerous Horseman.

NIX—A sprite, part human, part satyr, part fish. When he says "NIX" water turns to ice; when he says "NOX" it becomes too thin to swim in but too thick to breathe.

NORTH VILLAGE—Original home of Bink, and one-time capital of Xanth. It was evacuated during the Nextwave invasion. King Emeritus Trent retired there, and the author of these novels lives near it.

NOSE LOOP BUSH—Magical bush with loops that contract to quarter-size when an animal passes through, trapping it. In Mundania they are very small, trapping nematodes instead.

NYMPHS—Lovely nude young women, counterpart to the male Fauns. There are a number of varieties. DRYADS live in trees, having leaf-green hair; NAIADS are water Nymphs, with seaweed hair; OREADS live in mountains. Some are general-purpose Nymphs living elsewhere. Jewel the Nymph is in charge of gems.

O

OARY—Called the Imposter or Usurper King, he stole the throne of the Kingdom of Onesti from his nephew, King Good Omen. Has a private army of Avar mercenaries.

OCNA—The second largest castle in the Kingdom of Onesti, where Ocna Dungeon is located.

OGRE-FEN-OGRE FEN—The present home of ogres, who migrated there from Lake Ogre-Chobee.

OGRES—Humanoid monsters, twice the height of a man, gross and violent. They typically speak in rhyme, and lack facility with pronouns, which they take to be edible roots. Ogres are the strongest and stupidest and ugliest creatures of Xanth. The face of an ogress looks like a bowl of overcooked mush that some one has sat on, and her direct stare would rot the moon. Babies are called ogrets. The author was accused of being an ogre at fan conventions. *(See* FANTASY FANS), but at that time he had never attended one. So he wrote a novel with an ogre as the hero, *then* went to tear up the fans.

OLD ROATS—A form of breakfast cereal, somewhat backward.

OLEANDER ELF—Of the tribe of Flower Elves.

OMEN—Good King Omen, of the Kingdom of Onesti, who was displaced by his bad uncle Oary. A stunning young man who radiates charisma.

ONESTI—The Kingdom of Onesti, Mundania, seventh century A.D. in what is now known as Rumania, at the juncture of the Carpathian Mountains and the Transylvanian Alps, reached by way of the Black Sea and a tributary of the River Danube, the Siret. Beset by Avars, Khazars and Bulgars, it was in need of magic, hence was ready to trade with Xanth. Dor, a poor speller, located it by his spelling of "honesty," something he believes in. Evidently this contact was successful, as Onesti can still be found in some Mundanian atlases.

ONE WAY BRIDGE—One of the Gap Chasm crossings; like some paths, it only exists in one direction.

OPTICAL BUSH—Covered with bright glass disks that make contact with the eye: contact lenses.

ORACLE—The Cave of the Oracle is located on the south peak of Mt. Parnassus, and was originally guarded by the Python.

OUROBOROS—The monster serpent who circles the world, grasping its tail in its teeth. It served for a time as a guardian of Humfrey's castle. (*Every* type of creature owes the Good Magician for Answers!)

P

PANDORA'S BOX—One of the oddments the Good Magician accumulated. It was empty except for Hope, and Mare Imbri took that and now spreads it about in daydreams.

PARNASSUS—Home of the Muses, and a very strange place. No one of intelligence has ventured there in decades. On the north peak is the Tree of Immortality; on the south peak, the Tree of Seeds, guarded by the Simurgh. The Python and the Maenads, or Wild Women, are also there.

PASSION FRUIT—Avoid eating this when in the wrong company.

PASSPORT—A little book that transports a person instantly to the place marked on it. It doesn't work very well in Mundania, so is much used there.

PATHS—They come in all types. Some are enchanted, so that no one can be hurt on them, and some exist in only one direction, and some lead to tangle trees.

PEACE FOREST—In this region, people become so peaceful they lie down and sleep—forever. The best way to get through it is to have an unpleasant companion, such as a harpy.

'PEDES—A whole family of creatures. Centipedes are not worth two cents. Nickelpedes are five times as big and bad, dimepedes are slightly smaller but twice as bad as nickelpedes, quarterpedes are five times as bad as nickelpedes, and dollarpedes are a hundred times as big, but are not fierce at all, because they are made of greenish paper with or without a silver backbone, and have little staying power. As you might expect, it is the dollarpedes that are most prized by Mundanes, who collect them.

PEDESTAL—What men put women on, not entirely to the latter's discomfort. But little Sorceress Ivy put Stanley Steamer on a pedestal, changing his nature entirely.

PEEK—A female ghost horse with lovely eyes used by the Knock-Kneed Knights until freed by Jordan. Mate to Pook, and Puck's dam.

PEEPHOLE—*See* HYPNOGOURD

PHANTOM LAND—The home of those who remain too long in the hypnogourd.

PHOENIX—A bird of fancy feathers who lives 500 years, burns itself to death, and rises anew from the ashes.

PICKLEPUSS—Feline creature with a green prickly snout and eyes moist with brine, who pickles those who touch it.

PLANTS—In Xanth, plants are not necessarily passive. They have endless variety and magical powers. The most prominent are ones like the tangle tree and needle cactus, but there are useful ones like the shoe trees and blanket bushes. Castle Roogna has a whole orchard with ones like the cherry trees and pie trees and the guardian trees that move their branches to interfere with enemies of the castle. In addition there are curse burrs, fruitcups, knotweeds, the kraken weed, nosegays, pillbox bushes (for headache pills), pomegranates (with rock-hard fruit) and snapdragons. Irene makes much of plants, as her talent is to make them grow rapidly.

POOK—Male ghost horse, kept solid by the chains he wears about his barrel. Friend to Jordan.

POOKA—A ghost horse, such as Pook, Peek or Puck.

PSEUDO-MEN—Half-humans who inherited man's destructive tendencies: trolls, ogres, giants, goblins and such. Some, like the gnomes and elves, are not that bad, and ones like the fauns and nymphs are good.

PUMPKIN—A gourd that inflates things.

PUNS—Pundora's Box was emptied into Xanth, and the region is mostly made of puns. You have to watch where you put your feet, lest you step in a pun.

PYTHON—The nemesis and sometimes delight of females, he helps guard Parnassus. A huge serpent.

Q

QUARTERPEDES—*See* 'PEDES

QUEST—A special mission, such as Grundy's Quest to rescue Stanley Steamer that can lead to interesting things.

QUIETA—A tiny female imp who presents Smash with a useful little mirror. Her father is Imp Ortant. They are featured on the cover of *Ogre, Ogre*. The author likes to tell his daughter Penny that she was the model for that painting of Quieta.

R

RAINBOW—A magic arc of color in the sky, exceedingly choosy about when/ where it appears, and it always keeps its set distance from the viewer, even when there are several viewers scattered about. (An obvious impossibility, without magic.) To those on the ground it shows bands of red, yellow, blue and green; but when a person stands on it (a tricky business) the secret riches of it show: bands of polkadot, plaid and checkerboard. Some internal bands are translucent, while others blaze with colors seldom imagined by man, such as fortissimo, charm, phon and torque. It has a tight schedule, and must move from one showing to another, so seldom remains long in one place. Rainbows know no boundaries, so their magic spreads from Xanth to Mundania.

RAPUNZEL—Ivy's pun-pal, who lives in an Ivory Tower and has little contact with the real world, until she meets Grundy Golem. A descendant of Jordan and Bluebell, she is of mixed human and elven ancestry, so can change size readily. Her hair is magically long, capable of dangling the full length of the Tower, but it doesn't weigh her down.

REGION OF MADNESS—Caused by airborne magic dust processed by the Magic Dust Village. Reality appears to change there, and the constellations come to life.

RELEVANT—A large entity, with a long, sinuous nose, concerned about what is pertinent.

RENEE—The ghost-girl, Jordan's true-love in death. But when reanimated, she turns out to be TH-renee-DY.

RESURRECTION FERN—It resurrects memories of important figures in the viewer's life, causing an emotional experience. In Mundania its effect is much diminished.

REVERSE-WOOD—The spell reversal tree, and its wood, will reverse many magical effects. The tree was blasted by a curse from the curse fiends, who did not appreciate the way it converted their curses to blessings, but the fragments of wood retain the power. In Mundania these fragments are called lighter knot, and burn ferociously, still angry about being blown out of Xanth.

RIVER ELBA—Carried conveniently coiled about the elbow by Good Magician Humfrey. "Able was I ere I saw elbow." When the cord is untied, it is unbound and floods the region.

ROBBER FLIES—Flies who try to steal from people. Related to robber barons.

ROC-BIRDS—Largest of birds, they can be ferocious when aroused. They love rock gardens and rock music.

ROLAND—Bink's father, an Elder of Xanth. His talent is the Stun-gaze that freezes a person in place.

ROOGNA—A King of Xanth, whose talent was adapting living magic to suit his purpose. A pudgy, informal, gardner-type man with thinning, graying hair and a gentle manner. He fought off the Fourthwave and Fifthwave, built Castle Roogna, and ushered in the Golden Age of Xanth.

ROYAL LIBRARY—In Castle Roogna, where the lore of centuries is stored. King Trent values it highly.

S

SABRINA—A young and beautiful woman whose talent is holography. Bink's first romantic interest.

SALAMANDER—A fire-lizard that starts a magical fire that burns in the direction it starts regardless of other conditions. Water won't put it out, for it burns almost everything, even water. It can be put out by its own ashes, and it can't burn Salamander weed.

SALVE—A magic condiment that enables people to walk on smoke, if they smear it on their feet. But it is cursed: whoever uses it will perform some dastardly deed before the next full moon.

SEA HAG—A Sorceress whose talent is Immortality, which she accomplishes by taking over the body of some other person or creature after she dies. She holds Rapunzel captive in the Ivory Tower, for this purpose. A lovely body doesn't remain that way long after the Hag animates it, however.

SEA MONSTERS—Assorted large serpents who live in water and are always
hungry. Some are enormous.

SEA NETTLES—Plantlike animals that sting to death anyone who intrudes on
their channel. The headpart is gilled like a giant toadstool, with
driblets of drool.

SEA OATS—A crop that makes a foamy broth with a slightly salty taste. Sea
oats are restless and move with the tide.

SECRETARY BIRD—A bird used for secretarial services, at times bird-brained.

SEEDS—The Tree of Seeds has all kinds, but of particular note are the Seeds of
Doubt, Dissention and War, which are awkward to carry because of
their effects on the carrier, and dangerous to grow. They flourish in
Mundania.

SEL-FISH—A fish who sells instant gratification: don't worry about the welfare
of others. For some reason, the sel-fish isn't much liked by others.

SHADE—A half-spirit, ghost, or some unquiet dead, doomed to skulk in shadow
until its concern is abated. Donald the Shade helped Bink escape from
the Gap Dragon, and told of the Silver Oak.

SHIELD—An invisible, thin, but absolute divider between Xanth and Mundania,
causing instant death. It was adapted by King Ebnez, who caused the
Shieldstone to generate it to protect Xanth from further incursions by
Mundane waves. King Trent found other use for it, reopening the
border.

SHOPPING CENTAUR—A centaur who shops.

SIDEHILL HOOFER—A cowlike creature whose two left legs are shorter than the
right, to enable it to run around on the steep slope of a
mountain.

SILVER OAK—Its leaves are pure silver and repel evil magic. It reproduces by
means of silver acorns. The Mundane variety is less so.

SIMURGH—Wisest of all birds, she has seen the destruction and regeneration of
the universe three times. She is the size of a roc, with feathers like
veils of light and shadow and a crested head like fire. Her feathers
have magical healing properties. She is the Keeper of the Seeds, and
can read minds.

SIREN—A lovely young mer-lady whose song and magic dulcimer lured males to her island, but her sister the Gorgon turned them to stone. Deprived of her instrument, she did no more harm, and later married Morris the Merman.

SLOWSAND—The opposite of quicksand. It slows you down to a crawl, even if you try to jump over it.

SMASH—An ogre, actually a human/ogre crossbreed, son of Crunch. Stupid in the manner of ogres, he went to the Good Magician for an Answer, but forgot the Question. He married Tandy, daughter of Crombie the Soldier and Jewel the Nymph.

SNAILBOAT—A craft formed from a snail shell, used by Grundy to cross a dangerous acid moat. In Mundania it may be used to carry the mail.

SNEEZE BEES—Bees that make people sneeze, unlike Choke Bees that make people choke. Compare B's.

SNORTIMER—The Monster Under Ivy's Bed. He is composed mostly of five big, hairy arms and hands, that grab at ankles that come near the shadows under the bed. Monsters are under every child's bed, but disappear when the children grow up, and adults don't believe in them. They can't leave their lair by day, because direct light turns them to dust. Bad children tease their monsters by dangling their feet and yanking them out of the way when the monster grabs. The correct response to a grab is a piercing shriek, as good children know.

SNOW-BIRDS—Birds that carry and deposit snowflakes.

SNOWFLAKES—Dropped by snow-birds, they space out the mind so that things are seen that aren't really there.

SNOWSNAKES—Snakes formed of ice that melt in heat. Poisonous, carnivorous, silent.

SOPHIS-TREE—It looks like a regular tree, but is actually an animal masquerading as a tree by standing on its thick tail and spreading its limbs out. Truly a "weed creature."

SOULS—Souls are valuable and possessed mainly by creatures with at least some human stock. Night mares value them, though the acquisition of half a soul caused Mare Imbri to lose her edge with bad dreams. It's hard to be appropriately brutal when you have a soul, or even half a soul.

SOURCE OF MAGIC—The actual source is the Demon X(A/N)th; rock charged with his ambience slowly moves up to the surface and is spread about Xanth. But most of the magic radiates directly from him. When he departs for a while, the Time of No Magic devastates Xanth.

SPELLING BEE—Attracted by letter plants, there's nothing such a bee can't spell, but it won't necessarily tell a person about homonyms.

SPELLS—Varieties include the following (just a few) examples: anti-flea, anti-freeze, anti-rust, aversion, cleaning, coldness, happiness and curses.

SPHINX—A monster with the face of a human being, body of a bull, wings of an eagle and legs of a lion, who likes riddles. One retreated to Mundania for a nap of several thousand years, and the ignorant Mundanes thought it was a statue and knocked off its nose.

SPONGES—Some have magical properties that absorb agony and spread healing comfort.

SPRIGGAN—A giant ghost who haunts old castles and megalithic structures, tending to be destructive, which is why such structures break down. It can solidify its mouth and hands, to issue groans and shove stones.

SPRING OF LIFE—*See* **HEALING SPRING**

SPY I'S—White eyeballs hovering in midair. They whistle "Eye Spy!" as they depart on their mission.

SQUIGGLES—Of the family of voles. Cousins of the wiggles, but larger and they don't swarm. They travel rapidly underground and are harmless, leaving piles of dirt at the surface.

STANLEY STEAMER—After the dread Gap Dragon was youthened to dragonlet status by an overdose from the Fountain of Youth, he was befriended by Ivy, who named him. He helped save Xanth from the wiggles, and became a hero, with a statue on a pedestal.

STELLA STEAMER—Or Stacey Steamer; the author never did get her name quite straight. Female counterpart to Stanley. She assumes responsibility for guarding the Gap during his youth.

STEPPING STONES—Used to get across water. They sit on the surface, never quite regularly. Incorrectly used, they become "stumbling blocks."

STINK HORN—A plant in the shape of a horn, that makes a foul-smelling noise when blown. Children find it very funny when someone accidentally sits on one.

STONEMASON'S VILLAGE—Located in the gourd, where they make backdrops for the most formidable dreams. The masons are made of stone, and work with wood and metal and flesh.

STORK—A bird that delivers babies. It is a peculiarity of storkish nature that there is always a delay in the delivery, and it is always to the mother. The mechanism for summoning a delivery is a secret known only to adults; *See* ADULT CONSPIRACY.

STORM KING—Former King of Xanth. An atmospheric specialist who could brew dust devils, tornadoes, thunderstorms or hurricanes, making a draught or a downpour. But his power faded with age.

STUNFLOWER—A tall, disk-shaped flower whose song of conquest is "I'm the one flower, I'm the STUNflower!" At the word "STUN" there is a burst of blinding radiation.

STUNK—A goblin, recipient of one of Mare Imbri's bad dreams, who later delivers a message to her.

SUCCUBUS—Magical female creature who can assume any form, to seduce unwary males. It is surprising how many males are unwary.

SUGAR SAND—Edible sand, very sweet. In Mundania it is good for miring wheels.

T

TANDY—Daughter of Crombie and Jewel, she is a girlishly small woman. Raised in the underworld, she fled when the Demon Fiant (D-Fiant) had D-signs on her. Half human, half Nymph, her talent is throwing tantrums. She marries Smash Ogre, who really appreciates a good tantrum, especially when it hits him in the face.

TANGLE TREES—Large, tentacular trees in Xanth that grab and consume unwary people and animals. In Mundania they are harmless, having regressed into Live Oaks.

TAPESTRY—This was assembled at the Zombie Master's castle 800 years ago and taken to Castle Roogna, where it shows moving scenes of Xanth's history. Dor once entered the Tapestry for an adventure in the past. Ivy cleaned it by using crewel lye.

TARASQUE—A horse-sized dragon with an armored shell, six ursine legs, reptilian tail, and head like that of an ant lion with tusks. It lacks fire, smoke or steam, but is one tough creature.

TAXONOMY—The classification of living things, generally regarded as a centaur specialty. Possibly it has something to do with taxes.

TECHNICOLOR HAILSTORM—Storm with colored hailstones. Some such stones are formed of ice, but some are real rocks.

THESAURUS—A dinosaurlike creature given to the use of many words in lieu of one. Popular in Mundania.

THRENODY—A human/demon crossbreed who tells Jordan a cruel lie, causing his death. She has lustrous black tresses and midnight eyes and sings a song of lamentation. Her talent is demon-striation (which *see*). She is under a curse: if she ever enters Castle Roogna, it will fall.

THYME—The plant at the center of the Date Palm. It is the least dramatic but the most powerful plant in Xanth, the one that ultimately governs and brings down every other living creature. If trapped by Thyme, a person becomes a living statue, unmoving, unbreathing. Ivy was trapped for a while, but her magic enabled her to escape.

TIMESTONE—Operating for increments of five seconds, it opens the Shield so people can be sent through and exiled from Xanth. No longer needed.

TOPOLOGY—Magic which changes the form of something without changing the object; *i.e.*, stretching and folding an object changes its shape but not its nature. Vadne's talent.

TREE OF IMMORTALITY—On the north peak of Mt. Parnassus, guarded by the Maenads (Wild Women).

TREE OF SEEDS—On the south peak of Mt. Parnassus, guarded by the Simurgh. It has all the seeds produced by all the wild plants that have ever existed, including dangerous exotics like the Seeds of Doubt, Dissention and War.

TREES—Large plants, most of them magical in some fashion. Samples: BEER-BARREL, BREADFRUIT, PARASOL, ROCK MAPLE, SHOE, and TANGLE, producing beer, bread, parasols, rocks, shoes and horrible death.

TRENT—As the Evil Magician he was exiled from Xanth to Mundania, where he lived for 20 years and had a family. When that family was lost, he returned to conquer Xanth, and was recognized as the legitimate King. He is the Transformer, transforming others instantly to any other living forms. He turned out to be a good King, ushering in the Silver Age of Xanth.

TRIANGULATION—A magical means of locating something without actually going there. One of the few forms of magic that also work in Mundania.

TRITONS—*See* MERMEN

TROJAN—*See* NIGHT STALLION

TROLLA—Female Troll, leader of the Magic Dust Village.

U

UMBRELLA TREE—Has a giant canopy to shield itself against rain, and prefers dry soil. Its umbrella folds up when the sun shines.

UNICORNS—Equines, almost as rare in Xanth as horses, though whole herds of them range other fantasy lands.

V

VADNE—A woman of the past whose magic talent is topology, or the reshaping of things without changing their natures. Not quite Sorceress level. She converted Millie into a book, and was sent to the Brain Coral for storage.

VEGETABLE GARDEN—Discovered by Ivy, it contains horrors like spinach, turnips, radishes, onions and other stuff that exists only to nauseate children.

VOID—One of the five Elemental regions of Xanth. Its center is a black hole from which nothing escapes, not even light, except the soul. Its fringe is filled with altered reality. *See* ELEMENTS.

VOLE—A broad family of creatures ranging from the devastating little wiggles to the giant diggle. The extremes are wormlike, but the more central members, like the squiggles, are rodentlike. There is more to be learned of these.

VORTEX—A whirling column of water in Lake Ogre-Chobee draining into the nether caverns of Xanth. Gateway Castle was built around it by the curse fiends.

W

WATER CHESTNUT—Nuts filled with water.

WATER WING—*See* ELEMENTS

WAVES—The several Mundane invasions of Xanth, generally bringing horror to the population.

WIDOWMAKER—A tree with reddish sap that drops deadwood on victims below.

WIGGLES—Smallest and worst of the voles. They are flying worms less than the length of a finger, loosely spiraled, that hover in midair, then *zzapp*

forward, leaving a vacuum behind them. They drill through anything that gets in their way, instantly, which can be uncomfortable
for animals. They are indifferent to external things, but can be killed
by crushing, burning or cursing. Periodically they swarm, radiating
out in a great sphere. When one of them gets where it's going, it
incubates for a variable period ranging from weeks to centuries, then
starts a new Swarm. Thus it is important that every member of a
Swarm be exterminated—and just about impossible. In Mundania
they swarm mainly in buildings, and are contemptuously called ter-
mites.

WILD OATS—A type of plant that fascinates young men, who like to sow them.
Properly raised, they bring a Nymph who is bound to the man
and is good for only one thing. That's the attraction.

WILL-O'-THE WISPS—Faint lights that dance about at the edge of perception,
they are great teasers who will lure unsuspecting people
into trouble. Herman the Hermit was able to communicate with them, and with their help saved Xanth from a
wiggle Swarming.

WOODEN GEARS—The great clock in the gourd that measures out time for
every event in every dream. Once a Golem got in these
gears, and . . .

WOODEN KNOB—An unidentified object that reverses the emotion of those who
touch it, making enemies of friends and vice versa.

WORDS OF POWER—They command magic, but they must be properly pronounced, and few can do that. Examples: Schnzel (sneez-
ing), Amnsha (loss of memory), Skonk (foul odor), Krokk
(summons a crocogator), Bansh (disappear).

WRAITH—A nocturnal ghostlike creature who roams at night.

WYVERN—A small flying dragon with a barbed tail and only two legs. Vicious.
Not very smart, as any expendable weight is sacrificed in the interest
of lightness, and the heat of their fires tends to fry what remains of
their brains.

X

XANTH—A land of magic that has a suspicious resemblance to the Mundane peninsulas of Florida, Italy, Korea and the like. It is fashioned largely of puns, and everything makes sense in some magical way, such as Lake Wails supporting a whale with feet who makes the Prints of Wails. It has five Elemental regions and numerous special features, such as Mt. Parnassus and Lake Ogre-Chobee and the Isle of Illusions. Every person has a magic talent, of great or small extent, and most animals *are* magic. It is much easier to leave Xanth than to get into it. It represents the main link to reality for a number of zonkheaded Mundanes, such as the author.

XANTHIPPE—The Wicked Witch of the Wilderness, patterned after Socrates' shrewish wife. She is associated with Xanthorrhoed Trees, the root plants of Xanth, and with yellow things. She has a son, Xavier.

XAP—Xavier's steed, a golden yellow hippogryph.

XAVIER—Xanthippe's son, a robust and decent man of yellow complexion, who can zap things by pointing a finger. He marries Zora Zombie.

Y

YAK—A mooselike animal, who will talk your ear off.

YANG—Evil Magician, and twin to Yin. He makes negative spells, deceiving by indirection. Nevertheless, he became King of Xanth, so must be respected. All the stray spell-objects of Xanth date from his reign, even those appearing before his time. He ushered in the Dark Age of Xanth.

YIN—Yang's good twin, who lost out.

Z

ZOMBIE MASTER—The Magician Jonathan, who reanimates the dead to make zombies. Unlucky in love, he committed suicide and became a zombie himself for 800 years, but was subsequently restored to full life by a special elixir. He married Millie the Ghost and had two children, Hiatus and Lacuna.

ZOMBIES—The Living Dead, always sloughing off rotten bits of themselves. They were set by the Zombie Master to guard Castle Roogna, and normally rouse themselves from their graves only when the Castle is threatened. Living folk shun them, but zombies are not bad creatures, and could be almost alive if a living person truly cared.

ZORA ZOMBIE—A truly decent young woman who committed suicide when her true love was false, and was reanimated as a zombie. She was restored almost to life when she found love in the form of Xavier. Her talent is accelerating the aging process.

About the Author:

Piers Anthony, sometimes called Pier Xanthony, is the pseudonym of a Mundane character who was born in England in 1934, came to America in 1940, was naturalized in 1958, and moved to Xanth in 1977. He lives with his wife Carol and teenaged daughters Penny and Cheryl, who recently formed the "Anthony Ego-Buster's Society" to shrink his swelled head when he gets too much fan mail, which he now answers at the rate of about two letters per day. His first story was published in 1963 and his first novel, *Chthon,* in 1967. He reached the age of fifty while working on *Golem,* which will be about his fiftieth published novel. His first Xanth novel, *A Spell for Chameleon,* won the August Derleth Fantasy Award as the best novel for 1977, and his fantasy novels began placing on the *New York Times* bestseller list with *Ogre, Ogre* and have continued since. He shifted from writing in pencil to writing on the computer, and *Golem* was his first novel created on the machine; naturally the computer found its way into Xanth.